L'enforcier did things only one way…"The Drago Way"

Drago returned to Marya's side, but turned his back to the hotel clerk as he said, "The woman prefers to hear from you that one room is satisfactory. So we will return to the desk together, you will tell her that one room is fine, and you will give me a kiss convincing enough that she does not call *la police* on me. *C'est compris?*"

Marya couldn't believe what she was hearing. "I will do no such thing!" she whispered.

"Have a care, *mademoiselle.* An incident serves neither of us."

She had no choice, damn him. "All right."

She took a moment to take a deep breath and compose her features. Arm in arm they walked back to the desk. *This is never going to work.*

"One room is fine, ma'am. We had a little argument earlier tonight, but I've decided to forgive him and save him the cost of the extra room."

If I think about it, I won't be able to do it. So she just did it. She turned toward him, tilting her face up. He did the rest, taking her mouth gently with his. His lips were surprisingly warm and soft, but it was a quick kiss. Before she knew it, he was pulling away from her. She could see the desk clerk smiling at her in a way that told Marya she would be crazy not to share a room with this man. Drago winked at the woman, but before Marya's anger could flare again, Drago had her turned toward the hallway.

He smiled as he followed her into the elevator. "An excellent performance, *mademoiselle.* You almost had me fooled."

Once the door closed, she let her anger loose. "Why didn't you just cloud her mind into believing one room was fine?"

"Ah, an excellent idea. Why didn't I think of that?"

"I hate you."

He smiled again, this time showing teeth. "I know you do, *cherie,* I know you do."

Thanks to Jason and Gerry

Other books by Jaye Roycraft:

Rainscape
Double Image
Shadow Image (Coming in June 2002)

Afterimage

***

Jaye Roycraft

ImaJinn Books

AFTERIMAGE
Published by ImaJinn Books, a division of ImaJinn

ISBN: 1-893896-74-9

10 9 8 7 6 5 4 3 2 1

PUBLISHER'S NOTE:
This book is a work of fiction. Names, characters, places and incidents are products of the author's imagination or are used fictitiously. Any resemblance to actual events or locales or persons, living or dead, is entirely coincidental.

Books are available at quantity discounts when used to promote products or services. For information please write to: Marketing Division, ImaJinn Books, P.O. Box 162, Hickory Corners, MI 49060-0162, or call toll free 1-877-625-3592.

Cover design by Patricia Lazarus

ImaJinn Books, a division of ImaJinn
P.O. Box 162, Hickory Corners, MI 49060-0162
Toll Free: 1-877-625-3592
http://www.imajinnbooks.com

ONE

Vicksburg, Mississippi

It was still the witching hour when he broke into Marya Jaks' house.

He would have liked to believe that he chose the hour out of poetry for the occasion, but the truth was that he simply wanted to get this loathsome assignment over with before dawn so he could steal some well-deserved sleep before returning to Paris.

A shaft of moonlight speared him from the skylight high above. A pendulum clock somewhere in the living room announced the quarter hour with four funereal bongs.

Moments earlier, with the silence of a night shadow, he had slipped to the rear of the Louisiana-style raised cottage, searching for an easy way in. It had indeed been easy. French doors sprouted everywhere beneath the tin roof. Those leading from the rear porch into the living room were unlocked.

Negligent! His disdain for the subject of his visit grew.

He stood now in the living room, opening himself further to the nighttime whispers of the house. A refrigerator hummed from the kitchen to his right. The soft tinkle of wind chimes from the porch wafted through the open door. The clock ticked with the steadiness, if not the allure, of a heartbeat. He tilted his head back, closed his eyes, and drew a deep breath.

She immediately flooded his senses.

The beating of her heart, strong and rich with the promise of life, reverberated in his mind, drowning out all other sounds, save one. The resonance of her breathing tickled not only his eardrums, but danced along his skin, raising the fine hairs along his arms. But it was her scent—potent, heady, and full of life—that held his attention. His nostrils flared. Riding the sweetness of life was an acrid undertone.

Death.

He hated aberrations.

He opened his eyes, and his senses guided him unerringly across the living room through a bayed nook adjacent to an angled snack bar. A small kitchen table and two chairs sat empty beneath paintings that filled the walls with splashes of color, the hues subdued in the gloom of night.

A short hallway off the eating area gave access to a utility room on his left. He passed the utility room, stopped before a closed door at the end of the hallway, and took another deep breath. The scent of her blood was so strong he could almost taste it on his tongue. But this visit was business, not pleasure, and a rather nasty business at that. He ignored the age-old pull of the fluid of life and pushed the door open silently. He could see her in the blackness as clearly as if it had been daylight.

The aberration was stretched out on the bed, limbs and bedclothes alike askew. Dark hair fanned out along one side of her pillow and flowed across her neck to twist under her arm on the other side. The hem of a pale lavender nightshirt bunched at her waist, revealing long, slim legs and round hips. White bikini underpants left little to the imagination, but the image didn't interest him.

He had always hated aberrations. He sighed as he poured himself into a boudoir chair near her bed. There was no reason he should be handling a case like this that a local enforcer could dispose of with ease. It was only because he had once dared to prick the good will of *la directrice* that she relished giving him these detestable assignments. Their tiff had been almost one hundred years ago. He wished she would get over it.

Aberrations were creatures with tainted blood that were more than human, yet not quite damned to the realm of *Demi Monde,* the half-world of Midexistence. The aberration before him was the daughter of a *dhampir.* This *dhampir,* the offspring of a male vampire and his mortal widow, had been a particularly nasty creature. He had been human, but thanks to his sire, endowed with the ability to detect vampires. The *dhampir* had zealously hired himself out as a vampire hunter until he himself had fallen prey to one of those he hunted. The daughter, the aberration, had inherited her father's uncanny abilities and heightened sensory perception. She was a danger to the vampire community.

He sat and watched her.

Her long limbs were fetching eye candy, but it was her face that held his attention. He couldn't make out all her features, but what he did see was pleasing enough in its smooth, unblemished contours. She slept peacefully, just the barest trace of a smile curving her parted lips.

It had been his experience that female aberrations were disgusting creatures. Unable to handle the burden of their strange heritage, many turned to drugs. Ironically, these were the aberrations most often granted life, as their unappealing scent, made more so by the drugs, discouraged vampiric contact. But their destructive lifestyles often killed them when the Undead would let them live.

This aberration was different. He could tell from the tang that stung his nostrils that she was clean and healthy, and what his eyes beheld only supported the conclusion.

He flipped the light on.

***

Marya woke with a start, vaguely aware that consciousness was siphoning away a very pleasant dream. She cracked her eyes and saw a man seated not six feet away from her bed. The blue eyes that stared at her were so riveting they seemed to be no more than six inches away. She wasn't alarmed because she thought he was still part of the dream. She didn't want him to go away. It wasn't so much that he was beautiful. The long, aristocratic face and strong features hardly signified beauty, yet he was the most compelling vision of a man she had ever seen. She was afraid to blink for fear the vision would dissolve.

Her eyes blinked of their own accord, however. She

blinked again. The vision remained, but the dream ended.

He was a vampire.

The scent of the Undead didn't cleave to him as strongly as it had to the others she had met. In fact, the air she breathed carried no more than the faint spoor of a musty room, mysterious and beckoning, like her grandmother's attic. Yet she knew without a doubt what he was. His appearance screamed Undead, from the unnatural glow of his electric blue eyes to the attitude of superiority that clung more tightly to him than the black leather trousers he wore. How dare this creature invade the privacy of her bedroom?

She sat up, both angry and embarrassed that he should see her like this. In her culture, it was taboo for a woman to show her legs to a man. "Who are you? How did you get in here?" She reached for her blanket and yanked it toward her.

"Alek Dragovich," answered the creature softly, as if the name itself would answer all her questions.

It did. *Drago.* She wanted to laugh. He was no dream. He was a nightmare. There wasn't a vampire or a vampire hunter on Earth who had not at least heard of *l'enforcier.* He wasn't an executioner, wasn't even the only enforcer who reported to the Directorate. He was simply the Anti-God. For vampires, revenants, aberrations and ghouls, there was no appeal from Drago's decisions. "I know who you are."

"C'est bien! One explanation saved. Do I have to answer your second question, *mademoiselle?"* he asked, his silky voice skating the border between whisper and breath. His words would have been pure arrogance had not the look of total boredom been so evident in his hooded eyes.

She frowned. The fact that he was uninvited would mean nothing to a creature of Drago's age and strength. "You know perfectly well you don't. But would it have troubled you too greatly to call at a decent hour?"

Both his brows lifted just slightly, as if it would have been too much of an effort to lift them any higher. "My time is valuable. I can't afford to sit in a hotel and wait for what you consider 'a decent hour.'"

"And my time isn't valuable? Do you mind if I at least get

dressed?"

He said nothing for a moment, but the fingertips of one hand tapped up and down on the arm of the boudoir chair. When he finally spoke, he flattened his hand against the arm and slowly rubbed the pads of his fingers up and down the velvet upholstery. "There isn't anything I haven't seen in over five hundred years, but if you wish it, go ahead."

He obviously enjoyed being obtuse.

"I meant, in private."

At last the hint of a smile twitched one side of the perfect mouth. "Don't keep me waiting too long, *mademoiselle*. A lifetime's worth of patience was spent long ago."

In a motion so quick and smooth she couldn't register it, he was on his feet. He was tall, nudging six feet, but gave the illusion of even greater height. Perhaps it was the long face, longer hair, and lean body, or maybe it was the aura of power that shrouded him, but he seemed to fill the room. The hem of his black trench coat danced only inches above heeled boots.

"I'll hurry, I promise," she replied with as much dryness as she could summon. It wouldn't do to be overtly rude to a creature as powerful as this one, but if she was going to be flagged for termination, she wasn't going to go down without a fight, either.

He gave her a bow as sensual in its indolence as his previous movement had been dispassionate in its speed. Then he was gone from the room, her retinas retaining only the briefest image of long, black hair and the swirling pleats of his coattail.

She dressed, taking her time. It was not only her subtle way of rebelling against his orders, it gave her time to plan her strategy. Actually, there wasn't much scheming to be done. She had anticipated this day for a long time and knew all she could do was debate her stand for life with as much conviction and dignity as possible. Once the verdict was given, though, she knew she wouldn't have the physical or mental capacity to oppose even a local enforcer, much less *l' enforcier.* Whatever he decided, it would be final.

But just why was a vampire from the worldwide Directorate

here to interview her? She had expected a local enforcer from the Brotherhood, perhaps a regional officer, but surely no one with more standing in the hierarchy than that. But for *l' enforcier* himself to be here... She tried to decide if his presence boded good or bad for her. A chill washed over her as she slipped out of her cotton nightshirt. It couldn't be good. Nothing about Alek Dragovich was good news.

She put on a sleeveless white blouse with a low neckline, a long broomstick skirt in indigo, green, and violet, and added several handcrafted gold jewelry pieces that she herself had made. Even without high-heeled shoes, she estimated she'd be almost as tall as Drago. She didn't have the need or desire to dress up very often, but for an audience such as this one, jeans wouldn't do. Strangely, the simple outfit made her feel good. And confident. She would need every bit of confidence she could muster for her interview with Drago. She brushed her hair that fell to the middle of her back until the static electricity made it crackle and dance. Then she rinsed her face before putting on just a touch of makeup.

He was waiting for her in the living room, but instead of making himself comfortable on her wide sofa or overstuffed recliner, he was on his feet. He had removed the trench coat, revealing a white knit shirt as companion to the leather trousers. His long-sleeved shirt outlined the hard, elongated muscles of his lean arms and torso as he slowly circled the room, fingering her belongings as if they were goods in a market to be appraised for purchase.

At her appearance, he didn't turn toward her or even look in her direction. Instead, he ran his fingertips along the bottom frame of the large painting to the right of her fireplace. His touch on the satin-finished metal frame was almost like a caress, and Marya felt violated. It was bad enough that he was here for her, but must he also examine her every possession?

"Mar-ya, is it? Slavic, if I'm correct."

"Like Maria, but without the accent. And yes, it's Slavic. So?"

He continued fingering the frame, as if he were searching for a layer of dust. "Interesting. Not the kind of name I'd expect in this part of the country."

Was he intentionally trying to irritate her? If so, he was doing a good job of it. "Well, I'm not exactly your typical Southern belle."

"Remarkable artwork, *mademoiselle*. Is it yours?" His gaze slid over the painting. It was one of her ultra-realisms, done in acrylics, and showed a small girl and a woman standing at a gate.

She planted herself on the sofa and crossed her legs as slowly as she could. "It's one of my creations, yes. That one is called 'The Eternal Wait.'" She paused, waiting for the inevitable comment.

It came, but only after a moment of silence, and it wasn't about the painting. "Your English is very good, *mademoiselle*. And you live comfortably."

Comfortably? What did he know of how she lived? "Contrary to what you obviously believe, not quite all of us are illiterate and live in tents. But you didn't come all the way here to comment on my lifestyle or critique my art, did you." It was not a question.

His eyes finally acknowledged her—eyes so blue it hurt to look at them. It wasn't just what was there—color of a beauty and intensity rare in humans and Undead alike—but what was lacking in their depths. Life. Warmth.

"No...you know why I'm here," he stated, the softness in his voice at odds with the lack of emotion in his words.

He seemed to know everything she was going to say, and she doubted anything she could say would surprise him. "To decide if I live or die."

"Succinctly put and accurate. You've been interviewed every two years for the past twelve years. Six visits. Six recommendations. Three in your favor and three against. I perform the final evaluation. I make the final decision. Do you understand?"

Twelve years of her life. No, more than that. Her entire adult life, brutally summed up in a few brief sentences. *Three for and three against.* As if nothing else in the past twelve years mattered a whit. A sharp pang of anguish threatened to squeeze her throat shut. In truth, nothing much else *had* mattered. She forced herself to speak. "I understand that, but not a whole lot else. Am I allowed to plead my case, or have you already made your decision?"

Too late she realized her mistake as he sank to the sofa beside her. Why hadn't she thought to sit in the recliner?

"Mais certainement, mademoiselle. You will be allowed to speak."

He drew out the words seductively, but the hooded eyes gave her the distinct impression that he cared little, if at all, for anything she had to say.

The closeness of his body was suffocating. She wasn't sure if it was the aura of power that emanated from him and crawled over her skin, eating away at her defenses, or if it was her own fear drying her throat and scattering the unspoken words of her response.

She wanted to back away from him, but her pride held her still.

His voice filled the silence, his mouth only inches from hers. "I have read all the reports. I know the story of your father and grandfather alike. Rest assured that I will allow none of these things to sway me one way or another. My decision will be my own, and no, I have not yet made it."

Assured was the last thing she felt right now. He had leaned even closer to her as he spoke, and she hated him all the more for it. She was sure he knew his closeness was intimidating, and she well knew from past experience that intimidation was a favorite tool of the Undead. She had despised the six enforcers who had visited her previously, but what she had felt for them was nothing compared to what she felt now.

Her silence obviously prompted him to continue. "I will sum up for you what I have learned. That way, I can confirm that all previous reports were accurately made, and you will know that my decision is based on the facts."

He leaned back again, but the distance only gave her a better look at his face. Thick brows tented his hooded eyes, and double smile lines ran down either side of his face. A faint cleft shadowed his chin, above which rested a very dispassionate mouth. She wondered how he had ever smiled enough even in his five hundred years to etch such deep smile lines. She wanted to hurt him and scratch the lines even deeper into his face.

Instead, she finally found her voice. "That's all well and good, but I can guarantee you that my truth is very far from yours."

"I will try my utmost, *mademoiselle*, to see your truth." The antifreeze eyes, empty of compassion, said otherwise.

"Go ahead, then. I will correct you when you are wrong."

At that, one side of his mouth lifted, not enough to make the long smile lines pop, but enough to indicate amusement. All at her expense, she was sure.

He began her story. "Your grandfather, Nicolai, while living in Romania, was brought to the Other Side. Correct?"

"Yes."

"But even after becoming a vampire, he had an insatiable...appetite...for his widow."

She frowned. "Must you put it like that? He loved her. She was his wife."

"The Undead know little of love. It is a lust, *mademoiselle*, nothing more. Take my word on this, for it is something I understand only too well."

She wanted to argue further, but didn't. She wanted this whole thing over with, and she wanted this creature out of her house. "Go on."

"It is a lust, but a very powerful lust, a need that the vampire puts above all else. The vampire Nicolai continued to bed his widow until she bore him a son, your father Andrei. Your father was what many of you Gypsies call a *dhampir*, the human offspring of a vampire."

She interrupted him. Some things were too important to let pass. "Don't call us that. It's offensive. We're Roma, not 'Gypsies.'"

He held a hand to his heart. *"Pardon, mademoiselle! Je suis vraiment desole.* Sometimes I forget the era in which we live. We must be politically correct, no?"

She wouldn't have thought it possible, but her loathing

for the *l'enforcier* increased even more. How dare he reduce the centuries-long struggle against persecution to a snit over political correctness? She closed her eyes and swallowed. She mustn't fight with him. She mustn't. Her survival depended on it.

She opened her eyes. "Don't bother with apologies. Just do me a favor and call us Roma, all right?"

"*Comme vous voudrez.* As you wish. Andrei, the *dhampir*, had extraordinary abilities, did he not? He could detect vampires so well that he was hired by many of the...Rom to kill vampires, including his own father."

She swallowed again, but the tightness in her throat made it difficult. "Yes, but he only did that for a few years. He didn't enjoy killing, even creatures as foul as you are." She couldn't resist that last, even if it did anger Drago.

He blinked and paused in his recitation, but if he was angered, his hooded gaze didn't show it. "Andrei lived until five years after you were born. At that time he was killed by one of the vampires he had been hired to kill years before, but had failed to. Poetic justice, some might say."

She was trying to control her anger, but he was making it harder and harder. "Only a blood monster like yourself would call that 'poetic justice.' The Rom didn't feel that way, and my mother most certainly didn't."

He leaned all the way back against the sofa's cushioned back, stretching his left arm along the top of the backrest. His hand was directly behind her head. "You lost one father. I lost seven of my brethren to your father's vampire-killing career."

Her anger, still hot, helped her to ignore the proximity of his pale fingers. "'Brethren.' Don't make me laugh. I'd be surprised if you personally knew any of them."

"As a matter of fact, I did. But we regress. The story moves on to you, Marya. You have inherited your father's abilities. Those abilities have been well tested and documented by local enforcers over the years. You cannot only detect vampires by sight and smell, but you have an unusually strong resistance to the compelling gaze of the average vampire. Do you dispute any of this?"

She sighed. There was no point in denying anything. As he said, it was all documented. "No. When I saw you in my bedroom I knew almost immediately what you are. But the legends aren't as strong here as they are in Europe. Even if they were, I'm not an active part of the local Roma community. After my father gave up his career, he moved himself and my mother to France. When he was killed, my mother sold all his belongings, brought me here, and saw that I went to school. She wanted a better life for me than she had had. But I keep to myself. I don't seek out *gadje,* and I certainly don't seek out your kind. I've never had any contact with vampires outside the enforcers who have come to harass me. I am no danger whatsoever to any of the Undead."

"'No danger,' *mademoiselle?* I'm not so sure of that. You carry much anger within you. What assurance do I have that in an encounter with one of my kind that anger would not prompt you to use your abilities to do him harm?"

Marya couldn't believe what she was hearing. Now was as good a time as any to ask to speak her piece. "You told me I could speak. May I now?"

She felt rather than saw his fingers moving behind her head, stroking the fabric of the sofa. "You have been doing an excellent job of speaking thus far without my permission." He sighed, but continued before she could form a reply. "I have yet to perform the final test on you, but if you wish it, go ahead."

She took a deep breath. She was glad she hadn't prepared a set speech, for she knew she wouldn't be able to recite memorized words. What she wanted to say now came straight from her heart, and whether they helped her cause or hindered it, she didn't care any more. "You want to know why I'm angry? I'll tell you. If you had ever experienced the kind of persecution the Roma have, you'd understand all this."

Drago leaned his head back, and the motion narrowed his eyes. A muscle twitched in his cheek, but Marya barely took notice. She went on, neither caring if he had a response, nor wanting to give him a chance to respond even if he did have one. "My people have been enslaved, murdered, and denied the rights that most people take for granted. And should not some of that anger be directed toward your kind? What my grandfather and father did has nothing to do with me, and yet for the past twelve years you've held my life hostage. The fact that I'm not now part of the Roma community is because of the limbo you've put me in. If I were living with the Roma, I would be pressured to marry. Family is everything to us. But how could I allow myself relationships, knowing that in a few short years some vampire, who knows nothing of life, might arbitrarily decide I am to be denied mine?"

She paused to catch her breath, and the sudden silence was almost deafening until the clock announced the top of the hour with the requisite number of clangs. After the final bong, its echo hung in the air, giving nervous energy to the silence that descended once more. Still Drago said nothing.

Marya knew she hadn't made any brownie points with her speech, but she didn't regret a single word. It had needed to be said. Even if he didn't understand any of it, even if it meant her termination, it had been worth it.

He finally spoke, and his voice was very soft. "Tell me of your life, *mademoiselle.* In spite of your passionate declaration to the contrary, you do have a life. Quite a prosperous one. I see it all around me." He raised both hands in an acknowledgment of her artwork.

She shook her head. He would never understand. "My father's career was...lucrative. When he died my mother had enough money to give me a decent life. But I do have to make a living. My painting allows me to largely work at home. I attend arts and crafts shows and an occasional art club meeting. That's all. I have no social life to speak of and no close friends. I rent this house and most of the furnishings. I've never lived in any one spot more than three years. My mother is dead and I have no other family nearby. That is my life, if you insist on calling it such."

He leaned toward her again, his body nudging closer yet to hers. She was painfully aware that his leather-encased left leg was only two inches from her right leg. She dared not touch him, yet she rebelled at backing away.

"Oh, I do, *mademoiselle*. Only when life is completely stripped from you will you understand how much you have."

So that was it. He had already made his decision. She would be flagged for termination. Her throat constricted again, and she had to force the words out. "So that's it, then? Just like that?"

He threw his head back. "My comment was purely rhetorical. Only when I am finished will I make my decision. Tell me of this man whose name appeared in the last report filed on you. Jaime Buckland. He is a boyfriend?"

She took another deep breath. She hated bringing Jaime into this. "No. He's an acquaintance. He would like our relationship to be more than that, but I've made sure he remains a distant friend, nothing more, for the reasons I've already given you."

Drago's neon blue eyes seemed to burn into her. "And if you were granted life, you would have a relationship with this man?"

"Maybe. I don't know. As I said, I've kept him at a distance. There's a lot about him I don't know."

"But you would rejoin the Roma community?"

"It wouldn't be easy, but they're my people. The *gadje* certainly aren't."

"'*Gadje?*'"

"The non-Roma."

He tapped his fingers on the backrest behind her head. "And if someone in the Roma community were ever to approach you and want you to use your talents against one of us..."

She shifted her position, ostensibly to adjust her skirt, but the movement gave her the opportunity to move a few inches away from him. Those few inches of space were like a breath of fresh air, and the relief from his proximity gave her renewed courage. "I'm not my father. I'm not a vampire hunter. Much as I despise all of your kind, I have no desire to kill vampires. I would never hire my abilities out."

"In spite of all this anger and hatred that you seem to harbor."

Her eyes met his, a dangerous proposition, but she was not going to be the one to lower her gaze first. "My feelings are a part of me. I don't know that I would ever be able to change them. But I can control my actions."

"You are sure of this, *mademoiselle?*"

She held his eyes. "Yes."

"You would, for instance, make no move against me now in spite of your feelings for me?"

"Only in self defense. If, for example, you move your hand any closer to my hair, I would have no compunction against slapping your face."

He laughed out loud and brought his hand from behind her head. *"Bravo, mademoiselle!* I admire your spirit. Few would dare say such a thing to *l'enforcier.* Tell me something. How did you hear of me?"

Marya didn't smile in return. A left-handed compliment from Drago was nothing to be happy about. "I don't have any clear memories of my father, just vague impressions, but he told my mother all the stories of the Undead that he had heard, and she relayed them all to me when I was a child. Your name was mentioned more than once."

"In most unflattering terms, I am sure."

"If you're asking if you're hated among the Roma as much as you are among your own kind, the answer is yes."

The corner of one dark brow moved almost imperceptibly.

She shook her head. "Are you surprised? You dispense death as if it were nothing more than a pill from a bottle, designed to cure all ills, great and small." She paused. "Can I ask you a question?"

"Certainement."

"Why are you here for me? Surely the great and powerful Alek Dragovich has more important affairs to deal with than the future of one 'aberration.'"

Emptiness flooded the unblinking blue eyes, causing a shiver to invade the warmth of Marya's discomfort, and she wondered what, if anything, this creature felt.

His eyes shifted again, refocusing on hers. "Apparently not, as I am here. Perhaps it was felt that none of the local

enforcers have the competence to perform this final evaluation."
His voice was dry, filled with an obvious disdain for his co-
workers. No wonder they all hated him. "The reports filed on
you indicate quite a strong resistance to the domination of the
vampiric mind, even for a descendant of a *dhampir.*"

"And what is this 'final evaluation' you keep mentioning?"

"Are you ready, *mademoiselle?* It is what I will base my
decision on."

She swallowed, trying to summon all the courage she had
earlier felt, but her throat was tight with renewed fear. "Let's
get on with it, then."

"Very well. I warn you, though. It will not be pleasant,
but if it is any consolation to you, know that it is no more so
for me."

As if she cared how he felt. "You're right. It's no
consolation. Just what exactly are you going to do?"

"I will set the mirror before you, and to it you will reveal
all. Not the outward appearances you show to the world, but
your true self. Your reality, Marya Jaks. *Comprendez-vous?*"

More ribbons of chill ran down her spine, coaxing a bead
of sweat to form under her blouse. She felt it trickle slowly
down her side. "Mirror?"

"The vampiric mirror. Myself."

She was suddenly very afraid. She knew now what he
was talking about. She had never heard it referred to as a
'mirror' before, but she had heard countless stories of the
frightening power of the gaze of the Undead.

It wasn't that she was afraid he'd discover some deep,
dark secret, for, in truth, she had nothing to hide. There was
her 'double life' as she liked to call it, but for all the thrill of
the forbidden it gave her, her monthly visits to New Orleans
were innocent enough. Vampires infested New Orleans like a
disease, but while she had seen countless of the creatures on
her journeys, she had had no face-to-face encounters.

No, it was simply that her very soul would be laid bare to
this uncaring monster. For someone like her, who had long
sheltered herself from the world, it would be the ultimate
violation.

"There's no other way?"

"No, *mademoiselle,* regrettably not."

She was sure *he* had no regrets. She summoned her courage. She had no regrets in her life, either. There was nothing she had to be ashamed of, nothing she would do differently if she had it to do over. "Let's get this over with. Just don't touch me."

He merely nodded. "Gaze upon me, then, Marya, and the journey will begin."

She stared into his eyes and, as before, beheld their clear, cold depths. They were as beautiful as they were horrible, like some force of nature terrifying in its destructive power, yet impossible to turn away from. She shivered and tried to will herself to stand fast, but felt a stronger will intercede, compelling her to submit. The eyes before her grew opaque, as shiny and dark as black water, and for the first time in her life, she felt ruled by a mind other than her own. Beads of light reflected off his eyes, dazzling her, until she could no longer see him, but herself. She wanted to struggle, to fight, but had no power to transform her wishes to reality. She watched, helpless, as her life unfolded before her eyes.

She saw herself as a child, eager and full of wonder, listening to her mother's stories. She felt the pride and love for her father inherent in the tales, and the disgust for all things preternatural. She saw Marya the teenager, caught between the *gadje,* the Rom, and the Undead. Unwilling to shake off her past, denied a future, she fought for every moment the present lent her. But every instant spent in fellowship was followed by an eternity spent in isolation, and every minute of approval was followed by three spent in ostracism. She saw Marya the adult, trying to accept her fate, trying to forge a life, but only reaping anger with the passing of each bi-yearly visitation from the Brotherhood.

Suddenly she felt her mind released, and the vampire's composed features appeared once more before her. She felt exhausted, and her breath came in labored gasps, but she forced herself to search his eyes for her fate. All she saw revealed in his impassive gaze was a touch of weariness. Not sympathy for the tortuous journey he had just led her on, but his own lethargy, as if he had just completed a disagreeable task and was glad to be done with it. How could any being on Earth view a lifetime of emotion and react with so little empathy?

He's not human, she reminded herself. *He's a monster, whose job it is to dole out death.*

She blinked, and he was on his feet in an instant. He raked a hand through his hair, glanced at the pendulum wall clock, and sighed, his fatigue still evident in spite of the speed and boneless grace of his movements. "It is done, *mademoiselle.* You will receive no more visits from us. I will inform the Brotherhood. Know that my decision is final. No one in that esteemed organization or any other has the authority to take away what I have given. But know also that should you commit violence of any sort upon my kind, that I will personally come for you, and there will be no mercy. *Comprendez-vous?"* He pulled on the cuffs of his sleeves and grabbed his coat from the chair that held it.

What? She shook her head. "No, I don't understand. What are you telling me?"

He nodded toward the cocktail table in front of the sofa. "My verdict is on the table. I give to you what will never be mine. *Bonsoir, mademoiselle."*

She glanced down at the table and noticed a small white envelope sealed with a glob of red wax. *When had he put that there?* With trembling fingers, she picked up the envelope and stared at it. The wax had been sealed with the impression of a dragon's head. She broke the seal and pulled out the enclosed white card. It read *Alek Dragovich* and gave a phone number beneath the script of his name. She flipped the card over. There was but one word on the back.

LIFE.

She looked up, but he was already gone.

TWO

Drago didn't normally dwell on an assignment once he made his resolution. Maybe it was the boredom of the night drive to Jackson, or maybe it was the memory of another assignment in Mississippi last year. Whatever the reason, his mind chewed on the Jaks case. He put the car on cruise control, leaned his head back on the seat's headrest, and ran his hands up and down the leather grip of the luxury car's steering wheel.

It wasn't that he was displeased with his resolution. Any other enforcer worth his eyeteeth would have condemned the aberration to death without a second thought. Not only did she have forbidden knowledge of the extent and structure of the formal vampire community, but her powers to detect and resist the Undead were the strongest he had felt in a mortal in a long, long time. That in conjunction with her hatred of all things vampiric made her a very real danger.

He had relished giving her life, however, not so much for the girl's sake, but because he knew his decision would irritate not only those in the Brotherhood, but more importantly, Nikolena herself. It was *la directrice* who relegated these assignments—demeaning in their unimportance—to him whenever she felt piqued, which lately seemed to be all the time. To resolve a case in a decidedly unorthodox way was Drago's way of thumbing his nose at her. He couldn't do that on an assignment of real significance, of course. Nikolena would have his head. Literally. But on unimportant cases like this one, he took great satisfaction in using his discretion to resolve things "The Drago Way."

No, his unease with the Jaks affair wasn't due to his giving the aberration life. It was with the subject herself. Far from the disgusting creature he had expected, Marya Jaks nevertheless had been a disturbing find. He had hidden his feelings from her well and with the practice of centuries, but she, with the pain of her brief life and the passion of her youth, had stirred memories in him which were better left dead and buried.

She was young— barely more than a child even in human terms—and had grown up in the modern world. She knew nothing at all of real pain or persecution, yet she had pled her case with the kind of conviction that normally comes with age and experience. Her words had struck a chord deep within him.

He leaned his head forward and brushed a long, wayward lock of hair from his eyes. She was an aberration—a foul being as unnatural as any on earth. That such a detestable creature had the power to touch him shook him as nothing had in a very long time. He was glad he was on his way to his chateau outside Paris for a short vacation. He would relax, feast well, and think no more on black-haired beauties with tainted blood who spoke with an eloquence beyond their years.

***

Disbelief kept Marya awake for hours after Drago left. She stared at the white card over and over, afraid she was dreaming or hallucinating. Each time she looked at the word on the card she expected to see *DEATH* staring back at her in a mocking scrawl, but *LIFE* was all she saw.

She was almost afraid to try to go back to sleep. What if she woke up in the morning only to find that Alek Dragovich had really been nothing more than a dream after all?

She changed from the dress into jeans and a shirt and stepped out onto the rear patio. If she were still dreaming, maybe the brisk night air would snap her back to reality. Alek Dragovich— the Anti-God, the Black Death, the bane to all those who violated the laws of Midexistence—was much more believable as his namesake, the dragon, than he was as some kind of white knight.

Drago a white knight. The image was so preposterous she wanted to laugh. But each time she held the card to the moonlight, *LIFE* shone at her.

She had never really dared over the years to hope for life, and when Drago had appeared tonight any shred of optimism she still clung to had all but vanished. In spite of the arguments she had put forth, she had never counted on being spared. All she had expected Drago to see was the power of her abilities and her anger. *And the visits to New Orleans.* Those alone, she knew, were enough to constitute a great enough risk for her to be flagged for termination.

She wondered what had swayed his decision to the side of life. Mercy? Compassion? She wanted to laugh again. He knew no such emotions. Drago had appeared bored with the whole affair. Perhaps he just didn't care one way or another. Perhaps there was less paperwork to file in granting life than in taking it. This time she did laugh. It was by far the most plausible explanation she had come up with.

When Marya finally did lie back down to try to resume her interrupted sleep, though, Drago's image continued to fill her mind. Dream or nightmare, dragon or knight, the memory of the antifreeze eyes would not go away. Chilling in what they lacked, alluring in what they held, she wasn't sure if she was thankful she'd never have to tread their depths again, or sorry she'd never again be the object of his gaze.

***

Marya slept late that morning. Awareness gradually seeped into her foggy mind, and with it, fear. She was afraid to open her eyes. Light meant reality, and reality had always meant pain. She summoned the courage to crack her lids just enough to make out the rays of sunlight squeezing past the edges of the shades and drapes to form rectangles of brilliance on the walls. She opened her eyes a little wider and saw her boudoir chair. It sat empty, its velvet arms bereft of a body to embrace. Had Drago really sat there only scant hours ago? Now, in the light of wakefulness and reason, last night seemed even more like a dream.

But what a dream! Her mind's eye could still see the image of him in the chair, his long legs stretched out before him, his fingers rubbing along the velvet and his eyes doing likewise up and down the length of her body. Last night she had been too angry to worry about the impropriety of his visit, but now she felt her cheeks flame with the memory. Every detail of his appearance flooded her mind, from the long hair so black it glimmered with highlights as blue as his eyes, to the mouth that mirrored the indolence of his gaze. Could a dream conjure so much detail?

She squeezed her lids shut, took a deep breath, then opened her eyes and turned her head to her nightstand. The card was still there, propped against the base of the lamp, where she had set it before retiring. She squinted at the card. *LIFE.*

Marya sucked in another long breath and let her head fall back to her pillow. *It's all true. It's no dream.*

She covered her face with her hands, fighting a sudden impulse to cry. It was everything she had never dared wish for. *A future. Dreams. Goals. Relationships.* She bounded off the bed and let the shades snap upward. Light streamed into the room. She turned on her stereo, and music filled the silence. She barely knew where to begin. She had had no plan beyond this day. Her art. She had always been serious about her art. It was, after all, how she made her living. But too often it had become just something to pass time with, something to fill the hours between one Brotherhood visit and the next. Now she could set goals, both financial and artistic. She could travel, take workshops, really hone her craft.

She could make friends now, could allow real relationships to develop. She could make a commitment beyond tomorrow. *Jaime.* She could stop holding him off, stop giving him excuses. *If he's still interested.*

Sudden doubts shadowed her enthusiasm. Rejoining the Roma community would in truth be a challenge. She had no family nearby to claim, and with her schooling and artwork, she had assimilated herself into *gadje* society more than most Roma. Her only real chance was to marry into the Roma community, but her chances there were slim, too. She was well beyond what the Roma considered 'marriageable age,' and she had no family with whom a Romani family would wish to make an alliance. All she had was herself, her talent, and her unique heritage. She hoped it would be enough for Jaime. *And his family.*

The Buckland family had also been assimilated into *gadjikane* society more than most. They had run a successful horse farm near Jackson for a number of years, and Jaime, too, had received schooling. To his parents' eternal consternation, Jaime had not married and was now, like Marya, well beyond the age at which Roma couples united. She tried to remember the gossip she had heard about him. He had been seeing a Roma named Seline Smith for a while, but she wasn't sure if he was seeing anyone now. Marya tried to think how long ago she had heard the latest news. It had been at least two or three months ago. Jaime could already have met someone new and be a married man by now.

No. Romani marriages were grand events. Had such a happening occurred, even she would have heard about it. She reached for her small phone directory, then just as quickly put it down. She needed to have a plan. This had to be done just right. A thrill of excitement coursed through her. It was good to be in control of her life again.

Jaime. He had invaded her thoughts too many times over the course of the past two years. Always, she had pushed those thoughts aside. The luxury of dreaming about the good-looking young Rom was one she hadn't been able to afford. She indulged herself now, bringing forth the memories of her last meetings with him with as much vividness as she could summon. He was very tall and unusually slender for a Rom, but his dark, brooding looks easily made up for his lack of brawn. He wore his hair well above his shoulders, but its thickness made it appear wild and unruly in spite of its short length. His features were sharp, but regular, and only added to the intensity of his appearance. Schooling had given him tools of literacy and knowledge, but it had also bred anger. At his best, Jaime was severe, yet charming. Very, very charming. At his worst, though, he was hard to be around. Sometimes the chip on Jaime's shoulder was so big as to be nearly visible.

Marya frowned, realizing that from Drago's point of view, last night she had probably sounded like she had a chip on her shoulder, too. Well, if she had, so what? Who cared what a vampire thought? They weren't human. It irritated her that thoughts of Drago were intruding into her new life. She pushed the vision of his blue eyes from her mind and turned her thoughts back to Jaime.

What would have happened with Jaime if the Undead hadn't put her life on hold? Would they now be married? Would she already have children? She wondered if she would still have her artwork, or if horses would now rule her life. Was that the life she really wanted? She didn't know. She had never before allowed her dreams to progress far enough to ask herself these questions.

Damn the Undead! For how long would the twelve-year suspension of her life affect her future? Would she ever be able to lead a normal life?

Perhaps not, but she would lead *a* life. The vampires were gone. She was in control now.

Three hours later, she picked up her phone and called the number for the farm.

"Hello. Buckland Horse Farm." A male voice. Probably either Jamie's father or his uncle.

"Is Jaime there?" Better not to volunteer her name unless asked for it. Jaime's family had always frowned on her.

"Who is calling?"

So much for plans. "Marya Jaks."

"Marya." There was a short pause. "Jaime's busy with the horses right now."

No 'how are you' or 'nice to hear from you.' The censure came across loud and clear. Marya tried to ignore it. "Can you give him a message to call me, please?" She gave the man her number, but he neither repeated the number back to her nor gave her any other indication that he was actually writing it down.

She refused to let her excitement be dampened. She would wait a day for a return call, and failing receipt of that, would drive out to the farm. However, as it turned out, plan "B" was unnecessary. Jaime returned her call within the hour.

"Marya! This is certainly a surprise. What can I do for

you?"

Happily, Jaime's voice held none of the subtle rebuke she had heard from the man who had answered her call.

"I realized how long it's been since I talked to you last. I've been wondering how you've been doing."

"I've been well, thanks." Jaime's voice had the ability to range from a mesmerizing musical lilt to a harsh bark. So far it was cautious. Friendly, yet wary, as if he were dealing with a strange horse whose temperament he wasn't sure of. "Yourself?" he added, almost as an afterthought.

"Well. Listen, Jaime, I know we had our disagreements. I had...a problem I couldn't talk about. It kept me from doing a lot of the things I wanted to do. I'm sorry about the way we ended things."

He broke in. "No, the way you ended things."

"All right. The way I ended things. It wasn't good, or fair. I admit it. It was bad luck to leave things the way I did, and I want to make it right." She held her breath.

He was slow in answering. She heard the small noises in the background. A thump. A nicker. He must be calling from one of the barns. "What about these 'problems' of yours? Are you ready to face them?"

Not them. Him. And she had faced him last night and had won. Drago's image threatened to rise again. Damn those blue eyes! Marya had anticipated these questions and had carefully scripted an answer before she had made the phone call to the Buckland Horse Farm. She couldn't tell Jaime the truth, of course. Each of the enforcers who had visited her over the years had stressed that it was strictly forbidden for her to tell any human her knowledge of the realm of Midexistence. Even though Romani culture was filled with legends of the Undead, those legends prevailed predominantly in Europe. When her mother had moved the two of them here from France, she had been careful to keep the family heritage a secret. Neither the Bucklands nor any of the other local Roma knew anything of Marya's father or grandfather. So Marya had happily complied with the enforcers' directives, not because of their dire warnings, or to aid the Undead in the concealment of their existence, but because it was to her own advantage. The local Roma looked at her with suspicious eyes as it was. She had no desire to give them any more ammunition to use against her.

"I'm ready to face them now, but for a long time I didn't feel like I had good fortune at all. It turned out I was very sick."

"I hope you had the sense to go to a *gadjikane* doctor." She could hear the frown in his voice.

"Oh, sure. First the doctors told me it was serious, even life threatening, but it wasn't. Even the *gadjikane* aren't always right. Still, I felt rotten for a long time." In a way, it was the truth. She did feel her good fortune had deserted her. She hadn't felt right. She did think her 'problem' was life threatening. The only real lie was that Alek Dragovich had "cured" her, not some *gadjikane* doctor. Dr. Dragovich blessing her with renewed good luck and health. She wanted to laugh at the ludicrous image.

"You should've told me. I would have helped you any way I could. Hell, my whole family would have overwhelmed you with sympathy visits."

"The problem's been resolved. For good. Do you think we can meet and talk about things, Jaime? I would love to see the horses again. Do you have lots of new foals?"

Mention of the horses was very deliberate on Marya's part. It was Jaime's passion. She knew any mention of the animals would distract him from memories of their bitter last parting.

"Uh, yeah, we've had a good foaling so far." He paused. "Listen, Marya. What made you call me today?"

The question caught her a little off guard. She wasn't expecting him to turn the conversation back to her so quickly. "I want to put my life back on track. I've always regretted the way we parted." That much was only the truth. "As I said before, I want to try to make things right with us."

He paused before answering. "It isn't always possible to pick up exactly where one leaves off. Time passes. Things change."

"I know that, Jaime. I want to try. If you do, that is." She held her breath.

"What do you want from me, Marya?"

The million dollar question, as the gadje would say.
"There's an excitement to life that surrounds you. I want to be part of that. I want to be more than friends. I think you've always known that."

Jaime exhaled a harrumph into the phone. "'Excitement.' I doubt my parents would view my ways in quite the same light. Listen, I have to get back to work, but I would like to see you. How about Friday night? I'll pick you up at seven. We can play it by ear. Dinner, then maybe a show or a walk through the Garden District if it's nice out. How does that sound?"

"Wonderful. I'll see you then."

She set the phone down with a triumphant thump. She had truly missed Jaime. He was the essence of raw energy. He could shock, and he could spark debate all too easily, but his passion for life was contagious. Whether it had been a quiet walk along the horse trails of the farm, or a heated disagreement, Marya had come away from her encounters with Jaime Buckland feeling stimulated and revitalized.

And on those occasions when he had kissed her, it had been like touching a live wire. Places in her body she didn't know existed had responded first with an awakening, then a delight and a demand for more. He had offered the 'more' that Marya craved, but she had forced herself to reject him.

It had been one of the hardest things she had ever done. Jaime lived with the constant expectations of his family. Most of those hopes centered on Jamie's marrying soon, and to a proper Romani girl. In spite of his family, though, a spirit unbound by outside forces seemed to manifest itself in Jaime. He always somehow managed to do what he wanted to do. It wasn't recklessness, or a disregard, but a likening to a creature that runs wild across a field. The freedom and joy of that image was a powerful lure to Marya. Jaime embodied it, and she wanted to follow him, to touch him, to be a part of him. But she hadn't been able to. Not with the possibility of a death sentence hanging over her head.

So when Jaime had hinted at deepening their relationship,

she had backed off. And when he, in his frustration, had laid out an ultimatum, she had ended it. Jaime would accept no halfway measures. It was everything or nothing. He had left her no choice.

No. It wasn't Jaime. It was the vampires who left me no choice. Her anger, so close at hand whenever she thought of the Undead, threatened to spoil her positive mood. She was quick to control it. She ruled now, not them. Not *him*. Not Drago, the monster whose lassitude and indifference were opposite poles to the energy and ardor of the man she would soon be seeing again.

Marya was afraid that the next three days would pass with agonizing slowness, but in fact they fairly flew by with both plans and action. She went shopping, cleaned the house, painted, and, most of all, thought about Jaime. With every day that passed memories of the vampire and his visit intruded less and less into her daydreams. It was over with. He was a part of her dark past she was glad to put behind her once and for all.

Her nighttime dreams, however, were a different matter. Late at night, when her mind was drained and her will weakened, visions of the creature invaded. For the first two nights following *l'enforcier's* visit, she woke in the middle of the night in a sweat, her mind filled with strange phantasms dressed in long robes and warrior garb. The costumes changed each night, but all had black hair and blue eyes.

Thursday night, however, she slept peacefully, her dreams undisturbed by blue eyes filled with death. She took it as a good sign.

She woke filled with energy. She straightened up her studio, anxious to show Jaime her latest works of finished art as well as her sketches and thumbnails for new ideas she had. But it was a glorious, warm spring day, far too nice to spend entirely in the house. Marya passed the early afternoon in the backyard gardening, but came back inside in plenty of time to shower and change. She took her time dressing for Jaime, donning a silk wrap skirt with a floral design of tropical red flowers against a black background and a matching red silk blouse.

She just finished dressing when the doorbell rang. In a brief panic, Marya wondered how she could lose track of time so badly on such an important occasion. Perhaps her watch had just stopped. She checked the time on her watch with her bedroom clock, but the time was right. Jaime was an hour early. It wasn't like him to be so untimely, but she was pleased nonetheless. Spontaneity could be exciting. Maybe he was just eager to see her and couldn't wait. She would scold him for catching her without her hair done up and her makeup on, but she would let him know later how glad she really was.

She opened the front door wide without checking the peephole first. A handsome young man stood on Marya's veranda, but it wasn't Jaime. Light blue eyes squinted at her from beneath heavy brows drawn together in a sedate frown. The solemn expression contrasted with shaggy brown hair and a dimpled chin that bespoke carefree youth, but this was no youth before her.

If his inorganic eyes hadn't been a dead giveaway, the nasty scent was.

He was a vampire.

THREE

"Miss Jaks?"

She glared at him, shock parting her lips but slowing her response.

"My name is Revelin Scott," he said in a strange accent.

Marya found her voice with the anger that supplanted shock. "I don't care who you are. I know what you are, and that's enough. What are you doing here?"

A smile that had no doubt been charming when this beast was alive curved his mouth. "Perhaps an invitation inside would make this easier."

An invitation? Was he kidding? "And why should I want to make anything easy for the Undead? I'm surprised you didn't just break into the house like your partner did."

His smile took on a twist of disdain, seeming to indicate that she was the one confused, not him. "Partner?"

"Alek Dragovich."

The creature laughed. "Drago's nobody's 'partner.' He's from the Directorate. I'm from the Brotherhood, Southeast Region."

"I don't care where you're from. Drago promised me no more visits from *any* of you."

The smile faded. "Invite me in, Miss Jaks."

She doubted he was strong enough to compel her. From the strength of his scent, he was nowhere near as old as Drago, but then again, few vampires were. Still, she relented and held the front door open wide. There was no point in arguing on the veranda. It was clear he wasn't going to go away.

He stepped into her living room, and she took her first good look at him. He was the complete opposite of Drago in appearance. *L'enforcier* had a kind of updated eighteenth century elegance to him, and could pull off 'menacing' as easily as he could 'sensual,' but Marya didn't think the creature before her now could look menacing if he tried. He wasn't very tall, topping her height by an inch at best, and his build was hardly imposing, but it was his features and dress that would have made her laugh had the situation not been so serious. His shag haircut, long bangs, and sideburns embraced his face with errant locks, and the tunic-style shirt in a gold, green, and brown paisley design and flared brown pants were straight out of the sixties. Were all vampires caught in one time warp or another?

He turned to her. "Actually, I'm here on Drago's behalf."

She tried to place his accent. Somewhere in the British Isles. British, Irish, or Scottish, she wasn't sure which. "Then why isn't he here?"

"I'm sure *l'enforcier* has more important matters to attend to. But I am here on his orders. It's regarding your status."

Marya's heart started to pound harder. This had not been right from the moment she had opened the door, and it was getting no better. "My status has been determined. Drago gave me life."

"Well, apparently he thought better of his decision. He's reversed it. I'm here to inform you that you've been flagged for termination as a danger to the community of the Undead. Per standard procedure you'll be allowed two weeks to put your affairs in order."

"No! Drago himself gave me life!" *What had been Drago's exact words?* Frantic now, she tried to recall precisely what he had said to her. She forced herself to calm down, and as she did so, his words flowed into her mind, replete with the imperturbable French accent. "He said his decision was final. He said that no one in the Brotherhood had any right to change it!"

The creature smiled in triumph. "Exactly right! No one in the Brotherhood can overrule a decision made by the Directorate. And no one has. Drago himself reversed his own finding. I am merely here as the messenger."

This can't be happening. It was the nightmare all over again, but worse this time because she had dared to hope. "Wait here just a minute." She ran into her bedroom and grabbed the card she had stared at over and over the past four days.

Marya held the card out to the vampire. "See? It's Drago's card. It says 'Life.'"

He took the card and looked at it, flipping it over to see both sides. "It does indeed. Well, no one ever said Drago wasn't ruthless. Or eccentric. Typical of him, if you ask me. He isn't called the Black Death for nothing." He handed the card back to her.

"No! He can come back here and tell me himself why he lied to me!"

The creature laughed again. "That's bloody good. An aberration ordering *l'enforcier* around. Only one lady does that, Miss." He headed for the door. "I'll be back in two weeks. And don't think about running. You'll be watched the whole time." He turned the knob.

"Wait! There must be an appeal process."

"This isn't a court, Miss."

"There must be someone I can talk to. Who's your boss?"

"It wouldn't do any good even if you could talk to him. As you yourself said, no one in the Brotherhood can overturn Drago's decision. Good Day, Miss."

Before she could stop him, he was gone, and she was standing alone, Drago's card in her hand. She stared at it, and the single word, once so sweet, mocked her. *Life.*

She threw it to the floor just as the clock struck the half-hour, reminding her of the time. Jaime would be here soon. How could she go out with him now, knowing they had no future? Besides, she'd be miserable company, to say the least. If she canceled the date, though, Jaime would be furious. She wouldn't blame him. How many times would he forgive her contrary behavior and mixed signals, even with the excuse of returning illness? *Fool! What does it matter if he's angry or not?*

She looked at the clock. It was too late to call him and

cancel the date. She'd have to muddle through the evening the best she could and plead for an early night. She retreated to the bathroom to scrub away the quick tears of anger and frustration.

By the time the doorbell rang again, she didn't quite look her normal self, but she looked better. *Normal.* Now that was a strange word. There was no such thing as 'normal' in her life. She crossed the living room on the way to get the door, and her gaze fell on the rectangle of white nestled into the thick pile of her carpeting. She snatched the card from the floor and threw it into the fireplace, pausing to take a deep, calming breath. The bell chimed again.

This time she checked the peephole. It was Jaime. She pasted a smile on her face and opened the door.

"Hi, lady." His dark eyes flickered over her in appreciation. "You look very nice."

He didn't seem to notice the smile that felt so forced. "Hi. You look pretty good yourself." That much was easy enough to say. Jaime's hair had been combed back from his face, but the wind had tugged the short hair on the crown of his head into spikes that refused to lay flat. Dressed in black jeans, a black leather vest, and an ivory shirt, he looked good enough to eat. His trademark silver was evident in abundance. He wore a silver neck chain, earring, and rings on every finger. "Come on in."

She held the door wide and stepped aside, breathing in the mixture of scents that clove to him like an additional garment—leather, tobacco, and just a hint of cologne. It was a much more appealing fragrance than the musty odor of decay that had clung to her previous uninvited guest. The thought brought with it a renewed feeling of despair. As much as she wanted this man, she wouldn't be able to have him. All the desire, all the planning in the world wouldn't change that. She took a deep breath to try to keep the despair from building into rage.

Watching Jaime didn't help. She saw him glance at "The Eternal Wait," and the unwelcome memory of the last man to behold her work flooded her mind—Drago, fingering the frame and studying every inch of the canvas. She shuddered as she remembered the attention he had focused on her artwork. It had seemed far too personal, as if he had touched her instead of the painting.

Marya looked at the wall now and took quick refuge in her art. "Umm…you haven't been here in a while. I wanted to show you my work. I have lots of new pieces."

Jaime nodded absently, as if to himself. "It's very good," was his only comment.

In spite of the compliment, Marya was vaguely disappointed. She put so much of herself into her painting. If he didn't understand her artwork, would he ever understand her? *What did it matter?*

She swallowed hard. It mattered. It had to, or she'd never get through this evening. "Come and see my studio. Most of the rest are in there."

She led him to the east side of the house, where she had converted a spare room into her art studio, and flipped on the lights. A large, slanted worktable in a corner was flanked on one side by a taboret and the other side by a long table upon which brushes, palettes and miscellaneous supplies crowded. The paintings on the wall, however, dominated the room. She glanced from one to the next. The subject of each was a girl or young woman, usually alone—sometimes indoors, sometimes outdoors—but always with a sense of movement juxtaposed against the stillness of the scene. *Expectation. Hope. Strength.* Would Jaime see any of it?

She turned to watch him. His gaze flicked from one painting to another, spending little time on any one particular work until his eyes finally rested on the depiction of a young girl standing at a country crossroads, the surrounding landscape overflowing with cross vines and wildflowers. "Pretty somber stuff for a Romani artist, isn't it?"

Had he expected scenes full of dancing and celebration? She had thought that Jaime, who was as unconventional as any Rom she knew, would understand. "Crossroads" was one of her favorites. She took another deep breath. "I didn't exactly have a traditional upbringing. But it's not just sadness I try to portray, or even beauty, but the contrasts in life, you know?

Vulnerability and strength, tranquility and expectation, present and future." *Life and death.*

Jaime raised his eyebrows.

Did he just not see it, or didn't he care?

"The feminine mystique is something I don't profess to understand. But you're very talented. I can tell that much."

She forced a smile. "Thanks. Most of my customers, I'll admit, are women."

"Well, the subject matter *is* a little delicate for men."

She sighed quietly. "I suppose." Were her world and Jaime's really so far apart? A voice in the back of her mind answered that her world was apart from everyone's, but she didn't want to hear it. "Come on," she said, more brightly. "I'm hungry. Let's head into town and eat."

He smiled. "Whatever your pleasure, lady."

Marya returned his smile, and this one came a little easier. She turned off the track lights illuminating her art, led him back into the living room, and grabbed her shoulder bag from a chair. "Ready."

He took her arm and guided her out the front door and down the drive to where his truck was parked. The blue F250 was sporty with a push bar and grill lights, but looked to have done its share of work on the farm. The bed was from far from spotless, and a large hitch protruded from the rear bumper. The interior was clean, though, and Marya smiled anew as Jaime backed the truck down the long drive to the road. There were no memories of Drago or Revelin Scott outside her house. If this was to be her one and only evening with Jaime, she wanted to at least enjoy it.

The ride into town was brief, and their conversation alternated between the respective challenges of raising fine horses and selling artwork in New Orleans. Fifteen minutes later they were in Vicksburg's Garden District. Jaime parked the truck, lit a cigarette, and took her arm as they began their stroll down Washington Street. They passed the Biedenharn Museum, the Antique Doll and Toy Museum, and the Gray and Blue Naval Museum. The attractions were all closed for the day, but they walked slowly, peering in the windows and pointing out eye-catching memorabilia to each other as if they were tourists viewing them for the first time. When Marya was with Jaime, everything did have a way of seeming fresh and new.

It was Spring Pilgrimage in Vicksburg, when many of the antebellum mansions were open for tours. The sunny, balmy evening was tailor-made, and many couples and families alike were out and about, enjoying the weather, the historic landmarks, and nature's own beauty. Sunsets over the Mississippi and Yazoo Rivers were always spectacular.

Marya's gaze couldn't help falling on a couple several yards ahead of them who apparently cared little for the charm of the Garden District. Their attention was all on each other, and they halted midway through shared laughter to embrace and kiss. Marya tried to smile in response, but this time she couldn't, looking away instead. It was a too-cruel reminder of what could never be hers. *Damn all the Undead!* Who were they to take her life away from her? Her anger rose again, and the tightness in her throat made swallowing difficult. Why? Why her? She had done nothing, had committed no wrongs. Why was her punishment, for nothing more than being born the daughter of a *dhampir,* harsher than that of many violent criminals?

Jaime's voice intruded on her thoughts. "Marya, did you hear me?"

She gave her head a shake and faced him. "I'm sorry. What?"

A slight frown creased his face. He took a final drag on his cigarette and tossed it away. "I asked if you're feeling better now."

"Oh, much." She tried to instill a measure of enthusiasm into her voice she didn't feel.

"I'm glad. Well, do you want to eat here or walk down to the pub?" He cocked his head toward the café behind them. "I think they have a blues band here tonight, if you're interested."

It didn't matter. She was no longer hungry. She suddenly didn't relish walking another two blocks, but blues music definitely would do nothing to improve her mood. "The pub, I think. It'll be easier to talk."

They ambled back down Washington Street, but Marya found it hard to switch gears from brooding over her fate to making small talk with Jaime. They walked in silence. Five minutes brought them to the quaint English-style pub. A hostess showed them to a corner table, and when a waitress arrived a moment later, Jaime ordered wine for both of them and a grilled steak for himself. He raised a brow when Marya told the girl that all she wanted was one of the tavern's renowned gourmet salads.

"I thought you were hungry," he commented after the waitress left.

Marya stared at her water glass. "I guess I'm not as hungry as I thought I'd be."

Jaime leaned back in his chair, and when the wooden legs creaked, Marya looked up. He was studying her. His sharp eyes made her feel almost naked, a feeling she might have enjoyed three days ago. "Marya, what's wrong?"

She pressed her lips into the shape of a smile. "Nothing. I don't usually eat a big supper."

He frowned. "The day you called me you lit up the phone line with your smiles and laughter. I thought…" He paused and glanced around the room, as if searching for something elusive. His gaze settled back on her. "But tonight you don't even seem glad to see me. No more lies, Marya. Tell me what's going on."

She closed her eyes. She hadn't anticipated this. She had thought she could pull off this evening without betraying her feelings. What could she say? She took a deep breath and opened her eyes. "I'm sorry. I didn't want to worry you, and I didn't want to break our date. I really did want to see you, but I woke up this morning not feeling well. I was hoping as the day went on I'd feel better."

He pursed his mouth. "You should have told me. We could have made different plans. We didn't have to go to dinner. We could have even made it for a different night."

She reiterated her point. After all, it was as close to the truth as she could come. "I thought I'd feel better."

Jaime stared at his placemat then raised dark eyes to hers. "You know, your inability to be open with me is what sank our relationship last time. I thought you were going to change that."

"I'm not trying to hide anything, Jaime." *Liar!* She felt like she was sinking into quicksand, and she didn't know what to say or do to extricate herself.

"Then why didn't you just say you weren't feeling well when I asked you what's wrong?"

"I didn't want to worry you."

"Right. Marya, I was willing to try again with you, but I don't think this is going to work. I was hoping you'd changed, but I can see you haven't."

She felt tears threatening to build, and her throat constricted. Everything she'd spent the past three days hoping for was being snatched from her grasp. She was flagged for termination. Nothing was as devastating as that. Jaime's feelings shouldn't matter at all. But they did.

"My stomach is really feeling upset, Jaime. Maybe you should take me home."

"No 'maybe' about it. Let's go."

They canceled their order and walked back to the truck in silence. The ride home was the longest fifteen minutes of Marya's life. Jaime made no attempt at conversation, lighting up one cigarette after another, turning toward his open window to blow the smoke out. He didn't turn to her once. When the truck pulled into her driveway at last she could think of only one thing to say. "I'm sorry, Jaime. I really am."

"That makes two of us. Good bye, Marya."

She hopped out of the truck and ran into the house without a backward glance. Slamming the door behind her, she leaned against it and closed her eyes until the sound of tires spinning on gravel faded from her hearing.

It's over.

No, not yet. She steadied her breathing and forced Jaime Buckland out of her mind. Two weeks. She had two weeks left. She wasn't going to go without a fight. She opened her eyes. The fireplace filled her vision, and she stared at it. An idea started to take form in her mind. She ran to the fireplace, opened the screen, and pulled the white card from its perch atop the grate. Drago's card.

She sat on the sofa and studied the front of the card. *Alek Dragovich* and a phone number. A phone number. *Good.*

Next, she ascended a narrow staircase to the attic, excitement lending quickness to her steps. *It has to still be here.* She pushed aside cardboard cartons, wooden crates, and file boxes. Finally, she tore back an old blanket and found what she was looking for. The wooden chest was just as she remembered it. She dropped the blanket to the floor, knelt on it, and raised the chest's lid.

There it was. Her father's journal. The vampire hunter's diary. Many Roma of her father's generation had been illiterate, but her father had been an exceptional man in many ways. He could not only read and write, but his ability to render accurate drawings was extraordinary. Marya was certain she had inherited her artistic talent from her father.

She carefully removed the journal from the chest and carried it downstairs. It was the only item belonging to her father that Marya still had. After her father had died, her mother, in keeping with tradition, had sold all his possessions. Her mother had wanted to destroy the journal, calling it the book of *meripen.* Death.

But Marya, wanting to keep that which had been most important to her father, had saved the book and hidden it from her mother. It chronicled not only the vampire hunter's search for his prey, but detailed the methods used to kill each of his seven victims. It was a how-to book on how to kill a vampire.

Marya spent the rest of the evening studying the entries and drawings. At midnight she closed the book and stared again at the white business card. *Excellent.*

If she was going to die, she was going to make damn sure she took Alek Dragovich with her.

FOUR

Marya woke early the next morning, anxious to devise the best plan possible. She sat down at the kitchen table with the journal, a writing tablet, and a pen. She again went over the various methods for killing vampires, this time listing the advantages and disadvantages of each on a sheet of paper.

There were actually quite a few ways to send the Undead to the True Death, but not all were practical, and many required specialized weapons or great physical strength. She eliminated some methods from consideration right away. Decapitation. *Too gruesome.* Removal of the heart. *Too messy.* Sever the spine. *I'm not strong enough.*

The techniques involving fire and silver were more promising, although neither was a guaranteed success unless done just right. Fire in itself would only kill if the vampire was totally consumed. Likewise, silver wouldn't kill unless the heart was staked. Staking, of course, was the traditional tried and true means of killing a vampire. Silver wasn't the only weapon that was effective for staking, however. Certain types of wood also worked. Ash. Hawthorn. Oakwood.

A weapon called a "vampire hunter" was a lance constructed of one of those woods with a silver core. Her father had once had one, but Marya didn't know what had happened to it. Chances were her mother had disposed of it.

Using silver ammunition or a silver knife seemed to be the easiest to both acquire and use. She had no idea, though, how to obtain silver bullets. A sterling silver knife would be much easier to find, but harder to manage in the deed.

Marya re-read an entry that she hadn't quite understood the night before. Silver nitrate. Lunar caustic. The only thing that Marya knew about silver nitrate was that it was sometimes used by doctors in the eyes of newborn babies to prevent blindness. She read further. Her father had underlined several entries. "...a chemical used in medicine and industry that burns the skin and can cause severe poisoning or death in humans if swallowed...highly toxic to the Undead...lethal if injected close to the heart in a potent solution...dissolves easily in water..." Another entry was marked with an asterisk. "This will replace the stake as the future of vampire killing..." On the next page another paragraph was highlighted. "Silver nitrate is used to make the silver backing on mirrors, and most silver salts used in film are made from silver nitrate. Is this why vampires cannot see their reflection in mirrors and cannot be photographed?"

Marya was excited. *Not too messy, not too gruesome.* It didn't require phenomenal strength, and it sounded as close to a sure thing as any method listed. It sounded just right. If only she could acquire some of this 'silver nitrate.'

Her father's notes were written more than two decades ago. Perhaps she could find additional and more current information on how to obtain silver nitrate. She didn't own a computer, but the Vicksburg Public Library had several terminals for public use. She had often used them to order art supplies online, and she knew how to use the various Internet search engines.

She spent the rest of the morning at the library, taking copious notes. It wasn't long before she found what she was looking for. Colloidal silver. Minute silver particles in a colloidal suspension of deionized water. In dilute solutions, colloidal silver was a natural antibiotic, readily available at health food stores. She used the pay phone at the library to call the local store that handled such items, her heart pounding in time with the dial tone in her ear. After a couple moments she hung up the phone in relief. They had colloidal silver in stock. She drove to the store, bought the largest bottle they had, then stopped at a medical supply store and purchased several different types and sizes of syringes. By the time she arrived home, she felt better than she had in the hours since

Revelin Scott's visit. All she had to do now was practice giving injections, come up with a plan for getting close enough to Drago to inject him, and pray the concentration of silver in her magic bottle was strong enough to burn a vampire from the inside out.

***

Drago was tired. Tired and glad to be home.

His flight to Paris had been delayed by a whole week. After his Vicksburg assignment, Nikolena had called and sent him to New Orleans to investigate the death of a Brotherhood member. It had been a messy affair, resulting in two dead vampires and severe sanctions imposed on two more. Drago would have to make a follow-up visit to Louisiana as soon as he was done in Paris.

He immersed himself in the hot water of the in-ground bath at Chateau du Russe and let out a soft groan of pleasure. There were no castles in Russia, but there were palaces, and he had done his best to turn this ancient French castle into a true Russian palace. He leaned his head back on the pool's rim and let his eyelids drift shut. It wasn't that he needed the bath to relieve aching muscles or stiff joints. The warmth and buoyancy of the water just felt good.

The annoying bang of the door echoed behind him and broke his relaxed mood. Light, running steps grew louder, followed by a high-pitched feminine voice.

"Drago! You're finally back. I've missed you so much!"

He cranked his head to stare at the unwelcome intruder, who eased herself carefully into the water to stand next to him. It was Danielle, one of his 'guests.' Young women with an overabundance of time and zeal often stopped at the chateau in an attempt to win the favor of *mysterieux le Russe,* the mysterious Russian, as he was known locally. He had tolerated and often encouraged the visits, hoping perhaps to chance upon the elusive *affaire d'amour,* but lately it seemed that the women were interested more in his money than his charms, splitting their time between the chateau and shopping trips to Paris. He had already tired of Danielle long since, but she was more persistent than most in trying to secure his attention…and his francs. She was young, had flaming red hair, and wore the tiniest bikini he had ever seen. Suddenly she slapped her hand against the water, sending a spray to soak Drago's head and shoulders.

"That's for being a bad boy and ignoring me for so long."

He had seen what she was going to do, but had had time only to avert his face from the full blast of the splash. He slowly rotated his head back toward her, running a hand through his hair to pull wet strands from his eyes.

"How did you get in here, *mademoiselle?*"

She stood waist high in the water and started to raise her arms to embrace him, but his restraining glare halted her action, leaving her arms trembling in midair. Water dripped from her elbows back into the pool. Her red hair was piled high atop her head in a mass of carefully arranged ringlets. A few long tendrils spiraled down on each side of her head and along the nape of her neck, and sparkling brilliants were fastened to the coif in strategic places. Her makeup was a flawless match to the elaborate hairstyle.

Her exuberant voice lowered, almost to a petulant whine. "I followed you. I've been waiting sooo long for you, Drago! Almost three weeks! That housekeeper of yours is like a prison guard, but I…"

Three weeks? He had no doubt that most of that time was spent in St. Honore seeking out the latest in perfume, jewelry, and *haute couture,* not waiting for him. For a vampire to snarl was a novice affectation, but he didn't mind curling back his lips now and again at foolish humans. "First of all, Adelle is *not* a housekeeper. Secondly, you were *not* invited in here. Get out."

She looked confused. Her gaze drifted around the room, but she made no move to leave the pool. "But, Drago…"

"Get out, *mademoiselle.* I won't tell you again."

"I…" She never got the second word out. Her scream ricocheted off the walls as he used one leg to sweep her feet out from underneath her, but she was quickly silenced when her flailing arms weren't enough to prevent her head from dunking below the water's surface. She quickly bobbed out of the water, coughing and trying to peel the wet curls out of her eyes, but the damage was done. The coif was ruined.

"Out!" His shout was louder than even her shriek, and this time she didn't hesitate. In a frenzy of thrashing limbs, she half swam, half ran to the edge of the pool, hauled herself out of the water, and scuttled across the room, leaving a trail of puddles and wet footprints behind her. The door slammed.

He took a deep breath. She had thoroughly annoyed him, and the girl was lucky he hadn't done worse than spoil the work of a few hours in front of a mirror. He really must see to increasing security at the chateau. He closed his eyes and allowed the heat of the water to gradually restore a feeling of peace and stillness to his repose. The quiet lasted ten minutes.

Even with his eyes closed he easily picked up Adelle's approach behind him. Adelle Duquesne's step and scent were both unique and well known. His servant for forty years, she was now closer to a mother to him than a lover, companion, or any of the other roles she had played over the years. Her appearance now was not unexpected.

She sat down next to him at the pool's edge and ran her fingers through his hair. "I'm so sorry, Leksii. I don't know how she got through. She must have been hiding and waiting."

"Did you take care of the *coquette?*"

"Of course. She'll be escorted off the grounds, with instructions not to return."

He shook his head. "I don't know what I ever saw in her to begin with. Vapid, worthless mortal."

Adelle laughed. "She's a very beautiful girl. Very…hot-blooded."

He failed to appreciate the humor. "See to security, will you, *ma chere?* I cannot have this kind of thing."

"Changes will be made, don't worry." She tucked a long strand of wet hair behind his ear. "Can I get you anything, Leksii?"

"No, *ma chere,* nothing."

"You sound tired." Her soft voice held surprise.

He drew in a deep breath of the steamy air. "I am."

"And here I thought you were exempt from such frailties."

He felt, rather than saw, her sad smile and reached up to touch her hand. "It's not so much a physical exhaustion, Delle." No, his body was as strong and free from pain as it always had been.

"Your trip, then?"

It wasn't Vicksburg or even New Orleans. How could he explain it to her? "No, *ma chere,* it's just…something that has been settling in my bones, and, as time passes, it becomes more and more a part of me I can't shake." It was the downside to being almost six hundred years old.

"It's called boredom, Leksii. Perhaps you need a new job."

He sighed. "There's nowhere to go. You know that."

It was true. He was as powerful both in strength and position as any vampire on earth, save a handful of others in the Directorate. He was one of three Directorate enforcers assigned to North America, but more than that, he held the plum jurisdiction of all of the United States. He even had his own office in the Directorate building, albeit one that was occupied more frequently by his assistant Philippe than himself. There was no position carrying more power and prestige except for that of director, and he had no desire either to usurp Nikolena or hold a job that would effectively isolate him from the world. Nor could he 'retire' from his present position. The Directorate had a simple retirement system—it was called *la Belle Mort.* If one could no longer perform his duties, he was replaced. And killed. It was the only circumstance that justified a vampire's demise at the hands of another vampire. It would be just too dangerous to let loose in the world a former member of the Directorate without the supervision and sanctions that ensured obedience.

"So what are you going to do?" she asked.

"I don't know, my pet."

"Do you want me to let Cerise in? She's the only other guest here tonight. She's been eagerly awaiting your return, but with a great deal more patience than Danielle. You've always liked Cerise, haven't you?" Her voice was teasing now, but he didn't smile.

"All of them bore me. I just want to be alone."

She squeezed his hand. "All right. I'll see to it you're not bothered any more before you have to leave for your meeting."

"Merci, ma chere."

Adelle padded away from the pool area, and he was alone once again. There were few who understood his feelings when these dark moods descended on him, and even fewer who had the ability to meliorate those feelings. Adelle was the only mortal who knew and appreciated much of what he had been through in his life, but sometimes even she lacked awareness of his state of mind.

He sighed again. He was not looking forward to this evening's meeting with Nikolena. The affair in New Orleans had gone badly, but it had largely been over with by the time Drago had arrived. Little had been left for him to do save to clean up the mess and impose sanctions on those responsible. The Vicksburg case, however, had been one of Nikolena's 'punishment' assignments, and Drago's automatic response had been to amuse himself by resolving it in his own unique way. He was sure Nikolena would reprimand him, but he doubted there would be teeth to her bite. One aberration more or less in the world mattered little.

He frowned when he recalled his confrontation with the *mademoiselle*. She had displayed very little fear for a human in her precarious position and had spoken her piece with true conviction. *Persecution. What could she know of true persecution?*

He stared at the ripples in the water, and in their dancing ebb and flow, the centuries fell away.

Novgorod, 1471

He had been born a Prince of Novgorod, but in that year the nightmare that would steal his life from him began innocently enough. As a Prince, he had trained his whole life in the arts of riding, sword handling, and strategy. His command presence took no training—that had come naturally to the young man he was. When Ivan III, Grand Duke of Moscow, declared war on the city-state proudly named His Majesty Lord Novgorod the Great, Drago had relished the challenge, but his army, large as it was, could not live up to the grand and glorious name of the proud city. Largely composed of civilian militia, the Novgorodian army was disorganized and uncoordinated, and in July at the Battle of Shelon River, twelve thousand of his men were slain. Drago had fought hard, bloodying many a Muscovite foe without himself sustaining so much as a scratch, but it was only the first of Ivan's campaigns against everything the Prince held dear. Little did he know in 1471 that seven years later he would be wishing with all his heart and soul that he had fallen with his comrades at the Shelon.

The memories, always fresh, were never far away, but they were cold companions. He thought again of the Gypsy girl and how her dark eyes had flashed with passion. How different her eloquence had been from the inane squealing of the redhead.

He recalled the images that had flashed through her mind and his when he had set the vampiric mirror before her. He had seen loneliness most of all, and the pain and frustration that were offshoots of that isolation. Had the girl indeed known persecution? How could she? She was young. Worse yet, she was an aberration. He couldn't forget that.

He wrinkled his nose in disgust. It was disturbing to even think that he would give a second thought to such a foul creature as an aberration, even one as beautiful as Marya Jaks. It didn't matter anyway. It was over. He closed his eyes again, sank lower in the warm water, and tried not to think about growing old, Nikolena, or dark-haired Gypsies.

***

Drago dressed very carefully for his meeting with Nikolena. Her eyes were always appraising him, as if he were a prize-winning animal for sale at market. But he allowed himself the illusion that her pleasure at his appearance helped blunt any anger she felt disposed to direct his way. He dressed in snug black trousers, knee-high black leather boots, and a long black-velvet coat embroidered in gold, green, and blue silk in a pattern of peacock feathers. Underneath the coat he wore a gold brocade vest and, as usual, his sapphire collar pin at his throat. He left his hair loose in the manner he knew Nikolena preferred, checked the time, and called for his chauffeur. The drive to the chateau housing the Directorate offices outside Paris took less than an hour, but Drago dared not be late.

He wasn't, nor was he early, but Nikolena made him wait. Drago passed the time with Philippe Chenard, his assistant. Philippe, as all the Undead, looked the same as ever. His copper-brown hair hung straight to his collar and was combed neatly behind his ears. His dark goatee was trimmed with the same precision that his work was known for, and his tawny eyes gleamed with a feline shrewdness. And yet for all his debonair looks Philippe always somehow managed to look weary and put upon. Drago had often wondered exactly how he did it.

Drago sat on a corner of Philippe's desk. "So, tell me. What's madame's mood?"

Philippe lazily cocked his head and arched an even more indolent brow. "What do you think?"

"If I knew, *mon ami,* I would not be asking."

His aide leaned back in his chair. "Well, for starters she expected you three days ago."

Drago brushed a piece of lint from his black-velvet coat. "I can't help her unrealistic expectations. She knew I was delayed."

"Then there's your New Orleans report. It appeared she didn't think any better of your sanctions than those you imposed them on."

Drago flicked his brows in a quick dismissive gesture. "Nikolena wasn't there. Neither were you. A decision had to be made quickly, and harsh measures were called for. The deaths of two enforcers cannot be tolerated."

Philippe pursed his lips. "No, of course not. But sanctions so harsh that they inspire rebellion certainly cannot be any more desired."

Drago smoothed the velvet nap of the coat, as if daring another piece of lint to attach itself. "Then Nikolena should have sent someone else. She knows how I operate."

"Yes. We all do. But who would you have suggested?"

Drago smiled. "How about His Highness, King Evrard? Or was he too busy elsewhere?"

Philippe smiled. Drago knew his assistant didn't care for Evrard Verkist, the Brotherhood Patriarch, any more than he himself did.

At long last, the word was given from Nikolena's sanctuary.

"Wish me luck, *mon ami.*"

Philippe smiled again. "Good luck, Drago."

Drago drew a deep breath and strode into the airy chamber that comprised Nikolena's office, but halted well short of her grand desk. One didn't approach unless one was commanded to. He inclined his head in greeting. *"Bonsoir, Madame la directrice."*

Her dark eyes, even across the room, were cold and empty pits in her face. "You're late, Aleksei Borisov. Three days late. You know I don't like to be kept waiting."

He bowed low from the waist. *"Je suis desole d'etre en retard, madame.* My apologies. The incident in New Orleans was…complicated."

"'Complicated?' Your assignments always seem to complicate themselves. And two dead! The dead never fail to multiply when you are on a case. Why is that?"

"It's all in my report, *madame.*"

She picked up a stack of reports and slammed it down. The ringing slap of paper against wood echoed in the chamber like the report of gunfire. "If I could make sense of this muddle you dare call a report I wouldn't have to ask such a question, would I? Come here and explain yourself!"

He glided up to her and settled into an ornate chair, not across the desk from *la directrice*, but at her side. Nikolena liked to be close to those she chastised. As elegant as ever, she was dressed in a full-length ecru dress with a high collar and long sleeves, heavily embellished with hundreds of seed pearls and silver embroidery. A lace shawl hung from one shoulder. Though she barely topped five feet in height, Drago had to look up to meet Nikolena's eyes. Her chair, like a throne, sat on a raised platform.

"A votre service, madame. What can I clarify for you?"

She peered down at him. "Save your charms for your human

conquests, Aleksei Borisov. They win you nothing with me."

He tilted one side of his mouth in the barest of smiles. "I did not presume they would, *madame.*"

A matching shadow of a smile touched Nikolena's austere face. It was a never-ending game, played to perfection by both parties.

He patiently explained the circumstances leading to the two deaths in the Warehouse District that had been the result of a misguided power play between two of the city's newest enforcers. He emphasized the fact that both vampires had met the True Death long before he himself had arrived in town. The fact did nothing to mollify Nikolena.

Her gaze traveled the length of his body like a whiskbroom looking for dirt. "And just what took you so long to get to your assignment? I called for you because you were nearby."

"I was a state away. You called for me because Curt Deverick is inept." Deverick was the Brotherhood enforcer in charge of the Southeast Region.

"We're not here to discuss Deverick. It's your pretty head on the chopping block, my sweet, not his. I want to know why you took your time getting to a priority assignment, and so help me, Alek, if it's because you dawdled in Vicksburg, you will be sorry!"

Drago remained calm. It never served anyone to respond in kind to Nikolena's vitriolic censure. Many had found out the hard way. Her reference to 'chopping block' was not just a figure of speech. "I spent only one night in Vicksburg. I was in New Orleans within four hours of your call. The two vampires had already been dead twenty-four hours."

Nikolena tapped her pen on her desk, an irritating accompaniment to the equally annoying job she did of gleaning his intentions with the forceful gaze of her dark, narrowed eyes. After a moment, she dropped the pen and sighed. "Why, Alek? Why do you persist in defying me?"

"New Orleans…"

She shook her head. "I'm not talking about New Orleans. I'm talking about Vicksburg. What you did with that aberration is intolerable, and well you know it."

"Then you should have sent some neophyte enforcer to do the job. *Zut!* Any one of Curt Deverick's incompetents could have bungled their way through that assignment and made everyone happy in the process."

Her eyes slitted even more, yet Drago knew she saw into his mind with no less ease than before. "Have a care, Alek. You presume too much on my tolerance. One day it may not be there."

He didn't answer. There was little reason to. He hid no thoughts from Nikolena's piercing stare.

"Come closer, Aleksei Borisov."

The only way he could move closer to her was to get out of his chair and kneel by hers. He did as she bade. She reached out a small, manicured hand and fingered the velvet and silk of his coat, then lifted her hand and stroked his hair. A sad smile played across her mouth, softening her features at last. "You don't even care, Alek, do you? You persist in playing your role, but as time goes on you kick aside the rules of the game, one by one, don't you?"

"I live to serve only you, *madame.*"

"Oh, bullshit, Alek. You serve only yourself these days, and soon, you will tire even of that. Then what? I can't protect you forever. The others talk. There are whispers of your removal already on the wind. *L'enforcier* has made too many enemies."

He closed his eyes. "I made my reputation, Nika, and I've built it every chance I've had. I'm aware of what it's done."

"Are you? I think not. We are too alike, you and I—both Russian, both of noble blood. I understand the things you feel. My fortune is tied to yours. But I won't let you bring me down, Aleksei Borisov. You may be tired of living, but I am not. Fair warning, Alek, fair warning. Do you hear me?"

He stood. *"Oui, madame.*"

"Then to whom is your devotion?"

He took her hand, raised it to his lips, and pressed a kiss to the pale skin. "To you, *madame.*"

"Good. Then we understand each other."

He looked into her eyes and nodded. He understood.

***

Three hours later Drago stood in the courtyard formed by the private wings of his chateau. It was cool for early April, and a chill breeze swirled in the confines of the yard, setting the more slender tree branches to fluttering. The cold didn't bother Drago, though. He had removed the velvet coat, but still wore the high boots and brocade vest.

He canted his head and looked up at the moon, almost full, and did something he didn't often do. Considered his future. Tonight's meeting had signaled a subtle shift in his relationship with Nikolena, and it hadn't been for the better.

He heard Adelle tread up the stone path to stand beside him, and he acknowledged her presence with a long glance. Her hair shone more silver than blond in the moonlight, but she was still the slender, striking woman she had always been.

She adjusted her shawl to cover more of her arms. "Still pensive, Leksii?"

He looked away, a rumble in his throat his only answer.

"The meeting with Nikolena didn't go well, did it?"

"No."

She ran her fingers down the silk folds of his sleeve. "You look splendid tonight. How can you not have her eating out of your hand?"

He twisted his mouth into a rueful smile. "If I were naked, *ma chere,* I would not have her eating from my hand."

Adelle strengthened her hold on him, and he could feel the palm of her hand warming the muscles of his arm. "I doubt that," she whispered, but the smile quickly slid from her voice. She dropped her arm from his. "Is it that serious?"

Adelle was the only human he could share Directorate business with. She was bound to him by marks of blood, and as such, was not only unquestioning in her loyalty and faith, but shared a mental connection with him that no other mortal did.

"Talk of my removal is starting to circulate."

She shrugged her shoulders, setting the fringes on her shawl to dancing. "You've never been popular."

He sighed. "Unpopular. Now there's an understatement.

No, but there's a big difference between being disliked and being removed."

She gave him a short, mirthless laugh. "Disliked. Another understatement?"

"Very well. Hated. Hated by everyone except you, *mon chou.*"

Adelle put her hand on his shoulder and stroked the length of his arm. "That's because no one knows you like I do. But Nikolena..."

"Nikolena is afraid that if I'm ousted, her position is forfeit as well. So I am to behave myself. If I don't, her implication was clear. She'll distance herself from me any way she can."

Adelle shook her head. "But you and she have always held an alliance. You're like a favorite son to her."

"More like a favorite dog. Even the best alliances are hardly about loyalty or friendship. No, she would throw me to the pack in an instant if it meant her survival."

Adelle was pensive. Should he meet *la Belle Mort,* Adelle would die as well. Die or go insane. "Would forging a new alliance help? Perhaps then you would have help at your back instead of knives in your back."

He smiled, but it was more a rueful acknowledgement of the truth in her statement than any expression of hope over the idea. "I still have my old alliance with Philippe and Ricard De Chaux. There's no one else I trust even superficially enough to form an allegiance with."

"So what will you do?"

"*Je ne sais pas, ma chere.* I just don't know."

"Well, you're home now," she said with renewed liveliness. "If you're ever going to enjoy yourself, it's here. Let me send you Cerise, Leksii. She's not at all like Danielle. Really."

Maybe Adelle was right. He would accomplish nothing by brooding. His scheduled time in Paris was short, and then he'd have to return to the States. There would be no time then for relaxing, only for refereeing the never-ending power plays of vampires with not enough time on the earth to know real power.

He put his arm around Adelle and gave her a hug. "You're right, *ma chere,* as always." Cerise did have exquisite lavender eyes and a lovely, quiet voice. "Cerise, then."

He saw Adelle smile, but it was cheerless, doing nothing to light her eyes. Did she remember the times when she herself was the one to come to him? If only time could have stood still for both of them... He would much rather be with Adelle than any of the empty-headed young girls at the chateau, but it had been Adelle herself who had ended their intimate relationship a decade ago. It was her own comparison of his forever youthful appearance to her aging features that made her too uncomfortable to continue as lovers.

"Cerise," she acknowledged.

He gave her another squeeze. "Send her to the red room."

***

Cerise was a veritable feast for the senses. All but one. She was as quiet as the dead.

"Talk to me, Cerise," he begged as he kissed the side of her face.

She only laughed.

"Come, regale me with your day so I can experience both your voice and your mind." He nipped at her earlobe, a further entreatment to feed all his senses.

Cerise would have none of it. "You're a crazy *Russe,* you know that? Do you want to make love or hold a conversation?" She kissed him on the mouth to still any response.

Drago gave in and decided he could forgo the foreplay of small talk. Besides, what she did to his remaining senses more than made up for her silence.

He took his time, pulling away from her and taking in the sight of her beauty first. She had long, rich brown hair and eyes the color of spring violets. And she smelled like spring—fresh, fragrant, and full of the promise of life. His hands and mouth explored that promise first, feeling the softness and warmth that invited yet more. But he waited. This was not to be rushed. He started at her throat and worked his way downward. When he arrived, at last, at the moment of indulgence of the final sense—that of taste—he wanted her as badly as he had wanted any female in recent memory.

His cell phone jingled.

Drago groaned. *"Merde!"* His body drove him to ignore the interruption, but the mood was broken, at least on Cerise's part.

"Drago, maybe you should answer that. It could be important," she mumbled against his hair.

He didn't stop, but neither did the ringing, muffled though it was from beneath the jumble of his fine clothes on the floor.

"Drago…"

"Zut!" He rolled away from her and was on his feet in an instant. "Wait here, *cherie*. I will be right back." He dug the phone out from under his trousers. The ringing had stopped, but an icon flashed that a voice mail message waited for him. He slipped into an adjoining sitting room and closed the door. He could always cloud Cerise's mind later, but it was just less complicated if she didn't hear Directorate business to begin with. He played the message.

"Drago? This is Marya Jaks. Remember me? Or are all your cases forgotten as soon as the paperwork's done? Did you really believe that after what you did, you'd heard the last of me? Oh, and one more thing. When that vampire shows up later this week, I'm going to kill him. And if you don't think I have either the will or the ability, think again. I'm my father's daughter, and this will be for the both of us."

What? He stared at the phone as if it were to blame. *What was she babbling about? Was she insane, or playing some kind of sick joke?* Either way, he didn't need this. He groaned again at the denial of his pleasure, then let loose with every profanity in every language he knew. Either way, he couldn't ignore the call.

His vacation was over.

FIVE

Drago leaned back in the wide, leather seat and shut the distracting sounds of the plane from his mind. He needed to calm down.

Everywhere he had gone this morning, he had seen angry people, both human and Undead. Cerise had been upset over the loss of her pleasure. Adelle had lamented the loss of his company, so seldom had these days. Nikolena had been...there was no single word to describe Nika's anger. Tart, scathing, cold, hot—her anger was a brew of every kind of threat, rebuke, and cajolery possible. And it hadn't been only verbal. She had ripped at his mind with the power of her own until he had sat before her drained, exhausted, and unable to so much as form a thought.

This was what came, she had said, of not following protocol. This was what happened, she sniped, when he did things his own way. This was what he deserved, she proclaimed, for his defiance.

And at the end of it all, she had bid him kiss her hand, as usual, and begged him to have a care.

But by far the angriest person was himself. He was annoyed at having to be on the Concorde again so soon after his last transcontinental flight. He was wounded by Nikolena's lack of faith in him and incensed by her pointless show of dominance over him. He was furious at the aberration Marya Jaks for her foolish message. And he was mad at himself. Nikolena was right about one thing. He had selfishly catered to his own whims instead of resolving a case the way he should have. The Vicksburg assignment had been handled badly, and nothing infuriated him more than a job not finished. In his years of being *l'enforcier* he had taken many a vampire to task over doing a job poorly. He could be no less exacting with his own work.

Well, he would rectify matters swiftly. The aberration's threat to kill a vampire was an automatic death sentence. He had told her so. What had possessed her to call and leave such a damaging message? And what vampire was she talking about killing? Not that he would mourn the loss of any of the Southeast Region enforcers, from the lowliest novice to the head of the region, Curt Deverick. All of them were brutal and incompetent. It was the reason he spent most of his time in the states between Florida and Louisiana. He had complained numerous times in the past to Evrard Verkist, the Patriarch of the Brotherhood, but Evrard had done nothing to improve the quality of his enforcers. Evrard was as nasty a piece of work as Deverick, but Drago had sensed far more power in the Patriarch. Nowadays he tried to avoid dealing with Evrard Verkist whenever possible. Not because he was afraid of him. He feared no vampire, not even Nikolena. He simply didn't like Evrard. Never had. The feeling, of course, was mutual.

Drago allowed himself to doze. It was a risk, but a small one, and he had gotten little sleep last night following the aberration's call. There were no other vampires on the flight, of that he was sure. If there had been, the disagreeable scent of decay would have been a clear giveaway. Drago had looked over the other passengers as he had boarded. None looked to be a threat. The passenger seated next to him was an elderly Frenchman. So he slept, though lightly. His finely tuned senses, even in such a state, would warn him of any danger.

Less than fours hours later, the jet landed at JFK Airport. Drago heaved a sigh of relief. Not that he had risked and survived sleeping in a cabin with a hundred other people, but that the plane had touched down safely. Drago hated flying. Any kind of flying. A plane crash would just as effectively kill a vampire as a human. The flights between New York and

Paris were unavoidable, but once in the United States, he shunned airline travel whenever possible, much preferring to drive or even journey by train.

Drago retrieved his car from the long-term parking structure at the airport. It was a long drive from New York to Vicksburg, close to twenty-four hours, but he was counting on having the time. The aberration's message had been vague, saying that she would kill the vampire "later this week." She hadn't said "tomorrow," so he took that to mean he had at least a couple days.

He hoped he was right. He didn't even want to think what Nikolena's reaction would be if he ended up reporting the death of a vampire in this mess. But one dead aberration? A Gypsy with no family? Nobody, but nobody, would care about that.

***

The waiting was the hardest part for Marya. She had made her plan, she had made the phone call, and she had practiced injecting water into fruits a hundred times over. There was nothing more to do but wait. Either Drago would show up, and it would end with his death or hers, or Revelin Scott would show up and it would be him or her. She had no compunction about killing Scott. He was no more blameless than Drago as far as she was concerned.

In a way, she was glad she had left the message on Drago's voice mail rather than speaking to him in person. She hadn't wanted to hear his silk-lined voice, nor had she wanted to give him the opportunity to ask her questions. It had been much easier to leave the brief message and hang up. The only problem was that she had no way of knowing if he got the message, and if so, that he would even come.

She had thought long and carefully about what she could say to Drago that would assure his appearance. She had painstakingly tried to recall everything he had said to her during his visit, and she had written everything down, word for word, the best she could remember. The one statement she kept coming back to, time and again, was his warning that should she commit any violence against his kind that he would personally come for her. He had sounded dead serious when he had spoken those words, and she had no reason to believe he wouldn't live up to them. So, threatening to kill a vampire was the surest lure she had been able to devise to entice him back to her home.

It was the second day following her phone call. If he was coming, it could be any time now, and she couldn't assume he would come during the day and be polite enough to knock on her door. It was more likely he'd just break into her house again at night and sneak into her bedroom. She had to be prepared twenty-four hours a day, and that meant carrying the syringes with her at all times, even sleeping with them.

She waited up all that evening, keeping the radio and TV off so she could hear the smallest noise. She passed the time constantly checking the windows and entrances. It was a warm evening, so she kept one set of French doors in the living room open to get some air in the house. But she kept a close eye on the doors and the lit patio beyond.

The phone rang.

In the dead quiet of the house, the sound was more jarring than usual. Marya glanced at her clock. Almost eleven. Who would be calling her so late in the evening? She waited until the third ring, then, her heart pounding so loud in her ears it nearly downed out the sound of the phone, she picked up the receiver.

"Hello?"

"Is Bobby there?"

"Wrong number." She quickly put the phone down and drew a deep breath of relief. A wrong number. Her heartbeat quickened again. What if it wasn't a wrong number? What if someone just wanted to make sure she was home? The voice had sounded Southern, but...

She turned back to the French doors. They were still open. She had turned her back on them to answer the phone. How long had she had her back turned? Fifteen seconds? Thirty seconds? She looked around the room. Everything was as it should be. She would have heard if anyone had come in, wouldn't she? But the stealth and swiftness of a vampire was beyond human senses to detect.

This was ridiculous. She would go to bed. If he wanted to slink into her bedroom, she'd be ready for him. She closed and locked the French doors.

The grandfather clock sounded the top of the hour, and Marya jumped. She faced the clock, watched the pendulum swing back and forth, and silently counted along with the bongs. *One, two, three...* After the eleventh bong, she waited for the silence to swallow the final echoes of the chimes. All was quiet again.

She turned for the bedroom and ran smack into a figure in black.

The vision was that of Death, but it was no apparition. Drago was flesh and blood and standing but a foot away from her. *"Bonsoir, mademoiselle.* How very nice of you to leave the doors open for me. Almost as if you were expecting me."

She had made all her plans carefully, but the one thing she hadn't counted on was the fear that suddenly gripped her. This was one of the most deadly and powerful creatures on earth. What made her think she could defeat him? She forced herself to swallow and take a deep breath. *No, I've come this far.* She had a syringe in her pocket, ready to go, and she wore a loose duster over her shirt and drawstring pants. She figured the duster would help hide her hand movements.

She stared at him. He was dressed in black trousers and a black T-shirt that was snug enough to outline his pectoral muscles. *Good.* The thin shirt would be no impediment to the injection. All she needed was a chance to turn her back on him so she could prepare the syringe in her hand without him seeing what she was doing. She looked at his eyes.

A mistake. Their vivid, blue struck her anew, the only color in a sea of black, and he had one brow raised. She realized he was waiting for an answer.

"Don't be ridiculous. You're the last thing on earth I have any desire to see."

The second brow lifted. "And yet you called me. Did you think I would not come?"

She took one step back from him, trying to gauge the best distance to stand at. Too close and he'd see what she was doing. Too far away and she'd never be able to complete the injection. "Guessing a liar's motives would be difficult for anyone. I just wanted you to know I wasn't going to make it easy for you."

The tented brows lowered. "Liar, *mademoiselle?* What are you talking about? And what is this threat to kill a vampire? I could destroy you right now for that alone."

She had to make her move now, before he decided to do just that. "I was foolish to believe you when you were here. We humans don't mean anything at all to you, do we? We're just game pieces for you to amuse yourselves with."

She turned away from him, as if she didn't want to meet his eyes. She reached in her pocket for the syringe and positioned it in her right hand. With her left hand, she pulled out a long folding knife. She pressed against the thumbscrew, and the blade swung open. The duster still covered her hands, and she took a deep breath and whirled around.

She caught his gaze with hers in an attempt to keep him from looking at her hands. "I just wanted you to know that I'm not one to be trifled with."

She lunged at him, bringing the knife high in the air. He easily caught her wrist, but as he did, she thrust the needle of the heavy-duty syringe at his heart, pressing the plunger as hard as she could. With a cry, he ripped the syringe from her hand and threw it across the room. She hadn't completed the shot, but she was sure some of the liquid had been injected into him. She was glad. Whatever happened now didn't matter.

"Damnez-vous! What have you done? Silver nitrate?" Still holding her left wrist, he grabbed her right arm and pulled her to him. She winced at the pain his grip caused, but she didn't care. The knife fell to the carpet.

"Was it silver nitrate? Answer me!"

"It was, and I hope you burn in Hell!" She held her breath, waiting for him to kill her, but all he did was continue to hold her in his vice-like clutch, as his eyes closed, and his lips drew back in a grimace. *Of pain,* she hoped.

Suddenly he released her and pushed her across the room. "What concentration? Get me the bottle."

But she just stood there, trying to catch her breath.

"Get it!"

She ran into the bathroom and took the nearly empty bottle of colloidal silver from the shelf. He was right behind her, and he snatched the bottle from her hand.

"Ten parts per million," he said, reading the label. A line of sweat ran down one side of his face, paralleling a long strand of black hair that fell across his cheek from his temple.

She didn't know if that was good or bad for a vampire, and he made no comment either way. She met his eyes, and the things she saw warring in their blue depths scared her more than their previous emptiness had. *Rage. Disbelief. Confusion. Pain.*

"Stay here. Run, and so help me, I'll hunt you with no mercy."

With that he was gone. If he had tried to compel her with that command, it hadn't worked. Either he was weakened, or something in her *dhampir* blood gave her immunity. But even so, she stayed put. Marya knew she should run. She should just get into her car and drive. But where would she go? Everything she owned was here. There was no family, no close friends. She would not run and live in fear. Marya had done everything she had set out to do. She would accept the consequences. If Drago survived, he would end her life, but she would be free at last.

She went into her studio and looked at all her paintings one last time. She was proud of what she had accomplished in her life. Next, she said a prayer to the memories of her mother and father. She truly understood now what her father had lived with. That he had survived so long had been a tribute to his strength and will.

***

Marya was seated in the living room when Drago returned. His long hair was styled by the wind, and his T-shirt was torn and covered with dark splatters. *Blood?* Even though he was far from his usual immaculate, elegant self, he was alive, damn him! His pitiless blue eyes stared at her with all the condemnation of judges at the resolution of a Romani council, and in spite of her resolve, the fear returned.

He glided up to her and yanked her to her feet. "You have just signed your own *ordre d'execution, mademoiselle.*"

She tried to pull back from him. "I might have signed it, but *you* wrote it. You wrote it, damn you!"

His hold on her remained tight. "What are you talking about? Why did you do this? Do you hate my kind so much for what we did to your father?"

"Yes, but not just for him. For myself, too."

"I gave you life."

"And your messenger enjoyed telling me that you changed your mind and took it away!"

He stared at her. "My mandate stood. I told you this. Who told you otherwise?"

She twisted her arm again in an effort to free herself, but it didn't help. "A vampire. Who else?"

"Who? Where was he from?"

"Revelin Scott. He said he was from the Southeast Region."

"I know all the enforcers in that region, and I know of no such man. Tell me what he looked like."

"Let go of me, and I'll tell you."

His response was to pull her closer to him.

His aura of raw power flowed over her, carrying with it a magnetism that made her knees feel weak but also stirred her emotions into a confusing brew. The man—no, the creature—intended to kill her, but at this moment her body was feeling more than just fear and repulsion. "Let go, and I'll tell you what you want to know."

Drago let her go. She backed up until she bumped the sofa, but remained standing, rubbing her arms. She still tingled with the strength she had felt in him. "The guy was young. Not very tall. Shaggy hair and blue eyes, but not like yours." No one had eyes like Drago.

"What else?"

"He had an accent. British, I think. He dressed like something out of the Avengers."

"The what?"

She shook her head. "Out of the sixties. He didn't look like a vampire at all."

"But you're sure."

She nodded. "He stank."

"Tell me exactly what he said to you."

Marya recounted Scott's visit as closely as she could, watching Drago's eyes the whole time for his reaction. They glittered with a cold hardness when she told him that Scott had said Drago had changed his mind about granting her life.

"I told you no one had authority to reverse my decision."

"He said he was just a messenger for you—that you had made the change."

"And you accepted his word. You didn't think to check with me."

"Why would he lie?"

Drago was quiet for a moment. "Why indeed?" His eyes scanned the room, as if the answer were written on the walls. He looked back at her. "I gave no order to this Scott or anyone else to reverse my decision. Do you believe that?"

"Why should I believe anything you say?"

"Mademoiselle, if I wanted you dead, you would be dead. That, you can believe." He was silent for a moment more, then strode toward her. He grabbed her arm and pushed her in the direction of her bedroom.

Fear washed over her anew, and she planted her feet. "No!"

"I'm not going to touch you, *mademoiselle.* Your tainted blood holds no charms for me. Pack a suitcase with clothes and whatever else you need to travel. You're coming with me."

"No. Leave me here, please."

"I need you to help me find the truth, *mademoiselle.* Besides, you know too much. You'll be safer with me than if I leave you here."

"'Know too much?' I don't know anything!"

"You know that a vampire lied to you about me. Believe me, that alone ensures that whoever is behind this will want you silenced. They will have no compunction against killing you."

"And you will? Don't lie and tell me you wouldn't kill me

just as quickly."

"You want the truth, *mademoiselle?* Very well. Yes, I should kill you for what you did. I take it very personally when someone tries to send me to *la Belle Mort.* But someone else is behind this, and it's him I want to see pay, not you. Now pack. And start doing as I say. I have the means to enforce your compliance, and they're not pleasant. Be ready in fifteen minutes."

She went into the bedroom and started packing. There was no point in defying him further. She was alive, and it didn't seem he wished to harm her. At least not right now. She wouldn't trust him, but for now she would go along with him. She thought about Drago as she pulled clothing from her drawers and folded them neatly into her nylon travel bag. She had made so many trips to New Orleans that knowing exactly what to pack was second nature.

Had Drago really given her life all along? Her hatred for him had been so strong that it was difficult to think it had been misplaced. She had tried to kill him, and wrongly, it would appear. An unexpected wave of guilt washed over her. She had never before done any physical harm to another being. It was appalling to think that she was unjustified in committing such a horrid deed. And to Drago, who had only wanted to give her life... Just as quickly, though, disgust swept the guilt away. *No.* She was the wronged party here, not Drago. Someone apparently wanted her dead. If not Drago, Revelin Scott was to blame. She would feel no pity for the vampires.

She carried two packed bags into the living room and set them down on the floor. The lights were on in her studio. She stepped into the doorway and stopped. Drago was studying her paintings with the same attention he had paid them during his first visit, lightly running his fingertips over the texture of the canvas, like a blind man reading Braille. She watched his eyes shift up and down, side to side, on each image, and when his gaze lingered on a specific detail, it was almost as if she knew that he was seeing her intentions exactly. She wanted to laugh. How could he? He was one of the Undead. An unholy monster without a soul. How could he know what was in her heart when she executed each detail? And yet that was the feeling she had. He was standing in front of 'Crossroads.' Her favorite. The painting Jaime had called 'somber.'

He looked at her, and the way his eyes pored over her was just the way he looked at her art. *As if he knows me.* She didn't know what to say.

He saved her the trouble. "The crossroad. There is a very old legend in my native country that the Undead wait at crossroads to drink the blood of the unsuspecting as they chance by." He smiled, the first she had seen on him tonight. "Just a fairy tale, of course."

She drew a deep breath. She was wrong. He had no idea what the painting was about. "I had something quite different in mind when I did that one."

"Of course you did. But the crossroad is an endlessly fascinating subject, no? There is the symbolism of the cross, of course, but there are scores of legends involving crossroads, and most of them have to do with evil."

Marya was not amused. "I thought you were in a hurry."

"And so I am. While you were packing, I made some calls. Revelin Scott is indeed a Southeast Region enforcer. He was just transferred here within the past month from the Circle in England. Apparently the transfer was the Directorate's doing, not the Brotherhood's. A result, perhaps, of my complaining about the ineptitude of the local enforcers. Apparently the transfer stirred up quite a hornet's nest among the Brotherhood hierarchy."

She led him back to the living room. "I don't understand. What has all that to do with me?"

"I think, *mademoiselle,* that it has more to do with me. Come, then, if you're ready. Scott is stationed in Jackson. I think it's time we paid him a little visit."

At the door he stopped and faced her. "Oh, and *mademoiselle...*"

She picked up her bags and looked at him.

"If there is any more killing of vampires to be done, please leave it to me."

SIX

Marya settled into the leather passenger seat of Drago's car, and as he pulled onto Interstate 20 it struck her how completely her life had just changed. And in the most bizarre way imaginable. She had made no plans beyond this day. The only thing that had been on her mind for the past week had been killing Alek Dragovich. Now, somehow, she was in his hands. Figuratively speaking, of course.

She looked at him as he drove. She didn't want to, but he was impossible to ignore. She couldn't imagine a stranger traveling companion than a vampire. And not just any vampire. *L'enforcier.* She stared at his profile. The nose was just slightly curved. That, she thought, along with the peaked eyebrows which always seemed to relay boredom or incredulity, was what gave his face such a haughty cast. She was tired, but she certainly wasn't going to close her eyes and relax with him sitting so close to her. She decided that conversation was the best way to stay awake. Besides, there were plenty of things she was curious about.

"Where did you go when you left my house just a little while ago?"

He stared at the road, and for a moment she thought he wouldn't answer. "To heal," he finally said.

"I was hoping you had crawled away to find some deep, dark hole to die in."

With that, he did glance quickly at her. "You flatter yourself, *mademoiselle.* That solution you injected into me was extremely dilute. True vampire hunters make their own silver nitrate, and in concentrations much stronger than that drugstore concoction you bought."

"It must have done something to you if you had to heal

yourself."

"A precaution, nothing more."

Heal himself. She suddenly had a bad feeling. "What exactly did you do?" Her voice was sharp, but she didn't care.

"You have your father's knowledge. What do you think I did? I fed."

She closed her eyes, turned away from him, and covered her face with one hand. If one of her neighbors had died because of what she had done...

"Don't concern yourself. I have become very adroit in feeding without killing my victims. It's not wise to leave a trail of bodies in one's wake."

She didn't know if she believed him or not. "But I did cause you pain. At least admit that."

He shook his head. "Sorry to disappoint you, *mademoiselle.*"

Liar. She had caused him pain. She knew it. She had seen it in his face. *Vain, arrogant vampire.* Afraid to admit to a mortal that she had successfully struck even a tiny blow. She would have to be very careful about ever believing a word he said to her. They rode the rest of the way to Jackson in silence.

***

It was a quick trip to the state capital, though, and in less than an hour they found a motel to stay at. Marya's relief in arriving, though, was short-lived. At the desk, Drago requested one room instead of two. She interrupted him and politely told the desk clerk they wanted two rooms, feeling her cheeks flame with embarrassment as she did so. Drago took her arm and gently steered her a few feet away from the desk.

He kept his hand on her and pulled her close enough to whisper in her ear. "One room, *cherie.* Two beds, but one room. That's how it will be."

She shivered at his closeness and made sure she didn't look at his eyes. At this proximity, they would be too forceful. "There's no reason not to get two rooms. I'm not going to run away." Her anger made it hard to whisper, but she was already mortified and didn't want to make more of a scene.

"I need you where I can keep an eye on you at all times.

This affair is too important for me to take any risks. But don't worry. You'll be perfectly safe with me." This close, his voice was as persuasive as his eyes. All refined silk, smooth and sensual, but with that persistent undercoat of wickedness.

It was another battle it seemed she wouldn't win. She said nothing in return but exhaled a small sigh of resignation to let him know she wouldn't argue further.

"Stay here," he ordered. He returned to the desk.

As if she wanted another dose of embarrassment. Marya watched the desk clerk, but there was no smirk on the woman's face, only an obvious appreciation of Drago's unique appearance. Who was she kidding? Her gaze shifted to Drago. The man had stunning looks, damn him. She hated herself for the thought, and she felt another flush heat her face. She prayed this thing with Scott would end quickly and that Drago would let her go back home. She shifted her gaze to the clerk and saw the woman eyeing her in a questioning way.

Drago returned to her side, but turned his back to the clerk as he spoke. "The woman prefers to hear from you that one room is satisfactory. So we will return to the desk together, you will tell her that one room is fine, and you will give me a kiss convincing enough that she does not call *la police* on me. *C'est compris?*"

Marya couldn't believe what she was hearing. "I will do no such thing!" she whispered.

"Have a care, *mademoiselle.* An incident serves neither of us."

She had no choice, damn him. "All right."

She took a moment to take a deep breath and compose her features. Arm in arm they walked back to the desk. *This is never going to work.*

"One room is fine, ma'am. We had a little argument earlier tonight, but I've decided to forgive him and save him the cost of the extra room."

If I think about it, I won't be able to do it. So she just did it. She turned toward him, tilting her face up. He did the rest, taking her mouth gently with his. His lips were surprisingly warm and soft, but it was a quick kiss. Before she knew it, he was pulling away from her. She could see the desk clerk smiling at her in a way that told Marya she would be crazy not to share a room with this man. Drago winked at the woman, but before Marya's anger could flare again, Drago had her turned toward the hallway.

He smiled as he followed her into the elevator. "An excellent performance, *mademoiselle*. You almost had me fooled."

Once the door closed, she let her anger loose. "Why didn't you just cloud her mind into believing one room was fine?"

"Ah, an excellent idea. Why didn't I think of that?"

"I hate you."

He smiled again, this time showing teeth. "I know you do, *cherie*, I know you do."

***

Their room was a suite, spacious and well appointed, and the beds were queen size. No matter how nice the room was, though, the bottom line was that she was sharing it with a vampire. It would have been hard for her to share a room with any man, even a man like Jaime Buckland whom she liked and was attracted to. It was simply the way she had been raised. Women weren't promiscuous, and they didn't display themselves to men. But to share a room with a vampire…and after what this one just did to her…well, the thought was almost unbearable. Hopefully, by sometime tomorrow she would be going home. It was a pleasant notion, and she tried to keep it in the forefront of her mind. It was certainly better than thinking about the kiss that she could still feel on her lips. Drago's mouth had been soft and sensuous, and his touch had been tender—the last thing she expected from a vampire.

But as soon as she started to unpack he stepped to her side.

"Give me your bags. And your purse."

She froze. "What?"

"I need to make sure you don't have any more silver nitrate, needles, knives, or bazookas with you. I don't care to have a vampire-hating aberration try to kill me in the middle of the night."

She felt her cheeks flame all over again. "Don't be ridiculous. Do you really think I'd be so foolish?"

"You were earlier tonight." He held one pale hand out to her.

She gave him her bags and watched as he went through her things. She waited in silence.

He finished his task and looked at her. "Come over here."

"Why?"

"I need to make sure you have nothing on your person."

Her heart started pounding. "I don't."

"I have to be certain."

"Please…take my word for it."

"Ah, but trust is something you and I don't share, *non?* Come here. Surely it cannot be as bad as kissing me."

That was the problem. Kissing him hadn't been bad. And now he wanted to put his hands on her. She forced herself to remember what he was—a cold, Undead creature that survived from the living force of others. She stepped up to him and turned her gaze away from him. She felt his hands on her body, checking her pockets, her waistband, and even her brassiere. He wasn't rough, and there was a dispassionate efficiency to his movements, yet the feel of his hands on her was more disturbing even than she had feared.

"Done."

She looked at him and tilted her head to the side. "Satisfied?"

"Oh, I'll sleep much better now, believe me."

The chill softness in his voice cascaded over her like a winter rain, and she felt the resulting shiver down to her bones. She wanted to slap him, but resisted the impulse. She didn't care to know what his reaction would be to more violence on her part.

They both very badly wanted a shower, but Drago suddenly decided to play the gentleman and let her go first. The hot water felt wonderful—soothing and refreshing—but more than that she felt clean again, as though the water had rinsed away her improper thoughts of Drago. She scrubbed herself thoroughly, then dressed in clean, long pajamas and a long robe. Feeling almost right again with the world, she exited of the bathroom, eager for bed. Still, she forced herself to keep from running. Keeping what little dignity that wasn't already in shreds was important. She turned off the lights on her side of the room and slipped into bed. When she ventured a glance toward the bathroom, Drago was out of sight. Good.

Marya pulled the covers high and closed her eyes, but sleep wouldn't come. It had been too stressful a day, and the present situation wasn't any better. The sound of the shower running was soothing, and she hoped it would put her to sleep, but it didn't. The sound ceased, and contrary to what she knew she should do, she opened her eyes. A moment later he exited the bathroom wearing black silk pajama bottoms and nothing else. His black hair was wet and uncombed and fell in heavy, slick strands at the sides of his face. She couldn't help staring at him. She tried to keep thinking of him as the monster she knew he was, but in point of fact, he was a magnificent figure. He wasn't huge and brawny, but lean and muscled. The smooth, graceful lines of his torso seemed to perfectly match the refined elegance of his voice. If he was aware that she was watching him, he gave no notice. No doubt he was used to women staring at him. Only when he turned off the remaining lights did she finally slip into slumber.

***

They both slept late the following morning. Drago woke just before noon, and when he saw that Marya was still asleep, he remained in bed. He had driven nearly the whole way from New York to Vicksburg without a break, and he suspected that Marya was properly done in by her ordeal of the day before. He wanted to laugh. Her ordeal indeed! He was the one who had nearly been dispatched from Midexistence to Hell.

He hadn't dared admit to the girl just how close she had actually come to killing him. It was a basic maxim that all young vampires learned early if they wanted to survive. It was concealment—the ability to disguise emotions, mask intentions, seal up will, and to tame defects and hide them. One never allowed an opponent to know what one was thinking or feeling. Over the years Drago had elevated the ability to an art.

No doubt thanks to her father, the girl had stumbled upon one of the deadliest means to destroy a vampire—silver nitrate. Thankfully, she didn't have the experience or expertise of a true vampire killer. Professional vampire slayers, with the latest increases in technology, were discovering new and horrible weapons every day to use against the Undead. Some were even filling hollow point cartridges with silver nitrate or garlic, or scratching a cross into the business ends of bullets.

In truth, the girl, even with her amateur knowledge, could have easily killed him had she either been able to inject more into him or if the silver had been in a higher concentration. As it was, it had been a dilute solution and he had been able to feed immediately. He had found a man down the road from Marya's house from whom he had taken a healing quantity of blood—not enough to kill the man, but enough to negate some of the silver's effects. But the silver, as watered down as it had been, had burned. Burned like Hell. His immediate instinct had been to dispatch the girl right then and there, and it had taken all the strength of his will to overcome the rage of the moment. The only thing that had stopped him was his desire to find out why she wanted him dead. He was glad now that he had been able to control his lust for her death. It truly seemed that someone else was involved in this affair, and Drago very badly wanted to learn who that someone was.

Revelin Scott. He thought about the Brotherhood enforcer he would be confronting later that day. Scott was a day vampire, as few of the Undead were, but as most enforcers were. Tolerance to light made them more effective in their job, eased their travel, and made them harder to kill. Even so, the meeting with Scott would not be until this evening. Drago needed more information.

He had learned a little about Scott last night, but the brief run-down hadn't been enough. There hadn't been time before, but there was now. He eased noiselessly from the bed, picked up his cell phone, and called Paris. He spoke to Philippe and relayed his request. Philippe would call him back. Drago turned, and his gaze landed on Marya.

Her covers had been thrown off during the night, but her long-sleeved and long-legged pajamas revealed little skin, unlike her sleepwear of the first night he had seen her. He smiled at the memory. The girl was prudish in her dress and actions—a consequence, he imagined, of her Romani upbringing. Yet that first night the circumstances had been providential. He had seen her nearly naked, and the scent of her blood, even with the caustic tinge of her *dhampir* heritage, had aroused him. Even last night, with her very proper pajamas and robe on, she had roused not only his senses, but his blood. And the kiss... He knew she would never admit it, but he had felt her reaction to his kiss, and it wasn't revulsion. That alone had awakened an ardor in him he thought not to exist. How was it that this girl, an aberration, had more power to fuel his desires than the most beautiful girls in all of Paris?

His cell phone rang.

***

Somewhere in her consciousness, the sound of a phone intruded into her dream. Marya cracked her eyes open, and she vaguely wondered if the vision before her was truly real. She was sharing a room with a half-naked vampire. Drago.

It was real.

She watched him, much as she had done the night before. His hair was dry now, ruffled by sleep, yet still it fell in shiny, straight strands to flow across his shoulders. Other than his hair, though, his appearance was the same as it had been last night. He spoke on his cell phone, his voice as soft as a brush of satin against skin, but even if it hadn't been, she wouldn't have been able to listen in on his conversation. He spoke French.

Back and forth he paced across the end of the room, like a cat in a cage. Not like a lion, ponderous and slow, but more like a cheetah, lithe and bristling with latent speed and power. She shivered and wanted to pull her blanket higher, but she was afraid the movement would alert him that she was awake. And she wanted to continue her clandestine surveillance. She knew she shouldn't, but having done it the night before, she found it easier to do now. Besides, the role of covert observer gave her a strange feeling of power—a power that felt good in the shadow of such a forceful being.

She didn't want to admit it, but the very sight of him intrigued her. More than that, the sight evoked physical responses in her own body she was even less anxious to acknowledge. Yet she watched.

His skin was pale and flawed by faint linear scars on his back, but his chest and arms were unmarred except for a strange mark on his left forearm that she hadn't noticed last night. A tattoo? From this distance she couldn't be sure. His chest was smooth, and she watched the play of his pectoral and abdominal muscles as he moved. A thin line of black hair trailed downward from his navel only to vanish below the waistband of his silk pajamas. She should be embarrassed. She was fascinated.

He disconnected his call and turned to face her. *"Bonjour, mademoiselle.* Did you sleep well?" One lazy brow lifted just a little.

As if he cared. But his gaze lingered on her. Now she was embarrassed. "Yes. What was that all about?" She nodded toward the phone still in his hand.

"Business. Get dressed, then we'll talk."

She gathered items from her dresser and travel bag and retreated to the bathroom, donning a white tee with an open-weave lace neckline and a long silk skirt done in a pieced scarf pattern of pink, red, and gold. With her hand-made gold jewelry she felt comfortable, yet dressy enough to hold her own in a roomful of stylish vampires. She combed her hair, letting it hang to the middle of her back, then stepped into the suite.

Her eyes immediately met Drago's, and a strange feeling crawled over her skin at the intensity of his blue gaze. She finally remembered to breathe, and as she sucked in air she lowered her eyes. He was dressed simply in black trousers and a white shirt, but he looked no less stunning than if he had been in formal evening wear.

Marya took another deep breath. She really needed to get

her feelings under control. This was business, a rather nasty business, not a date, and this was *l'enforcier*, not some kind of white knight. His job was to compel obedience and punish disobedience, nothing more. That she was still alive was only because it was to his advantage, for now.

"I know you don't have this little problem, but I'm starving. Do you suppose we could have lunch?"

His cocked brows lifted, but a look of innocence failed to invade his world-weary eyes. *"Je suis vraiment desole, mademoiselle!* Why did you not say something earlier?"

She flashed him a smile that was as insincere as his remark. She could do without his snake oil charm.

He took her to one of Jackson's finest restaurants. His charm might be suspect, but the depth of his pocketbook seemed real enough. He ordered nothing for himself, but encouraged her to order anything she liked, even making suggestions to her. In the end, she made her own selections, pasta and a salad.

She felt strange seated across from Drago in such a setting and quickly searched for a topic of conversation. It wasn't difficult. "So have you figured out yet what this whole thing is about?"

"No. The only thing I'm certain of is that this is about me, not you. You're merely a disposable tool someone used to try to kill me. My death—my true death—is what someone wants, and very badly."

At first she thought his words to be pure arrogance.

"Disposable tool? Thanks a lot."

He didn't respond, and a glance at his hooded eyes, focused on a spot across the room, showed no conceit, only a lassitude that strangely frightened her.

"Drago?"

His eyes found hers. "If you had been successful, *cherie*, I would be dead, and no one would be the wiser. That is the truth of it, like it or not."

"And you say you don't know this Revelin Scott at all?"

He played with items on the table, tapping the crystal water goblet with his fingernails and fingering the texture of the cloth placemat, but she noticed he avoided touching the cutlery. *Must be sterling,* she thought.

"No. I have few dealings with the Circle, and know only of their highest ranking officers."

"Who did you call on the phone?"

He sighed, as if he didn't want to answer. "Philippe Chenard. My aide in Paris. I asked him for information on Scott. I like to learn about my opponents before I face them."

"So what did you find out?"

A smile curved his lips. "Now, *cherie,* do you think it prudent I discuss such things with you?"

His question irritated her. She picked up her fork and fidgeted with it just to annoy him. "I'm involved in this as much as you are."

He watched her hand with a smile that told her he knew exactly what she was doing. "You are, but I doubt that *monsieur* Scott would appreciate my telling a mortal his life's history."

"If he's your enemy, what do you care?"

His smile broadened, and she saw teeth flash. Teeth that were surprisingly white. And sharp. "He may not be an enemy."

"I don't understand."

"He may be a pawn, just as you were."

"Then who…"

The smile faded. "I don't know."

"All the Undead hate you. My father noted that more than once in his journal. Do you even care, Drago?"

He again looked at that elusive spot on the wall. "Those with power are often hated."

She tapped her fork to try to regain his attention. "You didn't answer the question."

Her salad arrived, and her question remained unanswered.

***

Hatred. Would a young mortal like Marya even understand if he tried to explain? He doubted it. It wasn't as if he had one day said to himself, "I'm going to become the most hated of the Undead!" It had just happened. Yes, those in power were hated, and yes, he had intentionally built a reputation of fear and respect. He was strong, but in his position, that was often not enough, so in the beginning he had employed ruthless tactics. He could still be ruthless if the situation demanded it, but more and more he felt that those up and down the hierarchy hated him more for his independence. He did what he wanted to do, with very few negative consequences. *Until now.* Now it seemed he was about to lose Nikolena's protection, and without that, regardless of his strength, he'd be vulnerable.

Marya's question had bothered him. It still did, as he watched her eat. Did he care? He didn't know anymore.

What he had told Marya about Scott had been true enough. Drago didn't think the ex-Circle member was behind the plot to kill him. Scott was just over two hundred years old, part Irish, part Scot, who had fought as a British soldier for Wellington in the Peninsular War against the French. In 1809 he was wounded in Spain and brought to the Other Side shortly after. Scott had fought against soldiers of Drago's adopted country, but Drago couldn't see that as a reason to hate him now. Scott had been an enforcer for the Circle for forty years and had a good record. It had indeed been Nikolena herself who had requested his transfer to the Brotherhood. If Nikolena had faith in the man, that was a point in his favor. However, Drago would test Scott's strength and intentions for himself soon enough.

He looked at Marya, and she raised her eyes to his, holding his gaze for a long moment before shifting her attention back to her meal. He would need to keep a close eye on her. Until this thing was over, he would have to safeguard her life. He had given her life, and he wasn't going to let someone else take that away. *Bodyguard to a mortal, and an aberration at that.* It was a strange feeling. Protecting her wasn't the only reason he'd have to keep an eye on her, though. As long as she carried such a hatred for all things vampiric, she was a danger.

Still, the danger from her was minor compared to the true danger. Somewhere out there a being with a lot more strength and hatred than Marya possessed wanted him dead. And he had no idea who it was.

SEVEN

They drove to Revelin Scott's office early in the evening. Drago smiled as he pulled up in front of the small, unassuming building. Most vampires, himself included, preferred to live and work in opulent surroundings, but Scott's office was an exception.

"Is this it? There's no sign," said Marya.

"I've been here before. Besides, can't you smell it?" He took a deep breath and slowly let it out. "Rot and decay."

She shook her head. "Not from inside the car and not with you sitting next to me I can't. How do you know he'll be in?"

"I called earlier today. He'll be here."

She cocked her head. "You're very sure of yourself. No one dares defy the great *enforcier.* Is that it?"

"If they're smart." He ran his gaze slowly down her body and back up again. She looked good enough to eat in her filmy silk chiffon. "Something you would be wise to keep in mind, *mademoiselle. "*

She didn't look one bit intimidated. "Tell me, do you always get your way?"

He gave her a small smile, but no answer. In the silence, Nikolena's voice rose in his mind. *There are whispers of your removal already on the wind.* He banished the memory. There was business to be done.

"When we get out of the car, I'll leave it unlocked. As soon as you verify that Scott is the vampire who came to your house, your part is over. You come back here, sit in the car, and wait for me. Understand?"

A pout started to purse her mouth. "This involves me, too, remember?" She stressed the final word, obviously wanting just that—the final word in all this.

He couldn't give it to her. "Scott and I will discuss our business in private. My way, remember?" He drew out the last word as well, mocking her.

She looked both annoyed and disappointed, but nodded her assent.

"C'est bien! Let's go."

He escorted her inside, and as soon as they entered, the stench of the Undead assailed his nostrils in full force. A pretty, young blond sat behind a desk. From the sharp stink that clung to her, she couldn't have been more than fifty years old. The instant she saw him, her attention never wandered. He watched her eyes and saw all her emotions laid bare in their widening depths—two seconds of curiosity, three more of dawning apprehension, and a dozen more of fear and awe. By the time he announced himself, he had no doubt she knew who he was."Alek Dragovich for Revelin Scott."

"Yes, sir. One moment." She picked up the phone, hit a button, and whispered into the receiver, but her eyes never left his. She hung up the phone. "He'll be right out."

"Merci, mademoiselle."

He no sooner got the words out than a man appeared at the head of an adjacent hallway.

"Drago. And Miss Jaks." A look of surprise flashed across Scott's face, but he quickly recovered. "No calls, please, Callie," he said to the young woman. He started to usher them down the hallway.

"One moment," said Drago. "Marya, is this the man who came to your house?"

She looked at Scott. The young man with the shaggy hair, dimpled chin, and outrageous outfit would indeed be difficult for her, or anyone, to mistake.

"He's the one."

Drago nodded. "Wait for me."

She took one last, long look at Scott, turned to catch Drago's eye, then left. He had no doubt Marya would give anything to hear the coming conversation.

"Follow me," said Scott.

They entered a large office that was as unique as its owner. The room had only one small window, but was brightened by several lamps, colorful artwork, and a color scheme of orange, aqua, and yellow.

"Drago. Welcome to Jackson. Have a seat. I take it this visit has to do with Marya Jaks?"

"It does. I prefer to stand, thank you. You paid a visit to her about a week and a half ago?"

Scott sat behind his desk, leaning back in his chair. "I think you know I did."

Drago examined one of the paintings on the wall. It was an original Peter Max. "Let's have no guessing games, *monsieur*. Answer my questions."

"Yes. I paid her a visit. On your orders."

The painting was extraordinary. "What did you tell her?"

"What I was bloody ordered to tell her."

Drago turned to face Scott. *"Monsieur,* if you persist in turning this into an amusement, I will glean what I wish to know without your cooperation, and I promise you won't find the game amusing."

Scott put his feet up on the desk and crossed them at the ankles. "Your threats don't scare me. My assignments come through all the proper channels, and I do as I'm told."

Drago admired the combination of strength and stand-up fortitude, but any time disrespect was an equal dose in the pot, a show and tell was in order. The 'tell' portion came first. Drago's gaze locked with Scott's, and the age-old clash for dominance began. Drago unleashed the influence of his eyes and mind, testing the younger vampire's response. "You will reveal all to me, Revelin Scott, all the things I want, and all that you want, so that I have not only my answers, but your every intention and desire."

Strangely, the enforcer didn't fight back with his own compelling gaze, but merely let Drago feel his power. "Go ahead, Drago. I want you to know me. I won't wage war with you, but know that I'm no novice to be rapped across the knuckles."

The control Drago felt in the brash young man was indeed

formidable. No match for himself, of course, but stronger than Drago had experienced in any vampire since Dallas Allgate last year in Natchez. Scott and Allgate were close to the same age, but vampiric strength had nothing to do with age. In Drago's experience, it had more to do with the physical and emotional strength the person had had in life.

The second half of the lesson, however, was still in order. The 'show' portion. Drago's body rose several inches off the floor, and he extended an arm toward Scott. Energy crackled across the room, and Scott's feet flew upward as he was thrown in a backward somersault to crash against the far wall. The dramatic display never failed to impress. Even those vampires who were the cockiest and most confident of their own power thought twice about opposing Drago after receiving such a lesson. Scott got to his feet slowly, and by the time he picked up his chair and sat down, Drago was already seated across the desk and brushing the lint from his trousers.

"Well, *monsieur*, shall we start again?"

"You bloody bastard! I'd heard you could do things like that, but I didn't believe it."

Drago shifted his attention from his fine linen to the young man, raising his brows.

This time Scott kept his feet under his desk. "All right. What do you want to know, Drago?"

"Who gave you the orders?" He let his voice drop to a purr. There was no reason now to shout.

"Deverick."

This was so much better. "Ah. And what exactly were you ordered to tell Marya Jaks?"

Scott pulled on the cuffs of his gold shirt to straighten his attire. "That you had reversed your decision regarding her evaluation, and that she was to be terminated. I told her she had the usual two weeks to put her affairs in order."

"And you didn't think to check with me?"

"I don't question my orders. I assumed Deverick had received all the proper authorizations."

"As a result of your visit, the *mademoiselle* tried to kill me."

"So? She obviously failed."

"Do you know who would wish me dead, *monsieur?*"

Scott laughed. "Let me guess. Half the world?"

The young man was becoming irritating again. "The trail led to you."

Another laugh, this one louder, burst from the young enforcer. "You think I cooked up this whole scheme to see you dead? First of all, I'm not that bloody stupid, and secondly, I've got no love for any Frenchie, but I don't have anything personal against you, Drago. I think you're making too much out of this. Somewhere along the line orders got mixed up, and I was sent to terminate an aberration. So what? She's alive. You're alive. No harm, no foul."

In about one more minute Drago was going to have to give another lesson in deference. "No one reverses my decisions. No one. Mistakenly or otherwise. That girl is to be granted life. Do you understand?"

"Talk to my boss. If there was a mistake, he made it, not me."

"Oh, I intend to. Where's Deverick now?"

"In New Orleans, seeing to two of our kind who ran afoul of more than just a paranoid delusion."

Enough was enough. Drago slashed out with the force of his mind, and instantly a drop of blood ran down Scott's cheek only to drip onto the front of his ruffled shirt. Before Scott could react, Drago was out of his chair and alongside the young enforcer, grabbing a fistful of gold ruffles. Drago gave a yank on the fabric.

"It's a pity that *Frenchie* soldier didn't do the job properly in Talavera. We'd have one less cocky bogtrotter in the world." He jerked again on the ruffles, released the man, and was at the door before Scott could utter a word.

"Sorry about the shirt, *monsieur*. Such a fine one it was, too. I'll see myself out."

***

Drago got into the car and turned on the engine. Instead of putting the car into gear, though, he leaned back against the headrest, closed his eyes, and let the engine idle. *Why is nothing ever easy?*

"Drago? What happened?" Her voice was soft, but he could hear the eagerness in it.

"There were many stories in your Old West of gunfighters—those who had the reputation of being the quickest and deadliest draws. Wherever they went, men wanted to prove themselves against the best, live or die. Sometimes I feel like one of those gunslingers."

"My God, Drago, you didn't kill Revelin, did you?"

His eyes still closed, he smiled at her question. If not for the prime directive ruling his kind... "No, *cherie*. But there is always the game to be played. I tire of it."

"Well, what did you find out?" Her eagerness was turning into impatience.

"I don't think he's involved. He said he got his orders from Curt Deverick. Did you ever have any dealings with him?"

"Deverick. No, the name doesn't sound familiar."

He raised his head and looked at her. "Well, remember it now, *cherie.* "

"You can take me home now, right? If Scott's not involved, there's nothing more I can help you with."

"Deverick's in New Orleans. I need to talk to him next."

"But you don't need me for that. It's not that far out of your way to take me back to Vicksburg. You can have me home in an hour and still be in New Orleans tonight."

He leaned his head back again and opened his senses to her, his eyes half closed, but his chest expanding with a deep, slow inhalation. Enjoying the sight and scent of her was much more pleasurable than considering her request.

She started to open her mouth, but he held up a hand. "I'm thinking."

Thinking, be damned! He was simply indulging. Her hair was a waterfall of silk he would have caressed had she not been so intolerant of his touch, and her dark eyes were wells that promised the granting of many future wishes. By far, however, it was her scent that tantalized him. After suffering the fetid stench of the Undead inside Scott's office, the sweetness of her life's blood danced over his skin, seeped into his pores, and invaded every inch of his being.

"Drago…"

He sighed. *If only she weren't an aberration.* She was one-quarter vampire, and her blood, now and forever, was poison to him. He put the car into drive and pulled away.

"Where are we going?" A note of hope softened her voice.

"Back to the hotel." She started to protest, but he cut her off. "Listen to me! Scott thinks I'm nothing more than paranoid, that his orders to kill you were just a mix-up, but I don't believe any of that. No one attaches my name to an order by mistake. Deverick may or may not be in New Orleans, and even if he is, he may not be the only one involved in this. You were an expendable pawn from the beginning, and whoever is behind this is not going to let you live now."

She was quiet after that, and they rode the rest of the way to the hotel in silence. When they reached their room, he offered to take her out to dinner, but she shook her head.

"Room service, then, *mademoiselle?*"

"I'm not hungry."

"You should eat. This ordeal may last longer than you think. You will need strength."

In the end she relented and agreed to soup and a sandwich from room service. After it arrived, he called Deverick's cell phone number.

"Deverick."

"Alek Dragovich."

"Drago."

Was there a note of surprise in the man's voice? Without the benefit of face-to-face contact, it was difficult to be sure.

"Drago, where are you? I thought you were supposed to be down here. Those sanctions you imposed did nothing but make matters worse."

"Where are you?"

"New Orleans, of course." This time the emotion in the voice came through loud and clear. Annoyance, backed up by good, old-fashioned hatred.

Drago strode across the room, swallowing its length much

too quickly. "I need you in Jackson, now. A matter of the utmost importance."

"I can't leave now. I have half my enforcers here trying to settle things down. I really thought you'd be here, too."

He turned and marched back across the suite. "I can order you to Jackson, *monsieur.*"

"Listen, Drago. I'm tired of your meddling in Brotherhood affairs. Go ahead and lodge a complaint against me. From what I've heard, it won't do you any good."

Drago snapped the cell phone shut with a growl.

Marya looked up at him, her mouth full of bread and turkey. She gulped down the bite of sandwich. "Did you really think Deverick would be cooperative?"

He smiled. She was right. "No. I was hoping, like you, for a quick resolution."

She put her sandwich down on the plate. "So what are you going to do now?"

He stopped pacing and sat on the sofa next to her. "There's no point in remaining here. First thing in the morning, I'll take you home."

Her face brightened immediately.

"But I'll have to stay with you. If I decide to go to New Orleans to meet with Deverick, I'll have to take you with me."

Marya couldn't eat the rest of her sandwich. Her pretty fiction of having this thing end quickly was gone. There was only one consolation. She was going home. And soon. If she clung to that thought, she might be able to get through one more night sharing a room with a vampire.

She withdrew to the bathroom to change. When she was safely in her pajamas and robe, she opened the room and hurried out, eager, once again, for the sanctuary of her bed. She made it without incident, and this time as she curled in her bed she kept her eyes shut. No more voyeuristic vampire-watching tonight. Even so, sleep was very long in coming.

***

Marya woke abruptly in the night. She opened her eyes, but could see nothing. The heavy drapes were more effective than the night itself in sealing the room in blackness. She lay still, listening, but heard nothing. Yet she was sure something had awakened her. She waited, not wanting to risk a light. Then she heard it. A word. A strange word.

It had to be Drago. She waited, thinking he was saying something to her, but there was nothing but disjointed sounds in a language she didn't understand or recognize. He was talking in his sleep.

She sat up, straining in the darkness to see him. *A vampire talking in his sleep?* She thought vampires were supposed to sleep like the dead. Either the legend was wrong, or Drago, as she was beginning to realize, was unique among the Undead. She eased out of her bed and opened the drapes a crack, just enough to let in some of the light from the parking lot lamps. Drago lay on his back, and the part of his body she could see above his covers was naked. She walked around to the side of her bed closest to his and looked at his face. A deep vertical furrow divided his brows, and the lines etched in his face that she jokingly thought of as 'smile lines' were deeper than she had ever seen them.

"Zaloznye."

She jumped back. She thought he was aware of her, but he was indeed dead to the world. What was he saying? She had heard him speak French enough to know it wasn't French. *Russian?* She couldn't be sure, but it seemed logical. She peered again at his face, and it looked almost contorted in pain. Sweat had broken out on his temple, and long black strands of hair were caught and trapped against his skin.

"Drago," she whispered.

"Zaloznye pokojniki. Ved'miak."

"Drago, wake up," she whispered, louder this time.

He only tossed his head, whipping a tangle of hair across his features.

She didn't want to, but she reached out a hand and touched his arm. "Drago."

It happened so fast she didn't have time to scream. A force grabbed her and sailed her across the room so fast she couldn't see her surroundings until her back slammed against the wall. The stun knocked the air from her lungs. She couldn't breathe, much less cry out. Fingers like the steel jaws of a trap held her arms, and a mask of pale skin, dark glassy eyes, and bared teeth swam before her. She struggled to get oxygen into her lungs, but the air wouldn't come. She started to hyperventilate when she felt his mouth against her neck, his smooth teeth raking her skin. She fought to get one word out.

"Drago!"

She felt herself being released, and she slid to the floor, having no strength to support herself. She vaguely wondered if she were dying, but no sooner than the thought formed she heard a voice.

"Marya, just relax and breathe slowly. Come on, breathe in."

She did as the voice instructed, and miraculously the air made it to her lungs. One hand supported her shoulder and another her head, but she didn't care. She was alive and breathing, and that was all that mattered. But the hands left her, and for a moment she was afraid. A light from the bathroom came on, and when she blinked and opened her eyes, Drago was on one knee at her side. His hair fell in a web of tangled strands, and a line of sweat still ran past one eye, but the look of pain was gone, and his eyes were clear again. And blue, even in the low light.

"Forgive me, *cherie*, I didn't mean to frighten you…or hurt you."

"For someone not meaning to, you did a pretty good job," she whispered.

He reached out and smoothed the hair away from her face, and she made no move to stop him. "Didn't your father ever write that it's dangerous to disturb a sleeping vampire?"

She managed a small smile. "I don't think I had ever planned on sleeping with a vampire."

He smiled in return. "Something to keep in mind for the future."

She pushed his hand away from her face. "I don't think so. Let me up."

"Not yet. Just relax a moment more and get your strength back."

"Relax? God, Drago, you almost killed me!"

"If it's any consolation, *cherie,* your blood would have poisoned me rather effectively."

"It's no consolation, thank you." She took a deep breath and closed her eyes. "You were talking in your sleep. I think you were having a nightmare. I was just trying to wake you up."

He sat on the floor next to her and leaned against the wall. "They come. Only *la Belle Mort* brings the true sleep of the dead."

"I couldn't understand what you were saying. It sounded like Russian."

"No doubt it was."

"What are the nightmares about?"

"Things you don't want to hear, *cherie. "* He was on his feet again in an eye blink. "Come. Back to bed." He extended a hand down to her.

She hesitated, but then reached a hand to his. He grasped it and hauled her easily to her feet. The movement brought her face to face with him. His mouth was only inches from hers, and this was the closest by far she had been to his bare torso. Her legs started to feel weak again, but his hand still held hers.

"Should you witness me in the throes of another nightmare, *cherie,* it is in your best interest to let me be," he whispered.

She shook her arm to free it from his. "You're welcome."

"I resisted killing you. Twice now. Consider that your thank you."

She looked down at the arm that held hers. She saw the strange mark again, the mark she had thought to be a tattoo. But the strange symbol was carved deep into his skin. She raised her eyes to his, and she knew he had seen where her eyes had been. He released her without a further word.

Sleep, once again, was very long in coming.

EIGHT

They left for Vicksburg at eight the next morning. Conversation was meager travel fare, but Marya didn't mind. No doubt Drago had a lot of plotting to do. She just hoped that in the final grand scheme, she would play a minor role.

It was a warm day, and she was happy just to buzz down her window and enjoy the feel of spring weather. In a quick hour Drago turned onto her quiet road. Marya had always loved her Creole-style cottage, but she had never been happier to see the tin roof, shuttered windows, and steps leading up to the raised veranda than she was when Drago parked in the drive. Only when he followed her into the living room and spoke did her enthusiasm at being home fade.

"If I were you, *mademoiselle,* I would not bother to unpack."

Her joyous mood broken, she nevertheless continued through the kitchen to the back hall. "Well, you're not, so if you don't mind, I need to wash some of these things. And there's not much food in the house, so I'm going to have to make a trip to the grocery store. I know these mundane chores don't concern you, but I have to deal with them."

He followed her to the hallway that led to the utility room and her bedroom. "Do what you need to do. But anytime you leave the house, I will accompany you."

He was right on her heels. "This bedroom is mine," she said at the room's entrance.

"Oui, cherie, I know it is," he purred. His voice was so soft it tickled her like a feather, and a shiver ran down her side.

"You can use the spare bedroom across from my studio,"

she said, entering her own room and slamming the door behind her. The memory of his first visit when he had seen her in a nightshirt and little else was as humiliating now as it had been then. She decided that the best way to put the memory—and him—out of her mind was action.

She spent the rest of the morning washing clothes, unpacking, and straightening the house, immersing herself as much as possible in the comforting daily routines. Thankfully, Drago didn't hover about her. In fact, he was out of sight most of the time. When it was time to go to the store, he was nowhere to be seen. Oh well, she thought. *Too bad.* She would not miss his company.

But as soon as she exited the side door to the carport, he was right beside her.

"You did not think to leave without me, *mademoiselle,* did you?"

"I was hoping you had disappeared for good."

"Come," he said, flashing very white teeth. "It will be my pleasure to drive you."

They took his car, and she directed him to the largest grocery store in town. What if someone she knew saw her with this man? She led a solitary life, but even so, she had neighbors and acquaintances from the art club. Vicksburg was a small town, and, as in any small town, people loved nothing better than gossip. What would people think when they saw her with Drago? Even in an outfit as simple as the black jeans and long-sleeved knit shirt he wore, he stood out—anywhere, in any kind of crowd.

Once inside the store, she tried to both ignore him and avoid eye contact with other customers or clerks. But even when he was behind her instead of in front, she was painfully aware of exactly where he was. Maybe it was the faint scent of the Undead he emanated. Every time she stopped to look at an item or put one in her basket she could feel him only inches away from her.

Finally, she could stand it no longer. She half-turned in his direction. "Do you have to stand so close?" she hissed.

His response was to move that much closer to her. "What

are you afraid of, *cherie?* That people will think I'm your lover?"

She felt her cheeks burning. "Well, they're not going to think you're my uncle," she whispered. But thankfully she didn't run into anyone she knew, and while she saw a few women giving Drago the once-over, she survived the outing.

By mid-afternoon, the laundry was done, the house was spotless, and she had eaten a late lunch. All in all, it had been a good day. Drago had been exceedingly considerate at the house and had stayed out of her way. At times she almost forgot he was there. Almost. It was impossible to completely overlook that one of the world's most fearsome vampires was under her roof.

She wondered why he was being so nice. Was he feeling guilty about nearly killing her last night? *A vampire feel guilt over a mortal?* She wanted to laugh. The idea was ludicrous. Drago was anything but a white knight. More likely he wanted something from her. Charm seemed to be one of his most potent weapons. Perhaps if she could wield the same weapon she could beguile him into relinquishing some information.

Tired of being cooped up inside cars and hotel rooms, she longed for some exercise. A walk. It would be the perfect opportunity. She sought out Drago. She found him in her studio, studying her paintings again.

"It's so nice out. I'd like to go for a walk."

He smiled, and she hoped he didn't have the power to see into her mind. *"Certainement, mademoiselle!"*

He was all gentleman, however, as they strolled down her lane. Marya lived on the edge of town, and while she had neighbors, the houses were set both well away from each other and the road. As they walked on the left side of the road, facing traffic, he stayed on her right, careful to keep several feet of distance between them. She actually found herself enjoying the exercise, the sunny afternoon, and his presence.

"Drago, will you talk to me?"

He seemed surprised at the question. His brows twitched upward, quite a different reaction from the lazy, bored look she usually got from him. "Of course."

"I mean, will you talk about yourself?"

"That depends on what you wish to know."

"Well, like when and where you were born...things like that."

"Ah, you want to know about someone else, not the man who walks beside you."

She felt oddly self-conscious, in spite of the fact they were talking about him, not her. She got the impression she had offended him and that he wouldn't answer. She had thought to preface her most burning questions with several about his past, both to put him off guard and to actually glean some information about him, but it seemed her plan had backfired.

It was his turn to surprise her. "In 1446 a boy-child was born to a prince in the city called His Majesty Lord Novgorod the Great. A privileged birth, wouldn't you say?"

She didn't answer, not wanting to presume she knew anything about medieval Russia.

"Tell me if you think so when I'm finished. Oh, Novgorod was indeed grand then, the capital of a vast territory and the oldest Russian city, but long before my father was born the princes had lost their influence. They existed and survived only at the whims of the citizens who held the true reins of power."

Drago paused for the length of three steps, gazing at the spacious yard of the house they were passing. "My father wasn't even allowed to own land. The boy-child was one of nine children born to the prince. Only three survived to adulthood. In the city, bread was dear. One-half ruble for two baskets, and that was when there was any to be had. There was crying in the streets and market place. Death from hunger. No law or justice. There were those who robbed in the villages and districts, and those who confiscated and demanded money. You would call them criminals today, but in that age they were neighbors and leaders. But the boy survived. So what do you say? Was he privileged?"

She suddenly found herself the one caught off guard. She had expected him to grudgingly give her a few facts and figures, but never thought he'd reveal details of his past. "The boy lived." It was the only thing she could think to say.

"Yes, the boy lived and grew to manhood. And in spite of what I just told you, yes, he was privileged. Novgorod, for all its problems, ruled itself. When the city fell, everything ended. Everything."

Marya was silent, and in spite of the warmth of the day, a shudder ran through her. She almost felt sorry for him, then she reminded herself that he was a vampire. Whatever pain he had suffered in life, he had paid back a thousand times over in death.

His final words hadn't exactly been a happy invitation for more questions, but she pressed on, eager for more information. "The mark on your arm. Will you tell me what it is?"

"No."

She looked down at his arm, but his sleeve covered the mark. "Why not?"

"It is not a thing to be shared."

Did he truly wish to spare her feelings? She doubted it, but it was the opening she was looking for.

"Drago, why are you being so nice to me?"

"Nice, *mademoiselle?*"

Apparently it was a word not in a vampire's vocabulary. "Why are you here? I'm sure you have more important things to do than baby-sit a mortal."

"I'm here to safeguard your life. What does the reason matter?"

"It matters."

She watched his profile carefully, but he gave nothing away. There were no sighs, no agitated shifting of the eyes, no muscle tics. Just the same alignment she had seen so often before to his features—the slight lift to his brows, the hooded eyes staring at nothing in particular, the chiseled mouth set in that irritatingly noncommittal half-smile. "You will not like the truth, *mademoiselle.*"

"I want to hear it."

"Very well. I should have had you terminated in the beginning. On any other day I would have, but on that particular evening it was your good fortune that I felt like amusing myself. I knew that giving you life would annoy a great many people."

She had expected something like this, but even so, to hear him state it so coldly gave her chills. "So that's the only reason you're keeping me alive? To annoy other people?"

He turned toward her, and the sight of his eyes cast even more of a shadow over the sun's warmth than his words had. Beautiful. And empty.

"You're an aberration, *mademoiselle,* and there is no aberration that generates more disgust among the Undead than a *dhampir.*"

Marya felt tears sting the back of her eyes. She couldn't understand why. She had known all along that he cared nothing for her personally. "And if I weren't an aberration?"

"You'd be food."

She asked no more questions.

***

Drago was disturbed. He hadn't intended to be so brutally honest with the girl. Perhaps it had been a reaction to the lamentable error he had made in telling her about his birth. Giving someone personal information was the same as giving that person a weapon. And while he no longer believed she wanted to do him harm, one didn't live to be over five hundred years old by making assumptions.

He wasn't sure why he had told her about Novgorod. He tried to tell himself that it was her Roma heritage that made him believe she would relate to his past, but even as an excuse the explanation didn't satisfy him. The one thing his naked honesty had accomplished was silencing her questions, but he wondered if the look of pain he saw in her dark eyes was worth it.

When they arrived back at the house, he watched as she worked in her garden, then retired to the kitchen to prepare her evening meal. She made no attempt at conversation, and he gave her plenty of space. But he caught her sliding surreptitious looks his way a number of times. On those occasions when he met her eyes she was quick to glance away.

He called Deverick several times during the afternoon and

evening, but the dialogues accomplished nothing except to give him the equivalent of a headache. Technically, Deverick was obligated to obey the orders of a superior, especially a member of the Directorate. But the man came up with one excuse after another for not agreeing to Drago's demands to return at once to Vicksburg. And over the phone, Drago lacked the compelling power of his eyes. Until he could meet face-to-face with the man, there was little he could do. He disconnected the final call in frustration, wanting nothing more than to smash something, but he quickly brought his anger under control. He would not win this battle of wits if he lost his temper.

It wasn't until nine o'clock that Marya appeared in the doorway to his room and spoke to him. "Are we going to New Orleans tomorrow? It would be nice to know if we are."

"Plan on it," he answered softly.

She let out a long sigh. "All right. I'll pack now, so I can be ready as early as you want."

He nodded, expecting her to turn around and head for her own room, but she lingered, glancing around the spare room he had made his.

"So…aren't you going to search my room before I go to bed to make sure I don't have any more silver or knives?"

He smiled. "Do you wish me dead, *mademoiselle?*"

Her gaze returned to him. "I told you at our first meeting that I have no desire to kill any vampire, even you."

He watched her eyes very carefully. "Can I trust you?"

She gave a slight shrug. "You didn't at the hotel. Why would you take my word now?"

He took a step in her direction, bringing his body to within a couple feet of hers. "I would like to. In payment for this afternoon, when I trusted you with a part of myself. Have I your word?"

She held her ground, and he wondered if it was pride or an answer to his question. *Trust.* He opened his senses to her, and the sound of her heartbeat thudded all about him like primitive music. A very fast heartbeat. *Fear? Or desire?*

She moved even closer to him, inches away. "You can trust me," she whispered. She gently prodded his chest with one finger. "Truth, you said, right? Well, there's nothing so foul as a monster who walks the night after death, but as much as I would like to be rid of you, I don't think killing you to do it would be in my best interest."

With that, she turned and swept out of the room.

***

He lay on the bed for a long time before summoning sleep. His sparring with Marya may be finished for the day, but his thoughts of her continued. He knew that her reference to him as a foul monster who walks the night was nothing more than payment for earlier in the day when he had refused to answer her questions and had referred to mortals as food. If what he had sensed in her was truly desire, her harsh words were as much a mask for her feelings as his detachment was for his feelings. His body told him the truth of the matter as he tried to relax.

He was glad, in a way, that the room he occupied was at the opposite side of the house from her bedroom. If she were any closer to him, he had no doubt the scent and sound of her blood would not only keep him up all night, but keep his body in a perpetual state of arousal. In his work he usually dealt more with vampires than humans, and he couldn't remember the last time he had spent so many nights alone with a mortal without taking his pleasure.

A million 'ifs' ran through his mind. *If only she weren't an aberration... If only her heritage didn't make them such natural enemies... If only...*

But the 'ifs' were better than sheep, and the sleep of the Undead finally stole over him.

***

"Drago?"

He thought he heard her calling him, but it couldn't be. Only in a dream would she call for him.

A scream jolted him from the half-sleep, and a fetid stink assailed his nostrils instead of Marya's fragrance. *Vampire!* He was out of the bedroom and across the living room in an instant. A tall figure in black loomed in the dining area. At Drago's approach the man whirled, hissing like a roused serpent.

Pale moonlight from the patio door illuminated short dark hair, a highly stylized goatee, and eyes that burned a dark red.

"Drago!" The creature hesitated in confusion. "What are you doing here?"

"I would ask you the same question, *monsieur.*"

But before the intruder could answer, Drago noticed that the door to Marya's bedroom was already open. He had heard her slam the door when she went to bed. Drago flew at the doorway as more screams pierced the night, but the vampire in black was just as fast, catching Drago in a bear hug. They crashed onto the dinette table, slamming it against the wall. The wooden tabletop buckled under almost five hundred pounds of fury, and Marya's painting sprang off the wall and bounced on Drago's head. The heavy canvas was nothing, though, compared to the beast that held him. Drago guessed that the vampire was at least four inches taller and one hundred pounds heavier than he was, but physical strength in life wasn't the same thing as vampiric strength. Not usually.

The impact had loosened the vampire's grip, and Drago twisted until he could fasten his hands around the man's neck. Drago squeezed, at the same time releasing the cutting power of his mind. He held nothing back, slashing at the red eyes until they ran even redder with blood.

The vampire cried out and released Drago, clutching at his eyes.

"Carlo! Carlo!" The shrieks from the bedroom were high-pitched and frenzied.

Drago cursed his blunder in being caught off guard. He threw the vampire he assumed was 'Carlo' against the far wall, soared into the bedroom, and collided with another body. The room was as dark as a nightmare, but his sense of smell told him instantly that the body in his arms was Marya's. He held her tightly, thankful that her renewed screams and struggling limbs meant life.

"Be still," he hissed into her ear. "It's Drago." She stopped fighting him, but he still felt the fear and tension in her body. "Are you all right?"

His hand on her head felt her nod.

"Where is he?" he asked, but she didn't answer. Her breath came in quick gasps, but no words. He shook her insistently. "Where?"

"On the floor," she panted. "The other side of the bed."

He drew her away from him, still holding her head. He waited until her eyes met his. "Stay behind me, but stay close," he whispered.

She nodded and slipped out of his way. Drago turned on a light and carefully circled the bed. The spread was on the floor, the blanket and pillow poised on the bed's edge to follow. A very young and very dead vampire lay sprawled on the floor, his shoulders and blond head propped against the wall. His sightless eyes were open and rolled up in his head, and his mouth hung slack, a line of spittle running down his chin.

"*Mon Dieu, cherie!* What did you do to him?"

But her only answer was another scream. Too late, Drago turned to see Carlo grab Marya from behind and pull her to him in a choke hold.

"She's leaving with me, Drago. If you try to stop me, I'll kill her."

Marya's eyes were round with both fear and silent entreaty.

"Release her, *monsieur.* You're already dead for what you did here, but if you harm the girl I'll make sure you die in the slowest way possible."

Carlo laughed. "You have no power over me, Drago. You're a fool! You just defeated yourself by cutting my eyes. As long as I can't see, you can't compel me."

"Ah, *mon ami,* but I don't have to compel you." Drago resorted to a very human trick. He reached down, grabbed a handful of braided rug, and yanked. Nearly three hundred pounds of vampire landed hard on the floor and cushioned Marya as she fell onto him. Before Carlo could react, Drago tore Marya from the vampire, hauled him to his feet, and pushed him out of the bedroom and down the hall to the kitchen.

"Who sent you here? Who?" growled Drago.

Carlo laughed again, a pained laugh that bordered more on hysteria than on delight. "I told you—the power of your eyes have no effect on me. I'll tell you nothing."

"Your eyes will heal themselves in moments, *monsieur.* In the meantime, I'm afraid you're going to bleed all over *mademoiselle's* clean floor." Still holding Carlo, Drago slashed out with his mind, creating a pattern of blood with a hundred strokes of invisible blades of energy. Carlo cried out, and in that instant of distracting pain, Drago reached for the longest knife protruding from the wooden block atop Marya's counter. *Stainless steel, but a knife was a knife.* One couldn't be choosy in a struggle to the death.

Carlo stumbled forward. "Drago!" His eyes had stopped bleeding, and a lurid gleam was returning to the healing orbs. Drago's gaze snared Carlo's restored sight, and he dazzled the larger vampire, setting before him the mirror of truth. It was Drago's own eyes, the polished surface upon which Carlo would see and relive every hell he had ever visited.

"Behold your existence, *monsieur.* You will tell me everything I want to know, or this hell will be your life from this moment on."

Carlo gave no answer, his mind and eyes alike seeing nothing but his own private nightmares. Blood glittered wetly on the front of his shirt, the result of the cutting power of Drago's mind, but Carlo ignored the wounds. Muscles in his face twitched, and cords in his neck strained with effort, and Drago knew that Carlo was pouring all his energy into battling the control over him.

Drago curled back his lips. "Who sent you for the girl, *monsieur?* Who ordered you to this house? Tell me!"

But the vampire was a Master, and his resistance was formidable. He lurched toward Drago. "You'll...get nothing..." His arms reached forward, but Drago knew it was not in surrender or supplication, but a final attempt to snare Drago and break his hypnotic hold. He allowed Carlo to reach him and drove the knife between the man's ribs.

"Then I'll have your death, *mon ami.*" Drago thrust the blade in up to the hilt, leaned forward, and twisted.

A guttural sound resembling nothing more than a laugh ground into Drago's ear.

Drago repeated his command. "Tell me who sent you, and I'll spare your worthless life!"

The creature spit at him.

Drago continued his deadly work with the knife, until Carlo's body slumped against his. Drago lowered the dead weight to the floor and made sure the vampire's heart was severed from his body.

"Bon voyage, monsieur. Enjoy the journey from Midexistence to Hell," he whispered, sagging against the counter.

He closed his eyes, exhausted. *Two vampires dead. There would truly be hell to pay now.* But he couldn't think about that now. *Marya.* He blinked. Was she dead as well? He inhaled deeply and closed his eyes again, letting his senses search for her. Life still rode her scent. He sat for another minute, then rose and headed for the guest bath where he washed quickly. He then changed his pajama trousers. The last thing Marya needed was to see blood all over him.

He found her in her bedroom, huddled on the floor in a corner. He knelt beside her, sweeping her long hair from her face. *"Cherie,* it is safe now. They are dead."

She raised her head and looked at him, her eyes wide with fright. She unwrapped her arms from her body, and he drew her into his embrace, cradling her against his chest. She circled his neck with her hands, pulling herself even closer to him, and in spite of his fatigue, hunger arose and demanded satisfaction. Sexual desire, bloodlust, and violence—they were the three notes of the chord that forever played in the vampire's mind. There was never one without the other, and right now he was too tired to try to separate them.

"Cherie..." His hands moved up to support her head and push her far enough away from him so that his mouth could reach her face. He leaned down and pressed his lips to her cheek. Her skin was so warm, so soft. *So sweet...* He kissed her, working his way toward her mouth. When her lips met his and parted for him, a groan rumbled from deep inside him. He tried to deepen the kiss, but there was tension in her body and a tentativeness in the touch of her lips that told him she

was by no means ready to surrender to him just yet. But his lust pushed him to increase the pressure of his mouth against hers even as he felt her hands against his chest.

She broke the kiss and pushed away from him. "Drago, no, please..." He loosened his hold and she scuttled backward across the floor until her back hit the corner. His body screamed in protest, but he let her go. Reawakening her fear would serve no purpose.

"Are they truly dead?" she asked.

He nodded. "I'm afraid so. Which reminds me, *cherie*. What exactly did you do to that one there?" He cocked his head at the far wall. "He's a novice, only twenty or thirty years old by his stink, but even so, he should have killed you easily."

"I used the same thing against him I tried to use on you. Colloidal silver. See, I didn't know when or where you would show up, so I had syringes hidden all over the house, including my bed. I couldn't sleep tonight. When I saw the door open, I thought it was you. But then I saw the blond hair. When he grabbed me, I was ready."

"I should say you were." He looked back at her, his eyes narrowed. "I thought you promised me you had no more vampire-killing weapons lying about."

"No, I promised I wouldn't try to kill you again. Not quite the same thing."

He gave her a wry smile, but it quickly faded as he thought about what would come next. "Listen to me. I have some unpleasantries to take care of, and your kitchen, I'm afraid, is something of a mess. I think it best you spend the rest of the night in the guest room."

"It doesn't matter. I won't sleep anyway."

He stood and offered her a hand up. "Try."

She took it, and he pulled her to her feet. She looked him right in the eye and whispered. "A bed might be nice. It seems you and I have been spending a lot of time on the floor lately."

"We could spend even more time on the floor, *cherie,* if you wished it."

She gave him a small smile. "I don't think so."

Was it his imagination, or was his reserved Gypsy quickly

learning the feminine art of flirtation?

He smiled at her again. "When you walk through the dining area, stay on this side of the kitchen island. And watch your step. You don't want to track blood onto the living room carpet."

She glowered at him, grabbed a few necessities from the room, and hurried out. He watched to make sure she didn't decide to take a tour of her kitchen, then went about business. He hadn't recognized either of the two vampires. It bothered him that he didn't know Carlo. Perhaps he wasn't an enforcer, simply a Master hired to do this one job. Drago took a good, long look at each vampire's features, committing them to memory. He would find out one way or another who they were. Next he removed the bodies from the house. They would be dumped tomorrow, where sunlight would make quick work of the remains. He cleaned up the kitchen, took a shower, and walked into the guest room.

Marya was hunched on the floor.

"Cherie! I thought you were finished with this business of the floor."

She was hugging herself, just as she had when he had found her curled in the corner of her bedroom. "I'm cold."

"Maybe if you used the bed you would find that a blanket is a very warm thing."

"Your scent is all over them."

He sat on the edge of the bed, having been surprised by her again. He thought...he didn't know what to think. She had allowed him to kiss her. And seemingly enjoyed it, until she had pulled away from him. Her banter had become increasingly bold, almost teasing. And yet she would not sleep in the same bed he had slept in, even without him.

"Am I that offensive to you, *mademoiselle?*"

"It's not that. I keep forgetting what you are. The bed reminds me. Your scent is very faint, but it's there, and it reminds me of death. The Roma have very strong beliefs about the dead. Ever since I was a little girl I was taught to fear the dead who might return in some supernatural form to haunt the living. That fear is so ingrained that the names of the dead are never mentioned. Oh, my mother told me stories, but she never spoke my father's name. The deceased are never touched. Fear is why my mother disposed of all my father's belongings after he died. She was very afraid my father, with his vampire blood, would return after death. She prayed every day for protection from the evil *marime* spirits."

He was silent.

She took a shuddering breath and drew her knees up to her chest. "Don't tell me you haven't heard some of our legends. That of the *mulo?* Like yourself, the living dead, who many fear will escape his body after death, take the form of a wolf, and seek revenge on those who either harmed him in life or caused his death. Even the mere sight of a *mulo* is bad luck. But the *mulo* is nothing compared to the fear of the vampire. And you wonder why I won't sleep in your bed?"

"So it's not my scent that offends you, but what I represent."

She nodded.

"But the Romani superstitions have nothing to do with you or I." He held out a hand to her. "If you're cold, come here."

Her eyes narrowed with suspicion. "Why?"

"Shared body warmth. Surely you've heard of it? Come, I promise I'll control my baser instincts."

"Somehow I don't think curling up with a cold, dead thing will make me feel warmer."

"First of all, I am far from dead." *Thus far, anyway.* "Secondly, my body temperature is virtually the same as yours. So come here. You don't really want me to join you on the floor, do you?"

She stared at him, and he waited. He would say no more. Either she would come to him, or she wouldn't. He settled back on the bed, laced his fingers behind his head, and closed his eyes. It had been one hell of a night. He had made so many mistakes that it was a marvel both he and the girl were still alive. First of all, he should have slept closer to her, whether she liked it or not. He had been too far away to sense the vampires' arrival until it had almost been too late, and he had allowed the intruders to get between him and Marya. If Marya hadn't been so resourceful, she'd be dead. His confrontation with Carlo had been a disaster. Cutting the vampire's eyes had indeed been a mistake, as had been turning his back on his opponent. He had failed to elicit any information from Carlo. But the worst failure by far was the conclusion itself. Death was never the preferred resolution. He began to wonder if what everyone was saying was true—that he was past his prime as an enforcer and too old to remain an effective Directorate member.

In the midst of pondering death, he felt Marya slide into bed next to him. Her movements were slow and tentative, and he remained still, not wanting to frighten her. She inched closer to him, first laying her arm across his chest, then pressing herself along his side. His body's reaction was instantaneous. None of his Paris beauty queens had ever made him feel like this. But he had promised Marya he would behave himself, and if it took all his control, he would.

She rested her head on his shoulder, and he brought his left arm down to hold her. Her body was still tense, but he didn't rush her. Besides, if she were truly to relax against him, it might be his undoing.

"I don't think I can sleep," she whispered.

Sleep was the farthest thing from his mind as well, but he wasn't about to tell her that. "Just rest then, *cherie.* "

"Talk to me."

Another pastime not high on his list. "About what?"

"I don't care. Anything. Tell me a story."

"You know anything I tell you is a lie."

"That goes without saying. I don't care. Finish the story of what happened after your city fell."

"Novgorod?" He resisted the idea. It was too personal. But what did it matter? It was far in the past, and she would never know that part of the truth was woven with the tall tale. "Very well. It was 1478. I was thirty-two years old..."

"The prime of life."

"Hardly, *cherie.* The French have a saying. 'If the young only knew, if the old only could.' I was very much lost between wisdom and the vigor of youth. No matter. My fate was decided for me. The history books call it 'annexation' or 'incorporation,' very bland, antiseptic words for what was nothing less than hell for every Novgorodian. Ivan Vasilievich confiscated the lands of every citizen—princes, boyars, even clergy. No one was spared. I had no lands to seize. I was a prince, yes, but in reality nothing more than a rather minor military leader."

"I don't believe that."

"As I said, do not look to a vampire for truth. Anyway, the Muscovites had to resort to creative means to get rid of me. They chose my eyes. My eyes were my downfall."

He felt her body shift, as if she wanted to gaze into the subject of his story. "Your eyes?"

Her movement pressed the warmth of her body closer to his, and his lust flared like a lit match, hot, fresh, and ready to consume. It was all he could do to piece coherent words together. "Blue eyes are a rarity in that part of the world, especially eyes as vivid as mine. Oh, the color you see now is enhanced by my Undead state, but even in life my eyes were extraordinary. Blue eyes were associated with vampirism and sorcery. It was said that those with eyes like mine were predestined to become vampires after death. Anyway, it was all the excuse needed for the Orthodox Church to condemn me as a heretic. My true faith mattered not the least. They had their pretext, and that was enough for them."

"But they were right. You did become a vampire."

"One of life's supreme ironies. I don't truly believe that my becoming a vampire had anything to do with my eyes or my having been marked a heretic."

"Then how did it happen?"

"Don't you think you've heard enough lies for one night?" The truth was that he couldn't concentrate on reciting stories with her soft breast against his chest and her long legs shadowing his.

"My grandmother used to tell me stories of the Vlach Roma in Moldavia. They were an enslaved people for five hundred years, bound to their owners' homes and farms. Not until the

1850s were they emancipated."

"But that was long ago and far away. You grew up in this country, didn't you?"

"Don't think there isn't persecution here. It's just more subtle. My mother wanted to keep me in school. She tried not to let anyone in the *gajikane* community know we were Roma, but people invariably found out. I remember when I was ten years old a boy sitting next to me in class was drawing pictures instead of doing an assignment. Another boy told him to stop fooling around or the teacher would sell him to my mother, the Gypsy Queen. When school was out I had a fight with that boy on the playground. After that, everybody called me 'the dirty Gypsy,' and no one would sit next to me."

She was quiet for a few moments, and he thought perhaps she had fallen asleep after all, but then her voice floated to him, almost like a dream.

"I killed a vampire."

"Yes, *cherie,* I know."

She squirmed, seeming to want to put more space between her body and his. Did she find the intimacy as difficult to bear as he did, or did she truly find the notion of lying with a vampire repulsive? "You said if I committed any violence against the Undead…"

"I know what I said. You have nothing to worry about. There's nothing at all to worry about. Try to sleep, *cherie.* " More lies.

Only in his mind did he tell her the truth. *Sleep well, cherie, because tomorrow there will be hell to pay.*

NINE

Drago couldn't have been more right. He heard the irritating sound of his cell phone long before the sun was even up. He was just into the time of day when he slept the most deeply, but listening for his phone's ring was a conditioned reflex. *No call at this time of the morning can be good news.*

It wasn't. It was Nikolena.

Marya stirred, but she didn't wake up. He took the call in the living room, both to avoid disturbing Marya further and to give himself room to pace. After he disconnected her call, he made one of his own. When he was finished, he sat on the sofa, propped his elbows on his knees, and rested his forehead in the cradle of his hands. He sat like that, not moving. He wasn't as successful at not feeling. After a few moments, he sensed Marya's presence. He looked up, running his hands through his hair to sweep the long strands from his eyes. She was standing in the hallway entrance leading to her studio and the guest room. Her dark eyes swam with worry.

"Drago? What is it?"

"Go get dressed."

She ignored him, crossing the living room to sit by his side. Her gaze traveled over him. He was still wearing nothing other than silk pajama bottoms. No doubt she was still adjusting to her reality's bump in the road of having a vampire as a bed partner.

"What's wrong? I have a right to know."

She was right. He just didn't know how to tell her. "That was Nikolena. I have to return to Paris. Immediately. She has me booked on the afternoon Air France One flight. I won't have time to drive to New York. I'll have to catch an early flight from Jackson to Kennedy Airport."

"Take me with you."

"I can't. There's only one seat booked. Besides, you don't have a passport, do you?"

She shook her head. "I don't even have a birth certificate."

He took a deep breath. "Get dressed. There isn't much time."

"Wait a minute. You're going to leave me, just like that?"

"I have no choice, *cherie.* I can't go against Nikolena's orders."

"Look. Until yesterday I didn't really buy your story about this vampire conspiracy against you, but last night convinced me. You don't think those two vampires will be the end of it, do you?"

"No, *cherie,* they won't be the end."

"So you're just going to leave me to my fate? It's no longer to your advantage to be here, so you're gone? Or maybe now my death will annoy lots of people, and that'll make your day, won't it?"

"Silence!" He raked his hands through his hair again, "If I could take you with me, I would, but I can't. And for me to disobey a command from *la directrice* would be death, something that would effectively defeat the purpose of this whole affair. I'm taking you with me as far as Jackson. I'll have Revelin Scott watch over you until I return."

"Revelin? That absurd young man?"

"He's a lot older than he looks. And looks and size don't have anything to do with strength."

"I thought you didn't like him any more than I did."

"Like or dislike has no bearing. He has three...no, make that four things going for him. One, Nikolena vouched for his integrity. Two, I know he's not loyal to Deverick. Three, he just happens to be in Jackson, and four, he's the strongest vampire I've encountered in a long time. There isn't anyone else nearby I would trust with you. I've already called him. He's expecting you. Now get dressed. You have half an hour."

"What if he doesn't want to be a babysitter?"

"Go, *cherie.* "

He couldn't blame her for her anger. He felt no better. He had promised to watch over her, and after only two days, he was leaving her. But he truly had no choice—he had been truthful with her in that. He had argued with Nikolena that he needed more time in Vicksburg, but she had been adamant in her wishes. She wanted him in Paris. Now. She wouldn't tell him the details, but she hadn't been happy. When Drago had told her about the two dead vampires, as he was obligated to do, the sudden dispassion in her voice was a bad sign. A very bad sign.

The only good thing about the conversation had been Nikolena's endorsement of Revelin Scott. In truth Drago didn't know if he liked the man or not. Scott had displayed strength, but also a brashness bordering on disrespect. However, disrespect was not an uncommon attitude among vampires, who were by their very nature egocentric. The Undead, also by nature, were masters of deception, but Drago had detected little dishonesty in his assessment of Scott's character. His appearance, as Marya had noted, was another matter. The last thing that anyone looking at the shaggy-haired young man would figure him for was a dominant vampire.

He only hoped he could convince Scott of the importance of safeguarding Marya. Most vampires cared little for mortals. Drago thought briefly about Dallas Allgate. Dallas was one vampire that Drago trusted and would have no second thoughts about leaving Marya with. The last Drago had heard, though, was that Dallas had moved out of Mississippi, and he wasn't sure where Dallas was now. Drago also trusted Ricard De Chaux, but Ricard was somewhere in the backwoods of Michigan. It seemed Drago was stuck with Scott. He wondered if there were enough compelling power or fear in the world to make Scott really heed an assignment like this.

Helpless. It was not often that he felt helpless. He had strength, wealth, and true power. He had an unlimited supply of some of the most beautiful women in the world at his disposal. And even within the rigidity of the Directorate, he had more independence and took more liberties than any other enforcer. Yet with everything he had, control over the present moment was not one of them. It put him in a foul mood.

Less than two hours later they were in front of Revelin Scott's office. Drago turned off the car's engine.

"Well, *cherie,* you have your wish. You are rid of me."

She sat gazing at her lap. "Yes, but you'll be back."

Her words came across more as a plea than the sarcastic remark he was sure she had originally intended. He reached over and ran his fingers down her cheek with the lightest touch he could manage. She closed her eyes and bit her lower lip. He slid two fingers to the far side of her chin and turned her face toward his. She allowed the touch, but kept her eyes lowered.

"Marya, look at me."

She raised her gaze. "Damn all of you," she whispered.

He dropped his hand. "I *will* be back, *cherie.* I promise you that. I can't tell you when. It depends on what Nikolena wants with me. In the meantime, trust Scott. And I know it goes against your nature, but try to obey him more than you did me."

She turned her head away and sucked in her lower lip.

He opened his car door. "Come. I have a flight to catch."

"Drago."

He paused and turned back to her.

"Whatever happens, and whatever your motives were, thank you for last night."

If only she knew how badly he had blundered last night. *"De rien, cherie.* But thank me again when I return."

Scott waited for them in the front office. The blond girl was nowhere in sight. Chances were she wasn't a day vampire. The look that Scott gave them, as well as his appearance, told Drago that he wasn't thrilled to be up at this hour, either. Scott wore flared blue pants, a matching vest, a white turtleneck, and several heavy, gold chains, but the vest was unbuttoned and his shaggy hair was more untamed than the last time he had seen him.

"Drago. Miss Jaks. I've been waiting for you." Scott put a noticeable emphasis on 'waiting.'

Drago turned his head to Marya. "Wait here. I'll have a word with *monsieur* Scott."

Less than a moment later they were in Scott's office with

the door shut behind them.

"You know, Drago, I'm not happy at being up and about at six-thirty in the morning. I'm also not happy about someone barging in here, making wild accusations, cutting my face, and then asking me for a bloody favor two days later."

Drago ignored Scott's complaint. "Two vampires tried to kill Marya last night, a master and his apprentice. Apparently they didn't know I'd be there. Their misfortune. The master, named Carlo, was about six-foot-two and between two hundred fifty and three hundred pounds. Short, dark hair and a goatee and mustache trimmed in a unique way. The novice was about my height and build, crossed over in his twenties, and had long, blond hair. That's all I know. Ring a bell with anyone you know?"

Scott sighed and sat on the edge of his desk. After a moment, he shook his head. "No. But then again, I've only been here three weeks. I know very few American vamps."

"Whoever sent them will know very soon that they weren't successful. Marya needs protection until I return, and there's no one else here I can trust not to be part of Deverick's scheme."

"Yeah? Well, lucky for you, mate, that this 'cocky bogtrotter' survived Talavera, hey?"

Drago leaned very close to Scott. "Heed my instructions in this, *monsieur,* and succeed, and I will make you a thousand apologies. Fail me in this, and I will have your head. *C'est compris?"*

Scott's gaze was unwavering. "I was a soldier. I know how to take orders. Even those I don't like."

"Good. Then we understand each other. This is between you and me, *monsieur.* I don't need to tell you not to say anything of this to Deverick or any of his men."

"Yeah, I got it."

"Good. Oh, and do be careful—not just with the girl, but yourself."

"Your concern is touching, Drago. Very heartfelt, I'm sure."

Drago leaned against the door and stroked his chin. "Deverick could have sent any of his other enforcers to tell Marya I had changed my mind, and she was to be terminated after all. Did you ever wonder why he sent you? I have. You're an outsider. A very unwelcome addition to his little group. I think he's set you up to take the fall in all this. So don't trust anyone."

"If it's got two legs, two fangs, and stinks of Undead, I don't trust it."

"C'est bien! I should be back the day after tomorrow if all goes well." He started to turn.

"Drago."

He paused, his hand on the knob, and faced Scott.

"Why all this fuss over the girl? A mortal. Worse yet, a bloody aberration."

He raised his brows. "I gave her life. She shall have it."

Scott snorted and shook his head. "Bloody Anti-God."

The words were whispered, but Drago heard them. It was nothing he hadn't heard a hundred times over.

Drago returned to Marya. She wouldn't look at him. He laid the back of one hand lightly against her cheek. "I have to go. Be careful, and behave."

She jerked her head away from his touch, meeting his gaze at last. "If you're going to go, then go."

"Au revoir, ma cherie. " The image of her face was already burned into his mind, yet he stared at her for a moment more. When he did leave, his vampiric gift of celerity took him swiftly away.

***

Damn all the Undead! She hadn't wanted him in her life and had been praying for the moment he would leave her. But now that the moment had come, she felt betrayed. All because of last night. He had saved her life last night, and she had been foolish enough to take comfort in his arms afterwards. She had reacted as if it had all been personal, forgetting that for him it was just a job. And now he was gone.

She glowered at Revelin Scott. At least she had trusted Drago's strength and power, if not his motives. She didn't trust Revelin at all.

His crossed his arms over his chest and sighed. "Well, Miss Jaks, what am I to do with you?"

As if she had any choices in the matter. She didn't bother

answering.

He sighed again. It wasn't a dramatic sigh, done for effect, as one gazing on his outrageous appearance might think. It wasn't the wistful sigh of one lost in thought either, but simply one of weariness. "You can't stay here, and you're not staying with me. I guess that leaves Callie. Won't she be thrilled."

Unlike Drago, Revelin made no attempt to be charming. In a way, she thought she preferred Revelin's demeanor. At least she would always know where she stood with him.

He buttoned up his vest. "Come on, then. I'll lock up, and we'll go out the back. My car's right outside." He locked the front door and headed down the hallway, apparently assuming she would follow. She hesitated for a second, then picked up her suitcase and dutifully trailed after him. Even if she had wanted to object, she had no alternatives.

He drove her across town, but all she could think about was Drago. She had been scared last night—more scared than when she had tried to kill him. That night she thought she was going to die anyway, so she had felt she had nothing to lose. But last night life had been hers again, and last night the two strange vampires had tried to take that away from her. And they would have succeeded if not for Drago. She had killed one vampire, but had no delusions that she could have dispatched the second on her own. And Drago, damn him, had played on her fear and had neatly seduced her into his bed. *No,* she thought. That wasn't fair. He had only held her, and he hadn't tried to press his advantage to try anything more. He had supported her and listened to her like no one ever had. And the kiss…once again, he had been surprisingly warm and gentle. She had always thought that vampires would be cold and clammy to the touch— warm, perhaps, only after feeding—but Drago's embrace had been a sanctuary of pleasure and comfort as well as safety. Still…he was gone and she was abandoned to a reluctant babysitter.

On the way, she asked Revelin if they could stop at a fast food restaurant. She hadn't eaten yet this morning, and she had no idea when she'd get her next meal. He complied, and soon afterward they pulled up at the rear of a large, well-kept house in a newer section of town. He unlocked the back door and punched in a code to reset the alarm system.

He led her into a spacious living room, and with a wave of his hand indicated that she make herself comfortable. The presence of two large sofas and numerous chairs gave Marya the impression that the occupant did a lot of entertaining. Either that, or hosted lots of meetings. It gave Marya a very bad feeling. If this house were well-known by vampires in the community…

Revelin's voice interrupted her thought. "Callie's my assistant and apprentice. She's only up at night, so I'll have to wait here with you until then. She'll watch you tonight. I'll stay as long as I can, but I might have to leave. In any case, I'll be back again tomorrow morning."

Marya's bad feeling worsened. *She was to be fobbed off again? And to an apprentice?* Still, Marya kept her mouth shut. To whom could she complain? Drago was gone, and Revelin certainly didn't care if she lived or died. So again, she made no reply.

Revelin's gaze tiredly flicked down the length of her body. "Not the chatty type, are you? Well, that's fine with me. The last thing I want to hear is a lot of moanin' and groanin' from a mortal. I am curious about one thing, though. What exactly did you do to land yourself in such a mess?"

She returned his appraisal, fastening her gaze on his pale blue eyes and letting it slide insolently down his body. "I didn't 'do' anything. It was my misfortune to be born with some of your blood."

He quirked heavy auburn brows at that, but his eyes, like Drago's, showed little emotion.

She decided that enlightening him couldn't hurt. "My grandfather was a vampire. Nicolai Jaks. Did you know him?"

"No."

"I guess you wouldn't have. He lived in Romania and only survived a few years after he was changed. His son, my father, killed him."

Revelin shook his head. "I've dealt with aberrations before, but their tainted blood has always been the result of vampiric contact, not birth."

"Listen, Mr. Scott, I don't want to be rude..." *Like hell she didn't.* "But I got only a couple hours of sleep last night. Is there a place where I can lie down and take a nap?"

"Sure. I've got plenty of work to do. And call me Revelin. Follow me."

He took her upstairs and gestured to a bedroom at the head of the stairs. "You can use this room. Bathroom's across the hall. I'll be downstairs."

The room was sparsely furnished, so Marya had little to do in checking out her new surroundings. There was a bed, dresser, and a table with a lamp. She checked the window and found it closed and locked. A quick look out the window was enough to determine that it would not provide a good escape route. It was a long way down. The closet was empty save for a spare blanket and several folding chairs. She pulled the bedcovers down, sat on the edge of the bed, and wrinkled her nose. The scent of the Undead permeated the room and the house as a whole, but the odor of decay was especially noticeable and abhorrent on the bed. It was the smell of hundreds of dead insects, dry and fusty. The thought of sleeping in the same bed some strange vampire had was almost unbearable, but Marya was too tired to allow the feeling to interfere with her rest. She slid between the spread and the blanket and closed her eyes.

Excerpts from her father's book of death ran through her weary mind. *Remember that though the vampire's appearance is human, he has little in common with other men. The illusory beauty of the vampire is its most powerful weapon over man, for though it appears real, it is not.*

Genuine or not, she wondered if she'd ever see Drago's austere beauty again.

***

Drago arrived at Chateau du Russe after midnight, tired and irritable. Adelle's greeting was both somber and without questions, nothing more than a quick embrace and the sound of his name on her lips.

"You don't seem surprised to see me, *mon chou.*"

"I've spoken with Philippe. There have been so many rumors taking to the air the past few days that he hasn't been able to counter but a few. None of them are good, Leksii."

He shook his head as he walked side by side with her to his private quarters. "I don't care about rumors. What's Nikolena's mood been? Has Philippe said?"

Adelle lifted one shoulder and let it drop. "He says she's been quiet since you left. Very quiet."

Nikolena quiet? La directrice was never quiet. The situation was even worse than he had thought. "What time does she want me?"

"As soon as you can be there. What can I bring to you in the meantime?"

"Nothing. No, wait…" He halted abruptly, and Adelle stopped at his side. "Send Cerise away. And anyone else who's here."

Her brow furrowed. "Well, there's only Cerise and Angelique. She just arrived yesterday, but…"

"Get rid of them. And don't accept any back in." He strode down the long hallway.

"But…" He heard her behind him, hurrying to catch up.

He held up a hand. "Enough, *ma chere.* Just see that it is done."

"Of course."

Something in her voice prompted him to stop and turn to her. "I'm sorry, Delle. It's been a bad week. I should not take it out on you. I'll make it up to you later on, I promise."

She smiled wanly. "Just promise me one thing. Curb your tongue tonight with Nikolena. She's all that stands between you and the mob that prays to Saint Guillotine."

He slipped an arm around her and gave her a squeeze. "Don't worry, *mon chou.* I'll hold on to my temper and my head."

***

Although Drago always dressed purposefully for his meetings with Nikolena, tonight he took extra time and care. The care was for how best to dress to placate Nikolena's mercurial temper, and the time was for himself—to calm his own mind. Adelle was right. He would have to choose his words very carefully tonight. He wouldn't beg for his life, but he'd have to be humble and sincere. Nikolena would know any spoken word—nay, any thought—that was not heartfelt. It wouldn't be easy. In fact, Drago wondered if he could pull it off at all. Dissimulation and deception were easy. Honesty and self-deprecation were hard for any vampire.

He donned loose, black silk trousers that tapered at the ankle and a white, silk shirt that hung open to his waist. Over this he wore a sky-blue satin *rubakha* that hung to his knees. The sleeves reached to the ground, with narrow openings for his arms to pass through at the elbows. The front opening of the *rubakha* ran all the way down the garment and was edged with silver embroidery, pearls, and semi-precious stones in every possible shade of blue.

Before he left, he stopped to have a final word with Adelle, but the moment was taken up more in silent appreciation. As her gaze soaked in every inch of him, the admiration and affection was apparent in her eyes, but more than that was the desire she couldn't hide. It was a desire that Drago knew Adelle would never act on, that in fact she hadn't acted on in the past ten years.

"There are no words, Leksii," she whispered. "Good luck."

"I don't know that luck will play a part, but *merci, ma chere.*"

***

He arrived at the Directorate offices at three in the morning, and for once Nikolena did not keep him waiting. He swept through the wide double doors and halted, as usual, to make his greeting and await her invitation to proceed.

"Bonsoir, Madame la directrice." He bowed gracefully and with every propriety, and there was not a part of his body that exaggerated or mocked.

"Ah, Aleksei Borisov. Come forward."

Her voice was friendly and welcoming, but he could feel the hairs rise on the back of his neck. When Nikolena draped herself with pleasantries and good cheer she resembled nothing so much as a sunning snake. Innocuous, but deadly. He strode to the side of her massive desk, and when she extended her arm toward him, he sank to one knee and kissed the proffered hand. Intricate gold rings appeared too heavy for her slender fingers and small hands, but her movements were as light as air.

"You look magnificent, Alek. Not that you don't always look splendid…" She ran her fingertips down the portion of his chest bared by the open-fronted shirt. "…but tonight you look absolutely delicious." She dragged out the final word, much the same way she dragged her fingers back up his chest and along his neck to cup his chin. "Good enough to eat…if I could but do so. Do I detect a design behind all this magnificence?"

"Only one, *madame,* and that is to please you."

She smiled a very slow Cheshire-cat smile. He again felt the hairs on his skin bristle, as if the room had suddenly gone cold.

"Sit, Alek."

He did, and she spent a moment staring into his eyes. He wanted to squirm under the inspection, but he held himself still, quieting his thoughts as well. He returned the scrutiny of her gaze. She looked no less regal than he did. Dressed all in gold, and with her straight, shoulder length ash-blond hair, she resembled a tiny tsarina. Her *rubakha* was of flaxen-colored silk, and the caftan she wore was of gilt brocade, heavily embellished with gold braid, gold embroidery, and hundreds of citrines and garnets in every shade of yellow, russet, and burgundy.

"So you wish only to please me, Aleksei Borisov?"

"Of course, *madame."*

Nikolena lifted an hourglass from her desk, turned it upside down, watched the sand trickle through the waist of the glass, then flung the instrument directly at his head.

He caught it deftly in one hand.

"Do you know what that is, Alek?" Chill replaced the cheer in her voice.

He steeled himself. "An hourglass, *madame."*

"Wrong! It is nothing more than the length of time you can go without getting yourself into trouble!"

He reached over to replace the hourglass on the desk, but said nothing.

"You left here less than a week ago. In the past two days I

have been inundated with phone calls, emails, faxes, and written reports. All had to do with you, Alek, and not a single one was good news. I got an official complaint from Evrard Verkist that you're harassing his enforcers for no reason. And well it seems justified! I received a complaint from Curt Deverick that you did not return to New Orleans to assist him there, and a grievance was filed by Revelin Scott stating you attacked him without provocation and made wild accusations against him. If that weren't bad enough, you yourself send me a report that an aberration—who should have been terminated long ago— is still alive, and that two vampires, one a Master, are dead at your own hands! Do you deny any of this?"

It was worse than he had expected. "I make no denials or excuses, *madame*. I do have an explanation, if you will hear it." He had fully anticipated that Deverick would lodge a complaint against him, but hadn't thought that the man who held the highest office in the Brotherhood, Evrard Verkist, would hear about the events of the week so quickly. Drago was especially chagrined to hear that Scott had reported him. *And this was the man he left in charge of Marya's safety.*

"Do you honestly believe that any explanation you could concoct would be reasonable enough or strong enough to counter all the adverse reactions your escapades have caused?"

He was silent.

She stood, picked up the hourglass, and hurled it at the stone wall behind her. The glass broke, and glittering shards fanned across the wall like fireworks, followed by floating trails of golden sand. "Well? Do you?"

"No, *madame.*"

Her black eyes burned with a cold fire, the only spots of darkness in a vision of gold and light. "You have no friends, Aleksei Borisov, none. Every Directorate member I've spoken with has called for your termination."

So. There it was. All the years of doing as he pleased had had a price, and now he was being charged. And the payment would be his life. "I am in your hands, as always, Nika. All I ask is that you listen to the story from my point of view."

She sighed. "Very well, Alek. Your service over the years

has earned you that much."

So over the next hour he told her everything—Marya's *dhampir* heritage, the forged order reversing her status delivered by Scott, her attempt on his own life, Scott's denial of wrongdoing, and the visit in the night of the two strange vampires. When he was done, it was Nikolena's turn to be silent.

"Many may hate me, Nika, but I think it's only one person who truly wants me dead. If he cannot conspire to kill me outright, he will start a campaign in the Directorate to vilify me until the mob mentality takes over and everyone calls for my head, including you. If this one person has in fact won you to his side, then I am lost."

"I am not so easily swayed as all that." She studied his face again. "You're tired, Alek. I can see it in your eyes without even looking into your mind. Answer me one question. Do you want to live?"

Do I want to live? He thought back again to everything that had happened during the past week, and his answer was there—across an ocean of time and space. *"Oui, madame. Je veux vivre."*

"Excellent. I think perhaps for once we are not at cross-purposes. I have one more assignment for you, Aleksei Borisov. If you are successful, I promise you that the mewling of all your detractors will be silenced. If you fail, your enemy will have won, and the repercussions will rock the Directorate as nothing ever has."

Another assignment? "Madame, I promised to return to Jackson."

"Did I not just offer you one last chance to live? You dare to object? Be silent and listen to me!" She stood and glided to the tall bank of windows that overlooked the lawns surrounding the chateau. The vista was dark. The only lights that vied with that of a sliver moon were a few garden lamps and the series of lights along the drive that, from the height of the window, looked like lustrous pearls strung on a curving necklace. "Stand beside me, Alek, and listen." The voice that was so strident a moment ago was as soft and beckoning as a lover's.

He stepped to her side, close, but not touching. The top of her pale head didn't even reach his shoulder, yet there was no mistaking the power that radiated from her petite body.

She stared out into the night. "The Brotherhood is rotten at its core, Alek. I've long known it, even before you began filing your complaints of ineptitude. I have suspected for quite some time that one of the high-ranking Brotherhood officials has been ascending the hierarchy by forbidden means. This man is powerful, Alek, and so far I've got no solid proof. You are to expose him, secure the proof I need, and, if possible, deliver him to me. However, if that is not possible and you have to destroy him…"

Drago understood. It was a fight to the death. *"Je comprends, madame. Merci."*

Nikolena sighed. "Don't thank me, Alek. I may well be sending you to your death after all. This man has all the manpower he needs at his disposal, while you have…"

"Only myself. I know."

"You will need help on this one, I'm afraid. I'm assigning you an apprentice."

This he had to protest. An apprentice would be worse than no help at all. *"Madame,* I work alone. I always have, you know that."

"Not this time. I'm dedicating Revelin Scott to you, for however long this takes."

"Scott? But…"

She held up a dainty, bejeweled hand. "Save your objections. I know. He doesn't like you. I'm sure the feeling is mutual. However, we've already discussed his merits. He's strong, and he'll do as you order. Come now. You must have some faith in him, else you never would have left your precious cargo in his charge."

She had a point, but not one he wanted to concede. Still, he knew objecting would only bring her wrath.

"Very well, *madame,* I will do as you ask."

"Good." She paused, and turned to him. "Aleksei Borisov, hear me. I have no one else who can do this. Not a one of my other enforcers has your strength, abilities, or your unique talent for getting a job done. I need you for this. Don't let me down. Or yourself."

He had rarely heard Nikolena admit her fondness for him in words. He answered her with his eyes.

"Just remember. This time, make sure you have your proof before you go killing anyone."

Drago smiled. For every caress there was a cuff.

"I have you booked on tomorrow's Concorde. Philippe has your orders." She held out her hand, the signal that he was being dismissed.

He took her delicate fingers in his and lightly kissed the back of her hand. *"Madame la directrice,* I will not fail."

***

As tired as she was, Marya slept fitfully. She woke briefly several times, but finally awakened, rolled over, and failed to fall back asleep. *I'm still alive.* And she was sleeping in a strange vampire's house. If the thought alone wasn't enough to urge her from the bed, the closeness of the room was. She felt like she couldn't breathe. It was like sleeping in a mortuary, except that the corpses were all still walking around.

She slid from the bed, feeling dirty in the clothes she had slept in. The house was very quiet. She padded to the window. Revelin's car was still parked in back. Feeling a little more secure, she used the bathroom across the hall to wash her face, comb her hair, and straighten her outfit. She then descended the stairs, taking a peek into the living room. Room-darkening shades and heavy drapes wrapped the room in a comfortable semi-darkness, as if allowing its occupants a peaceful respite during the warmest hours of the day. She couldn't see Revelin, though, and for a brief moment she wondered if he would leave her there all alone. *Don't be silly,* she thought. His car was still there.

"Revelin?" The sound of his name was no louder than a whisper.

"Down here, Miss Jaks."

With relief, she followed the sound to the kitchen. Revelin sat at a desk in the strangest kitchen Marya had ever seen. There was a countertop, sink, and cupboards, but no stove, refrigerator, dishwasher, or any other usual kitchen appliances. There was only the desk, cluttered with a laptop surrounded by papers, a few chairs, and a file cabinet.

He looked up at her as she entered. "Have a seat."

She sat down, and maybe it was the room, or the lack of what it held, but suddenly Marya was ravenous. "Listen, I hate to keep bothering you with this, but can you order me some take-out?"

He stared at her.

"Food." It was but one more reminder of how foreign the world was that she had unwillingly entered when she had awakened a week ago and found Drago sitting in her boudoir chair. But Revelin was gracious, and within an hour, fried chicken, biscuits, and soda were delivered to the door. She finished eating, cleaned the corner of the desk she had appropriated, and looked at Revelin. He was immersed once more in his work.

"Revelin…" She paused and bit down on her lip. "Is it all right if I watch TV?"

"Be my guest."

She wandered back into the living room and turned on the set. There wasn't much on that interested her, but she welcomed the distracting noise. The last thing she wanted to do was brood over Drago. It had been on the tip of her tongue to ask Revelin about Drago and why all the Undead hated him, but at the last instant she had kept quiet. Now, bored by the television, she was sorry she hadn't asked her questions. A little truth about Drago might counteract the illogical ache she still felt at the thought of never seeing him again.

A few hours later Callie and Revelin glided forward and were standing in front of Marya before she realized they had entered the room. Callie's pretty face wore a frown that was part puzzlement and part annoyance. Marya had little hope that the expression was solely due to waking up on the wrong side of the coffin.

Revelin looked tired and no happier. His introductions were brief. "Drago's orders. Our charge, Marya Jaks. Marya, Callie Monroe, my assistant."

A tight smile pulled unflattering creases around Callie's mouth, making her look suddenly older. "Excuse us, please," she said.

The two vanished as quickly as they had materialized, and Marya could hear angry voices from the kitchen. Callie was clearly not pleased to wake up and find a mortal cozily entrenched in front of her television set. *As if any of this is my idea.*

The shouting died down, and Callie reappeared without Revelin. She was wearing a red-paisley print, sleeveless mini-dress. A rather nauseating complement, Marya thought, to Revelin's retro styling.

Callie's smile was broader this time, but looked no more sincere. "I'm sorry, Miss Jaks…"

Marya interrupted with a smile of her own. "Oh, Marya, please. After all, I've been enjoying your hospitality."

"Yes…you have. I hope you can appreciate that this is a little out of the ordinary for me."

"Believe me, Miss Monroe, I am certainly not here by choice."

Callie sank onto one of the sofas. "I would be very interested to hear how all this came about."

Marya figured that telling the story couldn't hurt and would only help to pass the time, so she related the incidents of the past week. Finally, as midnight approached, Marya went upstairs. She didn't think she'd be able to sleep after having slept most of the day, but she could only stand so much of Callie. The woman was a very young vampire and, as such, had a most disagreeable odor about her.

Marya drifted in and out of sleep. She heard an endless series of sounds, but to Marya, in her semi-conscious state, those born of dreams were indistinguishable from those rooted in reality. Footsteps and voices came to her. She heard a car door slam, and a car engine started up with a rumble. An alarm sounded and startled Marya, but as soon as she woke and sat up, all was quiet. She waited a moment, then eased out of the bed and stepped to the window. Revelin's car was gone. She dressed quickly and edged the door ajar. Voices floated up the staircase to her—strange voices. Suddenly she felt as if she had just run a very long race. Her heart pounded, and she fought to get enough air into her lungs. Surely Drago couldn't be back already. Even if he could be, she hadn't heard his unique French accent. *Where was Revelin?* She told herself it was just some Brotherhood meeting, but even as she did, her feet took her down the hallway and away from the stairs. She quickly checked the other rooms, but they were either like hers, furnished simply, or used for storage. She examined every window, but all were closed tight. There was nowhere to go. She felt a soft vibration on the staircase, and Callie appeared before her.

Her dark eyes were like a doll's—round and slightly unfocused. "We have to go, Marya. Quickly."

Marya's heart still thudded in her ears. "Why? What's happened?"

"Rev wants us out of here. It's not safe."

"Who's downstairs?"

Callie didn't answer. "Come on. There isn't time."

Marya grabbed her bag from her bedroom and immediately regretted not taking a shower. She still felt sullied from sleeping in the vampire's bed, and now it seemed she must travel like this. She followed Callie downstairs. Two men waited. They were dressed casually and looked to be in their late twenties or early thirties, but neither one bore a friendly expression on his face. She assumed they were vampires, but at first she couldn't be sure. Callie's strong scent overpowered any vampiric stench the two men might exude. Her appraising gaze found each of theirs in turn, and glittering, cold eyes stared back at her. *Vampire eyes.* They weren't blue, like Drago's or Revelin's, but the emptiness was similar. It wasn't a blank look, or an uncomprehending one. They were simply windows, not to a soul, but to a very dark place.

"Callie, I think we should wait for Revelin to return."

It was one of the men who answered. "Let's go. We're going to take you to Scott now."

Marya hesitated. If they had wished her harm, wouldn't she now be dead? And Callie was agreeing with them. Perhaps they were friends of Revelin's. Just because they weren't friendly didn't mean anything. She was being paranoid. She picked up her bag and allowed the men to escort her to a waiting van, but as soon as she entered the rear of a panel van with Callie and saw the doors being locked, she knew it was all very wrong.

TEN

Drago returned to his chateau still buoyed by the confidence that had flooded him when he had vowed to Nikolena that he would not fail. In the back of the sleek limousine he swiftly reviewed his orders. It truly appeared that *la directrice's* assignment and his own quest were connected. He would not have to break his word to return to Marya. And if the corruption led all the way to Evrard Verkist and he could not be stopped any other way, Nikolena had sanctioned death.

Adelle was still waiting up for him when he arrived, and he gave her a long embrace. "Nikolena has stayed the drop of the blade, Delle," he whispered. "Come. I have to make a call, then I'll tell you all about it."

Once in his private quarters, the Russian Room, Drago took off his *rubakha*, handed it to Adelle, and dropped to a long, low divan. He called Revelin Scott's number on his phone and waited, finally getting nothing but a voice mail message.

"Zut!" Drago sprang to his feet and began wearing a path on the Oriental carpet.

"What is it?" Adelle quickly put the garment away and moved closer to Drago, though she made no attempt to match his pacing stride for stride.

"Scott's not answering his phone."

She gave him a blank look.

"I charged him with *mademoiselle* Jaks' safety."

Adelle's unchanged expression told him that he hadn't enlightened her at all. She pulled him back down to the divan and sat next to him, a restraining arm imploring him to sit still long enough to tell her the story. He gave her an abbreviated version of the week's events.

It took her less than one minute to digest the tale. "Tell me. Is this Marya the reason you had me send all the girls away?"

He quirked a brow at her. "Don't be ridiculous. She's an aberration."

"Leksii, you can lie to everyone else in the world, but when you can't tell me the truth I know you're not being truthful with yourself, either."

He gave her a hard look he knew she didn't deserve, but his anger begged an outlet. "The girls bore me. It's as simple as that."

"And this one girl does not."

He punched Scott's number again. There was still no answer.

"Drago, there's no sense in worrying. There could be a hundred reasons why he doesn't answer. There's no way faster than the Concorde, so there's nothing to be done right now. Get some sleep so you're ready for tomorrow." She stroked his arm, but, unlike Nikolena, she was careful not to venture too close to where his bared chest rose and fell in the center opening of his shirt. Ever since Adelle had made the decision many years ago to stop sharing his bed, she was careful not to touch him in any way that could be construed as sexually provocative.

He covered her hand with his own. "You're right, as usual, *mon chou.* What would I do without you and Philippe? The two of you brave the world for me."

She smiled. "Oh, it's easy for me. I'm sheltered here behind these walls. It's poor Philippe who must weather the daily storms."

"Even so, I value your loyalty no less." He leaned over to kiss her on the cheek, the most, other than an embrace or touch of his hand, that she would accept from him. "Make sure I'm awake in plenty of time for the noon flight."

"I will." She turned her hand to clasp his, and she sat there like that for a long moment before she pulled away and left the room.

Drago knew he had to rise in just a few short hours for his flight, but relaxation came hard. Was his assignment over before it had begun? Were Marya and Scott already dead? His incense over the possibility of Marya's death wasn't anything he was able to rationalize to himself any more than he could explain it to Adelle. Why should he care about an aberration? Her birth had made them enemies, and he couldn't forget she had tried to kill him. He fell back on the reason he had given Scott—that he had been the one to give her life, and he would see to it that she had it. It was an egocentric explanation, but right now egotism was something his vampire's tired and agitated mind could accept and understand.

***

Drago arrived in New York just before ten in the morning, local time. He tried Scott's number again, for the countless time.

"Scott."

Surprise almost had Drago speechless. Almost. "Where the hell have you been? I've been calling for the better part of twelve hours with no answer!"

"Drago." There was no surprise in the acknowledgement, but Drago could hear weariness and what almost sounded like resignation. "Never mind that now," continued Scott. "You may as well hear it right off. Callie and Marya have vanished."

It was all his fears come true, but rage ruled his response, for rage was a much more comfortable emotion than sorrow. "Vanished, *monsieur?* What do you mean, vanished? Weren't you with them?"

"I left Marya with Callie at her house. I had to go back to the office. I was only gone a half hour. When I returned, they were both gone."

Drago lowered his voice. "You left Marya with an apprentice?"

"Listen, Drago, I'm as upset about this as you are. Callie's been with me twenty years. I know that's not a long time, but she's more important to me than any mortal, and I…"

Drago cut him off. "Forget the rest. Where are you now?"

"At my office."

"I'm booked on the next flight to Jackson. We'll discuss it when I arrive. Oh, and Scott…"

"What?"

"Nikolena has officially assigned you to me for the duration of this affair. So, *monsieur,* think very carefully about where your loyalties lie."

***

Drago entered Scott's office to find him sitting behind the front desk, his elbows propped on a stack of papers and one hand supporting his head. He lifted a haggard countenance at Drago's appearance, but his expression swiftly restored itself, and the eyes that stared at Drago turned as sharp and cold as any he'd ever seen.

"I should kill you right now, *monsieur,* for your carelessness." Drago kept his voice very soft.

Scott collapsed his arms. "But you won't, because you need me, like it or not."

Drago dropped to a chair opposite the desk and leveled his gaze at the younger vampire. "How do I know you didn't help engineer this whole thing?"

Scott leaned back in his chair. "You talked about loyalty, remember? Well, it goes both ways. Trust me, or get yourself another bloody partner."

"Partner? You misunderstood me, *monsieur.* There is no equality here. You take orders from me." Drago flicked Nikolena's sealed order across the desk. "Just like I take orders from her."

Scott broke the wax seal, read the enclosed directives, and raised ice blue eyes to Drago. "At your service, then, *Master.*" No one could have missed the mockery in the last word. Before Drago could respond, Scott said, "A suggestion, then. Our time might be better spent in trying to solve this thing instead of bickering with each other."

Scott was right. Anger and temper would get them nowhere. Drago nodded. "Very well. Tell me what you know. Was there any blood at the house?"

Scott sighed and leaned forward. "None. Not a drop. The lock on the back door was sprung, but there was no sign of a struggle. Nothing out of place. Marya left nothing behind. Her bag and all her things were gone, almost as if she went willingly. There have been no calls, no messages left for me, nothing. I contacted all the vamps I know in Jackson, but nobody pretended anything other than total ignorance."

Drago spent a moment in thought. "All right. It's a game, then. Until we have proof otherwise, we assume the girls are still alive. Someone high in the hierarchy has them. It could even be Evrard Verkist."

Scott lowered his brows. "Verkist? Not Deverick?"

"Deverick's a *petit poisson,* a small fish."

"But where? Verkist has offices all over the country."

"It's me he wants. He'll let us know. In the meantime, we wait. And, I think, get some sleep—something which both of us have been very much lacking. I have a feeling, *mon ami,* that we shall need all our strength."

***

Ten hours later the van pulled to a halt, and Marya and Callie were ushered out of the vehicle and into the cool of the night. It had been a long, uncomfortable trip. The rear of the van had been converted into a small sleeping area, but the beds were narrow and hard, and there were no windows to relieve the boredom. A metal partition separated the rear of the van from the cab area. A small window in the partition had been kept closed for most of the trip, to keep the daylight from Callie, Marya figured, but also to keep Marya from knowing where they were going. Stops had been made for restrooms, but Marya had been closely watched the whole time, and there hadn't been any opportunity to make a phone call or leave a message. Food was brought to the van. She had tried talking to Callie, but the woman seemed dazed, and could answer none of Marya's questions.

Now, however, she stretched cramped muscles and prayed that the journey was indeed over. Lifting her head, Marya was stunned at the sight of her surroundings. Gone was the lush, green overgrowth of Mississippi. They were on a mountainside high in the desert, and the lights of a huge city blanketed the valley below like a layer of stardust. The black sky stretched all around her, the multitude of stars above a faithful image of the glittering lights below.

"Let's go." One of the vampires took her arm and turned her toward the face of the mountain. Before Marya was a vista as magnificent as the one she had just seen. Built flush against the rock was a huge house. The word 'house' seemed woefully inadequate. Dozens of lights illuminated the front of the building, adding sparkle to an otherwise stark, modernistic design of glass, stucco, and stone. Arched windows echoed the rounded curves of the russet roof tiles, and wings extended to either side of the grand entrance, like stiff arms trying to embrace the mountain. A landscaped courtyard and covered porch led to the entrance, and Marya was quickly guided inside. The interior was no less grand. A wide foyer sporting massive redwood beams in the ceiling and natural stone in the floors and walls gave the place a feeling of age and strength. The foyer opened directly onto a commanding sunken great room. Wide double doors to the great room were swung wide, revealing a very modern décor with colors of lavender, gold and gray.

She and Callie were turned over to a dark-haired female vampire who led them down the foyer to the northern wing of the house. Marya passed a small kitchen and a large dining room which looked to be more of a gathering room. The vampire undulated down the hall to the far end of the wing where she stopped and showed them a luxurious bedroom with a private bath and a connecting door to an adjoining suite.

"I'm Cheyanna. Make yourself presentable. I'll be back in exactly one hour. The Patriarch will see you then."

The door closed soundly behind Marya and Callie, leaving them alone in a cage as gilded as any she could imagine. Marya's thoughts weren't on the room, though, for as fancy as the furnishings were, the room stank of the Undead. No, her thoughts were on what the vampire had just told her. *The Patriarch.* She knew whom she was to see shortly. She didn't know his name, but thanks to her father's journal, she knew what he was—the most powerful, highest-ranking vampire in America. Indeed, there was no one more influential except for members of the Directorate itself. Leaving this room to Callie, Marya opened the connecting door and made herself at home in the neighboring bedroom. She opened her suitcase and took out the best outfit she had. It wasn't very elegant, but when she had packed she had no idea she would be having an audience with such a commanding creature. Of course the outfit wouldn't be out of respect for him—it would simply make her feel at her own best. She took a long, hot shower and scrubbed her skin and hair several times over. The room may smell of death, but it was heaven to have her body clean again.

She dressed in a long, narrow black skirt with a trail of embroidered red roses that wound downward from waist to hem, and a white blouse with long, flowing sleeves and a low cut neckline. At her throat she wore a red ribbon which held a black onyx pendant.

What could the Patriarch possibly want with her? He had obviously gone to great lengths to bring her here. *Ah, but this is not about me.* Drago had told her this was about him before he had left for Paris two days ago. Was Drago already here? Had he flown here, wherever 'here' was, while she had traveled by road? Would she see him in just a few moments? The possibility set her pulse racing.

In the dark van, Marya had tried not to think about Drago, but she had thought of nothing else. She knew she should hate him for what he was, but in truth he had not harmed her. Just the opposite. How many times in the past two days had her mind relived his saving of her life? His embrace afterward, soothing her fears? And the afterimage of his blue eyes, burned into her memory, was something she knew she'd never forget. So beautiful, yet so horrible. So empty, yet promising so much. Her heart pounding, she tried to think about the present.

Perhaps the Patriarch had learned of Curt Deverick's renegade schemes and wanted to personally apologize to Drago for the bad behavior of his underlings. After all, the Patriarch was ultimately responsible for those who worked for him. He would naturally want to make amends with the all-powerful Directorate. With the end of the long trip, the shower and clean clothes, and the prospect of seeing Drago again, Marya felt better than she had since she had left her own house. This huge misunderstanding would gracefully be resolved tonight, and they could all go home.

The door abruptly opened, cutting short her musing. It was Cheyanna.

"It's time. Come with me.

The woman led her to the large, airy great room. "Make yourself comfortable. The Patriarch will be with you shortly."

Cheyanna disappeared, leaving Marya alone to admire the raw beauty of the space around her. A waterfall was built into one rock wall, and skylights above opened the room to an expanse of night sky. The sofas and chairs were covered in fine gray leather and were smothered in pillows and throws of shades of lavender and spice. Hidden lamps illuminated the waterfall and abstract paintings which decorated two other walls, and gold torchieres lit everything else.

Mesmerized by the endless flow and splash of the water streaming down the rock falls, Marya heard nothing until she felt a presence directly behind her. It was the aura and scent of a very old vampire, and she thought it might be Drago. She spun around, and the man before made her forget the waterfall, Drago, and everything else.

Tall and well built, it was nevertheless his coloring that held her attention. Long, smooth silver hair cascaded to his shoulders, and gray eyes burned dark against a pallid complexion. Two long scars, one across either cheek, marred an otherwise rugged yet attractive face. "Welcome to *Fata Morgana,* Miss Jaks. Do you know the meaning of that name?"

His voice held the barest trace of an accent that, like Drago's, sounded French, yet the intonation lacked the silkiness of Drago's smooth voice. "No."

"It means 'mirage.' Isn't that what one expects to find in a desert?"

Marya blinked. "I don't know. I've never been to a desert. I'm not even sure where I am."

The vampire turned to the tall windows of the fourth wall and spread his arms to the side. "Below us lies the Valley of the Sun. I am a great fan of irony. Come. Sit down."

She sat in a huge leather chair, feeling small. He, on the other hand, poured himself into a similar chair, and it seemed to shrink in comparison. He wore a pale gray silk shirt adorned with a white lace cravat and white cuffs, and black trousers cut in the most current and expensive style. A huge diamond stick pin skewered the lace at his throat.

"My name is Evrard Verkist, the Patriarch. You do know what that means?"

She nodded. "You're the father of the family called the Brotherhood."

He smiled. "That's one way to put it, I suppose."

Enough of the pleasantries. "Why am I here, Mr. Verkist?"

"You've caused my people quite a bit of trouble the past few days."

"Forgive me if my trying to stay alive ruined somebody's day."

He smiled again, but there was no more warmth in the twist of his mouth than there was in the frost of his eyes. "You have no notion of what you've started, have you?"

She opened her mouth to protest, but he gave her no chance.

With one hand he stroked the cravat's lace as if it were a long beard. His hand was pale even against the white lace, and his lucent fingernails almost glowed. "Spare me. I know it's not your doing. The Directorate has long been meddling in my affairs, but this latest plot of Alek Dragovich to malign my people has got to stop. That's why I've invited everyone here. This crusade against the Brotherhood will end, one way or another."

Was he indeed here? Anticipation of seeing Drago did strange things once more to her body, nearly overshadowing the import of Verkist's words. *Plot of Alek Dragovich?* Verkist had it wrong, didn't he? It was someone else who had arranged for her death, not Drago.

"Then Drago's here?" She tried to keep her voice dispassionate.

Verkist's mouth twisted again, letting her know she wasn't

fooling anyone, and her gaze shifted from the froth of lace to the scars that angled in new directions with every movement of his mouth. "So, *l'enforcier* is still the ladies' man he always was. Even so, I'm surprised he was able to seduce a mortal with your *dhampir* blood. I would have expected you to be more resistant to his dubious charms than that."

"He did not seduce me."

Verkist laughed. "Denial is ever the response from those so conquered. Just know this, young lady. None of my people were responsible for changing the order regarding your final evaluation. I know this because I issued the order myself."

This man was as irritating to talk to as any vampire she had met. *Conquered, indeed!* "First of all, no one has *conquered* me. Secondly, by your own admission, you're the one who started all of this, not me."

He laughed again. "I would not be so foolish as to try to forge Drago's order. No, the order to terminate you came from Drago himself, just as Revelin Scott told you. Drago is going to use this affair as an excuse to wage war against me."

Marya was confused. "But why would he wage war against you?"

"The Brotherhood is mine. No one holds more power than the Patriarch. But the Brotherhood is also Drago's. He's the Directorate enforcer assigned to the United States. It has often put us into conflict over the years. You are but one more attempt on his part to exert his influence—to remind me that my position is technically subordinate to his."

"So where is Drago?" Since he was already aware of her interest, she saw no reason not to learn the answer to her most burning question.

"He'll be here soon, don't worry." He rose, seemed to float to the door, and opened it. Cheyanna stepped in. "You'll be called for when he arrives. In the meantime follow the instructions of my staff, and you'll come to no harm."

Back in her room, Marya took off her fine outfit and threw herself onto the bed. *Drago's coming.* She wanted to think of nothing else, but Verkist's words had been too disturbing for her to ignore. *L'enforcier is still the ladies' man he always was.* So what? She would not let that statement change her feelings. She herself would have guessed no less. Drago, with his wicked black hair, killer eyes, and lean, strong body, no doubt had had women falling at his feet for centuries. She had no illusions that she was anything but a promise to be kept. He had sworn to keep her alive, and he would do just that. *Seduced, indeed!* If Verkist only knew how wrong he was there. Drago didn't want her. She was an aberration. And even if he did want her…

For a brief moment she imagined herself in his embrace, feeling the deceptive power in his lean, hard body. Her mind replayed the memory of his kiss at the hotel, and she felt again his mouth on hers, warm and sweet. But also very controlled. She wondered what it would be like to kiss him when his control wasn't so tightly reined in. Just as quickly, she ended her fantasy. No, she was nothing more than a vow. He would come for her, resolve this misunderstanding, and take her back home. But Verkist's other words came back to her as well, and she knew none of it would be that easy.

Verkist was lying, of course. She had no doubt he was either covering up for one of his minions, probably Deverick, or that he himself was to blame for her termination order. To think otherwise would mean that Drago had been playing her for a fool all along. She didn't even want to consider the possibility. Not that she doubted Drago was capable of such deception…

Damn all the Undead! In the past week the four words had become her favorite curse.

***

Drago's phone rang, rousing him from a light sleep. He had taken a hotel room not far from Scott's private residence, and he rolled over and grabbed his cell phone. "Dragovich."

"Drago, it's Scott. You were right—the call came. It was Callie. She and Marya are on their way to Phoenix."

Drago sat up. "Then it is Evrard Verkist. He's got a stronghold there, *Fata Morgana.* I've been there. The place is a fortress. Did she sound herself?"

"No, that's what worries me. I'm sure she's been

bespelled."

"Call and book us for the next available flight to Phoenix. Call me back with the flight number and departure time."

"If we go, it's a trap. You know that, don't you?"

"Mon ami, I would be disappointed if it were not."

ELEVEN

A vampire knocked on Marya's door the following morning and informed her that she should dress again for the great room. When Marya asked why, she was told only that she would be waiting there.

Waiting for what? For another audience with Evrard Verkist? What could he want with her this time? Guilty thoughts of the vampire she had killed invaded her mind. Drago had assured her that there would be no repercussions for that act, but now she wondered. If the blond novice she had sent to the True Death had been one of Verkist's vampires, the Patriarch might well seek retribution.

As she showered, a new thought came to her. Maybe it wasn't bad news after all, but good news. Perhaps Drago had already arrived and was in the building even now. The thought prompted her to dress carefully, and, it being her best outfit, she once again put on the black skirt with the roses and the white blouse. When she was ready, Cheyanna escorted her to the great room.

Verkist was nowhere to be seen, but Callie was there as well as six other vampires, Cheyanna included. Special room-darkening blinds and drapes covered the windows, and closed panels sealed off the skylights. The only light came from the hidden lamps and gold torchieres. Marya sat next to Callie on one of the sofas. Thankfully, the confused look was gone from Callie's face, and the belligerent frown that Marya had seen at the Jackson house was again in evidence.

"Callie, what's going on? What is everyone waiting for?"

A fierce smile curved Callie's mouth. "Rev's coming for me."

"How do you know?"

"Rev would never let me down. Never. He'll come."

Somehow Marya didn't think that a reception this large would be for nothing more than a minor enforcer. "What about Drago? Isn't he coming, too?"

Callie scowled again. "I don't know anything about Drago."

Callie would say nothing more, but she looked daggers at each of Verkist's vampires. They ignored her. Finally, after an hour, Marya could feel the tension in the air rise to an almost uncomfortable level. Whatever the vampires were plugged into, Marya could feel it as well. She felt goose bumps on her arms, as if the temperature had just dropped.

The doors swung open, and Evrard Verkist blew into the room like a gust of wind. He was followed by six more strange vampires, all of them imposing in appearance, but none to match their master. His billowing silver hair was like a cloud, his flashing eyes like lightning. He wore gray trousers and a white shirt, and a lace cravat even longer and more elaborate than the last flowed down the front of his shirt like a waterfall. The diamond pin once again nested in the folds of lace. Marya guessed that Verkist was two or three inches taller than Drago and broader by about fifty pounds. The aura of power in the room became almost suffocating.

"Miss Monroe, Miss Jaks, please join me."

Marya looked around. Clearly, she had no choice but to do as he said. She went and stood at Verkist's right side, careful to leave several feet of space between them, and Callie stood at his left. Marya saw Verkist nod almost imperceptibly, and a vampire at the door swung it open.

Two more vampires strode through the doorway, and Marya's heart caught in her throat.

Drago wore knee-high, black leather boots and a midnight-blue, raw-silk shirt that reached mid-thigh. A black sash banded his narrow waist, and a huge sapphire winked at his collar. Revelin Scott wore a blue suit and white ruffled shirt.

Drago's eyes caught hers the instant he entered the room, and his gaze remained locked on hers for a long moment before it flicked away to sweep the rest of the room. There was no boredom in his blue eyes now, but an intensity that gleamed as dark as the jewel at his throat. He came to a halt in the center of the room. His attention was all on Verkist now, and he made no other gestures acknowledging her.

Verkist spoke first. "Welcome to *Fata Morgana,* Drago. I'm honored to have such a distinguished guest under my roof."

"First, I want my people returned to me."

Verkist raised a dark brow. "'Your people?' Isn't that a bit presumptuous? Miss Monroe works for the Brotherhood. That makes her mine."

"Not any more. Scott now works for the Directorate, under my orders. Miss Monroe is his apprentice. That makes her mine, as well."

Revelin nodded to Callie, and with one last look at Verkist, she skimmed across the floor to his side.

Verkist canted his head toward Marya. "You have no claim on this mortal, Drago."

"Then, *monsieur,* let her make her own decision."

She looked at Verkist, then at Drago. There was no decision to be made. It was a no-contest. She walked to Drago's side, conscious of more vampire eyes on her than she could count. Drago neither looked at her nor made any move to touch her, but again addressed the Patriarch.

"The rest is private business between you and me, Evrard, unless you really feel you need a dozen bodyguards surrounding you." Drago's voice was very soft.

Verkist glared at Drago, stroked the lace at his throat, then nodded. His vampires flowed toward the door.

Drago whispered to her, but kept his eyes on Verkist. "Go with Scott, *mademoiselle,* and stay with him."

"No." She didn't want to leave him, and she definitely wanted to hear what was happening.

"Go!" The ice in his voice told her he would brook no disobedience in front of Verkist.

Revelin grabbed her arm and pulled her to the door, and as quickly as she had won Drago's presence at her side, she lost it.

***

Drago began pacing the room, stepping first to the waterfall. "I am not pleased, *monsieur,* at the abduction of my people."

The Patriarch sank into one of the leather chairs, draping his arms on the armrests as though he were on a throne. "They came to no harm. Besides, as I said, I didn't consider them 'yours.' I merely wanted all participants of this latest debacle in one place so that we can resolve this before it goes any farther."

Drago held the fingertips of one hand under the streaming water. "You didn't think to simply ask me here?"

"You would have come? I think not. *L'enforcier* does only as he wishes."

Drago stared at the movement of the water over the rocks. "Now that I am here, what do you want, Evrard?"

"Your official assurance that this latest mad crusade against me and my people will cease immediately."

Drago turned around. Evrard was fondling the Brussels lace beneath his chin as though it were a cherished pet. It was a strange affectation for someone Drago knew had been a soldier much of his life, but Drago had never seen him without his trademark lace. "Someone forged an order and put my name to it. That order almost got an innocent girl killed, but more importantly, almost got me killed. Would you not have me investigate such an incident, *monsieur?*"

"Any incident that occurred was of your own making. There was no forged order. I sent the order. It came with your name on it, through proper channels. And as for someone trying to kill you..." Evrard shrugged, seeming to imply that an attempt on Drago's life should hardly be cause for surprise.

Drago moved to the drapes, drying his wet fingers carelessly against the heavy fabric. "I think you're a liar, *monsieur.* I think you would like nothing more than my death."

Evrard's eyes turned opaque and shimmered like mercury. "You want truth? Very well. You shall have it. Yes, I would love nothing more than to see you dispatched to Hell. You meddle constantly in Brotherhood affairs. You flaunt procedure. You damn consequence. And yet you manage to hold on to the most coveted position in the Directorate. Well, Drago, there are others with power as great as yours, if not position. We can resolve this peacefully, or we can settle it in the old way. The choice is yours. Think about it tonight. Very carefully. We'll speak again tomorrow." He rose from the chair like smoke and stepped directly in front of Drago.

Drago had to lift his eyes to meet the taller man's challenge, but he felt no intimidation. He greeted Evrard's silver eyes with his own power, and the two of them stood face-to-face for long moments. There was no dazzling, no unleashing of commanding or mesmerizing force, just the most subtle of prods—searching, testing, and assessing. For each nudge of force on Evrard's part, Drago jabbed back with an equal force. It was akin to a game of poker, to see who would bluff, who would call, but neither man seemed willing to show his hand. Not now.

Drago ended it with a smile. "I will see you tomorrow then, *monsieur.*"

***

Revelin had been questioning Callie. Marya, for her part, had sat quietly, her mind on Drago. What were the two men doing? Talking or killing each other?

Marya had seen a good number of vampires over the years, both enforcers and the young vampires who roamed New Orleans. Because of her *dhampir* blood, she was able to detect vampires by scent and was thereby able to guess their relative age. From the information in her father's journal and by her own experience, she was able to gauge auras of power. Once again she was thankful she had saved the journal when her mother had wanted to dispose of it. Her mother had called it the Book of Death, but to Marya, it was the only link she had to a father she had never known. Drago, by far, was the oldest, most powerful vampire Marya had ever encountered. Until Verkist.

The door burst open, and Drago stood in the doorway, his eyes as hard and opaque as the darkest sapphire. Marya jumped up from her chair, but wondered if her legs would support her. "Drago!"

His gaze settled on her the same way it had when he had first strode into the great room. His stare supported her, and she felt neither her legs nor the floor.

"Monsieur, I will speak with you later," he said to Revelin. Drago stepped into the room, took Marya by the arm, and propelled her into the adjoining bedroom, shutting the door behind them.

She couldn't get air into her lungs fast enough to breathe, and she stumbled and would have fallen had he not still held her arm. *He's here at last. Just like he promised.*

She stared into his eyes. "You said to thank you when you returned. Thank you."

"Cherie..."

He released her arm, but only so he could slide his hands around her waist and pull her to him. Marya circled his neck with her own arms and tangled her fingers in his hair. She rested her head on his chest, squeezed her eyes shut and heard his ragged breathing in her ear. She closed her fist over a handful of his smooth, heavy hair and felt the hard muscles of his body press against hers—felt the aura of his power, so close to being unleashed, wash over her. She thought wildly of that kiss she had fantasized about—the one that would not be as controlled as the last one was. She opened her eyes, unclenched her hands and pushed away from him, just enough to see him. She skimmed his face with one hand, then, with the lightest of touches, slid the tip of her index finger down across his parted lips. She looked at his mouth, marveling that such soft skin could be part of such a hard face, then shifted her gaze back to his eyes. They were the whole world.

He leaned forward, and his mouth, barely open, met hers. His lips closed on her own, then he pulled away, just slightly, to part his lips again and kiss her anew. He continued like that, increasing the length of each kiss a little more each time. Finally, he leaned back, and she struggled to catch her breath.

"I told you that you weren't rid of me for good."

She laughed, but his face turned serious. "Verkist didn't touch you, did he?"

She shook her head. "No, he's treated me well."

"He's not that great a fool, then." He paused, and his brows pushed against each other. *"Cherie,* does he know of your...feeling toward me?"

She nodded.

He released her abruptly. *"Zut!"*

"I didn't tell him. I didn't say anything. All I did was ask him if you were coming. He just knew."

"Cherie, it is spelled out plainly enough on your face so that a child could read it, never mind a four-hundred-year-old vampire."

She resented being made to feel she had committed some error. "So?"

He sighed. "So he will use it fully to his advantage. He will use you against me, and me against you."

He touched his fingers to her face, but she wrapped her hand over his forearm and pushed his arm down. "I don't understand."

"If he threatens to kill me, what will you do? No, don't answer. Just know this. If your answer is 'anything,' then we are lost, because he will have you in his power, and if he has you, he has me."

"I still don't understand."

He unwrapped the sash from his waist and took off the long shirt, throwing them both over a chair. He had a white shirt on underneath, but that quickly joined the pile draped over the armrest.

She was still piqued. "Are you just going to undress in front of me?"

"Ah, *ma cherie,* you are such an innocent."

She felt her cheeks flame, both at his words and at the sight of his bare chest. "If I am, it's because the Undead never allowed me a life."

He laughed and sat on the edge of the bed to pull off his boots. "I've never known visits from enforcers to prevent any aberration from living life to the fullest."

At the sight of his disappearing clothes, her whole body felt as if it were on fire. Verkist's words came back to her in a rush. *Still the ladies' man he always was...* "Well, unlike yourself, I don't consider several thousand one-night stands to be 'living life to the fullest.'"

The first boot dropped to the floor like a brick. The deep smile lines still showed on his face, but they embraced no smile. His eyes had paled once again to their transparent electric blue, fathomless and cold. "I'm tired. I haven't had much sleep in the past three days."

Marya looked at the bed. It was the only one in the suite. "Where am I supposed to sleep?"

The second boot fell to the floor with a dull thump. "It's morning, the time of day I sleep. Surely you're not tired? If you are, there's my bed, Scott's bed, or the floor. Take your pick." He stripped off his trousers and threw them at the chair, missing.

She stared at him, not able to help herself and hating her weakness. But he was beautiful. The mane of shiny blue-black hair, the wide shoulders tapering to the narrow hips, the lean, muscled legs, and everything between the top and bottom. He threw back the covers and stretched out on the bed, facing away from her. He was still wearing his shorts, but Marya's imagination took over, and she felt herself blushing at the vision in her mind of a totally naked male body.

But while the vision was inviting, his final words to her hadn't been. She picked up his clothes and hung them in the closet, then sat on the chair near the bed. There was nowhere else to go. She certainly didn't want to sit with Revelin and Callie. *What had happened just now?* She had been so glad to see him, and he had seemed no less happy. And the kiss…no man had ever kissed her like that, not even Jaime during his more passionate moments. Drago's kiss in reality had been more amazing than the one she had conjured up in her mind. It hadn't been the wild, out-of-control kiss of a young man driven by hormones, but the kiss of an experienced lover, one who knew what women wanted. *And who knew what he wanted?* Had he truly wanted her? *What had happened?*

He had blamed her for something he said would put them in Verkist's control. Something that wasn't her fault. Then he had chided her innocence, making her feel foolish. If that hadn't been bad enough, he had implied that she would have been better served living life in the fast lane instead of avoiding relationships she felt could never be.

Still the ladies' man... She had thought that Verkist's words wouldn't have the power to touch her, but they did. She hadn't thought to be anything more than a promise to be kept. She hadn't wanted to be anything more. So why did his words upset her?

She sat in the chair a long time, watching him sleep. In spite of her anger she wanted nothing more than to slide onto the bed and lie next to him. But she remembered the night in the hotel when she had awakened him from his nightmare. He had nearly killed her then. She had no desire to be slammed against a wall again. Perhaps if she was very careful and didn't touch him...

She stripped down to her underwear and eased onto the king-sized bed, careful to leave plenty of room between his body and hers. He rested on his stomach, his hair masking most of his face, but his left arm curled in front of him. She could see the strange mark. It looked like a scar, but it was deep and regular, a curved line with three perpendicular cross bars, almost like a stylized "E." The sheet covering him ventured no higher than his hips. She looked for other scars, but saw none except the ones on his back she had seen before. She looked at them closer. She counted six lines that crisscrossed each other across the pale skin that rippled over his contoured torso. *A whipping?* She was sure it was something Drago would never tell her about. She wanted to reach out and touch the faint scars, but she instinctively knew her touch would not be welcomed. Finally she closed her eyes and dozed on and off, opening them again only when she felt his eyes on her.

One blue eye studied her from beneath strands of hair that arced across his forehead. *"Je suis navré, cherie."*

She stared at him, not understanding and afraid to move.

He raked the hair from his face. "Sorry, I'm sorry," he whispered. He turned onto his back. "Come here."

She slid closer to him until she could feel the warmth of his body pressing against hers.

"Forgive my outburst. I was tired and frustrated. But most of all, the encounter with Evrard stirred the lust. The biggest challenge for any vampire, *cherie,* even myself, is controlling the lust."

So that was all the kiss was.

"You're not to blame for our situation, but I want you to understand the reality of it. It's not a good state of affairs. We are in the middle of the enemy's camp. This building is nothing less than a bastion, and Evrard has at least two dozen vampires here at his disposal—all very capable, experienced, and loyal to him. I have only Scott and Callie. Callie is a novice, and I have my doubts about how far Scott will go for me. Evrard holds all the cards, *cherie.* If he truly wants me dead, he could kill me easily and have more than enough witnesses to swear it was self defense."

A shudder ran through Marya, and she ran her hand over the muscles of his chest, just to remind herself of his strength. She had always thought *l'enforcier* to be invincible. Wasn't he the most powerful vampire on earth?

He closed his eyes. "I'm tired, *cherie.* I long for peace."

Those few words frightened her more than everything else he had said. She propped herself up on an elbow. "Drago, look at me."

He opened his eyes, but only halfway, as if he didn't want her to see into their depths.

She stroked the side of his face. "Tell me you still want to live. Tell me!"

He seemed to retreat behind the hooded eyes. "You are so young, *cherie.* You know so little of life."

She leaned down and kissed his mouth, not wanting to hear more. She felt his whole body respond under her and felt his hands reach for her waist, pulling her body flush to his. She heard his groan, but suddenly he flipped her onto her back and held her at arm's length. His hair slid forward and shadowed his face.

"No, *cherie.* Like fire, I am not to be played with."

***

Merde! Did she have any notion at all what her innocent kiss had done to him? She was scared. He knew that. But drowning her fears in misplaced passion was not the answer for either of them. She was too quickly forgetting what he was, seeing in him only some savior on a white horse, wielding an all-powerful magic sword. At any other time he would revel in her acceptance of the fantasy and immerse himself gladly in the sweet energy of her innocence, but the situation was too dangerous. She needed to be rooted in reality, and he needed to keep a clear head. He would need to build perfect control of his mind, his passions, and his body for his next encounter with Verkist, and each touch of Marya's lips and hands threatened to undo that control.

He rolled over and off the bed. "Yes, I want to live, but not for you. I want to find the bastard who wants me dead and see that he pays for his impudence."

She flinched, almost as though he had hit her, and something twisted deep inside him at the shock and humiliation that flashed over her face. He wanted to go to her, wrap his arms around her, and assure her he hadn't meant it. But he couldn't. If they were both to survive, she would have to think of him as the demon he was. There was no savior, only a creature trying to save himself, and no magic sword—only the weapons of cunning and command.

He pulled on trousers and a white shirt. "Get dressed. I'll tell you a story to pass the time."

She rose from the bed without modesty, and he could see that the look of hurt on her face had swiftly turned to anger. She stalked to where she had left the outfit she had last worn and snatched up the blouse and skirt.

"Then tell me another story about your city."

She yanked on her skirt, and he watched the enticing movements of her slim body as she did so.

"No." *Not Novgorod.* No stories of when he was human. She would know him for what he was now.

"Then tell me how you got the scar on your arm."

He had hurt her, and she, in return, knew exactly how to repay him in kind. "No."

She glared at him and gave him a twist of her mouth that could hardly be considered a smile. "Afraid, Drago?"

He gave her a wide grin, but not, he imagined, a very pretty one. "I would not allow Evrard to manipulate me with that trick, and I certainly wouldn't let a mortal trap me like that. You will hear only what I wish you to hear, *mademoiselle.*" He sat on the bed and leaned back against the headboard. "I will tell you a ballad. You like crossroads. This is a story of such a road, and of a warrior named Ilya who came upon it in his old age." He interlocked his hands behind his head and let his eyelids half close. "The signposts were of stone. Three stones at the intersection directed three paths. One led to a wife, one to riches, and one to *la mort,* death. Ilya was too old to care about a wife or riches, so he chose the road to death, but on the way he was attacked by thieves. He killed them all and returned to the crossroads. His second choice was the road to the wife, but she was a sorceress. Again, he was cunning enough to prevail, and returned to take the final road to wealth. Ilya found it, a treasure fit for an emperor, but he gave it all away to the poor." He paused and looked at Marya. Her eyes hadn't left his since the first word of the story had been uttered. "Each road had been taken. He was penniless and without a wife, but Ilya was unafraid. He went on to fight many battles in the years to come."

Marya sat curled in her chair, silent for a moment before she spoke. "So, Drago, is that you? The warrior who searches for death?"

He lowered his arms and smiled. "It's a *byliny, mademoiselle*, a folktale. Nothing more. A very common one, in fact, still told today."

Her answering smile told him she didn't believe him. "How does it end? What happens? Surely the warrior can't go on fighting forever."

He parried her smile with another of his own. "He is finally slain in a great battle and turns to stone, like those that directed him at the crossroads. But fear not that I am Ilya, *cherie.* The Undead cannot turn to stone."

She crossed her arms and hugged herself, as if suddenly

cold, but said nothing more.

"I need to meet with Scott. Afterwards, Evrard and I will make another attempt to resolve things. When I'm gone I want you to stay as close to Scott as possible and do whatever he says. You're under no obligation to do anything Evrard or his people want you to do, so if you're ordered to go somewhere, don't unless Scott tells you to. Understand?"

She nodded, somewhat reluctantly, he thought. The girl didn't like taking orders any more than he did.

"Stay here for now. I'll be back before I go to Evrard. If anyone knocks at the door, don't answer, just come into Scott's room."

***

Marya watched Drago go into Revelin's adjoining suite and pull the connecting door closed behind him. She swore under her breath, a very old Romani curse, then wondered why she was bothering to whisper. She didn't care if every vampire in the building heard her.

Damn Alek Dragovich! He had done it to her again. What had happened? She didn't have the slightest idea what she had done to transform the very hot man into the very cold vampire. Did he just enjoy torturing her? She hadn't had a lot of experience with men, true, but she was certain he hadn't been repelled by her kiss. His groan had not been one of annoyance or disgust. Of that she was sure. Did he simply resent a mere mortal taking the initiative to kiss him? She sighed and sat back down in the chair. And the story... In spite of his protestations, she was sure the story of the warrior had been about Drago himself. When his eyes had slid nearly shut he had looked every bit as worn-out as the hapless Ilya.

Trying to figure out men was a difficult enough task in itself. Trying to figure out a five-hundred-year-old vampire was next to impossible.

TWELVE

Drago stood on a broad patio that faced the city below and the heavens above. The obligatory southwestern privacy wall surrounded the patio, constructed of concrete block, but with numerous geometric holes to provide an artful touch to the cold barrier. He faced west and gazed at the evening sky. The sun had just set, the far off mountains on the other side of the Valley of the Sun having swallowed the final flare of coral fire. A halo of lemon yellow crowned the modest peaks, and above the yellow the western sky glowed a phosphorescent green. Higher still, the clear aquamarine sky was already deepening to its shade of night. The night lights of Phoenix were beginning to twinkle across the valley floor.

Evrard stood at the wall and watched as well. "I hope you don't mind our continuing our business out here. I don't fancy you tearing up my house."

Drago paced along the opposite end of the wall. "Is that what you're afraid I'll do?"

"Your temper is well known. As well as your ability to cause damage in unique ways."

Drago ran his hand along the top of the wall, feeling the rough texture. "I'll take that as a compliment. Let us hope it does not come to that, *monsieur.*"

"Then you've reconsidered your position?"

"I think you know me better than that, Evrard."

The Patriarch spread his arms and leaned against the top edge of the wall. "Then you and I are at a stalemate, Drago, because I don't have what you want."

"I think you do. How can I be sure you're not lying? Will you submit to my mastery?"

Evrard turned to Drago and laughed. "Now I think *you* know *me* better than that."

Drago did know him, at least as well as one vampire was able to know another. The two had fenced with each other many times over the years, yet Drago had always felt there was a part of Evrard's past that remained cloaked from him. It was what all master vampires strove to do—to veil their abilities and intentions from the world—and Evrard had done it well. "We have had too many stalemates over the years, my friend. No more. It ends tonight, one way or another. We will find out at last which of us is the stronger. Are you prepared for this?"

"I have nothing you want, but you have everything I want, Drago. I think that gives me the advantage, don't you? Yes, I'm prepared."

Something in Evrard's voice more than his words gave Drago pause. Not that he had instilled fear in Drago, but he had instilled caution. Drago's gaze panned his surroundings one more time. The patio was empty of furniture. A metal gate at one end of the wall led to a series of steps and landings that traversed the side of the mountain downward. Evening shadows swallowed the rust-colored rock, slowly erasing color and dimension from the landscape. Drago's vision, however, had no trouble discerning that which the light of day stole. Perceiving Evrard's true nature was a different story. Drago looked at him, and his opponent shone like a silver knight even in the shadows. How many of the rumors shrouding Evrard Verkist over the centuries were true?

Drago knew with a sudden certainty that Evrard had brought the battle outside not for fear of what he might do, but of the damage Evrard himself could do. Evrard was said to have been a sorcerer both in life and in death. It was time to find out.

"Then let the game begin, *monsieur.*" Drago opened his eyes wide, locked his gaze on his opponent's, and unleashed the dazzling energy of command. "The truth, Evrard. Did you have my order forged?"

Evrard laughed, a ringing sound that echoed in the evening's stillness, and his eyes swiftly altered, gleaming like polished chrome instead of living tissue. "Truth? There is no truth I can give you. We each take bits and pieces of reality and fantasy and forge our own truths, don't we? Our truths aren't for mortals, and mine is not for you!"

"You're mine, Evrard, as is everyone in the Brotherhood. You will tell me what I wish to know." It was a bold boast, but Drago had always had confidence that his mastery could indeed overcome any vampire's resistance. But Evrard was different, and thus far, Drago's commands were having little effect. Drago's mind reached out for Evrard's with increasingly stronger tendrils of dominance and command, but Evrard managed to stay just out of reach.

"Fantasy, Drago, fantasy. You think you have me, but you don't."

Drago circled his opponent. It was a movement more out of habit than anything else. On the empty patio, there was no way to gain a physical advantage.

"I'll tell you what's fantasy, Evrard, and that is any aspiration you have of ascending the hierarchy. You will never be chosen by the Directorate. Never."

"Coming from someone with so little Directorate support, that's as meaningless a statement as any I've ever heard. When your position becomes available, I will be the new *enforcier.*"

Drago's anger surged, and with it, a new release of power. The cutting blades of energy, Drago's most unique and potent weapon, slashed out at his opponent's mind. It was energy that could shred ideas and hack at a man's will until nothing was left except a muddle of confusion and disjointed thoughts. "How many other vampires have you killed in your ascension to Patriarch, Evrard?"

Evrard laughed again, and the sound seemed to come at Drago from every direction. "Killing is forbidden, Drago. You know that."

The invisible knives carved and cut, but their target always seemed just beyond Drago's range. Drago's mind hurled the force, over and over, but Evrard avoided every slash of power. It was almost as though Evrard was clouding Drago's mind, making him believe he was *here*, when in fact he was *there*.

"I know killing is forbidden, *monsieur*. But do you?" Drago tried another tactic. He extended one hand in Evrard's direction, then swung his arm in an arc, like a maestro conducting an orchestra. The flow of energy jerked Evrard's feet from under him, and he landed heavily on his back. Drago immediately worked on Evrard's mind again, hoping the jolt of physical pain would weaken his concentration long enough for the slashing power to do its deadly work. Evrard cried out and lifted a hand of his own at Drago.

Drago thought it was a "stop" gesture of submission, but immediately a fireball formed and appeared to hurl itself right at Drago's head. He dodged the flames, but surprise at such power broke his own hold on Evrard.

Evrard sprang to his feet. "I know more than you ever will, Drago. Are you even now asking yourself if that fire was real or just in your mind?"

Another white-hot sphere, like a tiny sun, flared and launched itself at Drago. Fire was as deadly to vampires as silver, yet somehow Evrard had found a way to harness a bane to vampires as a weapon. Drago, standing next to the wall, had nowhere to go. He used his arms to vault himself over the wall and fell a dozen feet to the ground below. The slope of the mountain lessened the hard impact of the fall, but his momentum as well as the loose stones carried him downward to the first stairway landing. With vampiric speed to match his own, Evrard was halfway down the stairs to the landing before Drago could get off the ground. Drago wasn't injured, but the break in concentration made him too vulnerable. Another fireball flew at him, and he rolled away, gaining his feet in the process.

Was the fire real? Drago didn't want to find out the hard way. There was only one thing to do. Drago hurled his mental knives again, this time at Evrard's body, simultaneously extending his arm and flicking his wrist in a 'come hither' motion. Evrard fell forward, as if pushed from behind, and somersaulted down the stairs. He tumbled to the landing, and when he stood, his lace cravat hung in shreds, and the front of his white shirt was covered with a crosswise pattern of blood.

"Damn you, Drago…"

But Drago was on his feet and ready for him. Evrard's eyes would be next. He couldn't hurl a fireball if he couldn't see his target. "I was damned over five hundred years ago, *monsieur*. Nothing you can do to me can surpass that." Drago loosed his cutting power on Evrard's face, not bothering to aim too finely.

Evrard screamed, trying to cover his face with his hands, but the only result was that they, too, became targets. Blinded, he never saw Drago whip behind him and catch him in a chokehold. The vampire's bloody hands tried to dislodge Drago's, but his hold was secure. And while Drago's size was no match for Evrard's, his superhuman physical potency was.

"I could break your neck before you draw your next breath, *monsieur.*"

Evrard's reply was a strangled cry. "You can't kill me."

"I've lost count of the number of vampires who have said that to me, thinking it would save them. It was their last words. So think carefully, Evrard. I've become quite adept at ripping spines out. You can die, or you can submit. Your choice."

"This round is yours."

Drago curled his lips back as he tightened his grip even more. "Say the words!"

"I submit."

"A good choice, *mon ami*. Your sight should restore itself in a few moments. Change your clothes and we will meet again to discuss our business without fireballs and knives. Yes?"

Drago felt Evrard's nod against his forearm. He leaned his mouth very close to Evrard's ear. "Play me false, *monsieur*, and I will kill you. Never assume for a moment that I won't." He flung the vampire's body away from him. Evrard smacked the far side of the landing and rolled into the red dust of the hillside.

Drago looked down in disgust at the splatters of blood on his shirt. He ripped the shirt off just as Evrard stood up and flung the shirt at the man's head. "I detest the stench of vampire blood."

Drago made his way back through the great room and across

the foyer to his room unescorted. None of the vampires he met in the hallway dared to challenge him, and most went so far as to show him deference by lowering their eyes. Drago didn't know if it was the sight of the blood on his hands or the look he imagined was on his face. It didn't matter. If he was smart, he would take Marya, Scott, and Callie and leave now. He had the upper hand, something he may not be able to maintain. But there was still Nikolena's assignment and his own mission. He hadn't found out if Evrard Verkist was responsible for Marya's order, and he hadn't learned if Evrard had risen in the hierarchy through forbidden means. The thought spoiled any pleasure he had derived in besting the Patriarch.

He pushed in the door to Scott's suite without knocking.

Marya jumped from her chair. "My God!"

Scott kept his seat, but raised his brows. "Bugger me!"

"There's blood all over you. What happened?" asked Marya.

Drago strode into the bathroom and washed his hands and arms. "The Belgian's wardrobe is short one overpriced shirt and one very expensive lace necktie."

Scott stood and leaned against the doorjamb, crossing his arms over his chest. "As apparently is yours, Drago."

Drago dried his hands and looked at Scott. He had done him the same disservice, in a much smaller way, to be sure, but he knew Scott hadn't forgotten. "Just so, my friend. But I didn't bleed all over my shirt the way Evrard bled all over his." It was vital that Scott understand that. Drago had no misconceptions about Scott's loyalty. Orders notwithstanding, if Scott detected any weakness in Drago at all, Drago had no doubt the younger vampire would back Evrard Verkist if forced to take sides.

Scott didn't smile. "You didn't kill the bugger, did you?"

Drago shook his head. *"La directrice* would be proud of me. I exercised restraint. Something I'm sure she believes to be totally lacking in my character."

A small smile finally pulled at Scott's mouth. "So what now?"

Drago exited the bathroom and paused at the connecting door. "Now that the posturing is over, we will sit down and play at being gentlemen. He will tell me what I wish to know, and then we can leave this godforsaken desert. I don't much care for the heat." He opened the door, crossed into his own suite, and slammed the door shut behind him.

Marya opened the door and followed him. It was, he supposed, to be expected. He said nothing.

"You're all right?" she asked.

He avoided her eyes and went about the business of pulling a fresh outfit from the closet. "I'm a vampire, *mademoiselle.* Nothing hurts me."

"When you came in with that blood all over you…"

"All of it was Evrard's. Every drop of it."

He heard her inhale a deep breath. "I'm glad."

"You're glad. I'm glad. Even Scott's glad. Only Evrard is put out. So let me take my shower, *mademoiselle,* will you?"

He felt her warm hand on his arm. "Something's not right. Look at me and tell me you're okay."

He turned to her, and her dark eyes were filled with as much worry as if he had told her all the blood was his. Very few people either saw or cared what lie beneath the image he presented to the world. Only Adelle, who had been with him forty years, and Nikolena, who seemed to see through him only at the most inopportune times. This girl had known him for mere days and already saw what only Adelle and Nika had ever been capable of seeing. A part of him wanted to reach out and touch her face, wanted to pull her to him and feel the warmth of her body against his chest. But another part of him recognized the danger, so he resisted.

He looked her in the eye and spoke very softly. "I told you, *mademoiselle.* Nothing hurts me."

He turned, grabbed a handful of undergarments, and went into the shower, closing the door behind him. *Restraint again. Nika would be proud.*

***

Marya sat on the edge of the bed and fingered the trousers he had carelessly thrown there. *They'll wrinkle,* she thought, automatically picking them up to straighten them. But she stopped and brought the material to her face instead. The silk carried the scent of the Undead. *No,* she amended. *Of Drago.*

When he had burst through the door with blood on his hands and bloodlust on his face she had feared for him. She believed him when he said the blood was all Verkist's, but something was nevertheless wrong. The lust propelled him, but there was something else he carried—something that weighed him down. A bone-wearying kind of fatigue. When he had looked at her just now, she had been all too aware of the furrow in his brow and the lines etched on either side of his mouth. She had been hoping that when he returned his attitude toward her had changed from this morning, but it hadn't. For some reason he had closed himself off from her, and he seemed determined to keep it that way.

When she had followed him into their suite, she had expected him to shout at her to get out. She could have handled the anger. The quiet declaration instead that nothing could hurt him had chilled her to her core.

She laid the trousers down carefully and picked up the shirt he had likewise flung to the bed. It was of white silk, like most of the shirts she had seen him wear. She straightened it, too, and waited for him. He wasn't long. She heard the water turn off, and a moment later he stepped out of the bathroom wearing nothing but shorts. Unlike her surreptitious glances of before, she now gazed at him openly. Regardless of his feelings for her—or lack thereof—and despite any weight of the world he might be shouldering, he was a magnificent figure.

He could hardly fail to notice her appraisal. "What happened to the shy little Gypsy I met not so very long ago?"

She cocked her head. "She met a man. And don't call me a Gypsy."

She caught the barest trace of a smile before he repressed it. "And I shall correct you, as well. You met a vampire, *mademoiselle*. Don't forget it."

"You're tired."

He pulled the trousers on. "What if I am?"

"Sit for a moment. Verkist can wait."

He surprised her and sat next to her on the bed, close enough so that the scent of soap and shampoo overpowered that of what he was. But he didn't touch her and made no invitation for her to touch him.

He sighed. "I just expended a great deal of energy, *cherie*. The equivalent of your running a marathon."

She stared at his profile, willing him to at least look at her. "If you don't want to talk to me, then don't. But don't lie to me."

He obliged her, turning so that he met her eyes. "It's no lie."

A long ribbon of damp hair hung over one blue eye, and it irritated her that he didn't bother to dislodge it. "But there's more to it than just that, isn't there?"

"Are you afraid I won't get you out of here?"

She very badly wanted to smooth the careless strand from his face, but knew the gesture wouldn't be tolerated. "No. I'm afraid I'll lose you."

He stood up and put his shirt on. "You never had me. Go wait in the other room." He said the words very softly.

Intentionally, she had provocatively answered his question of what she was afraid of, hoping for a response that was either passionate in his denial or angry at her presumption. A heated retort either way would have heartened her. The cool rejoinder shook her, and when he had turned his eyes on her, their apathy had scared her.

She stared at him, telling herself it was the exhaustion, or perhaps just the natural aftermath to an encounter with another of the Undead, but she didn't believe either excuse. She left the room.

Revelin looked up at her and cocked one brow.

She stared at him, trying to control she panic she felt. "I hope you have a plan for getting us out of here, Revelin, because Drago's going to die."

THIRTEEN

Drago sat across from Evrard in the latter's office, a room at the far end of the southern wing to the building. A huge desk separated the two, a massive polished beast almost as grand as Nikolena's. Evrard was impeccably garbed and groomed, and there was no trace of blood, scars, pain, or injury on his face. A new fall of lace flowed from his collar. Only the flint in his gray eyes gave evidence that he was far from happy with the events of the day. He flicked a square of heavy paper at Drago.

Drago caught it in one hand.

"Go ahead, Drago, look at it. Your order to me to terminate the girl."

Drago examined the outside of the folded paper. His seal, the dragon's head, in broken red wax, was affixed. He opened the order and read it to himself. It called for a reversal of Drago's judgment and an immediate notification of termination. His signature was at the bottom. He tossed the paper onto the desk. "I didn't send this. Seals and signatures can both be forged. You know that."

"I have to go by what I receive. It was all in order. As were these." He flipped another paper at Drago. "My order to Deverick." And another. "Deverick's order to Scott."

Drago snatched both easily and quickly glanced at them. Both had the correct seals and signatures.

"Satisfied, Drago?"

He threw the two orders to the desktop. "Submit to my mind. Then I'll be satisfied."

Evrard glared at him, his features composed, but his steely eyes full of hate. "As you wish." He raised his arms in a gesture of openness.

Drago opened his own eyes wide and set the vampiric mirror before his adversary. When placed before mortals, the mirror revealed fantasies, but when set before the Undead, only naked truth was revealed. Drago would have his answer. The mirror never lied. "Gaze upon me, Evrard, and see the truth. Did you forge my order?"

"No."

"Do you know who did?"

"No."

"Have you killed to advance your rank?"

There was only the slightest hesitation. "I've only killed when I needed to kill."

Drago released his subject. It was pointless to continue. "Our business is concluded, *monsieur.*"

"Just like that?"

Drago pulled on the cuffs of his shirt. "Just like that. You were right. You have nothing I want."

Evrard leaned all the way back in his chair and steepled his fingers in front of his face. "Yes, but at the moment that isn't very consoling, because as I also said, you have everything I want."

Drago sat very still. "Say what you mean, *monsieur.* These games bore me."

"Do they? We shall see. The girl—the mortal you chased in such hot pursuit—she means something to you?"

Drago's blood ran cold. "Of course not. She's an aberration."

Evrard slowly lowered his hands. "Good. I'm glad to hear it. Then you won't mind if I keep her as compensation for your unfounded accusations and the embarrassment of being humiliated in my own house."

It was what Drago had feared all along. Evrard was going to try to use Marya against him. "I do mind. I gave her life, and she will live it freely."

A slow smile spread across Evrard's face, twisting the long scars. "Oh, she'll go free. But first she'll be my guest for awhile."

Drago kept his own features dispassionate, a habit, luckily, he had perfected centuries ago. "She's an aberration, Evrard. She's foul. Her blood would poison you."

He fingered the folds of lace as if it were a woman's skin. "I know. But she has other charms which I'm sure you haven't failed to notice."

Drago fought to keep the lie of dispassion on his face. "She is not a point for negotiation, *monsieur*. End of discussion." Drago stood.

"Sit down, Drago. You're not giving orders here anymore."

Drago didn't sit, but strolled to a teakwood shelf along one wall. He took a small clay horse off the shelf and tossed it into the air, catching it neatly. Then he walked back to the desk. "I warned you not to play me false, Evrard." He squeezed his hand, crushing the figurine. "*Mademoiselle* Jaks leaves with me." He dropped the broken pieces on the desktop.

Evrard smiled again. "Your threats are meaningless, Drago. You can't kill me over a mortal, and if you so much as try anything against me, I'll use every vampire at my disposal to stop you. You have only one option if you want to leave here with Scott and his apprentice, and that's to do as I say."

The Patriarch was wrong. Drago had no options. None, anyway, that didn't involve *la Belle Mort*. Drago had built his reputation early in his career. Since then his two weapons had been intimidation and strength. When the first didn't work, he fell back on the second. Unfortunately, this was a situation where intimidation was fast proving to be ineffectual.

Still, he persisted. "You will not have the girl, *monsieur.*"

"And how do you think to stop me without consequence to yourself?"

Drago wandered to a nearby sofa, picked up a pale gold pillow, and wiped the dust of the clay figurine from his hands onto the silk. He tossed the pillow back to the sofa and quickly scanned the room for possible weapons. Heavy furniture of wood and leather. No fireplace with fireplace tools. No tall candlesticks, no ceremonial Indian lances or hatchets on the wall. Just lots of throw rugs, pillows, and artwork. And one very tall, narrow torchiere lamp. He turned to face his opponent. "You proceed from a faulty premise, Evrard. You assume I

care. I don't. I don't care about you, Nikolena, or rules and
regulations. I don't even fear the True Death, *monsieur.* You
see, I'm Russian. Russians don't fear something will go wrong,
they expect that it will. There is an old saying, 'God is too high,
and the Czar is too far.' So don't presume that anything you
can threaten will scare me or coerce me."

For the first time, Drago saw uncertainty flicker in Evrard's
gray eyes, and for a moment, Drago had hope that the weapon
of intimidation would carry the day after all.

The moment passed. Evrard's eyes steadied, as if he came
to a final decision, and he pressed an intercom button on his
desk. "Secure Miss Jaks in my quarters."

Drago drew his second weapon. Strength.

He flew over the desk and lunged at Evrard, knocking the
larger man to the floor. Their bodies rolled to the wall, each
trying for the other's most vulnerable spots. Drago reached
for Evrard's neck, who countered by trying to gouge Drago's
eyes. Drago was forced to hurl the larger man's body away
from him. Evrard landed on a throw rug, slid into the sofa,
and was on his feet in an instant, but Drago was ready for him
and unleashed the power of his mind before Evrard could ready
his defenses. It was the mirror again, and Drago hoped to blind
his foe long enough with the mirror's revealing visions to
secure a physical weapon in hand.

"Take a good look, Evrard! See every hell that's ever
embraced you. I know you, Evrard. You were a Walloon
mercenary, weren't you? Do you remember the massacre of
Magdeburg? Of course you do. So relive it now, as if 1631
were yesterday. Do you remember that great and splendid
German city? Your imperial troops burned and plundered it in
a frenzied rage, didn't they? What part did you play? Beating?
Torture? Or were you one of the soldiers responsible for
carrying off the property of murdered citizens? What was your
booty? Gold chains and jewels? Was the hell worth it?" Drago
kept his eyes on Evrard even as he stepped backward across
the floor. Evrard's wide eyes glittered at him, and Drago knew
his opponent was indeed seeing nothing but the nightmares
of his past. He dared not take his eyes from Evrard. It would

sever the hold.

Evrard was doing a good enough job of breaking the hold on his own. The glassy eyes started to blink rapidly, and his mouth worked silently. The lines of his scars twitched up and down like writhing snakes. Drago could feel the resistance building and could see the cords in the man's neck and the vein at his temple strain with effort.

Drago kept backing, adjusting his position solely by memory. He was almost there. It stole from his concentration, though, and with a roar Evrard shattered the mirror's hold.

"You highborn bastard! What do you know about being a real soldier? My men died every day of hunger and disease!" He raised a hand at Drago, and a ball of flame grew and flew across the room.

Drago ducked and grabbed the torchiere next to him, smashing the top of the lamp against the edge of an adjacent table. The shade and bulb exploded in a shower of broken glass, leaving the long, narrow lamp base. "'Your men?' You were a mercenary, Evrard. You were only out for yourself. And I very much doubt if you ever went hungry."

Drago whirled toward Evrard just as another fireball hurtled toward him. He twisted to the side, but he was too slow. He felt the heat from the flames sear his chest, and an instant later Drago's shirt was on fire. With a scream Drago soared at Evrard, the lamp held in front of him like a battle lance. Drago's momentum drove the end of the lamp through Evrard, pinning him to the wall. The Patriarch's shriek drowned out Drago's, who was trying to rip at the burning shirt with one hand and keep his enemy affixed to the wall with the other. Evrard was bleeding and thrashing like a fish caught on the end of a spear, but as bad as the injury appeared, it wasn't life threatening unless Drago could reach Evrard's heart or spine. But the fire's touch had sent a debilitating wave washing over him, and he couldn't find the strength needed to finish the job. The two men struggled against the wall, their frenzied cries and movements sapping their strength.

Evrard wrenched himself free from the wall and lunged toward his desk. "You'll pay for that, Drago. That, and everything else!"

Too late, Drago remembered the intercom. He pushed Evrard away from the desk, but not before Evrard's hand stabbed at the button.

"Now, dammit!"

Drago stood and spun toward the door, but again was too late. The door flew open with the force of a storm, and a dozen vampires streamed into the room like a gale.

"Stop him, now!" Evrard shouted.

A vampire raised a semi-automatic weapon and emptied a clip of bullets into Drago. The shots didn't burn with silver, but they knocked him off his feet and kept him on the floor writhing in pain. He heard someone yell not to kill him, but when he felt silver shackles bind him and a silver helmet take his sight, the burning pain would have made him beg for death, had not it first taken his consciousness.

***

Marya knew something was wrong. Even without the feeling of foreboding she had had earlier, it took no great insight to know something very bad had happened.

Drago had been gone for four hours. Three hours ago one of Verkist's vampires had knocked on the door, wanting Marya to change rooms. She had refused to go without Revelin and Callie, and when the vampire had looked into Revelin's eyes, he had decided not to argue. Thus, all three of them had been moved. The new room was in the southern wing, but like the old one, had no windows.

"Revelin, is he dead?"

He was slouched in a chair, his eyes closed and one hand on his head. Callie sat next to him in a companion chair. "If he is, there's nothing we can do for him. We have to take care of ourselves now."

That wasn't what she wanted to hear. "But do you think he's dead? Can you sense his aura? You can do things like that, right?"

Revelin sighed. "Yes, but...I don't have the kind of connection with him I have with Callie."

At that Callie leaned over and put an arm on his. He looked

at Callie and smiled. "And in a building this large with so many vamps nearby…it's difficult. I don't sense his True Death, but I could be wrong."

Marya resumed her pacing, but to her surprise Revelin was out of his chair and beside her before she could take two steps. "Marya, listen to me. Drago's survived for hundreds of years. The chance of him meeting the True Death in this place, at this time, is remote."

She wasn't reassured. "But…"

"Look. If Drago had nothing to rely on except good sense and winning personality, he'd have bloody gotten himself offed a long time ago. But he's strong. He's so strong he can afford to live his life tweaking the devil's nose. Besides, Verkist wouldn't dare kill him. Even if he had, don't you think the bugger would have come here by now to gloat?"

"I suppose you're right. But if something did happen, what will Verkist do with us?"

Callie spoke up. "About time you started worrying about yourself."

Marya and Revelin both ignored her, and Scott answered Marya's question. "I don't know. Your average vamp wouldn't consider harming me or Callie, but Verkist's far from average. Any vamp willing to take on *l'enforcier* certainly isn't going to have second thoughts about doing us wrong."

"He'd have to kill Drago, then. If he didn't…"

Callie stood up and interrupted. "I've had enough. This is making me sick."

She stood next to Revelin, almost pressing herself against his side, and it crossed Marya's mind that Callie was piqued because Marya was monopolizing Revelin's attention. The female vampire was most certainly too used to having him all to herself. Callie wasn't finished with her two cents. "Why are you so worried about Drago anyway? Has he got you that dazzled?"

"Dazzled?"

"Come on, don't be stupid. Under his spell. Seduced by the mirror. You know, what we vamps do to you mortals."

Revelin put a hand on the girl's arm. "Callie, that's enough."

Marya was quick to break in. "No, Revelin, it's okay. I want to hear what she has to say. Are you telling me, Callie, that the only reason I'm worried about Drago is that he has seduced me into thinking he's something he's not?"

"Of course. Why else would you give a damn about him? He certainly doesn't give a damn about you. He has little enough respect for his own kind, much less mortals. And you're an aberration besides."

"Callie…"

"No, Rev, let her finish." Marya took perverse pleasure in calling Revelin by Callie's pet name for her Master.

Callie's dark eyes glittered. "Let me introduce you to Vamp 101. Mortals are at the bottom of the food chain. And you're not even that. The only reason he'd ever show any interest in you would be for his own amusement. That's our entertainment, you know. Creating little fantasies for our prey to wrap themselves up in. So, please, no more moaning about 'poor Drago' or 'poor Marya.'"

Marya stared back at Callie. "He's still your Master, Callie. I hope for your sake he doesn't find out how little respect you really have for him."

"I think he's got slightly bigger problems right now than my disrespect."

"Ladies, ladies. I don't think this is going to help us any."

A noise at the door caused them all to swivel their heads in that direction. Someone was unlocking the door. Marya's heart started to pound, and her mind's eye already saw the lean, elegant vampire with the jet-black hair and the neon blue eyes. The door swung wide.

It was Verkist. Framed in the doorway, he looked taller and more massive than Marya had remembered. The blood seemed to drain from her head in a rush, and she grabbed Revelin's arm for support.

Verkist stepped into the room and closed the door. "Mr. Scott, Miss Monroe, it is my duty to inform you that you are again working for the Brotherhood."

"No!" Marya didn't realize the word had slid from her lips until Revelin shushed her.

"Be still," he hissed at her before turning to Verkist. "I work for Alek Dragovich and the Directorate until he or one of his superiors tells me otherwise." Revelin paused. "If Drago's dead, show me the body."

Marya felt lightheaded and wondered how she was able to stand. She still held Revelin's arm, amazed that she felt so much support from the vampire who was four inches shorter and a couple hundred years younger than the creature in front of them.

"He's not dead. But he is incapacitated. Quite severely. So you see he is in no position to tell you anything."

"What happened?" asked Scott.

"Our business, to my mind, was concluded. He chose to extend our confrontation. His attack on me was unprovoked. I was merely defending myself. I ask you again, Scott, will you show loyalty to me?"

Revelin looked at Callie, and an understanding seemed to pass between them. Scott looked at Verkist. "When you put it like that, yes, of course. We are at your service, Patriarch."

Marya let go of Revelin and backed away from him, feeling as if she had just found out he had the plague. *How could he?* If Revelin was indeed abandoning her, any hope she had was lost.

Marya stepped forward, careful not to stand anywhere near Revelin or Callie. "What about me? What are you going to do with me?"

"You've committed no wrong, Miss Jaks. You will remain my guest for a period of time, and then I'll see to it that you get back home safely."

"I want to see Drago." She had no leverage and no bargaining power—nothing to make her believe he'd do anything but laugh in her face—but she had to try. It was obvious that Revelin wasn't going to stand up to Verkist.

Verkist did laugh, a rich sound that seemed much too loud for even the spacious room. "The aberration and the fallen Anti-God. Yes, I like that. I think that can be arranged, Miss Jaks. I'll send one of my men by later to take you to him. Miss Monroe, you will come with me now."

A look of fear washed over Callie's face. "No. I'll do as you want, just let me stay with my Master, please."

"No, I think it's best I separate you. It will assure compliance on both your parts."

Revelin turned to Callie. "Go on. It'll be all right. Trust me."

Callie hesitated for a moment, but with both Revelin's and Verkist's eyes on her, she was soon prompted to action. She gathered up her things and went out with the Patriarch, looking back at Revelin the whole while. After they left, the door was locked behind them.

Marya fell into one of the chairs, marveling that her legs had held her as long as they had. She felt stunned, as if someone had just slapped her across the face. "How could you? How could you swear loyalty to that beast? You didn't even ask to see Drago! You don't know what really happened to him. Until you do…"

Revelin cut her off. "How could I? Easy. A long time ago I fought a bastard called Napoleon. He said that God is on the side of the biggest battalions. Always back the winner, Marya. It's called survival. Verkist bested Drago. I wasn't going to bloody argue and have my head cut off as well."

"So whose side are you really on?"

Revelin sighed and sat down in the other chair. "You go see Drago. If he's lying in Mistress Death's embrace, I don't have much choice."

"But if he's alive?"

"I'll answer that after you see Drago."

"How do I know I can trust you?"

"Vamp 102. I'm a bloody vampire, Marya. Never trust me."

***

Marya was curled on the bed, which Revelin had been gracious enough to let her have. She had thought to try to get some sleep, but rest of any kind was impossible. Verkist hadn't said when he would let her see Drago, but she had thought he meant that evening. Several hours had passed, however, and now she realized that he just as easily could have meant tomorrow, a week from now, or a month. With his one promise, he had the power to string her along indefinitely. Perhaps it was nothing more than his way to ensure that she would remain his obedient 'house guest.'

She tried not to think about Drago, but she did. Perhaps she was being foolish in worrying about a five-hundred-year-old creature that no one else seemed to care about. Callie had told her she was being silly. Maybe she was, but if she had to weigh Callie's offhand remark against Drago's kiss, she was willing to bet on the kiss. And if she had to assess Drago's own cold words to her against what she had caught once or twice in his eyes, she would put her money on his eyes. She had seen pain and an emptiness that longed to be filled, and those rare glimpses into a man's private hell were something that all the dismissive words and bored countenances in the world couldn't disguise.

She wondered where he was. Was he locked away in some dark room? Was he even conscious? In a way she hoped he wasn't, for it would save him from whatever pain Verkist had inflicted on him. And Marya was certain that Drago could feel pain, in spite of his unemotional statement about nothing hurting a vampire.

When the knock came, followed by the unlocking of the door, Marya was too caught up in her thoughts to hear. She didn't raise her head from the pillow until Revelin said, "Marya, he says you can see Drago now."

She jumped off the bed, still dressed, and quickly put her shoes on. Revelin came over to her while Verkist's vampire waited at the door.

"Listen, Marya. Don't pay any attention to what Callie said to you before. She was scared, that's all. She's never been through anything like this before."

"And the rest of us have? Don't worry, Revelin. I considered the source when I heard her words."

Revelin steered her into the bathroom and closed the door behind him.

"What are you doing?" she whispered.

"I don't want that vamp to hear what I have to tell you. If Drago can hear you, tell him what I said about Napoleon. And also tell him to remember what Voltaire said."

"Voltaire?"

"He'll know. Just tell him Napoleon and Voltaire." He opened the door and preceded her out.

Marya took a deep breath and nodded to the vampire at the door. "I'm ready."

"Follow me."

It occurred to her that this whole thing could be a trap, and that Verkist was luring her away from Revelin for some purpose of his own. But she had no way to know for sure, and she figured it was worth the risk.

It was late at night, but there were plenty of lights on, and she could hear voices and laughter from various parts of the house. She wondered where Verkist was, and what he was doing. Was he celebrating his victory over *l'enforcier?* Her vampire guide took her to the end of the southern hallway and outside to the patio behind the great room. He led her down the stairway that traversed the hillside, and the voices gradually died away. Her guide stopped outside a doorway one floor down from the great room.

"In here." The vampire unlocked the door, turned around and ascended the stairway.

He's just going to leave me down here alone? No, not alone. With Drago. She watched until her guide was out of sight. Another thought came to her. Maybe her guide was afraid to be in the same room with Drago. But what could be here that would frighten a vampire? Marya tasted sudden fear in her mouth, hard and sour. She tried to swallow, but couldn't. She wondered again if it was all just some elaborate trick. Maybe Drago was dead, and Verkist was sitting upstairs laughing at the thought of her viewing his mutilated remains. The thought almost had her running back up the stairs.

"Drago?" Marya opened the door and peered around the edge of the frame. The room was dark. Her probing hand found a light switch, and after a heartbeat of hesitation, she flipped it. The concrete room was barren except for a lone figure slumped on the floor. "Oh, my God."

Tentative steps brought more details to her eye, and each

one she saw brought new despair. He was chained to the wall by both wrists, and his bare chest and trousers were covered with dried blood. A strange metal helmet covered his eyes as well as his head.

"Marya." His voice was barely a whisper.

"God, Drago, what did he do to you?" She kneeled beside him and looked from the massive rings embedded in the wall to the wide armbands that covered half his forearms.

He raised his arms a few inches, then let them drop, as if they were weights too heavy to lift. "The shackles are silver. They take my strength."

"And they burn, don't they? The silver burns."

"Like fire," he breathed. "Like the hottest fire you can imagine."

She touched the helmet, a quick touch, as if it would burn her, too. "And this?"

"All silver. It weakens my mind and negates the power of my eyes. *Cherie,* how did you get here?"

"I just said I wanted to see you. I didn't actually think Verkist would allow it."

He turned his head toward her, and she imagined his eyes, blinded by the silver, but still seeing her with his mind's eye. "He knows you can't help me, and it amuses him no end, I'm sure, to have a mortal see me like this."

She hadn't thought of that. She hadn't thought that Drago would be humiliated to have her see him in such a state. "Do you want me to leave?" She didn't want to, but she would if he asked.

"No. Stay."

"There's no guard. He went back upstairs."

"As I said, he knows you can do nothing for me."

She shook her head, stupidly forgetting he couldn't see her. "No, Drago, there must be something I can do. Tell me what to do. I'll do anything."

"There's nothing."

"I don't believe that." She looked at his chest and saw numerous red welts among the streaks of dried blood. She tentatively brushed her fingertips over his skin. He flinched at her touch. "What happened? Verkist said you attacked him unprovoked."

"So, he's not only a coward, but a liar. I was through with him, ready to leave. He started making threats—threats I couldn't allow. He wouldn't back down. He left me no choice. I would have had him, but he changed the odds. He called for his vampires, and I couldn't fight them all. One of them shot me, slowing me enough that they got the silver shackles on me."

She touched his chest again, and this time he didn't start. "These red marks on your chest…"

"The bullet wounds. They healed. By tomorrow the redness should be gone. Not that it matters."

"What is Verkist going to do with you? He can't leave you here like this."

Drago leaned his head back against the wall. His muscular neck looked as it ever did, but the movement made it seem as if he truly lacked the strength to hold his head up. "That's exactly what he's going to do. It's the slowest, most painful torture that can be inflicted on one of the Undead. Don't tell me your father never wrote about it in his journal."

"No. But I don't understand. What will happen?"

"The silver helmet will slowly eat at my mind. It'll weaken my will, block thought, and destroy memory. Eventually there will be nothing left but the pain, and I'll go insane. Evrard will cover his tracks, and the world will only know that I disappeared. Eventually the Directorate will replace me. Most likely with Evrard, and he'll have what he's always wanted."

"But what about Revelin and Callie? After I tell Revelin what happened to you, he'll know the truth."

"Evrard won't let Scott leave here until he's sure of his loyalty."

"Revelin already swore his allegiance to Verkist."

"I figured as much. Scott is smart. He won't risk himself for me."

"Oh, I almost forgot. Revelin told me to give you a message. He said you'd understand. Something about him fighting Napoleon and his battalions, and then he told me to mention

Voltaire."

Drago tilted his head forward. "'God is on the side of the biggest battalions.'" There was wonder in his voice.

Marya was buoyed by the first spark of curiosity she had seen Drago exhibit. "Yes, that was it."

"Napoleon said that. What Voltaire said was that God wasn't on the side of the biggest battalions, but the best shots."

She had no idea what that signified. "So?"

"It means that Evrard has the advantage of numbers over us, but that we're stronger. It's also Scott's way of saying he'll try to help me if he can. Where are Scott and Callie now?"

"Verkist took Callie away with him, but Revelin is still with me."

"Good. Remember when I told you not to be fooled by Scott's appearance? Scott is a very powerful vampire. Evrard might not have sensed it yet with his obsession with me, but he will soon, so you and Scott will have to act quickly."

"I don't want to leave yet. Verkist might not let me return." She reached over and grazed her index finger across his cheek to a wayward strand of black hair. She rolled the shock of hair between her finger and thumb, feeling its texture. It was smooth and heavy, but with a stiffness to it that made her think of filaments of spun glass instead of hair. She skimmed the hair to the side of his face. "Do you mind?"

"Mind what, *cherie?*" His voice sounded as if his mind were far away.

"My touching you. You flinched before."

She saw a small smile twitch the corners of his mouth. "After fire, bullets, and silver, your touch is…almost a shock. But don't stop. Your hands are like the light—a very guilty pleasure for one such as myself."

Marya inclined her body closer to Drago's and ran her hand along his chest. His skin was warm, the muscles as hard as ever. He tilted his head back again, and his lips parted.

She remembered again what Callie had said. "I thought…never mind."

"What, *cherie?*"

"It's nothing. Just something Callie said."

Drago sighed. "Callie is very young and, I suspect, in love with her Master. She scorns mortals, forgetting she was human not so very long ago. What did she say to you?"

Marya dropped her hands back to her lap. "Nothing that you haven't told me yourself."

"Ah. That I care nothing for mortals."

She leaned over and kissed him. The helmet with its metal chinstrap made it awkward, but she managed to catch his lower lip between hers as he did the same to her upper lip. She drew on him, and felt the strength imprisoned in both his body and mind. She pulled away just enough to give him his answer. "I've also been told never to trust what a vampire says, so I don't."

He smiled. "The kind of answer a vampire would give."

She returned the smile. "I guess I've been in the company of the Undead for too long." She paused, still looking at the mouth she had just kissed. His lips were again parted, and she could see his sharp eyeteeth. She looked down at his shackles in frustration. "So what would you need? To defeat Verkist?"

"My eyes, first and foremost."

She took a moment to examine both the shackles on his arms and the helmet more carefully. It appeared that both operated by key. A key that only Verkist would have, she was sure.

"Go, *cherie*, please. Talk to Scott. Trust him for now. As long as he believes there's a chance I'll prevail, he won't give Evrard more than lip service."

She didn't want to leave. What if Verkist refused her more visits? The thought that this might be the last time she saw Drago scared her. "Drago..."

"Tell Scott I understand Voltaire's words. Go now."

It wasn't much of a reassurance, but it wasn't his words that scared her. It was what he hadn't said. He hadn't promised her he would overcome the pain and hopelessness of the situation. He hadn't reassured her that he was stronger than Verkist. And he hadn't said he wouldn't give up.

She touched his cheek one more time then ran out of the room and up the stairs. She prayed that Revelin hadn't been moved from her room, because as far as she could see, it would all be up to Revelin and her.

***

Drago drew in a long, slow breath and let it out just as slowly. It didn't help. He leaned forward, balled his fists, and yanked the chains as hard as he could. Over and over he pulled and jerked at his bonds, until the silver armbands bit into his skin. The burning pain shot up his arms, and he slumped against the wall. He welcomed the agony and exhaustion. It masked the bittersweet anguish and sexual frustration he had felt during Marya's visit. He had to give credit to Evrard Verkist for one thing. Evrard had known exactly how best to torture him, both physically and mentally. There was only one thing Evrard could have done that was more cruel than the silver apparatus, and that was allowing a mortal to see him like this.

Drago had always been strong. As a human, he had never known humility, even during the darkest months of the Muscovite invasion and with all the horror they had inflicted on him. He had held his honor, dignity, and self-esteem through every human nightmare. But his journey to the *Demi Monde* of the Undead had perverted everything he had been, as was the way of such things since time immemorial. Self-respect had become arrogance, and dignity had become conceit. All vampires by nature were proud and vain, but Drago had had more years than most to nurture and dwell in that pride. For a mortal, especially an aberration, to see him brought so low was the ultimate humiliation.

And yet, as disgraced as he had felt, he had been glad to see her and to know that she was thus far untouched by Evrard. And the simple touch of her hand had pervaded his entire body with waves of desire that not even the silver burn could match in intensity. For him to feel her and not be able to respond had indeed been every torture Evrard could have hoped for, and more.

Time meant nothing in the silver prison. It could have been fifteen minutes after Marya's visit, or six hours afterwards when Evrard appeared. Regardless, it was an unpleasant moment when his nemesis' odor assailed his nostrils. As was the way of older vampires, Evrard in fact exuded very little scent, but the odor was recognized and hated nonetheless.

"Come to gloat, Evrard?"

"As a matter of fact, I do find I'm enjoying this even more than I had anticipated. The great *enforcier* Alek Dragovich chained to a wall like a dog. Where's your power now, Drago? You're no vampire anymore. The noble Russian, so proud of your glorious, tragic country. You're no high and mighty prince now, either. You're not even a man—just an animal, a beast, tied to a wall. I wish every vampire you've ever administered your twisted form of justice to could see you now. Well, as long as your memory functions, I want you to remember that it was the Belgian who did this to you. The lowly mercenary." Evrard no longer bothered disguising the vehemence in his voice. "I heard a song long, long ago. 'Every one who flies too high is sure to go amiss; presumption, aiming at the sky, must pay in hell's abyss.' You're paying now, Drago, aren't you?"

"Why, Evrard? You and I have had our differences over the years, but nothing to merit this."

Drago heard a laugh, but bitterness tightened the sound. "That's just it, though, isn't it? To you I was nothing. Just like my country meant nothing to its oh-so-powerful neighbors. For centuries Belgium was nothing more than a convenient killing field for everyone else. And I've been nothing but a convenient dumping ground for all the muck you've stirred up in the Brotherhood."

Drago heard the scrape of a boot and realized his foe had stepped closer to him. "Yes, all our encounters were of scant importance in your mind. But to me they were everything. You never conceded a thing to me, not even the smallest point. You said earlier that all our meetings ended in a stalemate. Well, not from my point of view they didn't. You cut me off at the knees every time, and never thought twice about it. Remember Memphis two years ago? You unilaterally decided to transfer half my Southeast enforcers. Eight years ago in Chicago? You publicly chastised me in front of two dozen of my top officers. I could go on and on. But all that was nothing compared to Paris in 1935. The Directorate meeting to choose a new

Patriarch, remember? You championed the *Coterie* Paramount Ricard De Chaux instead of me. And where is De Chaux now? Playing amongst the mortals in some northern burg, local Overlord to a handful of backwoods vamps. You were the only vote against me, Drago. I've never forgotten that." The vitriolic words seemed to drip from Evrard's mouth to fall right on Drago's head.

"De Chaux's got more integrity than you or I will ever have."

"No matter. Because now it's more than payback. You know that, don't you? I've always yearned for the power and position of the Directorate. Well, now I'm going to have it."

"Then do it properly this time. Unchain me. *Guerre a l'outrance, d'egal a egal.* Fight to the finish, man to man. No interference."

"Yes, you'd like that, wouldn't you? I'll admit, the thought of inflicting more pain on you is tempting, but then again, I think that all I have to do to accomplish that is send that mortal in again to see you. How did that feel, Drago? In five hundred years has such a lowly being as an aberration ever looked at you with pity and disgust? There isn't a fantasy in all Midexistence that would make that girl see you now as anything other than what you are—a foul creature brought to a just end."

Drago didn't answer.

"Good. I'll see that she comes again." Drago suddenly felt a cloth being stuffed inside his mouth. He swung his head, but had no strength against Evrard. "In the meantime, Drago, feast on this."

A Belgian lace handkerchief. Drago spit it out. Only after Verkist's scent was long gone from the room did Drago allow himself a small smile.

FOURTEEN

Revelin was still in the room when Verkist's vampire unlocked the door and let Marya in. She described Drago's condition to him, but neglected any mention of the pain she knew he was in. She thought Revelin would be more inclined to try to help if he thought Drago was in better shape than he really was.

"He told me to trust you. He said he understood about Voltaire. That it's the best shots that count, not the biggest battalions."

Revelin smiled a cocky grin that lifted only one side of his mouth. "I knew he'd understand. He's lived in France too long not to."

"But what can we do? Even if you were to overpower the guard and get into the room, there's no way to unshackle him without a key."

"Describe the mechanism to me. How big are the keyholes?"

She told him. Revelin sat back in his chair and looked thoughtful. "I was a bloody soldier in Wellington's army. Did you know that?"

She shook her head, but refrained from asking what that had to do with anything.

"But before I was a soldier, I was a thief. The reason for my fighting for the king's shilling, as a matter of fact. I was a picklock. Quite a good one, actually. 'Til I was caught, that is. Anyway, you know what they say about habits." He bent down and twisted the heel of one boot. It came off in his hand. "They're bloody hard to break."

He showed her his varied assortment of picks. "Everything from some very old skeleton keys to some very new picking needles and tension wrenches. I never leave home without them. One of these should do the trick."

"But we still have to get you into Drago's room."

Revelin shook his head. "Naw. Too risky. If I'm caught, we lose all chance of succeeding. You'll have to do it."

"I don't know how to use any of these things."

"By morning you will, one way or the other. Tell me more about this very unusual *dhampir* blood of yours."

***

Drago floated in and out of consciousness. The pain was too great to allow a deep sleep, but he was too drained to remain fully awake. During those moments when he was alert, he tried to concentrate on what he needed to do to survive, but he couldn't. He was tired, but now it was more than that. The silver prison slowly consumed each idea as he tried to form it, like a slow fire catching a piece of kindling. The periphery of thought burned first, darkening slowly, until nothing was left but the essence. Then that died, too, and grayed to ash. His will tried to latch onto something that wouldn't wither under the assault, but there was nothing he cared for enough to fight the pain. Nothing, except the one thing in life he had always sought. The one thing that made Eternity bearable. The elusive *affaire de coeur.* A matter not of principle or self-interest, but of the heart.

A vision of the slim, sable-haired Gypsy with eyes that made the dark come alive arose before him and kept him from madness.

A draft of air, created by the opening of the door, carried Marya's scent to him. He thought he was dreaming. Slow to realize the truth, he lifted his head in wonder an instant before his ears heard her voice.

"Master."

It wasn't her voice. Yet his mind persisted in the dream. It was Marya. Her scent was unique among mortals. No one else exuded the bewitching combination of the sweetness of innocence and the bitterness of death.

"Cherie?"

"Call me 'cherie' one more time, and I'll change my mind about helping you."

"Scott?"

"Your faithful apprentice, at your service."

His mind refused to function. "How?"

"Possession. You have your talents, I have mine. I simply imposed my will on her and took control of her body. However, with the help of her *dhampir* blood, I can also see the world through her eyes. But I'll have to hurry. Neither one of us has the strength to maintain this for long."

"The helmet first, then."

Drago felt Marya's body next to his; felt her hands at his head. But it was Scott's dexterity that manipulated the lock.

"Hold still, Drago. This device must be as old as you are."

Drago heard the lock pop open, and seconds later the chinstrap was pulled free and the helmet was jerked from his head. Relief flooded his body and his mind, and he drew a deep breath, trying to summon the energy and power that had been so cruelly held at bay. He blinked his eyes and saw Marya's face before him, but the dark eyes that stared back at him were vampire eyes.

"Don't thank me. We're not out of here yet."

The shackles were next. When they dropped to the floor Marya slumped into his arms. Scott was gone. He held her like that for several moments, knowing she needed time to recover her strength as much as he did. What surged through his veins first, though, wasn't strength or energy, but lust. He desired this warm female in his arms more than he'd wanted a woman in years. But it was the unthinking lust of the Undead for sustenance and survival, not the desire to cherish the woman who had just saved his life. He had been badly injured, and if the scent of her tainted blood hadn't reminded him of what she was, he would have burrowed at her neck, sinking his teeth into her soft flesh and drawing on the rich life force of her blood.

But he couldn't take her, and he spent the moment instead shackling his base instincts as ruthlessly as the silver had bound his body. A sound escaped the binds of his control, the half-moan, half-growl of a beast in pain, but Marya didn't stiffen in fear or revulsion. If anything, she held him all the tighter. He waited, not thinking, not feeling, but summoning the vestiges of his control. He sealed his senses from her, lest her fragrant, yielding body undo everything his mind was trying to muster.

A moment later, he drew a deep breath and grabbed her by the shoulders. To wait any longer would give the power of her heated body time to assault his control again. *"Cherie,* can you hear me?" He pushed her away just far enough to read her eyes.

She nodded. "Vampire, can you see me?"

He smiled. "You look beautiful."

"You look horrible."

He could well imagine. And yet Marya didn't seem put off by the vision in the least. "What time is it?"

A small pout pursed the mouth he wanted nothing more than to ravage. "You're welcome, vampire," she said in response to his unspoken thank you.

"We're not out of here yet. What time is it?"

She sighed. "Morning. The sun's up. Rev wanted to do this when as few of Verkist's vamps as possible would be awake. Rev doesn't think more than three or four of the vamps here are day vampires."

"Including the guard that brought you down here."

She nodded.

"Scott is smart. Good odds. I want you to go outside and call for the guard. Tell him I'm dead, or that I'm bleeding all over the floor. Anything to get him to come in here." He held her face. *"C'est compris?"*

She dipped her head again. "I've got it."

He rose to his feet and drew her up with him. He felt the lust stir again with the prospect of battle, and he couldn't resist pulling her to him. He bent his head and kissed her mouth, opening his senses enough to savor her soft heat. It was Marya who pulled away, and a questioning look puckered her brows before she turned and ran out the door. Seconds later he heard her voice on the stairway, calling up to the patio above.

"Come quickly! I think he's dead! He's not moving, and

there's blood all over the place."

Drago heard the vampire on the stairs. An instant later, the heedless vamp rushed into the room. Drago was ready and waiting behind the door. He grabbed the vampire by the arm and whipped him into the concrete wall.

Still pressing the man against the wall, Drago growled in his ear. "If you value your life, you'll be quiet, *monsieur*. Understand?"

The vampire nodded. Still holding him by the arm, Drago snapped a silver shackle on the vampire before he could recover from being slammed into the wall. A quick search of his pockets produced a room key. He tossed it to Marya, who waited just inside the door.

"The key to your room. Let Scott out and tell him what happened. Tell him I authorize him to kill any vamp who gets in his way."

"What about you?"

"I owe Evrard payback. And Marya…"

She looked at him expectantly.

"Once you set Scott free, lock yourself in that room. Understand?"

She nodded.

"Let's go." They exited the room, and he led the way up the stairs, opening his senses fully to the scents and sounds around him. They traversed the patio to the door leading to the hallway running through the southern wing. There was no one in the hall, and Drago could hear no voices emanating from nearby rooms. He signaled for Marya to run down the hall to Scott's room. She did, and unlocked the room. Drago paused outside a closed door just down the hall. *He's here.* Verkist's scent was faint, but present. Scott appeared in the hallway, and Drago cocked his head. Scott glided to his side.

"Watch my back." Drago silently mouthed the words, and Scott nodded. Drago tried the knob. The door was locked. He raised a booted foot and lashed out at a spot on the door near the lock. The door shattered, and Drago was inside before the splintering sound faded away. Evrard jumped out of bed, but Drago was on him before he could react or prepare a mental defense, knocking him backwards. Both men bounced heavily on the bed and were launched to the floor. They rolled into the wall, and by the time Drago gathered his feet beneath him, he had his hammerlock hold on Evrard.

"No games this time, *monsieur.* It's simple. Life or death. I either kill you right now or you tell me what I wish to know, and I allow you to live." Drago tightened the hold for emphasis.

"Go to hell!"

"I was hoping you'd say that." With an expert twist, Drago snapped his neck. "One more and I'll sever the spine."

"What do you want?" The words were little more than a croak, but Drago heard them.

"The names of the brethren you killed to ascend."

Evrard answered through teeth gritted together in pain. "Just three. Michael Caley, Franco Loria, and Cain Rogan."

"Did you hear that, Scott?"

Scott's voice floated to him from the doorway. "Bloody hell. I knew Caley and Rogan. I always wondered how they came to meet the True Death."

Drago kept the hold's pressure and addressed Evrard again. "And if De Chaux had ascended to Patriarch, he would have been the fourth?"

Evrard nodded as best he could.

"Say it!" commanded Drago.

"Ricard De Chaux would have been the fourth." The words were nearly spit out.

Drago loosened his grip, only to crank it tighter than before. "And was I on your list as well, Evrard?"

"No. Not until I saw the opportunity to bring you here. But I didn't forge that order."

Keeping the compliance hold on his opponent, Drago escorted him to the door. "Scott, help me get him downstairs. He's going to know the burn of *l'argent.*" Evrard struggled, but it was a poor effort against the combined power of Drago and Scott. Once in the concrete prison, Drago shackled the Patriarch to the remaining silver armband, and fitted the helmet to him as well.

"Search him, Scott. Make sure he has no keys on him."

The search took only a couple of seconds. Evrard was wearing nothing but silk pajama bottoms.

"I'll have my revenge on you yet, Drago. This won't be the last of it. The Directorate will never forgive you for what you've done here."

"Perhaps not, but neither will they forgive you." Drago dug in the pockets of his trousers. "I'm sorry I don't have a souvenir for you…" His fingers touched something small and cold. "Ah, but I do. I'll leave this with you." He pulled the coin out of his pocket and gazed at it. *His lucky kopeck.* It was just a one-kopeck coin, dated 1990, but it was one of the last issued before the collapse of the USSR. "Here. Something as obsolete as you are soon to be, *monsieur le patriarche.*" Drago flipped the coin at Evrard, and it landed on his lap.

Drago and Scott left and closed the door behind them, but Drago could hear the cry of pain and frustration all the way up to the patio.

"Scott." Drago stopped at the end of the patio.

Scott came to a halt as well. "We need to find Callie."

"We will. First, there's something I want to tell you. I don't say this very often, but *merci beaucoup, mon ami.*"

A wry grin twisted Scott's mouth. "I just follow bloody orders. Thank your lady friend. She took the risk."

Drago nodded. There was a lot he was planning on doing to Marya, and thanking her was only one of the things on his list. "I will. Let's get what belongs to us and get out of here."

They met two of Evrard's vampires in the hallway, but the two didn't seem inclined to challenge either Drago or Scott. They found Callie in the bedroom in the northern wing of the house. Scott gave her a quick hug.

"Grab your things, Cal. We're going home."

They made their way swiftly back to Marya's room. The door was still locked. *"Cherie,* it's me. Open the door."

He heard the key in the lock, and an instant later she was in his arms, not seeming to mind the dried blood on his body or the wild manifestation of bloodlust he was certain was still apparent in his appearance. His senses were open, and the beating of her heart, her quickened breathing, and the warmth of her slender body assaulted him in a mad rush of sensation. The control he had fought so hard for nearly deserted him in the ease of one quick embrace. But now was not the time. They were still in the enemy's camp.

"I was so afraid…" she whispered.

"That Evrard would best me a second time?" As soon as he asked the question he was sorry. It was unfair to question her faith in him. Especially since she seemed to believe in him more than he himself did.

She pulled away from him and said nothing, but her dark eyes answered him all too well. He had hurt her again.

He looked at Scott, not wanting to see any deeper into Marya's eyes. "Give me ten minutes to clean up, then we're out of here."

Marya let out a long breath. "We'll need the special van for Callie. The van with no windows. It's what they brought us here in."

"We'll get it, don't worry," replied Scott, giving Callie an embrace almost as ardent as the one Marya had given Drago.

Drago was already heading for the bathroom, clean clothes in hand. The shower he took was quick, but very, very cold.

***

Marya watched Drago retreat to the shower then shifted her gaze to Revelin and Callie. Marya had no doubt that if Callie hadn't been so glad to see Rev she would have made it a point to show her disdain of Marya's affection for Drago.

Affection? What exactly did she feel for Drago? He had promised to keep her safe, nothing more, but he had lived up to his word. Was it simply gratitude entwined with a strong physical attraction that she was mistaking as something deeper? Or was it just that she found it easier to hold her fear at bay by immersing herself in fantasies of fondness and desire?

And what about him? Certainly he had rebuffed her every time she had tried to get close to him. Did he still think of her as the repulsive aberration? The mortal with the tainted blood? Perhaps Callie had been right all along—she was just being foolish in trying to paste a layer of humanity onto a being who was far from human. What could Marya possibly expect to happen? Assuming they made their way safely out of 'the mirage,' was there any future other than going home to Vicksburg, saying good-bye to Drago, and never seeing him again? Yet how could she accept such a future when she knew she'd see the afterimage of his haunting blue eyes every day for the rest of her life?

He stepped out of the bathroom wearing snug black jeans and nothing else. She stared at him, and it was the wrong thing to do. Her physical response to the sight of his dripping wet hair creating thin rivulets of water down his bare chest was so immediate and powerful that it swamped any logic her mind was trying to exert over the situation.

Drago glanced at her, but only to ask her if she was ready.

I'm ready. Could he read her mind? She felt her face flush. *Well, if he can't read my mind, he can certainly read my face now.* "I'm packed. I've got your things packed as well."

"C'est bien." He quickly rummaged through his suitcase, pulled out a black T-shirt, and pulled it over his head, giving her one last look at the undulating movement of his abdominal muscles. "Let's go, then. Marya, stay right behind me. Scott, you follow the ladies."

They swiftly made their way across the house to the northern wing. Cheyanna was the only vampire they encountered. She opened her mouth as if to ask something. But at a look from Drago, she snapped it shut and slunk away like a dog chastised by nothing more than a stern look from its master. Beyond the kitchen was a door to the garage. It was locked, but a kick from Drago's boot proved just as effective, if a little messier, than a key. The van was in the garage, and the van's key was hanging on a rack on the wall.

A half hour later they were off the mountain and down into the heat of the Valley of the Sun. Drago drove and Marya sat beside him. Revelin was in the back with Callie. Drago hadn't spoken since they left the house.

"Where are we going?" she asked at last, curiosity overcoming her unease at his silence.

"We'll fly back to Jackson if there's a night flight. In the meantime I think an inn is in order. We could all use some rest."

"Is it over? All of it?"

He let out a long breath. "Nikolena's assignment is done. Mine isn't. Verkist wasn't the one who forged your termination order. None of his people did."

"So now what?"

"Simple. I look under a new rock."

Simple. None of this had been simple, and she doubted Drago thought so either. She studied his profile as he spoke. He did look exhausted. It showed in the heavy smile lines framing his mouth and the shadows under his eyes, made darker, perhaps, in contrast to the paleness of the rest of his face, but there nonetheless. It was also apparent in his body language. At red lights she noticed he leaned his head back against the headrest.

It wasn't long, though, before they found a hotel. Getting Callie inside was a bit of a problem. Drago pulled the van as close to the door as possible, and Rev wrapped Callie in a long, black coat, completely covering her head with a second coat. He hustled her quickly inside, and except for some dizziness, Callie was no worse for the experience.

Drago ordered two rooms—one for himself and her, and one for Rev and Callie. This time Marya made no complaint about being in the same room with Drago. She followed him into their room and set her suitcase down. Drago dropped his on the floor and leaned back against the wall, his eyes closed, as if he, too, had been dizzied by the sunlight. Marya wasn't sure what to do. The Anti-God of the vampire world was hardly what she had expected. He was strong, to be sure, but far from invincible. Right now he looked like a man who had just run the race of his life but didn't care in the least that he had won. It made him seem human, and whether he was or not no longer mattered.

She moved closer to him, then stopped, unsure of herself. He had warded off all her previous attempts at intimacy. If she went to him now and he were to push her away, she didn't think she'd be able to stand it. Yet she couldn't look at the need in him and see him supported by nothing but a wall. She tentatively stepped up to him and slid a hand along his waist. The fabric was soft, the muscle beneath hard.

His eyes opened at her touch, and the double barrel of longing and fatigue that aimed at her eyes launched her heart into her throat with renewed fear that he'd turn away. But he didn't. He lifted his arms to her head and drew her to him. She slipped her arms around his waist and ran her hands up his back. She buried her face along his neck and inhaled deeply. He smelled clean, but his own scent prevailed as well—warm, close, and familiar.

She felt him gather handfuls of her hair and draw them to his face, as if he, too, wanted to drown himself in her scent. She gave a shuddering breath and relaxed against him, shifting her feet to bring her entire body into contact with his. He groaned in her ear, but then suddenly pushed her away from him. A feeling of dread sank her heart to her toes until she saw what his intention was. Grabbing the bottom of his shirt in both hands he stripped it over his head and off in an instant. As he lowered his arms he did the same to the cotton tank she wore, then pulled her body flush against his.

He said nothing to her, asked no questions. This was not the time for a discussion of what they meant to each other. Talk of feelings could wait. As could the future, if they had a future. This was pure need, and she felt it as strongly as he did. It was a primal thing, raw and undeniable, like a raging river, and yet it wasn't out of control. A kind of restraint banked the river, containing and directing it. But just barely.

His hands moved to either side of her head, and he positioned her to give his mouth access to hers. It was the mouth of the experienced lover she had tasted once before, but this time she could feel the underlying tension. His lips drew on hers, pulling away, then increasing the pressure, never still, never in one spot too long. Finally he dragged his mouth to her jaw and sucked at a spot halfway to her ear. A shiver coursed down to her toes, and her whole body trembled. His response was a groan against her skin, and the vibration of his voice tore all the way through her, as if her body were trying to soak up every part of him she could.

He glided to the bed, drawing her by the hand, but he didn't pull her down to the covers. Instead, he stood next to the bed and took both her hands in his. His hands were sure, the fingers long and slender, and they guided her hands to the waistband of his jeans. She took a deep breath, trying to slow her racing pulse. She grazed her fingers along his abdomen, feeling the smooth skin, hard muscles, and line of hair that disappeared beneath the heavy denim. She undid the button and zipper of his jeans while he brought her long hair from either side of her head across the space between them to his mouth. When she started tugging his jeans down, he dropped her hair and ran his hands across her shoulders, dragging her bra straps down to her upper arms. With a renewed urgency he wiggled and stepped out of the jeans and pushed her skirt down to the floor.

She backed up to get a wider view of his body, and in doing so hit the bed with the back of her knees, toppling her to the mattress. She had only the blink of an eye to marvel at his lean body, so perfectly proportioned, before he followed her onto the bed. He lowered himself onto her, splaying his fingers against the mattress on either side of her head to take some of his weight off her. He took her mouth with his again, parting his lips and kissing her more deeply than before. She wrapped her legs around his and encircled his neck with her hands, weaving her fingers through his thick hair. Frustrated with the space between them, she tried to arch up to him, at the same time releasing his hair and grabbing his shoulders, trying to pull him down to her. He collapsed the brace of his arms and let his weight press fully against her, and a small cry of pleasure escaped her lips. But there was still clothing between them, and she wanted to feel all of him. A sweet but demanding ache set parts of her body throbbing, and her hands struggled to satisfy the demand, tugging at the waistband of his shorts.

She didn't have to worry. It was clear he wanted the same thing she did. He rolled her a little to the side, enough to unhook her bra and untangle the straps from her arms. Her panties and his shorts were next, and the sudden exposure and vulnerability sent a quick tremor of fear through her. She had never been this intimate with a man before, but when Drago's hands covered and warmed her, the waves of pleasure overran her apprehension.

His mouth kissed hers as his hands caressed her breasts. His long hair hung forward on either side of his face, shielding the light from her eyes. In the darkness his lips and hands and body were everything, and they told her stories more magical than those he had communicated with his voice. His mouth relayed euphoria and passion, and his hands spoke of a possessiveness of all he deemed his. In his body she felt his strength, but strangely it wasn't the strength of force and power, but of endurance, patience, and courage. His lifted his head, and she saw his eyes, as blue as the clearest lake. The fathomless depths enraptured her with their melancholy. She saw loneliness as interminable as a long, gray winter, and an emptiness as vast as the cold plains.

"Love me, Drago."

"The vampire will love you. The beast. Your tainted blood won't satisfy the bloodlust. I swear I won't hurt you, *cherie,* but you may not like what you see." The sentences came almost as gasps.

"I don't care. I need you, Drago, please," she begged.

She felt him tremble as he lowered his mouth to just below her earlobe. His lips and tongue unfurled a ribbon of pleasure down her throat, but suddenly she felt a tension in his body, and his breathing became labored. He raised his head and shifted his gaze to hers. His eyes darkened to the color of the night sky, and his skin shone with a pale luminescence. It was the manifestation of the vampire, but she didn't want him to stop now. She raked her fingers through his hair and silently willed him to continue.

He dropped his head to the well between her breasts and pressed a line of kisses downward. In between each kiss he murmured sounds against her skin, some words in French, some in Russian, and some that were no words at all, but purrs and growls. His voice created a vibration in his lips that her skin absorbed and conducted to every inch of her body. She squirmed beneath him, wanting more with every kiss he bestowed on her.

His hands cupped her breasts, teasing her nipples with his thumbs, but with every awakening of her desire she demanded more. He gave it to her, skimming his mouth over the curves of her breast. His hands streamed down her body like rushing water, cool and energizing, flowing over her ribcage, across her belly, and along her hips. When his hands reached her buttocks and thighs, jolts of electricity ran through her, and when his mouth closed over one nipple, the current she felt surging between them threatened to erode the remaining banks of her restraint. He suckled her, holding her bottom and pulling her tightly against him. She felt him hard against her softness, as rigid and unyielding as the tension that tightened her body in an almost painful grasp.

She felt him press against her again, and suddenly his mouth was at her ear.

"Relax, *cherie.*"

She shook her head, frustration and fear abruptly intruding where only desire had reigned. "I don't know how."

His fingers stroked her softness, and a groan next filled her ear. "Why did you not tell me you had never had a man before?"

She shook her head again, tears against her eyelids coming easier than words. "I don't know."

"Shhh...shhh, *cherie.* It's all right. Just relax."

She tried to, and he waited, but not easily. Suddenly she felt his teeth pressed against her skin, as sharp as the ache deep within her, and she had the insane desire to feel his canine teeth pierce her flesh. But he didn't. He shifted his body, his quickened breaths heating her skin in time to the blood pulsing through her veins, so close to his mouth, yet forever out of reach. But his frustration was immediately followed by his salvation and hers. He held her hips and drove into her, slowly but steadily, and she cried out with him in both pain and pleasure.

His thrusts were slow and deep, and he trembled in her arms as if he, too, were making love for the very first time. He buried his face in her hair, and she wrapped her hands around his neck, feeling the tautness building again in his body. His rhythm quickened, and his strokes became progressively harder and faster. The physical sensations assaulted her with an intensity she couldn't assimilate, sending her mind to a place of light and shadow it had never been before. Flashes of brilliance strobed behind her eyelids, and with each flare of light, she saw images of life and death—flames and fortunes, charnels and churches, invaders and icons, birch-barks and blood. She didn't understand what she saw. She only knew that they came from his mind. But as quickly as the visions came, they disappeared, shattering in an explosion of awareness. He had given her life, and a freedom she had never known sent her soaring above all the darkness of the world.

His rhythm broke, and she was aware again of the man in her arms. He drove into her hard one final time and trembled with the release he shared with her. His weight settled on her, and she held him, stroking him as though he were anything other than the Anti-God of the Undead.

Too soon, though, he pulled out of her and rose from the bed. He scooped his clothes from the floor and vanished into the bathroom. She climbed underneath the covers, cold without his warmth. She closed her eyes, trying not to think. She, for one, would not regret what had just happened.

A moment later she felt the edge of the mattress dip under his weight and felt him gather a long strand of her hair. She opened her eyes. He had put on the shorts, but was still naked above the waist. She watched him twirl his finger, wrapping the strand of hair around it. He let go, and the hair uncoiled slowly and fell from his hand. His gaze met hers. His eyes had paled once more to the color of blue glass.

"Forgive me, *cherie.* I know I hurt you. I should have warned you. But if I had, your fear would have increased, and you would have never been able to relax. The next time will be better, I promise. In the meantime I can erase the memory of the pain if you wish."

Better? She didn't know if she could stand 'better.' And she certainly didn't want any part of the experience erased. "No. I'm all right. But you…you didn't…you couldn't…" He hadn't been able to consummate his bloodlust. This she did know, if little else.

"No. Feeding for me isn't as vital as it is for a younger vampire, but even so, it's difficult to disconnect bloodlust from lovemaking. And lovemaking such as that was…well, you must understand if I separate myself from you for a while. Yes?" He was off the bed before he spoke the final word.

She nodded, though in truth she understood little other than the fact that reality had already dropped on her like an unwelcome downpour.

FIFTEEN

Drago hadn't planned this. In the beginning, she had been nothing more than an aberration. Unique, to be sure, but not the kind of mortal female that the Undead chose as objects of entertainment. Somehow, in the course of serving as her protector, he had come to realize just how unique she was. It had been years since he had made love to a woman who knew him for what he was and accepted him for it. With Marya, however, it hadn't been mere acceptance, but true desire. True desire for him when she had never before made love to a man. He hadn't wanted to hurt her, but even if he had known beforehand that she was untried, he didn't know if he could have resisted her. His craving had been just as strong as hers.

He had been exhausted—still was—but when Marya had come to him he hadn't been able to refuse her. He hadn't wanted to, and the result shook him even now. He thought of the vampire game of fantasy—the sport of seduction that began with allowing a mortal female to see in the vampire what she wanted to see and ended with the vampire's satisfaction in destroying her. He had never wanted to play this game with Marya. She saw beyond any fantasy he might project, and harming her was the last thing he wanted. Still, the beast was hard to control. He dared not go near her just yet. When he had realized she was a virgin, feelings had risen so powerful and elemental that the bloodlust had arisen as well. And the lust was not so easily tamped down.

He sat on the bed and told her he'd have to keep his distance, and the look in her eyes had reached deep into him and touched places he thought didn't exist. It would be a problem, but not one he was able to think about now. He still hadn't slept, and right now the desire for sleep pushed all else aside.

He called the airport and inquired about a flight to Jackson. There were no direct flights, but a connecting flight to Memphis at nine o'clock this evening. He booked reservations and hung up. Next he called Scott's room and relayed the message regarding the evening flight. The last thing to be done was to call for a wake up at six o'clock.

Everything done, Drago drew a deep breath. He couldn't recall being this fatigued in a long, long time. A vampire's exhaustion was generally mental, not physical, but right now Drago swore every muscle in his body ached and every joint was stiff. The days on end without sleep, the battles with Evrard, and the assault of the silver on his body and mind had taken a toll greater than he wanted to acknowledge, even to himself.

He glided to the bed and knelt by Marya. She was curled at the edge of her side of the bed, but her eyes opened as soon as he came near her.

"I need sleep, *cherie.* I would love nothing more than to fall asleep with you in my arms, but the things you do to me would prevent me from resting. Do you understand?"

"You don't want me to touch you."

He wanted nothing more, but he couldn't tell her that. "The only way I can rebuild my strength is by getting some uninterrupted sleep. The game is not over, *cherie.* If I am to find and defeat the vampire who forged that order, I will need to replenish what I have lost."

He knew she didn't understand. He could tell by the injured look in her dark eyes that she felt like she was nothing more than an unwanted distraction, but he didn't know how else to explain it to her right now. His mind felt like a road of mud, and the simple task of thought and communication was like trying to trudge through the muck one laborious step at a time. But it wasn't just the weariness. Sleeping with a mortal who knew what he was just wasn't something he was used to doing. He had slept with Adelle, true, but that had been years ago, and there had been no one since.

She broke eye contact—the only reply to his statement. He stood, circled to his side of the king size bed, and lay down.

Sleep was longer in coming than he thought it would be.

***

Hours later, needs other than rest gradually reached deep into his vampiric sleep and roused him to wakefulness. In his frequent travels he had learned to sleep where and when he could, but rarely was his restorative sleep disrupted by something as mundane as a mortal's presence.

Yet there was nothing mundane about Marya. Even with his eyes closed, consciousness flooded him with the intensity of her spirit. She hadn't touched him, but in the cool of the air-conditioned room, her scent enveloped him, warm and musky, and her life force sang to him, a siren song of seduction.

He turned his head and looked at her. Her eyes glinted at him in the gloom of the curtained room, but there was no guile in the forthright stare. Unlike his Paris beauties, she didn't want his money or the glamour of being seen in the presence of *mysterieux le russe,* 'the mysterious Russian.' She knew what he was and understood the world of the Undead better than all but a handful of mortals, and still she wanted him. As innocent as she was of men and the ways of love, her desire reached out to him, as tangible as her fragrance.

"Did I wake you when I rolled over?" she whispered.

How could he explain that it was a gap she had bridged that woke him, not a creak of the bed? So he nodded. "But it's all right, *cherie."* He glanced at the bedside clock. "I slept seven hours. Enough to nourish my control and tame the beast. Come here."

She hesitated, but he sensed it wasn't out of trepidation or lack of want. She was simply no more used to this than he was.

"Come." He pushed the covers down in invitation.

She slid across the sheet and eased into his embrace, but he felt a tension in her body stiffen her muscles.

"What is it, *cherie?* Why do you not relax?"

"Are you kidding? I just made love to a vampire. I don't know if what I did will bring good fortune or bad."

"There's no good or bad, no right or wrong. Each of us had a need, and together we found fulfillment. It is a rare thing, so cherish it, *cherie*, don't question it." He scooped a handful of her long hair to his face and breathed in its perfume before smoothing it back down across her shoulders.

"Don't ask questions. I can read between the lines. There's no future for us, is there?"

He let out a long, slow breath. "Just enjoy the moment, *cherie.*"

"You're a master of evasion, you know that? Tell me, is that a vampiric or a Russian trait?"

"Both." It was nothing but the truth.

She laughed softly, and though there was a touch of sadness in the sound, with her amusement came a relaxation of her body. She pressed herself against him, wrapping her long legs over his, and her warmth swirled over him as though a genie had uncorked a lamp and granted him his fondest wish.

"*Marya.* Did you know that your name is quite famous in Russian literature?"

She made a sound against the bare skin of his chest, and the vibration awakened every part of him not already roused. "Sorry. Russian literature isn't at the top of my reading list."

"Tolstoy had a Princess Marya in both *Anna Karenina* and *War and Peace.*"

She laughed again, and her voice was like the flow of water across his skin, cool and cleansing. "Maybe if I were a vampire I'd have time to read *War and Peace.* But it doesn't matter. One thing I'm sure of is that there aren't any princesses in my ancestry. Just a vampire." The laughter died a shuddering death against his heart.

"Maybe your hate for him has lessened a little, yes?" His voice was very quiet.

She hesitated before answering. Perhaps the new twists in her reality were not so easily traversed.

"I didn't know my grandfather. All I know is that he killed people to feed his hunger."

"He was a very young vampire then. He had to feed often. At that stage it is an uncontrollable need more than a controlled pleasure. Besides, you told me you believed he loved his wife. So much so that he fathered a child even after the change. So he can't be all bad in your eyes, can he?"

"And you told me that was nothing more than lust." She sighed, torturing him again with her breath against his skin. "I don't know. When my father grew to adulthood he was hired to kill my grandfather for the good of the community. Everyone saw him as evil."

"And when the Brotherhood visited you it was for the good of the vampire community. We each look out for our own. How can you applaud one side for wanting to survive and hate the other side for wanting the exact same thing?" He knew he was steering the conversation into dangerous waters, but he truly wanted her to understand that the Undead were more than just killing machines. Of course, he hadn't shown her anything but the violence in his world. And, as she loved to remind him, she saw too easily in him the quest for death— not a pretty picture.

"I don't know. It's how I was brought up."

"Cherie, you can't love me and hate the vampire."

"Tell me a story."

It was clear. In spite of everything that had happened between them, she still could not fully accept him for what he was. It was forever the way with mortals. Perhaps she had not bridged that gap after all.

He sighed. "Very well. There's an old Russian fairy tale of a warrior-princess named Marya Morevna. Her army had just been victorious over its enemy, and the white tents of Marya's soldiers sat ringed by the bodies of their slain foes. Into this battlefield rode a lonely young prince named Ivan who was in search of his three married sisters. Ivan told Marya he came in peace, and he stayed and feasted for three days and nights. Ivan and Marya fell madly in love, married, and moved to Marya's kingdom. Many tales would end there, but Ivan and Marya's happy years together are just the beginning of their story." Drago could feel Marya's smile in the relaxation of her body, and it felt good.

"For years they lived in peace, but one day Marya told

Ivan she would have to leave to battle an army in a faraway part of her kingdom. Before she left, though, she implored Ivan not to enter a particular room in the deepest, dankest part of the castle dungeon under any circumstances. But after she left, curiosity got the better of Ivan, and he unlocked the cellar door. Stretched out on the floor was a giant who was held down by numerous chains to both his arms and legs. It was no commonplace giant, but the famous Koshchey the Deathless. Koshchey implored Ivan to give him water, saying he had been without food or water for ten years, and the tenderhearted Ivan gave him not one bucket of water to drink, but three. Koshchey drank it all, after which he broke all his chains as if they were made of straw. He told Ivan he would never see Marya again, and the giant flew out the window. Koshchey the Deathless did indeed capture Marya, and Ivan had many further adventures in trying to rescue his beloved princess."

"You just made that whole thing up."

He smiled. "Believe what you will, *cherie*. It is a story." He reached his left arm over her to caress her side, and she brought her hand up to finger his forearm. He flinched, moving his arm away.

"Can't you tell me about this now? This mark, and how you got it?"

"I got it when I was human. It has no bearing on what I am now."

"I think it does."

"You know nothing of the world, young one, and even less of me."

He felt her stiffen again in his arms. "I see. I'm good enough to bed, but not to trust with your past."

"It's not the way of the Undead to reveal themselves to mortals."

She rolled away from him. "Fine. Then have it your way, vampire. I'm going to take a shower."

He closed his eyes and sighed as he felt the mattress shift from the release of her weight as she rose. *Master of evasion.* He had indeed told her the truth. Certainly the art of evasion was standard to a vampire's repertoire. Truth was a scarcity.

What wasn't outright lie was deception or dodging. As for being a trait of his homeland, no *rubakha* could drape more naturally from his shoulders than the cloak of evasion. The average Russian just wanted to be left alone. But with centuries of rule by a very small elite that the typical Russian had little understanding of or identification with, survival meant paying lip service to whoever was in power and then proceeding to do exactly as he wished. It was a strategy Drago had employed for years.

The thought of those in power reminded him of Nikolena. She was Russian, too. Drago had long believed that their shared heritage was the reason for her tolerance of his methods and the affection that occasionally glowed through the chinks in her armor. A call to Nikolena regarding Evrard Verkist was in order. Drago slipped from the bed and picked up his cell phone, daring to hope that this one time she would both be pleased to hear his report and proud of him for resolving an assignment without shipping a brother to *la Belle Mort*. It was after midnight, Paris time, a good hour to call. He would not be rousing Nikolena from sleep and, therefore, wouldn't be rousing irritation at being awakened as well. He hoped.

She answered.

He gave his report matter-of-factly, without conceit over his victory or pride over the swift completion of the job. But while he hoped for Nikolena's good will, he never presumed to have it. He told her that Evrard had confessed to the murder of three vampires in his rise to Patriarch, and that Scott had been witness to the confession. Drago gave her the names of the three victims and also told her of Evrard's plot to kill Ricard De Chaux in the event De Chaux had been appointed Patriarch. Drago knew that Nikolena, like himself, had always had a penchant for the Frenchman De Chaux.

Silence greeted Drago from the Paris end of the call. Sometimes silence was preferable to Nikolena's words. Sometimes it was a very bad thing.

Her voice, raised in question, finally floated to his ear. "And what of the forged order, Alek?"

He swallowed. Something told him she wouldn't like his

answer. "Verkist had nothing to do with it. Neither did Deverick. The seals and signatures all looked to be true."

More dead air.

"Are you certain, Aleksei Borisov?" The words were drawn out carefully and clearly, implying she wanted an answer just as deliberate.

There was no hesitation in his voice. *"Oui, madame.* I am sure."

Two beats of silence. "You know then what needs to be done."

"I know. When I arrive back in Jackson I'll call for Philippe to bring all the files. I don't want to leave Marya behind again to travel to Paris until this thing is over."

"I understand. I'll give permission for him to make the trip. And I'm anxious for your report on all this. Send it directly to me, not to Philippe. Oh, and Alek…"

"Yes?"

"Have Scott call me."

"Nika, where is your faith in me?"

Laughter, crackling like burning wood, erupted from the phone.

He sighed. "I'll have Scott call." His response was as dry as her laughter. It was clear that the young vampire glittered in Nikolena's eyes. Revelin Scott would go far in the hierarchy.

"Don't screw this up, Aleksei Borisov." There was never a pat on the head without a box on the ears.

"I'll try not to, *madame.*"

He disconnected the call and glanced at the clock. Almost six o'clock. He called Scott's room and delivered the message. As soon as he hung up the phone, it rang. The wake up call. Marya stepped out of the bathroom, and he replaced the receiver by feel alone. His eyes were all on her.

Her body—meagerly covered by a sleeveless blouse and tight skirt—was soft, but the gaze that flicked his way could have cut glass. Her damp hair spilled over her shoulders and down her back in shining ribbons, and drops of water glistened on her arms.

He lifted a brow at her. "All finished?"

"Finished." Her voice could do a pretty could job of cutting glass as well.

"Cherie..."

She cut him off. "I know. There's no time to talk now even if you didn't feel like being evasive."

He stood before her. It wasn't so much that he was sidestepping her remark. He simply didn't know what to say.

***

Marya was never so glad to be back in the Mississippi, the Hospitality State. The trip had been long and tedious. On the flight from Phoenix to Memphis she hadn't had a seat next to Drago, Rev, or Callie. On the second leg she sat next to Callie, but that was as bad as sitting alone. Callie was no more friendly now than she had been before. The layover in Memphis had been almost two hours, and during that time Drago hadn't been inclined toward conversation. Memphis International Airport was nearly deserted so late at night, so there had been no one to overhear them, but he had merely sat, his eyes staring at a spot far down the concourse.

At the Jackson airport they retrieved Drago's car and drove Callie home, just before dawn's pale fingers reached over the eastern horizon. The next stop was Revelin's office. Drago dropped him off and spent a half hour talking to Scott while Marya waited in the car and greedily downed a fast food breakfast big enough for a starving artist.

Drago strode out of the office and to the car just as she was savoring the first bite of a biscuit with jelly. He slipped into the driver's seat and started the car without a word or more than a cursory glance in her direction. She chewed on the doughy mouthful, washing it down with coffee. She sent darting looks Drago's way. *What does a vampire think about?* Was he plotting for the future? Was he thinking about her? Or was his mind forever locked in some nightmare of the past he could never free himself from?

She, for one, had thought of nothing but Drago and the way he had made love to her since it had happened. Yesterday she had never felt closer to anyone. Today never further away. Vampire or no vampire, how could he feel so differently about what had happened than she did? It had been a glorious joining of two bodies attuned to each other and needing each other, but it had also been a joining of minds. She had seen his past, as though he had seen each image, then closed his eyes and transferred each afterimage to her mind. Why was he so reluctant to share those feelings now?

She dispatched the last of her biscuit with a final gulp of tepid coffee and cleared her throat, unable to stand the silence any longer. "What happens now? You said it's not over, but what's the next step?" He may not have thought about her, but she had no doubt he knew exactly what he was going to be doing next.

"I'll call my assistant Philippe to bring all my files from the past couple weeks. I'm sure something will enlighten me."

She drew a deep breath. Another slippery answer. "What about me? Surely my part in all this is done."

"Not until I find out who wished you dead."

Well, at least she'd be in her own house. And Drago, for all his hot and cold ways, wouldn't be leaving her yet. She didn't want to even think about his leaving.

"So when will Philippe come?"

"Tomorrow, if it can be arranged."

One more night alone with Drago. Don't think about it. She tried instead to think what more to ask him. His Spartan answers weren't doing much to feed the conversation. "What exactly will you be looking for?"

"The lie. When it faces me, I'll know my enemy."

Patience, patience... "And then what?"

"One of us will be sent to the True Death. No quarter this time."

At least that was specific enough. "Just like Ilya. You're going to keep traveling roads until you find it, aren't you?"

"Would you rather I allow my enemies to prevail without a fight, *cherie*? That would be a shorter road yet to *la mort.*"

She was quiet after that, but the trip was a quick one to Vicksburg. When Drago pulled into her driveway and stopped the car, she jumped out, happy to see her cottage with its tin roof and French doors. She was even more glad to see green leaves instead of cactus spikes, and grass instead of sand and stone. Drago followed her into the house, but he clearly didn't feel the same joy she did. She suddenly wondered if he had a home. Did he ever feel the same kind of delight she felt at being in a particular place? Did five hundred years on earth bind him more than ever to a certain city, or did he tire of places over so much time?

She brought in her mail and her suitcase, and then she checked the refrigerator. There wasn't much food, but enough for a day or two. When she went back into the living room, Drago was slumped on the sofa, his eyes closed. She sat down next to him. What she was beginning to think of as the 'Ilya' look was back. It was the look of the traveler, weary but determined to find what lay at the end of the road. The lines on his face were tight, not relaxed, and even in repose his brows were drawn together, creating twin vertical furrows between them.

"Drago?"

His eyelids slowly rose, almost mechanically, and when he faced her, the startling color of his eyes struck her anew. She realized that half the trouble in seeing into his soul, if he had one, was getting past the distraction of blue so clear and bright that, like a sunny sky, it hurt to look at it.

"Do you have a home?"

He closed his eyes again. "I call Paris home now."

"What's there?"

He opened his eyes and gazed out the French doors at her garden. "A chateau. It's an old French castle, not a very big one, but I've scandalized the locals by turning it into a Russian palace rather than preserving it as a hallmark to French history."

There were a million questions she could ask him. And he seemed willing to answer as long as it didn't involve his past. "How often do you go there?"

"Usually twice a month."

"And for no more than a day at a time, I'll bet."

He turned to her and his eyes flicked down and back up as if he could see her without her clothes on. If his memory was as good as he claimed it was, her naked body was exactly what he was seeing. "Actually, I was there on a very nice vacation when you called my number and left a very odious message about killing vampires."

She felt her face flame. "For which you can't blame me."

A slow smile curved the chiseled mouth. "You don't want to know what I thought of you at the time."

She decided to change the subject. "Do you ever visit Novgorod anymore?"

"Sometimes. I try to visit Russia once a year." A different kind of gleam came into his eyes when he talked about Novgorod. Something heavier, almost a burden, but something he embraced nevertheless. "Travel's easier now than it used to be. Novgorod is a modest industrial center today, but it's a wonder it has endured at all. The centuries have not been kind to the city, but every time it has been invaded and destroyed it has survived to rebuild itself."

Marya thought that the city and its one-time prince had much in common, but she kept the thought to herself. No doubt he would only chide her for how little she really knew.

His cell phone rang, startling her.

He pulled it from his belt and answered. "Alek Dragovich. Ah, Philippe!"

The rest of the conversation was in French. When he disconnected the call ten minutes later, she looked at him expectantly.

"That was my assistant. I had left a message for him to call. He's on his way. In the meantime we have a day or two of rest. Starting right now. Do what you want, *cherie,* but heed two things. First, don't leave the house, and second…"

She put up a hand. "I know. Don't disturb you."

He finished the thought anyway, gazing into her eyes. "Let me sleep until six tonight."

She nodded. She was catching onto the drill.

He reached out and stroked her cheek twice, once with the back of his hand and once with his fingertips. She closed her eyes. His touch was cool, but far from dispassionate. Did he know what he did to her with just the slightest contact?

By the time she opened her eyes, he was already gone.

She unpacked her suitcase and did a load of wash. She thought about working on her art, but Drago wasn't the only one who was tired. She had been up all night with the flights from Phoenix and hadn't nodded off for more than a half hour in the lounge at the Memphis airport. Finally she gave up trying to stay awake and lay down on her bed.

I'm as bad as a vampire—awake all night and sleeping all day.

***

Slanting rays of afternoon sunlight crept into her room and woke her. Unlike the vampire, she was too unused to resting by day to get a full complement of sleep. The first thing she did was check on Drago in the guest room, but she was careful not to do more than crack the door. A glimpse of dark hair and pale skin in the dim of the curtained room was enough.

She put on old clothes, ate a late lunch, then cleaned and scrubbed her bedroom as thoroughly as she could, trying to remove all trace of the strange vampire she had killed. She changed all the bedding and opened all the windows to air out the room.

A shower and another change of clothes later, Marya wandered outside to sit on her back patio. The warm sunlight felt good after being cooped up in the suffocating, closed rooms of vampire houses. She glanced around at her carefully tended garden and spacious yard. *Drago was right.* She did have a good life. She had her nice cottage in a lovely, quiet spot on the edge of town. She had her talent and her art, and she was able to support herself doing what she loved to do. And now she had freedom. Once this was over, she could do what she wanted. She could travel and forge as many or as few new acquaintances as she wanted. *Would it be enough to make up for Drago's absence?*

Like it or not, she had to face his leaving. One or two days more, and this whole affair would end. Drago would be gone forever, one way or another, either having finally found the end of the road, or off to do battle again somewhere else.

You can't love me and hate the vampire. Did she love him? She had never felt such an attraction to any man, not even Jaime. But was it love? She wasn't sure. *He's leaving. Better that it's not.*

She smiled as she realized a more appropriate thought would have been, "He's a vampire—better that it's not." Had she truly accepted the vampire side of him? She thought about her grandfather, Nicolai, the vampire, wishing for the first time that she had known him, but he had died at the hands of his own son before she was born. Her mother had never told her anything about Nicolai, and when she had asked, curious, her mother had hushed her and recited a quick prayer against evil.

Marya retrieved her father's journal from a cabinet in the living room and looked through it, hunting for entries Andrei had written about Nicolai. There were very few, and those that did exist detailed the *dhampir's* search for his father and his eventual execution. Unable to live life as a mortal after crossing to the Other Side, her grandfather hadn't stayed with his wife after siring Andrei. But the journal detailed very little written in the way of thoughts, feelings, or anything that gave Marya insight into the character of her vampire grandfather.

She read part of the longest entry.

August 5, 1968

It is done. The Evil One is dead. Death itself is unnatural, but in this case, death could not be a better or more fortunate happening. The Evil One will prey no more upon the innocent who were once his own people. He seemed surprised to see me, but quickly hid his astonishment in mockery. He was strong, but young, and with youth he was careless and overconfident. He did not believe his own blood capable of killing him. His mockery died when he did, but it would not have been so with one wearing the experience of more years.

It would also not have been so had he taken a Master to properly instruct him, but it is the way of the Roma to be independent of the shackles of another. Thus, there is no one to mourn him. For I will not.

The rest of the entry detailed the exact time, place, and method of execution. She skipped down to the method, lines that she had already read over and over, when she had been searching for a method to kill Drago.

I emptied my revolver into his chest, and it took all six of my silver children to knock him down. The Vampire Hunter piercing his heart prevented him from rising up again, and the following was done to the body in the grave to stop him rising in the future: I placed bits of iron between his teeth, fingers, and in his ears and nose, placed a rosary on his chest, and covered the body with a fishing net. When the grave was filled in, I sealed it with boiling oil and pounded hawthorn stakes into the ground over his head and stomach.

The grave is well hidden. My work is done.

Marya wondered if it was just coincidence that Nicolai was the last vampire that Andrei killed. Perhaps her father felt more for the vampire than he let on in his writing. How could anyone, even a *dhampir*, think of his own father as nothing more than an 'Evil One?'

Marya herself had been raised to think of all vampires, including her grandfather, as evil. *Dhampirs*, especially those like her father who took to vampire killing, were revered almost as saviors. And while she had never actually cherished her *dhampir* blood, she had accepted it and had thought of her father with pride.

Yet what really distinguished the blood of one from the blood of the other? *Nothing. My grandfather's blood flows through my veins. Am I any different from him?*

She was different. She didn't kill people for need. Her human blood gave her the control to make choices. But was that alone enough to separate herself from those the Roma considered 'evil?' Even if it were, could Nicolai, who she believed killed only as a result of an uncontrollable need, truly be deemed wicked?

Could she ever again think of her grandfather as evil? And what about Drago? For all her initial hatred of *l'enforcier*, if she no longer thought of Nicolai as evil, how could she think of Drago as malevolent? She couldn't.

She closed the book and put it away. She had never

questioned any of these things before. She wasn't sure she had any of the answers now, but there was one thing of which she was certain. No amount of logic, no adherence to the teachings of her youth, could continue to make her believe Drago was evil. She glanced at the grandfather clock. It was after five. She stepped softly into the guest room and pulled up a wooden chair next to the bed. She had left the door open, and enough light poured through the doorway to illuminate the subject of her fascination. He rested on his back like a corpse. At first appearance he certainly looked more vampire than mortal. His skin clung to his facial bones with a translucent pallor. Life, as well as humanity, seemed to have sunk far below the surface of his being. If he breathed, she couldn't tell.

But try as she might, even with the mask of the vampire so evident, she couldn't think of him as either dead or evil. Stillness bathed his features, but it was a tranquility of peace and innocence, and she associated these things more with the life she couldn't see than the death she could. She craved nothing more than to touch him, to break the calm and swirl the current of life to the surface. She wanted to see his energy breathe animation into the handsome features. She yearned to see his desire for her again, and she wanted to know that it was stronger than his death wish.

Most of all she wanted to see all the parts of him kept hidden from the world under the layers of denial and deception that she surmised had only hardened more and more over time so that they were nothing less than rock now. What magic could she or any mortal wield that would be powerful enough to shatter those defenses?

She pulled her chair closer yet to the bed and reached her fingers toward his mouth, stopping them just inches short of their destination. Suddenly she saw his bare chest expand with the inhalation of a deep breath, and his lips parted to exhale. His eyelids slowly lifted, exposing the blue sentinels that guarded the entrance to those depths she so wanted to explore. Her hand froze in midair, and she felt like a thief caught trying to steal a sacred treasure.

Wakefulness pumped life into his face, and the waxy

translucence of vampiric sleep melted away to reveal the firmness and texture, if not the rosy glow, of living tissue.

"Go ahead, *cherie.* It's all right." His whisper, like a newborn creature, snuggled against her and sent shivers cascading down her body.

She stretched her fingers forward until they grazed his mouth, and his lips parted again under her touch. The corners of his mouth curved slightly upward, giving the appearance of wry amusement, but the full lower lip seemed firmly anchored in solemnity by the shadowed cleft in his strong chin. His skin felt cool, and yet she sensed an underlying warmth that, like his features, just needed the stimulation of life to awaken.

"What do you find so fascinating in my appearance, *cherie?"*

"You're beautiful." She felt strange saying such a thing to a man, and the amused bow of his mouth under her fingers only strengthened the feeling.

"I have been called many things over the centuries, *cherie,* but I don't think beautiful has been one of them."

She pursed her mouth in skepticism. "I don't believe that. With all the women I'm sure you've made love to…" She swallowed. "What female wouldn't be mesmerized by those blue eyes or pulled under by those waves of black hair? Not to mention sex appeal that goes off the scale."

Something in his eyes shifted. "All those who know what I am."

The words were stated so matter-of-factly that an almost uncontrollable sorrow gripped her. She rose from the chair so quickly it toppled over backwards, and she fell against the edge of the bed, her mouth seeking his. He pushed himself up to meet her, but the momentum of her weight drove both of them to the mattress. His arms snaked around her and pulled her entire body onto his, and she groaned in between his kisses. She drew on him as fiercely as he did on her, determined to invoke the spell necessary to break through to those parts of him he so zealously guarded.

He rolled her over so that she was beneath him, and it was

he, rather than she, who worked enchantment with his hands and lips. Desire immediately flared deep within her, a result not only of his current endeavors, but of the memory of yesterday's union, still so fresh and powerful in her mind. Tingles surged outward in waves to the tips of every extremity, sensitizing her to his slightest touch. Other parts of her body reacted in different ways to the anticipation of what was to come, and an ache almost painful in its intensity made itself known in a most pressing way.

There was nothing slow or easy or controlled in either her movements or his, but a desire and need that wove together and drove both of them to abandon the luxury of ease and leisure. His fingers, usually so deft, tripped with the recklessness of hunger and tore one of her buttons. She didn't care. His goal was hers, his impediments hers as well.

A rush of victory washed over her even as her heart and body raced on. No death wish on Drago's part could possibly be as powerful or elemental as the forces now urging his body to ride the limits of his control. She felt his body tighten with the strain and marveled that she, so young and inexperienced, had both the ability to arouse and the power to undo a being as ancient and skilled as Drago.

But it wasn't a contest of power or a test of expertise. It wasn't mortal against vampire, youth opposed to age, or female versus male. In this they were partners, equal in their passion and longing. They each took, and they each gave, and when he joined with her in a cry of both possession and release, her feelings became indistinguishable from his. She felt his pain, his joy, his victories, and his defeats, and the heat and sweat and musk that cocooned them were a part of them both. At last, when her mind and body could take no more, she surrendered to her release, and his followed immediately.

His final shudders faded away, his body relaxed, and she despaired, knowing he would once again leave her side. But this time he didn't. She didn't question him, but simply enjoyed the pleasure of lying in his arms. Perhaps it was nothing more than the two days of rest repairing the damage the silver had done him.

Whatever it was, she took a deep breath and delighted in the afterglow of his lovemaking. She felt safe from the world, but more than that, at peace with herself and who she was. She felt accepted for the first time in her life, and she felt a oneness with another being for the first time. That he was a vampire no longer mattered.

In a day or two, he'd either be dead or gone from her life. She didn't want to think about either possibility. She had shared something miraculous with him, and right now nothing else mattered.

SIXTEEN

Drago's left hand held the back of her head and stroked her hair. She caught a glimpse of the mark on his arm, and she had the strange impulse to kiss it. But she knew he'd only pull away from her if she did, so she lay still, moving nothing but her eyes.

He started talking, and for a moment she reveled in nothing but the silky sound of the soft words flowing over her. She quickly realized, however, that he was not telling a fairy tale this time.

"In 1478 Ivan the Great began his second invasion. *Great.*" Drago sounded the last word as if it were a piece of sour fruit he wanted to spit out. "When Ivan and his Muscovites invaded, they not only swept a land clean, but also a way of life. The city-state of Lord Novgorod the Great included thousands of square miles of wilderness beyond the Volga, and Ivan took it all—the land, the houses, all our possessions, even the churches. But he went beyond that. He took our independence and abolished all our democratic institutions. Go ahead and smile. It always shocks Westerners to learn what a grand democracy we were back then."

"And the people?"

"We were purged from the land like a disease. No one was exempt. Merchants, clergy, boyars—the aristocrats of the day—were all deported to the far wilderness. The land left behind was converted into service land and given to cavalrymen from Moscow. Reward for loyalty and service rendered. Even the archbishops of the independent Novgorodian church were replaced by Russian Orthodox leaders from Moscow."

"And you?"

She felt his chest rise underneath her with the long inhalation of a deep breath. She was sure this was something he never talked about.

"Princes, who had no great power to begin with, were certainly not exempt. Some went quietly. Many did not."

"I can imagine that you were not one to go quietly." She tilted her head and saw his mouth twist in a bittersweet smile.

"No, *cherie*. I did not go quietly. I would have preferred to die bravely in battle, but I was denied even that dignity. Many perished, it is true, but most who died did so not in battle, but by deprivation, hardship, and the ignobility of torture."

He was silent for a few moments, but she saw his Adam's apple work, as if he struggled with choosing his next words.

"So what happened to you?" Somehow she knew Drago would not kowtow to those who wished to conquer him. She was coming to know not only Drago's stubborn streak of independence, but the cruelty of the ancient Russians. A feeling deep in her gut told her they would make him pay dearly for his defiance. Pay with everything short of his life.

"Most who would not go quietly were taken before the Church. We were labeled heretics under any pretense the Orthodox Church could come up with, no matter how far from the truth it was. The Church was all-powerful. What I told you before about my eyes was no mere story, but the truth. They took one look at my eyes and proclaimed me one of the Undead. The supreme irony, for at that time I was still human. Solely by virtue of my blue eyes, I was deemed to have at least dabbled in black magic, or witchcraft, or, at some point during my life, have sold my soul to the devil. All of this, of course, was more than enough in their righteous eyes to prove I had seriously deviated from the teachings of the Russian Orthodox Church."

"What did they do with you?" She spoke softly, because her throat was already tight with the pain she felt in his voice.

"I was *cleansed.* Purified."

She waited for him to continue, fearing that if she said

anything he'd stop telling her the story.

"Over the centuries Russians have become very adept at unusual ways to torture without killing. The *knout,* for example. It was nothing more than a kind of flail—a wooden handle attached to a thick strip of rawhide that had been boiled in milk until it was as hard as metal. With only three strokes an experienced wielder of the *knout* could kill a man."

He paused and tilted his head away from her. She closed her eyes, but the images she saw in her mind were as raw and agonizing as his voice was. "They did that to you," she whispered, no doubt in her mind.

He nodded. "Six times. Just short of death. They only stopped because they didn't want me to die. That would have been too easy on me."

The scars on his back. There was more. She knew it. Her stomach knotted in anticipation of his words.

He turned to her and shifted her body upwards so that she could better see his face. "Look at my eyes, *cherie.*"

She looked at the incredible color, so unique. It was always the first thing her mind's eye saw when she thought of Drago.

"These blue eyes, which you seem to think have won me the adoration of females through the centuries, had me branded a heretic."

She stared at him.

"Branded. Literally. Like an animal." He held his left arm before her, his hand fisted, so that she could see the muscles and ligaments pop in his powerful forearm. He rotated his arm slowly so that she could see the mark. "A red-hot brand was pressed against my flesh and held there. This is the brand that has forever damned me as an outsider. The mark stands for 'heretic.'"

"It looks like an 'E.'"

"It is."

"I don't understand."

"In Russian the word is *eretik.*"

She drew a shuddering breath and reached a tentative hand to his arm. This time he didn't flinch or pull away, but allowed her to trace the ridges of the letter burned into his arm.

"I was banished to the north. Three years later, in 1481, I died and was reborn into the *Demi Monde*. The half-world of the Undead. So tell me. Was the Church right about me? Was I unclean—unholy—all along? Predestined to become a vampire? Or was it just a twist of fate? A coincidence?"

She was silent. She had no answer.

"No, I don't expect you to know. In over five hundred years I haven't found the answer. I don't suppose I ever will. But it still gives me nightmares."

"The nightmare you had in the hotel room."

He nodded. "I'm not sure what you heard me say, but I can still hear the bishop's words when he declared me one of the unclean. A blood-monster. Now do you understand why this was a story I was not eager to tell you?"

She dipped her head.

He folded his arm back down and slid it behind her. "I've only told one other mortal this story, and Nikolena also knows. I didn't tell her, but she knows what the mark signifies."

"I'm glad you told me. Thank you."

"Just one thing, *cherie*. Don't presume to think you know me because of one story. And don't feel sorry for me. I didn't tell you all this so you'd pity me or be more willing to give yourself to me. I could tell you many stories that would just as easily horrify you. Some that would no doubt send you running for another syringe of colloidal silver with which to purge the earth of me."

"I doubt that."

"Ah…no judgments, *cherie*. I am simply what I am."

There was nothing 'simple' in what he was. "Then why did you tell me the story?"

He paused, and his eyebrows quirked upward. "I don't know. Maybe so you wouldn't tell me again how beautiful my eyes are."

She frowned. She had forgotten how exasperating he could be. "I'll remember that," she said with as much dryness as she could muster.

"I'm not a knight, a savior, a villain, or a monster. And don't be fooled by anything you see. You can put a rhinestone collar on a tiger, but that doesn't make it a house cat. I'm a vampire, not a human, and anything you see that glitters of humanity is just a rhinestone collar. Don't forget that."

"I won't." She added a hard edge to her dry tone. What was he so afraid of?

"On to a new subject, then. The evening is yours, *cherie.* What would you like to do? I will take you anywhere you wish to go."

Personally she'd be happy with spending the evening in bed with him, but somehow she didn't think that would be such a good idea. She needed to get a grip on her feelings, and she couldn't do that with his naked body putting her hormones in charge of her brain. Besides, he seemed more amenable to conversation than he had been before. *Drago and amenable.* Those were two words she imagined were not often part of the same thought. She might do well to take advantage of his mood while she could, but she really didn't know where she wanted to go. She'd have to think about it. She looked him up and down, sucking on her bottom lip, but the contours of his body didn't inspire too many ideas other than under the sheets.

"I'm not sure. I'll take a shower, think about it and let you know." She leaned forward and kissed him once on the mouth, just to torture him for his comment about the cat. A house cat was the last thing she would ever compare him to.

An hour later she stepped quietly into the living room. Drago was pacing back and forth in front of the French doors, dressed in a white long-sleeved shirt and black trousers. Both made of silk, if she knew him. He turned toward her and froze. His feet didn't shuffle, and the fingers of the hand held at his chin stopped mid-stroke. Only the flick of the blue eyes she wasn't supposed to mention told her he was taking in every inch of her appearance.

She shifted her weight from one foot to the other, feeling more self-conscious in her floral bustier and skintight skirt than she had with no clothes on at all. No man had ever looked at her like this.

Finally he dropped his hand and glided up to her. "I've known a lot of women in my life, *cherie.* You make me forget them all."

She smiled, feeling her face take on a color she was sure would not look pretty with her tangerine skirt. "I bought this last year for one of my trips to New Orleans, but I never wore it." Maybe it had been modesty, or perhaps a lack of confidence, but Drago erased all those feelings now. She felt just as sexy and beautiful as the outfit.

"Where do you want to go?" he whispered, smoothing her loose hair over her shoulders.

"Well, there's a big restaurant called The Quay right over the river. I've heard they have dancing and live bands."

"This is really where you want to go? You know I'll take you anywhere in the world."

She smiled again. It was unrealistic, of course, but a pleasant thought. "You know I don't have a passport."

He curved his mouth in return, showing very white teeth and putting the smile lines to work. The deep creases dug out an otherwise invisible dimple on the right side of his face.

"It'll be fine, really. I don't go out much," she added.

The dimple disappeared with the fading of his smile. "'Much?' Not at all, I think. Come. We will fix that."

He escorted her to his car as though it were a royal carriage and she were Princess Marya of a fairy tale, decked out in satin and jewels instead of nylon and beads.

"You would really do that, wouldn't you?" she asked before he backed to the end of her driveway. "Take me anywhere?"

"Bien sur. Of course."

"But why?"

He cocked his head toward her, and a sickle of shiny, black hair fell over his right eye. "Because you've seen so little. There is so much beauty and art in the world. It would please me to see the joy on your face at such sights. For me, through your eyes, the world is fresh again."

That gratified her more than anything he had said earlier, even his claim that she had made him forget other women. For this remark showed an interest in life on his part, something she thought he had lost forever. It was a very un-vampire-like thing for him to say, and yet, she realized, it was just a pretty fantasy. And wasn't that what vampires were best at? Like ringmasters, they were experts at presenting flights of the imagination. Tonight, though, she was willing to indulge herself in the pretty pictures. It was all she would ever have.

"So if you could take me anywhere in the world, what would you have me see?"

He thought about it for a moment. "I would take you first to St. Sophia's Cathedral in Novgorod."

She raised her eyebrows. "A church? Don't vampires hate churches? And I would have thought that you especially…"

He cut her off. "I'm thinking what you would enjoy. St. Sophia is a thousand years old—even older than I am. The exterior is very austere—all in white—but it has five naves, six domes, and frescoes, icons and murals second to none in the world."

He had neatly evaded her question, but she pressed on. "Where in the world have you lived?"

"The past fifty years have been spent mostly working in your country. The early part of the century was spent in France. Before the Revolution I split my time between France and Russia."

"I was born in France. My mother moved us here when I was small, so I don't remember anything of the language or the country." She paused. "But you know all that, don't you? I told you that the first night you came to see me."

Had it really been only twenty days ago? All her thoughts and words to Drago that night came flooding back to her—her hatred and her frustration with her life. She had blamed it all on the Undead. She glanced at Drago's profile. Somehow the most despised vampire on earth had changed everything for her. The hate was gone, and she now accepted her heritage—all of it—her *dhampir* and vampiric blood as well as her Roma legacy. Was that to be Drago's final gift to her? What gift could be better? He had not only given her life, but *a* life. She had a past she could be proud of, and a future she could look forward to. It was more than she had ever had, and more than she could have ever hoped for. Yet when she looked at Drago she felt selfish and ungrateful. She wanted more. She wanted him.

She drew a silent, deep breath and leaned back against the leather seat. She couldn't have him, so there was no point in even thinking about it. His remark about humanity and the collar had been his way of telling her that, in spite of the union they had shared, he wasn't capable of love. But she had known that all along, hadn't she? From day one she had had no illusions about the nature of the being seated next to her.

She was silent for the remainder of the drive, but it was short. Five minutes later they were at the edge of the Garden District, and Drago found a parking space along the river. They exited the car, and if true feelings of love were foreign to him, the trappings of chivalry and romance were not. He took her hand in his, and even when they stopped to look at something, his fingers found a home at her waist or the small of her back. When they strolled, he didn't try to pull her along or even guide her, but adjusted his pace to exactly match hers. If she slowed, he slowed, and when she paused at some sight, he did nothing to hurry her along. Not that there was any danger in the quaint little town of Vicksburg, but it was reassuring to know that even if there were, he would allow no harm to come to her. More than that, his touch was a constant reminder that she was not alone. For someone who had led the lonely existence she had, nothing else he could do for her could mean more.

The low sun bathed the world in warmth and light, and when they could see the great river, it was like a rolling mirror, reflecting back all the color and grandeur of the evening sky. They arrived at The Quay, and Marya enjoyed an excellent meal of crab cakes and lobster, ordered at Drago's insistence. They sat on the open deck—built out from the rock and literally hanging over the river—and watched the sun go down. The ball of fire deepened from gold to coral to scarlet, and the sky and water took on each new cloak of color in its own unique way. The sky added shape and dimension with finger-like clouds of lavender and rose, and the water swirled the color in an ever-changing kaleidoscope of sapphire and gold. When the sun nudged the horizon, the western shore and everything around them was a silhouette of black, and only the edge of the sky and the river held any remnants of golden light.

Colored lights strung on poles and on the deck railings glowed with a bright gaiety, replacing nature's colors, and a blues band started playing inside the building.

The evening was indeed a fantasy. Between the large meal and the music, she hadn't been able to engage Drago in a lengthy conversation, but it didn't matter. Marya noticed several admiring glances from men who were out of Drago's line of sight. She didn't acknowledge any of the looks, but they made her feel good. Men had seldom ever paid attention to her, except for the occasional lout in New Orleans who had imbibed in too much alcohol. Marya could also hardly fail to observe the many female glances thrown Drago's way, which ranged from blatant stares to furtive peeks.

Maybe it was his jet-black hair and pale skin, but unusual as his coloring was, she didn't think it was that which drew the women's attention. She didn't even think it was his blue eyes. She was sure that Drago didn't care about any of the women in the room, so there were no come-hither looks, provocative body poses, or any other signals that men sent out to attract the opposite sex. No, it was something totally intangible. She hadn't had a lot of experience with men herself, but on her trips to New Orleans she had spent hours studying the subtle interactions between men and women. She had told herself it was so she could capture expressions for the subjects of her paintings. An observer of life. That's all she had ever been until now. Now she was a participant.

She smiled, looking at Drago and pretending the pleasure was due to the music. Did he know what he did to women? He had to. The sensuality that clung to him was more than akin to just another garment he could put on or take off. It was a natural part of him, no different from his skin or eyes. It was what had reached out to her the first night she had met him, undeniable even knowing he was the hated Anti-God of the Undead.

The band started playing a slow song.

"Come, *cherie*. Dance with me."

She hesitated, but this time he didn't let her have her way.

He stood, as if pulled by strings from above, and reached for her hand. He drew her to him, and in a heartbeat she found herself at the edge of the dance floor, pressed to him. She wound her arms around his neck, burrowing her hands through his thick hair to feel the skin of his neck against her fingers. She gazed past his head at the crowd and saw every female at the bar staring at them. She closed her eyes, hid a smile against his shoulder, and let her feet follow his, all the while breathing in his scent and feeling the hard muscles under his shirt rub against her body. Desire quickly flared low in her body, and by the hardness she felt pressing against her, she knew Drago was dealing with a similar reaction.

When the song was over Drago tilted his head and kissed her, just once, but as unhurried as if he had all night.

His kiss fired the ache she felt, but it was nothing more than pleasurable tension, and part of the evening's magic. The hours passed too quickly in slow dances and moments spent on the deck, watching the night sky above and the dark water below.

Both of them were quiet during the short drive back to her house. Marya leaned her head back against the headrest. She could only think about one thing—making love to Drago, without either the fear and momentary pain of the first time, or the overwhelming need and frantic pace of the second time. Tonight, this last time, would be, well…if not perfect, then as close to perfect as one could get making love to an Undead creature with no soul.

When Drago pulled the car into her long driveway, she lifted her head in anticipation. She saw the strange car caught in the headlights' beams just as Drago spoke.

"You have company."

He stopped his car well back of the strange one, shutting off the engine but leaving the headlights on. She pushed her door open, but his hand snaked out and clamped onto her arm.

"Wait, *cherie.* Stay here."

He let go of her and exited the car. She stayed in her seat, but continued to hold her door open so she could hear. A stranger stepped out from the driver's seat, and a too-familiar stink assailed her nostrils before she could hear any words. *It's a vampire*. A second later a woman exited the passenger side of the car. She heard Drago's voice, but he was speaking French. It didn't matter. Her eyes told her enough.

Drago's smooth, unhurried steps took him to the woman, and after a quick swap of words he held her in a gentle embrace. Marya sat numbly watching the strange exchange. After a moment she saw Drago look her way, and he motioned for her to come ahead. She did, shifting her gaze back and forth between Drago and the strangers.

"Ah, Marya, this is my assistant, Philippe Chenard, and a...good friend of mine, Adelle Duquesne. They've just arrived from Paris. Philippe, Delle, this is Marya Jaks."

Drago smiled as he made the introductions, but the curve of his mouth looked forced, and his words had seemed to snag more than flow like they usually did. These people were friends of Drago's, yet Marya felt a strange dynamic between the three. Like her, was he disappointed at the prospect of their postponed lovemaking? Despite her disappointment, Marya greeted the visitors politely.

Adelle took both her hands and squeezed. "We apologize for the lateness, and don't worry, my dear, we won't be staying over. We have a hotel room in town. It's just that I've been so worried about Drago I couldn't wait to see him," she said, her gaze anchored on the subject of her concern. Her English was good, but she had a strong French accent. She was a handsome woman, in her fifties by Marya's guess.

"It's fine, really. I'm sorry you had to wait. Come in, please." She unlocked the door, flipped on the lights, and led the group into the living room. "Make yourselves comfortable." She turned to Adelle. "Can I get you anything? I'm sure you've been sitting in that car a long time." Philippe was a vampire, but Marya knew Adelle was human.

It was Drago who answered. "Ladies, would you excuse us? Philippe and I are going to have a word."

The two vampires escaped to the rear patio, and Drago eased the door shut behind them with a definitive snick. Marya watched them until shadows swallowed their faces. Drago hadn't looked very happy.

"Come to the kitchen with me," she said to Adelle. "I'll make us some coffee."

Adelle smiled. "I'm sure Drago's going to give Philippe a dose of 'The Drago Way' for both bringing me from Paris and to your house. Philippe's instructions were to check into a hotel and contact Drago from there, but it wasn't Philippe's fault. I insisted on coming."

Marya had no idea what the woman was talking about, but she tried to keep her features neutral. She started water to boil, sparing several glances out the bay window, but the men were out of view. "'The Drago Way?'"

"Drago likes things done his way. Those who disobey can always count on a correction."

"I'll try to remember that. With Drago I'm getting used to the unexpected."

"I'm sure you are. Has he told you who I am?"

Marya sucked in a deep breath. Drago had mentioned Philippe and Nikolena, but no other women. "No."

"I would have been surprised if he had. He introduced me as his friend, and I am that, but much more. I'm his chatelaine. Do you know what that means?"

It was becoming obvious to Marya that she knew very little about vampires, and about Drago in particular. Marya set two sets of cups and saucers on the counter and turned to face Adelle. "Not really."

"I've been his servant for forty years. I take care of his chateau outside Paris, and I run all his affairs that aren't directly related to Directorate business. But it's more than that. I've pledged my life to him. I would die for him if he asked it."

Marya suddenly felt self-conscious standing there in the revealing bustier and sexy skirt. This was the woman in Drago's life. What must Adelle think of her? She spun back to the counter to hide her embarrassment, and poured water over instant coffee. "He's an extraordinary man. You must care for him a great deal." Her voice felt as tight as her clothes. She turned and offered a cup to Adelle.

Adelle's voice was soft. "He is. And I do. When I heard

the report and the details of the injuries he sustained in Phoenix, I had to see with my own eyes that he was all right. I also know that you saved his life. Thank you. I have the feeling that I'm not the only one who cares for him."

Marya felt her face flame even more. She blew on her coffee and tried to hide the heat of her emotions in the steam from her cup. This woman seemed to know a whole lot about her, and she, in turn, knew nothing about Adelle. Did Adelle know Marya was Drago's lover? Dressed in the provocative outfit, a guess on Adelle's part wouldn't be very difficult. How many other lovers had Adelle seen come and go in past years? Most likely so many that it didn't bother her to see one more.

"Am I right, Miss Jaks?"

"Call me Marya, please. And I'm sorry, but right about what?"

Adelle sipped her coffee. "You do care for Drago, don't you? A great deal, if I'm not mistaken."

Was it that obvious to someone who had only seen her for five minutes? She nodded. "You must think me pretty foolish. After all, in another day or two I'll never see him again."

"You're only foolish if you abandon your feelings for him."

Marya was about to reply when Drago and Philippe came in. Neither man looked any happier than before they had gone outside. Had Drago indeed given his assistant a tongue-lashing? Adelle also seemed to notice the lack of joy in the friends' reunion, because she was quick to squeeze Philippe's arm and give him a smile of encouragement before she stepped up to her master.

"Leksii, a private word, please?"

Drago didn't answer right away, but looked first at Marya, then Philippe. A slow burn seemed to fuel his stare, but what did he have to be upset about? Marya understood Adelle wanting a moment alone with Drago, though, even if it meant she would be alone with Philippe. Small talk after midnight with a strange vampire wasn't something she looked forward to.

Drago's gaze settled back on Adelle and seemed to soften.

"Outside, then, Delle."

The French door to the patio got another workout, and Marya was left to share the sofa with a vampire whose lingering gaze on the low neckline of her bustier made her feel more exposed than the garment did.

***

Drago's anger still threatened to boil over, but he didn't want to take it out on Adelle. "Philippe had no business bringing you here. I told him that in no uncertain terms."

"Please, Leksii, don't blame him. I insisted. And how can you be angry with him? He's the only one who supports you. Do you have any idea what he's been through the past few weeks? He's got the chiding of every vampire who passes through the Directorate to contend with, along with phone calls and letters of protest from every vampire you look sideways at. And not least of all, he's got Nikolena breathing over his shoulder and taking all her frustration with you out on him."

He stared past her through the door. Marya looked decidedly uncomfortable with the vampire in question. "How can I be angry? Easy. Because it's dangerous, and Philippe's brought you right into the thick of it. You'll be just another pawn for my enemy to use against me, and I've already got my hands full with Marya."

He saw Adelle's gaze flick toward Marya, who sat with her arms folded across her chest.

"Yes, that's quite obvious, isn't it?" asked Delle. Her voice took on a sharpness, and Drago wasn't sure if it was because of his anger at Philippe or his all too evident relationship with Marya. It wasn't like Adelle to be jealous of other women, but then again, his liaison with Marya was no mere vampire game, and he was sure Delle knew it.

"Delle…"

She turned back to him. "No, Leksii, I'm sorry. It's not for me to question your affairs of the heart. And this girl does love you. I hope you know that."

"L'amour?" He didn't want to be hearing this.

"Yes, love. Don't pretend you can't recognize it in others

just because you can't see it in yourself." Her voice lowered, but kept its edge. "Though it amazes me that any female with a brain strong enough to battle the army of hormones you set to raging can love an exasperating creature like you."

He smiled and smoothed back a strand of graying, blond hair that the breeze had curled across her face. "You did, *ma chere.*"

"Yes, I did. And sometimes, after forty years, I'm still astounded that I fell for you. You didn't bespell this girl, did you?"

"No."

"I didn't think so." Her voice softened at last. "What are you going to do with her?"

This was getting far too complicated. He had too many things to worry about right now. "*Mon chou,* even if I had the capacity for such tender reflection, I don't have the luxury of time for such things. Evrard Verkist is a very bad apple, but he didn't forge my order. Neither did Deverick nor any of the other Brotherhood bad boys."

"How do you think Philippe can help? He brought all the files, as you requested, but the order to have Marya terminated didn't come from your office. You know that."

He sighed. "There's very little I'm sure of, Delle." He glanced again into the living room. "Come. I think Marya needs rescuing from Philippe's charms."

Adelle put a hand on his arm, and the warmth of her touch threatened to bring memories of four decades ago to the present. Of course, forty years was no more than a blink in time for him, but for Adelle it was a lifetime. "A moment more, please, Leksii. It's the reason I wanted to see you alone in the first place. When I heard what happened with Verkist...well, it..." She paused, and Drago put a hand on her shoulder. "It was almost more than I could bear. I just want to know you're all right."

Dear Adelle. It had amazed him, too, over the years, that such a beautiful, strong woman as she could love a melancholy Russian who had lost his soul so long ago. He slid both arms around her and drew her gently to him. She didn't resist the move. In fact, he felt her joy in touching him in every part of the soft body that pressed against his. But he also knew that she would tolerate nothing more than an embrace. "Do I not look all right, *ma chere?*"

"You look magnificent, as you always do, and you know it." She pushed away from him. "Let me look into your eyes, Leksii. Your eyes cannot hide anything from me, and you know that, as well."

"Look, then, Delle, and satisfy yourself."

She gazed at him with an intensity and scrutiny that only Nikolena could best. After a full minute she smiled. "Hmm. I can see that you don't need my mothering after all."

He kissed her lightly on the cheek. *"Ma chere,* I shall always need you."

She pulled on a strand of his hair. "I won't be around forever. I think it's that Gypsy girl in there that you need right now." She glanced inside the house. "But at the moment I think she needs you. Philippe is not used to being around mortals. Especially beautiful females."

Drago gave a dramatic sigh and looked through the glass doors, but his sigh quickly turned to laughter. While he had been embracing Adelle, Philippe and Marya had risen from the sofa. Philippe had Marya backed against the wall. He didn't have her totally boxed in. He'd only braced one arm against the whitewashed drywall, but Phillipe's smarmy grin told Drago that he would like nothing more than to corral Marya. But Marya had fisted her skirt in each hand and pulled the material up to her thighs. Perhaps Philippe saw only skin, but Drago saw one knee cocked and aimed right at his assistant's manhood.

"Do you know, Delle, that Marya nearly killed me? And that she did manage to send some other poor bastard to *la Belle Mort?* I pity Philippe if he makes so much as one more wrong move."

Delle smiled as well. "Rescue him, then. Philippe has suffered enough tonight under the whip of your tongue. A knee in the crotch from a mortal would be adding salt to the wound."

"Very well, my pet. Only for you, though. Philippe's actions win him no pity points with me."

They entered the house, and Philippe immediately stood up straight.

Drago strolled up to Marya and looked his aide in the eye. "It would seem, *mon ami,* that you forgot to pack your manners when you left Paris."

Philippe raised both brows and stared back with hazel eyes that glowed with an almost golden fire. Logic may have told Philippe that Marya was an aberration with tainted blood, but that apparently hadn't mattered to Philippe. A beautiful mortal was a beautiful mortal, and Drago knew bloodlust when he saw it.

"Manners? She's nothing but an..."

"Careful, *mon ami.* You would be well advised to taste your words before you spew them out. Adelle is done with me. I will see you tomorrow. Call me in the afternoon, and we'll arrange our meeting—without the women."

He escorted them out the door, bid them good night, and moved the car so that Philippe could back out the driveway. A moment later he was back inside the house. Marya was opening all the windows and French doors.

"Your friend not only stinks, but his behavior is no better than that of an undisciplined child. I can't believe that man is your aide."

Drago smiled. "He's efficient, but he's used to dealing only with the Undead. I would venture to guess it's been a long, long time since he's been in a room alone with a human female who looks the way you look."

She sidled up to him and put her hands on his shoulders. "Is that some sort of backhanded vampire compliment?"

He slid his hands around her waist, and his lips pressed his answer against hers. "Philippe is very lucky," he breathed when he released her.

"Umm. Why do you say that?"

"Because if it hadn't been for Adelle, Philippe would have received either an excruciating lesson in comportment from you or an even more painful one from me."

Marya pushed away from him and her expression shifted

with the speed of an angry female. "You didn't tell me about her. Never even mentioned her. Is having a flock of lovers a Russian thing, a vampire thing, or just *The Drago Way?"*

The restraint that Nikolena had implored him to have was wearing thin, but Marya was not the person he wanted to lose it on. *The time will come, and soon, when I can abandon care and unleash the beast.* Until then, composure and control held the reins. Still, Marya's misconceived anger needed an answer. He sighed. "First of all, I would never betray Adelle's trust in me by discussing her with a mortal, any more than I would discuss my relationship with you with another vampire. Secondly, I have no other lover who knows me for what I really am. I haven't for ten years now. The others mean nothing. They're entertainment for the vampire, nothing more."

She slumped against the same wall that Philippe had thought to have her cornered against. "I'm sorry. I have no hold on you and no right to be jealous. There's so much I don't know…I don't know what to believe anymore."

He walked up to her and mimicked Philippe's move, yet taking it one step further. He leaned forward, and splayed the fingers of both hands against the wall on either side of her, effectively boxing her in. Thankfully she didn't look in the mood to shoot a knee at the bull's-eye on his body. "Marya, listen to me. The Russian might be evasive, and the vampire might lie. But Alek Dragovich tells you the truth. There is no one else in my bed who knows what you know."

He leaned even closer to her, and she bent forward to meet his kiss. All the passion and longing of her previous kisses echoed in the warmth and urgency he felt in her now. He pulled away just far enough to whisper in her ear. "Come, *cherie.* It has been a very long and frustrating evening. Let us hope there are no more interruptions to thwart our lovemaking."

She smiled against his cheek, and the simple gesture almost undid him. He pushed away from the wall and took her by the hand, leading her into her bedroom. He unbuttoned his shirt by practiced feel alone, for his eyes as well as his thoughts were all on Marya. There was serious thinking to be done later about tomorrow, but that was tomorrow. Right now the only thing on his mind was easing the tension that had been building in his body all evening long. He threw his shirt to a nearby chair and beckoned Marya with his eyes. It wasn't a compelling gaze—it didn't have to be. She came to him of her own accord.

Her hands rode up and down his chest as he unzipped her top, warming him in places her fingers didn't even reach. She helped him with her skirt, squirming out of the tight sheath like a snake shedding a skin. He helped her in turn with his trousers, but not much. Undoing his clothes was a skill he selfishly wanted her to perfect as much as possible on her own. There was so much he wanted to teach her...

He closed his eyes, chastising himself for his thoughts. He was assuming that he had time, as he had always had in the past, but it was now a luxury he might not possess for long. Time...the one thing the Undead take for granted more than anything else. He had always had it in abundance. Like too many rubles burning holes in his pockets, he had often squandered the hours of the day either in restless boredom or frivolous pursuits, but now that tomorrow hung so precariously, each moment seemed all the more precious.

Divested of their clothes at last, he pulled her to him, wanting to feel all of her body against his. And again, he pushed tomorrow away. He opened his senses to their fullest and moaned into her hair as the feel and sight and smell of her assailed him all at once. He pulled away long enough to step to the bed and stretch out on it. She was right beside him, her movements almost as quick as his.

He drank in her lustrous hair, flawless olive skin, and dark eyes. Especially her eyes. He saw desire—yes, a passion he had seen feeding many a woman's gaze—but in Marya's sable depths he also saw unfamiliar things. Vulnerability. Trust, something the vampire didn't inspire. When was the last time anyone had trusted him? Revelin Scott, perhaps, at *Fata Morgana* and, of course, Adelle. Did Nikolena even trust him? He doubted it. How was it possible this girl trusted him after so short a time?

He kissed her long and deep, as if he could thusly draw an answer from her. But her warm, wet softness conveyed his mind and body further from rational thought, not closer. His hands played over her shoulders, arms and back, and her smooth skin and tender curves were chords to the song of heat and life that sang to him. When he cupped her breasts and felt her arch up to him, the bloodlust rose in him, hard and unrelenting.

"Talk to me, *cherie.*"

"Talk? About what?"

The surprise in her voice was no shock to him. Talk always seemed to be the last thing women expected from him. "It doesn't matter. Just talk to me. Concentrating on the sound of your voice will help my control." He wanted to make the moments with Marya last.

"The first time you made love to me I saw things. Pictures in my mind. Unfamiliar things that weren't part of my past."

"What kind of things, *cherie?*" He whispered the question in between kisses to her soft flesh.

She hesitated, and he didn't know if it was because of the images she tried to remember, or because of what he was doing to her body.

"Some beautiful things. Wide rivers, rolling plains, deep forests, and tall buildings with golden domes rising above the trees. And art, beautiful art, with deep, dark colors, but very solemn and sad."

"Icons." He nestled his head between her breasts and tried not to think of all he had lost. "What else, *cherie?*"

He ran his hands down her back to her bottom, and she squirmed under him.

"Horrible things."

He lifted his head and hands to her face, but she tried to turn away from him. "It's all right, *cherie,* it's all right."

"No…there's fire and blood and death all around…" She shook her head, but he knew she was battling the images, not him. He held her tight. "Shhh. It's all in the past, far, far away. It can't hurt you, *cherie.* No more talk now. There's only pleasure now, no pain." He turned her face back toward his and kissed her mouth, his fingers feeling the tears that crawled down her cheeks. His ploy for maintaining control had backfired. He wanted her more than ever. He gave up any further attempt at restraint and buried himself in her warmth, letting the sensations of sheer ecstasy banish all thoughts of loss and suffering. Her warmth and life enveloped him and nourished him, but it was more than mere sustenance. Her unique combination of human and vampire blood that he had once thought of as tainted now thrilled him with its intoxicating mix of innocence and perception.

She moaned against his cheek, and her fingernails dug into his back, but he felt no pain. The vampire, unbound, emerged and took his fill of all he could, save her blood. But everything else was his, and he took it—her energy, her sweetness, and her unspoiled youth. He drowned himself in her until he could take no more. With a final thrust, he took his release. She cried out and clutched at him, then slowly relaxed, her own tension liberated as well.

He sagged to the mattress next to her and held her, waiting for the beast to submerge once more, sated in all but blood. With the release of his body, his mind drifted, at peace, thinking no thoughts of yesterday or tomorrow, but merely sunning, like a creature at ease, in the warmth of now.

Her voice stirred him. "Those images I saw. How did you do that?"

He thought a moment, readjusting his mind. "Your heritage, I think. It gives you a measure of control against the vampire. You have the ability to resist bespelling, yet at the same time it gives you the gift, if you so choose, to be open to our thoughts. It was the reason Scott was able to possess your mind so readily, and also the reason I was able to inject a part of myself into your memory. Like it or not, *cherie,* you are open to us as few mortals are. You have had this gift your whole life, I suspect, hated though it may have been."

He felt her head nod against his chest. "Yes. It was one of the reasons I was certain I'd be flagged for termination. It was a true shock that you gave me life. It still is."

He smiled. "It was a shock to a great many people, I fear."

"It's what started this whole thing, isn't it? And you still have a price to pay for it, don't you?"

"Yes. It's far from over." Thoughts of the next day were

already seeping back into his mind. "By the way, what did my friend Philippe say to you that had you ready to do battle with him?"

She scooted up on the bed so that her eyes were level with his, and she propped herself up on an elbow. "He's a prime example of why I've always hated your kind. He kept asking what I thought about you and what my feelings were. He also asked if I knew how you truly viewed me."

He hoisted himself on an elbow as well. "And how did you answer him?"

She smiled, her mouth and eyes alike dancing with a wicked delight. "I lied."

He laughed. "No more than what he deserved. What did you say to him?"

"I told him I hated all vampires, and that I was only pretending to go along with your fantasies out of self preservation."

His mirth faded. "A lie very close to the truth, I think, *cherie.*"

She looked at him steadily, her eyes not even blinking. "Once, maybe, not so long ago."

He reached out a hand and smoothed a wayward strand of hair.

"Drago, tell me something. Why were you so mad at Philippe? When he first arrived, I mean."

He fell back to the bed, drew a deep breath, and stared at the ceiling. "Because he brought Adelle into danger."

"She said it was because Philippe disobeyed your order."

He smiled, but it was a somber gesture. "Adelle knows me too well."

"Something was all wrong tonight. I could feel it in the air."

"Your perception is even more acute than Adelle's." He rolled to his side and looked at her. "Get some sleep, *cherie.* You're tired, and I have much thinking to do."

"I don't want to go to sleep."

It was late. He could see the weariness in her, and yet she fought to stay awake. For him. She knew, as well as he did, that this was their last night together. He told her the lie anyway.

"Rest then. I'm not going anywhere."

The vampire could lie better than any mortal could.

SEVENTEEN

Marya finally fell asleep in his arms. He looked at the bedside clock. Almost three in the morning. In less than twelve hours he would be meeting with Philippe. He would have to sleep, but first he would have to prepare his mind for the encounter.

He let his eyes drift shut. He was tired. It wasn't just the exertions of the past couple weeks, damaging as they were. He was tired of the game. In days and years past he had only thought about winning and pleasing himself in the process. His confidence had perhaps been arrogance, but he had never considered losing. He had never thought about what he had lost when his life had been taken from him so long ago. He had never mourned his humanity or his soul, had never lamented living the half-life of the Undead. Until now.

Marya had described the images she had seen that had come from his memories. The icons. The memories would always be present, but that's all they could be now. Memories. The reality was gone forever. It was the same way with the churches. They represented the antithesis of everything he was. The thought now of all he had truly lost hit him hard. For when he had passed through the mirror to the Other Side, he had left the essence of being Russian behind with his soul. In life, the icon had been an ever-present companion, the visualization of everything the Russian held most dear—compassion and love, the prevalence of justice, and the triumph of Good over Evil. But he was the Evil now, and all that the icons represented were gone forever to him.

But none of that was as important as what he could lose now—Marya, Adelle, his position in the Directorate, even his life, such as it was. The possibility of losing the game had never before been a consideration, but now it was the only thing on his mind. Maybe it was a sign he was getting too old to remain on top.

He looked down at Marya. She would not want him to give up, and he wouldn't. He would fight whatever battle fate had in store for him, but for the first time in his life he would do it for someone other than himself, for something other than his pleasure.

He fell into sleep at last with his arms wrapped around the only future he cared about. A future that would last no more than twenty-four hours.

***

He awoke to find the lamp on and Marya sitting a few feet from him, a large sketch pad in hand.

"You moved," she scolded with a smile.

He didn't know what to make of it. No woman had ever tried to draw his portrait before. On the other hand, it was already past ten, and he could ill afford the luxury of a sitting now. "I'm afraid you'll have to make do with what you already have, *cherie*. This promises to be a rather busy day."

She tilted her head. "It's all right. I'm almost done anyway." She closed the pad. "I just wanted to see if I could capture something on paper before you woke."

Now he was curious. "Capture what? And come, you cannot hide it away without showing me what you did."

She shook her head. "No, it's…it's personal. Besides, I don't know if I got it quite right."

He smiled. "I'll make you a deal. A kiss for a look."

She smiled in return. "You play dirty. You get both—the kiss and the look."

"I do what it takes. I'll tell you what. If I live through today, you can draw all the pictures of me you wish. Do we have a deal?"

She sighed. "You always get your way, don't you?"

He let his smile drop. "Not always. But today I hope I do. Come, *cherie*. It's a fair deal. We both get what we want." It was, in fact, a poor substitute for what he really wanted, but he had to take what he could get.

"Very well. Here." She opened the pad and turned it so he could see.

It was just a vignette done in pencil showing his head and upper torso against the pillow, but the contrast of light and shadow was dramatic. More subtle was the juxtaposition of life and death she had somehow managed to capture in his features.

He looked at her, but her gaze was on the floor, and her cheeks were full of color. "It's quite remarkable, *cherie.*"

She raised dark, gleaming eyes to his. "I was inspired. Come on. My turn."

He reached over, took her hand, and pulled her to the bed. "I am yours."

She leaned into him, and he parted his mouth for her. She caught his lower lip and sucked on it as though it were indeed a prize. "Mmm. Does that mean you're offering more than a kiss?" she whispered at last.

It was tempting, and though he was willing to offer himself, time was not his to give. "I would like nothing better, but I can't, *cherie*. Not now."

She sat up straight on the bed. "So, what's going to happen? You're just going to meet with Philippe?"

"Umm. Something like that."

Her lips pressed together in an acknowledgement of the vague answer, but she pursued in her quest for answers nevertheless. "Where?"

"I don't know yet. Not here, certainly, and not in some hotel room."

"What about Revelin's office? Isn't that what's it for? Meetings like this?"

He stood and went to the windows, pulling back the curtains and opening the blinds. "Ordinarily, yes. But this is no ordinary meeting. I'm getting close to the truth now, and whoever wants me dead knows it. Unexpected company may show up, and I don't want any mortals nearby who might interfere by calling the police or becoming hostage bait." It had been a lesson he had learned the hard way many times in the past, and as recently as earlier this month in New Orleans when the death battle of two enforcers had encompassed a myriad of human complications.

"It sounds like you don't trust Philippe."

He turned to her. "Now, *cherie.* What did I tell you about trust?"

Her smile reached him from the bed, as warm and sunny as the light that spilled in through the windows. "I get it. But where else does that leave for a meeting place?"

He sat next to her again. "I will need your help with that. I'm going to shower and dress. While I do, think of a place for me—quiet and out of the way."

She nodded. "And I'm coming along, right? You're not leaving me here." A note of harsh determination had crept into her voice, a reminder that she, like the sun, could be relentless.

He reached over and stroked one finger down the side of her face. He had already plotted this part of the plan. "No, I'm not leaving you here. But don't think you'll have any input or control over what happens. Revelin Scott will be keeping you safely away from the proceedings."

She flicked her gaze up and down his body. "Interesting. You don't trust Philippe, whom you've known for years, yet you trust Revelin after knowing him only a few days."

That extraordinary perception again. "It's not that I mistrust Philippe, but whoever wants me dead has had some connection to my office in order to so perfectly counterfeit my orders. As for Scott, he could have very easily left me to die at *Fata Morgana.* So, yes. I trust him." He stood up. "Go now, *cherie.* I have to make a call and get ready. Think of a good meeting spot for me, will you?"

She rose, and he kissed her once more before she left. He picked up his phone and called Scott.

"Scott."

"It's Drago. Are you ready for more games, *mon ami?*"

"I am. Are you?"

Even if he wasn't recuperated from the Arizona ordeal, he would never admit such to any vampire, even Scott. "I'm ready. Philippe Chenard is in town. I'll be meeting with him this afternoon. I'm working on the exact location now. I want you there with me, *mon ami.* Philippe has brought my servant, Adelle, from Paris. I instructed him that our meeting was not to include her, but I'm sure he'll disobey my orders. Marya will be there as well."

"I got it. You want me to be a bloody babysitter again."

"What I want is your help, *monsieur.* I don't ask for that easily."

"No, I don't suppose you do. I'm still in your service, Drago, so just name the place and time, yeah?"

"Come to Marya's house right away. By the time you get here I'll have details."

"I'll be there in an hour." The call disconnected.

***

Marya sat at the dinette table in the breakfast nook, staring at the drawing she had made. It was a gorgeous day outside, warm, clear and bright. She was sitting in her own house with a more cheerful future than she had ever had, and yet, as she studied the drawing, all she felt was dread. The uneasy feeling had crept over her last night at the sight of Philippe and Adelle with Drago, and even now, in the light of day, the anxiety persisted.

She hadn't liked Philippe. That was no great surprise. With the exception of Drago and maybe Revelin, she had never held anything but hatred for any vampire. Yet her dislike wasn't the source of her foreboding. It was something she couldn't put a cause or definition to. It was just there—slowly destroying all the thoughts of happiness she should be having.

And no scenario she could picture in her mind could put the dread to rest.

If Drago prevailed once more—and she was sure he would as he always had—he would be leaving her to return to Paris and his job. The thought of not seeing him again, of imagining him in the arms of other women, tore at her. Even if she could dismiss the selfish feelings of jealousy, there was his pain. She had felt it in his stories, in the images he had transmitted to her mind, and in his eyes. Those blue, blue eyes. A student of color, she knew every association for the color blue. *Gloomy and dreary. Strict. Aristocratic and patrician. Risque.* Somehow each of them fit Drago. And every one conveyed a pain she knew he'd carry with him the rest of his life. The despair she felt at that thought was as great as her green-eyed thoughts.

Would it be better, after all, if he lost this final battle? Her father had commented on the existence of the Undead many times in his journal. She knew many of the passages by heart, and one was: *The Evil Ones, in creating others of their kind, sow immortality, yet reap nothing but damnation. For surely it must be God's punishment to damn these creatures to loneliness, shadow, and the endless winter of an existence with no soul to guide it. For all their arrogance and grand trappings, they are but slaves to Mistress Death, and until one such as I can free them, they are forever bound to toil under the whip of destruction.*

Was her father right? Would Drago be better off meeting the True Death? Would he find peace, if not redemption, after hundreds of years of bearing the yoke of his unnatural life?

A movement at the periphery of her vision startled her, and she raised her head. He was standing in the entranceway to the kitchen, dressed in black jeans and a black-ribbed T-shirt. His hair was combed, but still damp. It might be a selfish thought, but she didn't want this magnificent creature to die.

"What? No silk or linen? No power outfit for your meeting with Philippe?"

He cocked his head. "If I were French, I suppose I would want to go out in style. I've no doubt Philippe will be decked out in his finest, but I have no need to try to impress him. Did you think of a place for our meeting?"

She nodded. "It's about an hour's drive from here, but it's what you wanted—quiet and out of the way. It's the Grand Gulf Military Park. It's got hundreds of acres. There's a museum and some historic buildings, but also lots of trails, camping facilities, and even a pavilion. There are never too many people there at any one time, so you should be able to find a private spot with no trouble. Here. I brought a map in from my car. It's easy to get to from here." She showed him the map and traced her finger down the line that was Highway 61. "See? It's just about thirty miles south."

A wide smile brought out his hidden dimple, and a wink

brought a return smile from her. "Good girl. It sounds perfect."

A half hour later Revelin Scott arrived, wearing faded, flared blue jeans and a sleeveless U-2 T-shirt. He somehow didn't quite look like a typical 'good ol' Suthun boy,' but with his youthful good looks and irreverent hair, he fit into the Mississippi landscape better than Drago did. Marya couldn't picture Drago fitting in no matter how he dressed.

Revelin had brought a pair of two-way radios with him. He gave one to Drago.

"Excellent. Listen, *mon ami,* when we get there, stay behind and out of sight if you can. I don't relish my opponents knowing you're there. If I should need you, I'll call on the radio. Come up in the car as quick as you can, but then leave the keys with Marya. Marya, if that should happen, take the car and get as far away as you can. *C'est compris?"*

"I've got it."

Shortly after that, Drago's phone rang. He didn't bother taking the call in private, but he spoke French, so the result was the same. However, he volunteered the contents of the conversation without her or Revelin asking.

"That was Philippe. I instructed him to meet me at one o'clock just inside the park entrance. I also told him not to bring Adelle, but I have no doubt he'll bring her."

"He's never been here, has he? I hope he finds it all right," she said.

"He's a big boy. He'll find it. We'll take two cars. I'll go in Scott's van, and the two of you will go in my car. *Cherie,* a word."

He led her into the guest room and closed the door. He paced the room once and stopped before her. His features were as solemn as ever. "Listen, Marya, and listen well. This is not a picnic in the park we're going to. It's business, and deadly business at that. No matter what happens, you're to stay with Scott and do exactly as he says."

She tilted her head back, not quite a dramatic head toss, but enough to let Drago know she wasn't happy with his words. "Don't talk to me as if I were a child. I know what this is about, and I think I proved in Phoenix that I can do as I'm told."

He stared at her, and for a moment she thought he would reply in anger, but a small self-deprecating smile curved one side of his mouth. *"Bravo, cherie!* I always admire those who have the heart to stand up to me."

She folded her arms in front of her. "Really? I thought defiance was always frowned upon and insubordination always punished."

"There's a big difference between showing the courage of one's convictions and the disrespect of disobedience. But I apologize, *cherie*. You did more than handle yourself well in Phoenix—you saved my life. And I know you understand the importance of this meeting. It's just..." The silky voice faltered, something which Marya hadn't often heard.

The anger went out of her, and she ventured a guess at his thought. "Just that you're concerned about me. But it's a lot easier for the vampire to chide than to admit to a human emotion like worry, isn't it?"

He smiled again. "Perhaps. But promise me..."

She cut him off, nodding her head. "Yes, I promise to behave myself and do everything Revelin says." It would be an easy promise to keep. She had no real wish to be anywhere near any meeting between Philippe and Drago. Her previous feeling of dread had only deepened, and she knew with a certainty that something was very, very wrong.

***

Marya sat in the passenger seat of Revelin's car, watched the lush beauty of the Mississippi landscape slide past, and tried to let the view instill a feeling of peace into her. The gently rolling hills and green sculptures formed by the ever-encroaching kudzu vine relaxed her. Each time it did, though, she'd turn her head and catch a glimpse of the van behind them, and a reminder of Drago's mission would disturb the serenity of the moment.

Revelin drove almost due south on The Great River Road, turning off at last on Grand Gulf Road. Marya, unlike the average Mississippian, cared little about the American Civil War, and had had little interest in the subject as a child. She had considered the war a *gadjikane* affair, and not relevant to either her own heritage or present life. However, it had been a subject oft-taught, and even with her passive attention she could not have failed to learn of Mississippi's role in the Late Unpleasantness. The battle of Grand Gulf, as well as the siege of Vicksburg, of course, had been regaled in each grade, and she had participated in more than one field trip to Military Monument Park.

"Have you ever been to Grand Gulf, Rev?"

"No. I've only been in Mississippi a month. How well do you know this place?"

"Pretty well. I've been here several times, but not for a number of years. Still, I know the roads through the park and how to get to the main attractions."

"'Attractions?'"

"The pavilion, cemetery, forts, things like that. Rev, do you know this Philippe?"

"Not really. I've met him a few times at the Directorate office, but that's about it. I used to work in England for the Circle. I tried to avoid Directorate entanglements as much as possible."

"Do you know how powerful he is?"

"Any vamp chosen for the Directorate, even in the role of an assistant, has to have power and influence, or they aren't chosen. Not to worry, though. I wouldn't put the bugger in Drago's class."

"We're almost there. The entrance is just ahead. Let Drago pass. He can't miss it from here."

With his hand, Rev motioned out the window for Drago to pass, and a moment later the van pulled ahead of them. Revelin dropped his car back, still keeping the van in sight but careful not to follow too closely. When Marya saw Drago pass through the entrance, she told Rev to pull over to the side of the road. A few moments later Rev's radio crackled.

"Scott?"

Rev picked up the radio. "Yeah, Drago."

"Philippe's here. He's in a silver coupe, and it looks like he's alone. I'm going to lead him down the road to the historic tour, as Marya suggested. Stay just inside the park entrance unless I call. When I stop I'll try to give you an exact location. Keep a watchful eye, *mon ami.*"

"Understood."

Marya and Rev pulled inside the park and into the first parking lot they came across. Rev kept the engine running and the air conditioner on, but the difficult game of waiting had begun. Grand Gulf, once thriving, was now all but extinct. She prayed the same thing didn't happen to Drago.

***

Drago stopped the van in a deserted spot sheltered by giant moss-covered oaks. Historical markers on posts stood as solitary reminders of events and days long gone. He radioed Scott with his position, exited the van, opened the rear doors, then strolled to Philippe's car. Philippe swung his door open and flowed out, rising to his full height like a swirl of golden smoke. With his neatly styled copper hair, hazel eyes, and butter-colored brocade vest, Philippe was a vision of sun-drenched elegance. Drago smiled. It was exactly how he had expected Philippe to dress. Drago took a quick look inside the car. Adelle was not there.

Drago reached out a hand in greeting. "Philippe, my old friend. I failed to say so last night, but it's good to see a familiar and welcoming face. You brought everything?"

Philippe's bland expression hardly looked welcoming, but at least his gaze didn't have its usual weary, put-upon cast. Instead, his gaze flickered over Drago's apparel. When a small smile finally curved his thin mouth, Drago suspected it was more in amusement at his uncharacteristic casual dress than in any gesture of welcome.

"Of course. It's all in the trunk."

"Bring the files into the van, then, where we can be comfortable."

Philippe easily hauled a carton of paperwork into the van. "I don't know what you expect to find, Drago. I tell you, there's nothing here."

Drago looked through the tightly controlled book containing copies of all Drago's orders. They were all numbered in sequence. He flipped back an entire month, but no numbers were missing or duplicated. "Very meticulously kept, *mon ami,* as always. However, I saw the faked order that Verkist had. My seal was on it and a very good imitation of my signature.

Not only that. The paper was Directorate stock. I'm sure of it."

Philippe shrugged. "Anything can be duplicated. Look how easily currency is forged."

"That doesn't help me, *mon ami*. I need both your insight and some helpful suggestions. Who, for instance, has my seal?"

No dismissive shrug this time, but a lazy arch of dark brows. "You and I, of course, and Nikolena. And, I would assume, Adelle."

"Yes. Adelle has one."

"Your chateau has lots of…visitors, if I may so delicately put it as such. Perhaps one of them was light-fingered. Or perhaps Adelle…"

"No. What about your office? What's the possibility someone borrowed my seal when you were away?"

"I suppose there's a chance of that. Everything is kept locked, but locks can be picked, just as documents can be forged. Know any picklocks?"

As a matter of fact, he did. Someone taught well by the mean streets of Dublin. Revelin Scott. Scott had been transferred about a month ago, just before all this madness started. The transfer would have meant a visit to the Directorate head office and an audience with Nikolena. Everyone seeing Nikolena goes past Philippe's desk. *And Scott has the attribute of possession.* During his visit he would have had both the skill to steal the seals and paper stock himself and the ability to control another vampire's mind to do his own bidding. Drago himself had admitted that he had not met a vampire as powerful as Revelin Scott in a long, long time. *And I've just left Marya in his care.*

Philippe was waiting for an answer. Drago wasn't ready to make a judgment—not yet. Nor was he ready to reveal his hand. The vampire lie was always best. "Half the enforcers in this country are probably picklocks from Great Britain or Europe, but no one specifically comes to mind. What about you? You see everyone who comes through the office."

Philippe nodded. "True, but I don't exactly hold revealing conversations with any of them. Most who come my way do nothing but complain to me about you."

Drago took a deep breath. *"Oui, bien sur."* His mind drifted back to Phoenix and *Fata Morgana*. Scott had saved his life. Why save it then if his intention was to see Drago die the True Death? Or was there some other objective better served by Drago's death occurring at a different time and place? What motive could Scott even have for wanting him dead? Until a few days ago, he had never met the man. Perhaps Scott wasn't working on his own, but under someone's direction. He couldn't have been working for Evrard Verkist, though. He had betrayed Evrard too thoroughly for that. *This is getting too complicated.*

Drago stepped out of the van into the shade of the oak trees and motioned for Philippe to join him. "What about Nikolena herself, Philippe? Does she want rid of me enough to go to such trouble?" He didn't really believe that Nikolena had anything to do with it, but he wanted to keep Philippe talking while he tried to think.

"It would be treason for you or me to even consider such a notion. You know that."

Drago waved a dismissive hand. "Yes, yes. I know. But this is just between you and me, Philippe. Is she capable of such a thing? A political move to get rid of me without appearing to turn her back on one of her own?"

"Good God, Drago. Such a thing is unprecedented. Unthinkable."

All of it was unthinkable. And yet someone he trusted was behind all this. "Well, Philippe?" Drago turned and faced Philippe, his gaze riveted onto his aide's face. "What other possibilities are there? No matter how unthinkable?"

Philippe's eye caught his. "I'm surprised you haven't named me as a suspect. Am I not the obvious one?"

"Too obvious, I should think. Besides, you're my right hand, my confidante. Part of *l' alliance*. My friend."

Philippe smiled broadly. Only white teeth filled the space encircled by the dark mustache and goatee, prominent among which were extraordinarily long eyeteeth. The display was not lost on Drago. "I don't know which reference amuses me more, Drago, *l'alliance* or the human concept of friendship. Tell me, did you consider me your friend or yourself my friend?"

Drago smiled as well, but showed no teeth. "Such things are mutual, I thought. But you are right. A human notion. Nothing like that binds us, does it, Philippe?"

Philippe's smile faded, but his eyes took on the lost passion. "The vow of *l'alliance* did. At least I thought so. Do you remember 1875, Drago?"

1875. *L'alliance* had been three men—Drago, Philippe Chenard, and Ricard De Chaux. Drago had just been promoted from the *Coterie* to the Directorate. De Chaux held the position of Paramount in the *Coterie,* and Chenard was the head enforcer for De Chaux's region of Champagne-Ardenne. Alliances were common up and down the rungs of the hierarchy, but Philippe was right—they had nothing to do with a shared past, friendship, or trust. At best such partnerships were masked with a veneer of camaraderie and dependence, but they existed for one reason only. Advancement. Still, a formal alliance was a serious affair, and any vampire who betrayed his partners usually found himself on the pointy end of retribution. Drago had no trouble remembering Paris in the fall of 1875.

Three men sat in the salon of the private club operated by the Coterie. Two were Frenchmen, and the third was the adopted French son, the Russian, Alek Dragovich. All three were elegantly turned out—Philippe, perhaps, most of all. He wore a shawl collar, double-breasted waistcoat of buttercream satin, and a small white neck tie. Drago was all in black and white, the only spots of color his sapphire collar pin and lavender gloves. Only the tall, broad-shouldered De Chaux, with his mane of bronze hair uncharacteristically tied back, looked uncomfortable in the pretension to beauty and elegance.

Philippe, the most eager, spoke first. "We're agreed then, yes? We will support you unconditionally, Drago, and you, in return, will ensure that your coattails are broad enough to carry us with you to Directorate standing." Drago studied each of them in turn. Philippe, despite the frivolous ornamentation of his outward appearance, weighed a glance on Drago as cold and calculating as round shot aimed at the heart. De Chaux, nicknamed le docteur la mort, Doctor Death, by his peers, sat with the stillness of his namesake. Since there was no trusting the future actions of either man, Drago could only look to their past deeds. The two men were opposites. Philippe was efficient and relentless in his work, but his way with words far outclassed his way with people. Ricard, on the other hand, was a chameleon. He could blend into society with grace and good humor, or he could stand out with the presence of a force to be reckoned with. But he lacked Philippe's fire.

"I agree to nominate and back both of you for Directorate positions. Ricard, your vow?"

The Doctor's hazel eyes were as ever-changing as his demeanor—at different times green, gray or golden. His gaze rested lighter on Drago than Philippe's leaden stare, but no less steady. "I will always be yours to command, Drago. You have my support."

"Philippe?"

"I will back you and assist you in any way I can."

Drago stood. "We have an alliance, then, gentlemen. Our toast." He raised a goblet shimmering with the dark fire of life.

Philippe and Ricard both rose, and each in turn lifted a goblet.

Drago gave the toast. "The oaths of an alliance are sacred. May we all keep our vows and prosper in the effort. To l'alliance!"

The crystal chalices rang against each other, the blood was downed, and the pact sealed.

Drago studied Philippe now as he did then. "I never broke my vow. I backed De Chaux for Patriarch all I could. And you, Philippe—you wear the mantle of Directorate status."

"As a clerk!" Chenard's fists were balled at his sides as tightly as his words were flung.

Drago gave a casual shrug of one shoulder. "You have no people skills, *mon ami*. Everyone knows it. Your wretched tête-à-tête with Marya last night showed that hasn't changed."

"She's...an...aberration!" The three words were drawn

out, as if Philippe were trying to explain a basic fact of life to a child.

Drago turned his back on his aide both to hide his anger and give him time to calm it as well. He wandered to one of the markers. Confederate rifle pits. *Brother against brother.* His suspicions had proven true. Perhaps this was a fitting setting after all. What was this, if not brother against brother? He stared at the faint depression in the ground, grass covered and green with life. He must do no less now, nearly 140 years later, than what these soldiers had done. He must dig in and persevere.

He took a deep, cleansing breath and walked slowly back to Philippe.

"Nevertheless. I did all I could for you. I never broke my vow. Why do you break yours now in this ill-begotten attempt to have me killed?"

Philippe laughed. "How did you know?"

"As you said, you were the obvious choice. No one else could have executed the forgery so precisely. Your own meticulous attention to detail gave you away, *mon ami.* But why? I never broke my promise to you."

A muscle twitched under the fair skin. Somehow Philippe's passion seemed at odds with the perfection of his fussy grooming and appearance. Perhaps it was just that Drago had never seen him display anything other than cool efficiency.

"You don't have any idea what I've had to endure these past fifty years, do you? The consequences of everything you did fell on me. Me! Not you. I've suffered the fallout day after day, while you travel in blissful ignorance of your actions. And when you do come to Paris, you spend more time at your pleasure than business, then complain when you have to spend a moment under Nikolena's lash."

"What can you hope to accomplish with this, Philippe? What is it you want?"

"It's not just me, Drago. I'm part of a new alliance now. We all feel your time is past, and we want your position opened up. I don't expect to be chosen as an enforcer, but there are others I back who would do your job and get the results without the mess to clean up afterwards."

Drago stood silent. Had he really been so blind as to what had been happening around him? Or had he sensed it and just not cared? How many were in this 'new alliance?' Even if he dealt with Philippe, how many more would come after him?

"Answer one question for me. Is De Chaux part of your new alliance?"

"No. He cares nothing for the Directorate now."

Drago was glad. He had always had a true liking for Doctor Death. "Or perhaps it is just that *he* remembers *his* vow?"

Philippe ignored the barb. "Enough of this. It's time."

"Time for what? You can't kill me, Philippe. Not and get away with it."

Philippe smiled the carefree grin of one without a worry in the world. "We shall see. It is my hope that you will take care of matters for me."

Drago hadn't feared this encounter with Philippe. Perhaps it had been the 'death wish' Marya had talked about, or maybe it was just a feeling of inevitability—that whatever was to happen would happen. But now a new sensation of dread stole over him. Philippe would not have been so rash as to proceed without a plan. *Adelle.*

"Say what you mean, Philippe. I am in no mood for guessing games."

"Ah, but it is my game we play now, isn't it? But it's simple. End your own existence, and your women live."

Was he serious? End his own life? "If I die, no matter how I die, Adelle, as my servant, will perish as well. The bond between us is too great for her to survive without me. You know that."

"I do. But last night was very enlightening. It became all too clear that there is another mortal you care for, though for the life of me I don't know why. Take your own life, and the aberration lives. Force me to kill you, and both women die as well."

The feeling of dread deepened, pervading his mind and body like a disease. He felt light-headed, almost dizzy, yet his feet felt mired in iron boots. "You may have Adelle, but I have Marya."

Philippe laughed again. "You say that as though you don't really believe it. But go ahead—find the truth."

Drago slowly pulled his radio from his pocket and depressed the call button. "Scott."

"Yeah, Drago."

"You have Marya?"

"Of course."

Philippe stroked his goatee, a wisp of a smile curving one side of his mouth. "Are you reassured, Drago?"

He didn't answer.

Philippe held out one hand, curling his fingers in a 'come hither' motion. "Give me your radio."

Drago wasn't about to hand over his lifeline to an enemy. "How long have you known me, *mon ami?* Almost two hundred years? Do you really think I'm going to lay down and die for you?"

Philippe laughed. "Oh, I think I know you better than you know me. The radio is of no matter." He pulled out a cell phone and hit a programmed number. "Scott? Chenard. Bring the car and the girl up right away." He disconnected the call and hit another button. "Bring her. Now."

Seldom before had Drago felt not only so totally helpless, but so frozen by indecision. Once upon a time he would have never hesitated, but would have lashed out at his enemy with every bit of his power. And he would have shown no mercy. At another time, in another place, Philippe would be dead by now, his spine severed and his heart torn out. But now Drago merely stood, his anger having no outlet, his energy having no clear course of action. So he controlled both as tightly as he could. The result was a feeling of numbness in his limbs where there should have been quickness, a conflagration in his mind where there should have been cold clarity.

He stood, powerless, and watched Scott's car pull up the narrow track, stopping about twenty-five feet away. He saw Scott say something to Marya and saw her shake her head in disagreement. *She knows something is wrong.* Suddenly she looked through the windshield at him, a question clear in her raised brows. He made no sign to her. She shook her head in confusion, took one more look at Scott, then shoved the car door open and jumped out, running back down the road. No mortal can outrun a vampire, though, and in seconds Scott caught her. He slowly escorted her back to the group, gripping both Marya's arms behind her back as if she were handcuffed.

The deadness Drago felt extended to his voice. He could only stare at the young enforcer and focus all the accusation and rage at the vampire's betrayal through his eyes.

If Scott felt any of it, he gave no outward sign. "Make one wrong move, Drago, and I'll bloody well kill her right now."

Marya's eyes were dark saucers filled with confusion and disbelief. They pleaded with his, but he had no answers to give her.

A high-pitched laugh, almost like that of a hyena, escaped Philippe's lips. An undignified sound, but he didn't seem to care. "You look surprised, Drago. I can't tell you how much that pleases me."

"I suspected that either you or Scott was behind the forgery. It never occurred to me that it would be both of you." The honest statement was a tactical mistake, and Drago knew it, but no lies slid from his tangled thoughts to his tongue.

Patches of afternoon sunlight poked through the oaks and lit Scott's head, warming the color of his shaggy hair to a gleaming bronze. The blue eyes, though, shone pale and cold. "Sorry, Drago. This *cocky bogtrotter* found a better offer than to be bloody babysitter to an aberration."

EIGHTEEN

Marya had sat in the car with Revelin, trying to convince her heart and pulse that she was perched calmly in the middle of a nineteenth-century time capsule, not running the New York City marathon. The sound of the cell phone ringing startled Marya and accelerated her heart rate even more. She turned to Scott as he unclipped the phone from his belt and answered it. The conversation lasted only seconds, and Revelin answered with only 'right' before disconnecting the call. He put the car in gear and started driving up the road.

"What's happening? Who was that?"

He didn't look at her. "We're wanted."

Something didn't make sense. "Why did Drago call when he was just on the radio a moment before?"

"Mine to obey, not question."

She panned her gaze through each car window, even turning to look behind them, but all was as it should be for a peaceful sanctuary. *But there will be a battle today.* She was sure of it.

"Rev, something's wrong, isn't it?"

"Just stay close to me, Marya. Everything'll be rum."

She looked ahead and saw the van, its rear doors thrown wide open. Drago and Philippe stood nearby, watching their approach. Revelin stopped the car well back of the van.

"Get out, Marya."

She stared at him and blinked. "Drago said for me to stay in the car."

"He wants you out there, now."

She shook her head. "No. Something's going on." She looked out the window at Drago, silently begging him for direction, but he stood as motionless as one of the park's monuments.

"Get out of the bloody car, Marya. Now."

She swung the door open, pushed off from the door frame, and ran back down the road, not looking back. She hadn't taken twenty steps, though, when Scott's hand grabbed her arm and jerked her to a halt. Her breath came in gasps, and she couldn't get enough air. "No..."

He held her tightly and pulled her to him. "Shut up and calm yourself down! Just do as I say, yeah?"

Before she could think to fight, he had her arms bent behind her back and marched her back to Drago and Philippe.

Revelin's voice grated in her ear. "Make one wrong move, Drago, and I'll bloody well kill her right now."

After that she heard none of the taunts. All she could see was Drago's staring eyes, their blue touch as empty as she had ever seen them—bare of power, uncomprehending. The look scared her like nothing else ever had.

Philippe started talking again, and she tried to concentrate on his words.

"Really, Drago, you shouldn't be so surprised. I've been planning this for months. It was I who long ago planted the seeds with Nikolena to have Scott transferred from the Circle to the Brotherhood. Over time she came to think of the idea as her own. Not a small feat for someone with no people skills, wouldn't you say, Drago?"

He didn't answer.

Why doesn't he do something? Marya wondered, bewildered. But the answer came to her as quickly as the question had formed. *Because of me. Fear for me has him frozen.* Her own tongue was plenty loose. She twisted in Revelin's grip.

"You lying, two-faced bastard. How could you?"

Revelin laughed. "Is that the best you can come up with? I was called worse when I was still bloody human."

She heard a car engine, and everyone turned as another vehicle pulled up behind the car. A dark-haired man exited the driver's door, glided to the passenger side, and pulled

Adelle none too gently from her seat. Adelle's furrowed brow and darting eyes showed the same bewilderment Marya herself had felt a moment ago. The man held Adelle in front of him with one arm around her neck and the other around her waist. Adelle's mouth worked silently, but no words came forth. Her eyes, though, were everywhere, finally settling on Drago.

Marya looked to Drago as well, but it was Philippe who spoke. "Excellent. Now that we are all assembled, you can see, Drago, that like it or not, you really have no choice. Perform the deed, and I'll let them live."

Drago shook his head and started circling Philippe slowly. "No, you won't let them live. Marya will have seen too much, and Adelle will die anyway. I do have another choice, and that will be to take as many of you with me to *la Belle Mort* as I can, starting with you, Philippe."

Philippe was quick to respond, backing up with each step that Drago took in his direction. "I'll cloud the girl's mind. She won't even remember today."

"She has *dhampir* blood. She won't cloud."

"Then how's this for incentive? End your life and they both will die quickly. Fight me and they will be subjected to every pain and indignity my imagination has concocted in three hundred years." He glanced at Marya and Revelin. "But of course all the members of the new alliance will share in the spoils. That would please you, Scott, wouldn't it?"

"Bloody right. Taking anything belonging to Drago would please me."

All the names Marya had called the enforcers that had interviewed her over the years came flooding back to her. "You damned abomination! Unholy perversion of everything right and just!"

Philippe frowned. "Scott, do us all a favor and shut her up, will you?"

Revelin pulled up on her arms, and she cried out, but more in anger and despair than pain. A draft of chill air washed over her, and Marya could barely breathe, but she knew it wasn't Revelin's doing. The warmth and fresh air of the glade was gone, replaced by a suffocating shimmer of energy that made the hairs on the back of her neck stand up and cold sweat run down her spine. It was the aura of vampiric power, and there was only one vampire here with enough age and authority to exude such a tangible force.

They all felt it, for all eyes shifted to Drago before he even spoke. "Chenard, I promise you one thing. Regardless of whatever else happens here today, you will die. That is no pretty vampire lie, *monsieur,* but truth, bald and ugly."

The words crackled through the air, sending a shiver through Marya's body, but before Drago could make good the promise, Scott's voice rang out like a gunshot. "Drago!"

Drago's gaze shifted from Philippe to Revelin. The vertical groove between Drago's brows extended well up into his forehead, and his blue eyes were rounded with the look of a madman. *The bloodlust,* thought Marya. Philippe would die, but she had no doubt she would perish as well. Drago couldn't save both her and Adelle, and Marya knew that his first loyalty was to his servant.

Eddies of cold chased through the trees, bringing darts of pain she felt on her face like frozen rain driven by the wind. She gasped for air and wanted to turn her face away from the stinging assault, but she couldn't. Her gaze was riveted on the source of the storm, and there was no escape.

"Mon ami, don't think I have forgotten you. Philippe will have company on his journey to *la Belle Mort."*

Revelin snaked one arm around her neck in a perverted embrace and laid a cheek against her hair. A staccato burst of laughter peppered her ear. "Drago, listen to me! In my life, I have prayed but one prayer: 'Oh Lord, make my enemies ridiculous.' And God granted it."

A strange stillness settled, and Marya felt a shift in Drago's aura. She drew a deep breath at last and waited, watching Drago's mad dog eyes. They were still on Scott, as if Philippe all of a sudden had ceased to exist.

"Do you understand, Drago? You have but one bloody choice. Finish it."

There was a tension in Drago's face that released, and Marya saw a subtle shift in his eyes, but she couldn't decipher what the change signaled. *Resignation? An acknowledgment? But of what?* His earlier display of power hadn't frightened her, but this strange calm did.

"You are right, *monsieur.* I will sacrifice no more innocents to my lust. When we have lost everything, including hope, life becomes a disgrace, and death a duty."

She understood all too quickly. "No!" This time the shout ripped from her own mouth. "No, Drago. You can't!"

Drago ignored her, turning to Philippe. "What instrument of death would you have me use?"

Adelle's anguished cry sounded behind Marya, echoing her own feelings. "Leksii, don't, please. Let them take me, but save yourself!"

Drago looked past her to Adelle. "No, *mon chou.* We will do this with dignity, if nothing else. What weapon, Philippe?"

Adelle was crying now. Marya felt too stunned to cry.

"Nothing less than a death's-head would be appropriate in this case, I think," said Philippe, the gloat in his voice adding to the pain his words caused.

"Bring it, then."

Philippe seemed to float to his car, his steps as light as air. He opened the trunk and took out a long bladed weapon. When he returned to Drago, he held the apparatus point up and rotated it for Drago to see. Marya recognized the instrument from her father's journal. It was a Vampire Hunter. For those who stalked vampires, it was salvation. For the Undead it was the wicked manifestation of mortality. Death. The most ancient of weapons for the killing of vampires. This one appeared to be of silver instead of wood, and was elaborately carved. The sunlight winked off the silver blade with white fire.

"One condition, *monsieur.* Allow me to say my farewells."

Philippe held onto the polished, wooden handle and brandished the death's-head as if he were about to fight a duel with it. "Agreed. A small enough price for your true death." He motioned with a jerk of his head for Scott and the other vampire to bring her and Adelle closer.

Marya was able to get a closer look at Adelle and the vampire holding her. Adelle had stopped crying, but silent streams of tears still coursed down her face. The vampire was one Marya didn't recognize. He was about Drago's height, with short dark hair and a small goatee. He still held Adelle firmly to his body.

Drago took a step closer to Adelle, prompting the strange vampire to speak for the first time. "No closer, Drago."

Drago halted. "Reno. A pity you're involved in this."

Reno laughed. "That's rich. The great *enforcier* having pity on a brother. Say what you want to say to the woman."

Drago ignored him and shifted his attention to Adelle. *"Mon chou..."*

She started to cry softly again. "Leksii, please don't do this. I beg you."

"It will be all right. No good-byes, *ma chere*. Do not be afraid. It will be over soon." He turned and took a step in Marya's direction.

Revelin pulled her backwards. "That's far enough, Drago."

Drago's feet brought him no closer to her, but the power of his blue gaze reached out and touched her as if he were but inches from her, sending a torrent of shivers raining down her back. There was no sadness in his eyes, only a calm acceptance of his fate. A fleeting image of the warrior Ilya flashed through her mind. *Drago, like Ilya, at the end of the final road.* The thought robbed her of strength, though, and if Revelin hadn't been gripping her so tightly, she would have collapsed to the ground. But she would not cry.

"My brave little Roma. What I do is right, *cherie.*"

She didn't know what to say. If Adelle's heartfelt pleas couldn't sway him, clearly nothing she could say would change his mind. "Damned vampire," she breathed.

"Do one thing for me, *cherie*. Forgive your grandfather." His gaze shifted just slightly, and she knew he was fixing a long stare on Revelin.

An instant later Drago stood once more before Philippe. In one fluid motion Drago peeled his T-shirt off and tossed it to the ground. "The finale, then, to this macabre play, Philippe."

She watched the bright badges of sunlight dance over the lean torso she had so recently adored with her lips and hands.

He had reeled in the power he'd cast out moments ago, and his eyes had lost some of their mad light, but the muscles of his abdomen and arms were still contracted with tension. More images marched across her mind like the shutter of a camera opening and closing. Drago, being declared unclean and unholy. Drago, officially damned by his fellow man. *Branded a heretic for all eternity.* Her mind saw the glowing brand forced against human flesh. She heard the hiss of living tissue seared by unbearable heat. *He would not go quietly, then.* She stared, holding her breath.

Philippe struck a pose with the death's-head held at an angle, his arm cocked as if waiting to deliver a blow. "No, Drago, I'm not going to hurry. I've waited too long for this moment. I'm almost tempted to do the deed myself, but it's better I don't. This way I can never be accused of murder, and I have two witnesses who will swear you took your own life on my command without so much as a compelling glance." He paused, rocking the flat of the blade lightly against his right shoulder. "My reputation will be cemented forever with this one act. Perhaps I'll be chosen for your spot after all."

Drago reached out a hand. "Then do it. Give me the death's-head."

Philippe smiled. "In good time. I'll be savoring the memory of this moment for decades to come. I want it to last." With that Philippe brought the blade forward and drew the point across Drago's chest. The touch was light enough not to draw blood, but the cords in Drago's neck stood out with the pain of the caress. The silver blade continued to stroke Drago's skin like the hand of a lover. He emitted no tortured cry, but she knew the narrowing of his eyes and the tightening of the lines in his face showed only a small part of the agony he felt.

Philippe raised the tip of the blade to Drago's face, tracing a line of fire down across his cheek and throat. Then the blade flashed, a blur of white so blinding she had to turn her head away. Drago's silence was finally ruptured by a groan of agony, and when Marya looked back at his face, blood ran down both cheeks.

Marya struggled in Revelin's grasp, but his only reaction

was to clinch her tighter than before. Her breath gone, she sagged against him. *It doesn't matter what happens now. I've already died.* She closed her eyes, but Philippe's voice forced them open again.

"A parting gift, Drago. Something to remember me by. *Au revoir.*" Philippe took several steps backward and tossed the weapon to Drago. He caught it deftly by the wooden grip. Marya took one long, last look at Drago's eyes, trying to ignore the blood that trickled like the tracks of red tears, then squeezed her own eyes shut again. Of all the images that would haunt her until her own death came, she didn't want the sight of the silver blade piercing his heart to be one of them. She couldn't watch him die.

NINETEEN

Drago held the Vampire Hunter, feeling its heft and balance. It was a good weapon, as such evil devices went. The silver cutting edge, as he knew only too well, was razor sharp. The blade itself, about a foot in length, was heavy but well balanced, and the grip was sturdy and comfortable. It would do.

He took a deep, calming breath and blocked the pain of the scorching silver burn from his mind. He looked at each of the people around him in turn. Philippe stood poised like a general drinking in the victorious execution of his battle plan. Adelle's eyes were closed, but her mouth worked in the silent recitation of a final prayer. Marya caught his eye briefly, then shut her eyes as well. Reno's rounded eyes and creased brow showed a tense expectancy. Only Scott's expression was cool and detached, as if the death of a vampire, as dramas went, was neither comedy nor tragedy, but a mildly boring affair. Drago nodded once, almost imperceptibly.

Scott yanked on Marya's arms again. "Come, girl. You have a bloody front seat. Open your eyes!"

She cried out, and Drago felt all eyes on her.

His were on David Reno. Drago flew at Reno with the speed of the gift of celerity, hurling the death's-head at the side the vampire had exposed when he had turned toward Scott. Reno and Adelle both screamed, their voices merging in a gruesome harmony.

Scott's voice rang out above both Reno's and Adelle's. "Philippe!"

Drago had no time to react. He felt a body slam into his, and the momentum carried him to the ground. He rolled forward into a somersault, gaining his feet in the process. He spared a quick glance at Reno and Adelle. Both were on the forest floor, but while Reno writhed in pain, Adelle was still.

Reno jerked the Vampire Hunter's blade from his side. "Scott, damn you, help me!"

Revelin ran to Reno, knelt beside him on one knee, and took the death's-head from the hand still clutched around the handle. "I'll help ease your pain, mate." With that, Scott, in one smooth-as-silk motion, lifted the weapon, flipped it in midair, grabbed the handle so the blade faced point down, and staked David Reno through the heart.

A high, keening cry rent the stillness of the glade. When the final death rattle gurgled from Reno's throat, Scott stood up. "You've a level playing field now, Drago."

Philippe, like Drago, had stopped to witness the subplot in the drama. "You Irish scum! Your alliance was with me!"

Scott smiled, and the chilling power that glimmered in his ice-blue gaze was the only reminder in a face full of dimples and white teeth that he was more than a flippant young man. "My alliance was forged long before you came along, Chenard."

Philippe cast an accusing stare at Drago. "You knew about this the whole time!"

"No. But you didn't really think I'd sacrifice myself for you, did you?" Without waiting for an answer he lashed out at Philippe with the cutting power of his mind, aiming right for the golden eyes and pretty face.

Philippe snarled, more an animal sound of defiance than a human laugh. Drops of blood barely reached the white collar of his silk shirt before the wounds healed themselves. "Had you forgotten, Drago? My invulnerability is a match for your power of destruction. Any injury you attempt to inflict on me is no more than a nuisance." By the time he finished his declaration, only the drying blood was evidence he had ever been cut.

It had indeed been a mistake on Drago's part. Philippe had been an ally, not a foe, for so long that Drago hadn't thought of all he was capable of. Philippe Chenard was no mere desk clerk. He was a member of the Directorate, and the fact that he wasn't an enforcer had nothing to do with his lack of power. Drago called on a different weapon in his arsenal, the most basic of all, but eminently effective. Simple dominance. He widened his eyes, loosing arrows of command more forcefully than if his mouth had shouted mandates.

Philippe's own eyes took on the dull luster of tarnished brass, but Drago could see the muscles twitching in Phillipe's pale face and knew he was fighting the power. "No more…will I do your bidding, Drago!" The words tore from Philippe's mouth in a supreme effort of defiance.

Drago added weight to his compelling stare, the kind of look that could wither a man as easily as the cold hand of Death. "You will stay your onslaught at once, *monsieur,* and submit to me. You have not the power to challenge me, and you know it!"

Philippe's gaze remained trapped by Drago's dominance, but even as his eyes strained against the snare of supremacy, Philippe tilted his head back. He held his chin high and flared his nostrils, like a beast of prey testing the wind. Drago could afford to lose no more time. Philippe's resistance was formidable.

Drago soared at Philippe, circling to position himself to snatch his quarry. But just as Drago closed in, Philippe broke the hold of Drago's eyes and sprinted into the trees, his movement so fleeting he was no more than a haze of foul, mummy-brown smoke. Drago gave chase without a second thought, his own progress no less swift. He wove through the trees, a kaleidoscope of life spinning around him with the lushness of the canopies of the giant oaks above him and the verdant carpet of emerald below. And mixed throughout was the dappled sunlight, sprinkling brilliance and energy like a trail of bright crumbs to be followed. Drago pursued blindly until the overpowering stench of death drew him to a sudden halt.

Drago stood, struggling for breath, and turned his head from side to side to take in his surroundings. It wasn't just the shadows or the aged oak trees, covered with a patina of verdigris moss. It was the cold aura of Mistress Death herself, presiding over the tombstones, family plots, and monuments that encircled him. Philippe stood some fifty feet away, a wide smile cutting a swath of white across the dark of his beard.

Too late, Drago recalled Philippe's fascination, along with *le docteur la mort,* Ricard De Chaux, with death. The obsession with unlocking the mystery of the fatal hour had been the common thread linking the two together long before *l'alliance.*

Philippe raised his arms and prayed to his Mistress.

> *The hour of death is a pretty lie,*
> *For time crosses not the threshold.*
> *Of decay of age and days gone by,*
> *You are surely uncaring and cold.*
> *Sensible still, today as yesterday,*
> *Undiminished by that which touches you not.*
> *Rise, then, my children, to the light of day,*
> *And heed the commands long forgot.*

Drago laughed, but it was a nervous laugh. He had indeed forgotten about Philippe's ability to call spirits. "You fool! There are no fresh corpses here. These graves are too old to hear your babbling, Philippe. You're on your own."

Philippe's mouth curled downward in disdain. "What do you know about such things, Drago? Long ago, while you were touring the continent, I was roaming the cemetery at les Innocents. Even now, for every hour you spend making love to courtesans in your grand castle, I spend two hours in the catacombs with the dead. Revivification is a reality, not a fantasy, and the passage of time means nothing to them, as they themselves will tell you." He spun in a circle, his arms raised again, and when he next spoke, his voice was as cold and hollow as a winter wind. The words weren't French, Latin, or any other language Drago recognized, but an incantation of sounds as primitive as life and death.

Drago's laughter died in his throat. Whether or not anything could or would respond to Philippe's summons, the time to press the attack was now. Philippe was distracted. Besides, the blood was still running freely down Drago's face, and the burn of the silver was as debilitating to him as a gunshot wound would be to a mortal. He leapt over the ornate wrought iron fencing of a family plot, but as he did so, a wraith rose up before him. As formless as mist, as insubstantial as shadow, yet the creature was as real as Philippe had boasted. A whistle, like a gust of air through a drafty house, tore through Drago. He had no defense against such a being, and when the gray specter reached out feathery arms and passed through him, there was nothing he could do to stop it. Dizziness washed over Drago, and he fell forward across a table-type gravestone. The cool granite felt good against his burning skin, and he wanted nothing more than to rest against the stone, but he forced himself to his feet. He stepped out of the fenced square of the family plot, but as he did, another spirit rushed at him and through him, sapping his strength. Drago gasped for breath, the odor of decay robbing the air around him of oxygen. The silver wound burned more than ever.

His only hope was to reach Philippe, who was still chanting to the netherworld. Drago stumbled forward, winding his way around boxed tombstones, the crumbling brick walling of plots, and monuments that were nearly twice his height. The wraiths seemed to have the power to appear only for a short time, but as soon as one dissipated into a plume and vanished, another one rose to confront Drago. Some whistled, some wailed, and one even shrieked, but all took their serving of life when they touched him.

Philippe was only twenty feet away. His eyes were closed, his face was slack, and the mouth that had beckoned the spirits moments before hung open. Perhaps Philippe was summoning more strength, or maybe he was simply in rapture. It had been long seconds since the last apparition had wafted away, and another one had not yet formed. *Now.* Drago flew at Philippe will all his available speed, and the collision of flesh and blood bodies did more than knock the wind out of Drago—it propelled both of them over the edge of the high, steep ridge housing the cemetery. Drago, unable to hold onto Philippe, tumbled and rolled down the embankment. Fallen logs and dead branches tore at Drago's bare skin, but the pain only helped to rouse the bloodlust for Philippe's demise. Drago rolled to his feet and saw Philippe, only yards away, trying to scamper back up the hillside on all fours.

"What's your hurry, *mon ami?* Your friends can't help you any more. You don't have the strength to call them again, and even if you did, they're far too old to bridge the gap between worlds a second time."

Philippe turned, his teeth clenched and his fangs bared. A wild gleam lit his eyes, and all pretense at civilized elegance was gone. "You know nothing of what I can do! You never concerned yourself with me unless there was some menial task to be done. De Chaux and Scott were no better. Only the spirits have been faithful. They will rise again!"

Drago allowed Philippe to expend energy in climbing the slope, while he himself followed at a more leisurely pace. Each time Philippe got too far ahead of him, Drago reached out an arm and flicked his wrist, the resulting energy knocking Philippe's legs out from under him. Philippe finally reached the top of the ridge, but kept running in spite of his words. At the rear of the cemetery a long, narrow trench ran along the ridge. When Drago came upon a historic marker mounted on a square wooden post, he paused just long enough to wrench the post from the ground. The end tapered to a convenient point.

Drago pursued again, but unhurriedly. Exercising any vampiric discipline was tiring, but Drago imagined that summoning the dead for roll call was more draining. He ran down his prey at last, using a final wave of energy to send Philippe's silk covered knees to the grass again. Drago stood beside him and waited.

Philippe eyed the marker with its sharpened post. "I'll not meet *la Belle Mort* on my hands and knees. Grant me that, at least."Drago dipped his head.

Philippe pushed himself to his feet and brushed his hands together to dislodge the dirt. "You never understood. None of them ever did—not even De Chaux." A lurid gleam came into his eyes, and they focused on a point somewhere over Drago's shoulder. "It was never about death, but the *élan vital,* the impulse of life. Don't you see? It's not just the beating heart that sustains us, but the spark of life, the vital force that animates everything around us."

"Believe it or not, *mon ami,* I do understand."

Philippe set his gaze on Drago's. "Perhaps. If that's true, then sing no *chant du cygne* for me. No swan song. No death song."

"I won't."

"Good." But there was no finality in the word, no peace. And the flicker of defiance had not been snuffed.

Philippe lunged at him before Drago could heed the warning in the vampire's eyes. Philippe clamped his hands on the wooden post, nearly wrenching it from Drago's grasp before Drago could tighten his hold. Both men twisted and tugged, spinning around and fighting for a strong foothold on the uneven ground. No longer was it a contest of disciplines or mind power or psychological gamesmanship. It had come down to raw physical strength, endurance, and will. Drago's eyesight blurred with bloodlust, and he fought on the instinct of the beast alone.

His exhaustion, the burn of the silver wounds, and all the ennui that had gripped his mind for so many years faded into the backdrop. Drago planted his feet and whacked Philippe to the ground with the square post's flat side. The quick movement nearly tore the post from his hands, though, and Drago was forced to fall on Philippe to maintain his grip. He raised the post to Philippe's neck and pressed downward, trying to choke the man. Philippe clenched his teeth and pushed up, and Drago could see the muscles in Philippe's neck tighten and strain with the effort.

Drago reversed his energy, pulling up on the post and catching Philippe off guard. Drago immediately slammed the post down again. Philippe cried out, but when Drago lifted the post for another blow, his opponent was ready. Philippe shifted his grip and propelled the tablet portion of the marker against Drago's head. A splintering of wood echoed through Drago's head, and he felt himself reeling to the ground, his hands free. He rolled and saw the business end of the post dive straight for him. He rolled again, feeling the post being driven into the ground mere inches away. His momentum carried him away from the weapon, yet he tried to lunge back to it. His fingers just grazed the painted wood when Philippe snatched the post, bereft now of the tablet marker, and yanked it out of the ground.

Philippe stood above him, his feet wide apart and the post securely in his grasp. "How does the truth of the final hour feel after so many centuries of cheating death, Drago?"

The one advantage to not holding the weapon was that Drago's hands were free. He whipped his arm out, turned his wrist, and just as quickly pulled his hand back to his chest. Philippe's feet jerked out from under him as if pulled by invisible strings, and he landed with a heavy thud on his back. Before Philippe could regain his feet, Drago straddled him and wrapped his fingers around the wood. He twisted the post up and over in a hooking motion and broke Philippe's grip. "I'll cheat death a little longer, but you, *mon ami…a la mort!"*

With that Drago raised the post and thrust the pointed end into Philippe's heart. A shriek of agony burst from Philippe's lips, followed by a more subdued death groan. Drago kept his hands on the post to prevent the vampire from removing it with the last of his energy . "You sing you own *chant du cygne, mon ami,* but I will cant no death song for you. I leave that to the invisible choir. May your lost soul join them in peace."

Philippe's glassy eyes focused on his, and an understanding of sorts bridged the chasm between their minds which were, after all, not so disparate. Philippe's hands fell from the post, and his head lolled to the side, his eyes still open, but unseeing. The improvised stake had effectively severed the heart. Drago dragged the body into full sunlight and watched. The light, no longer held at bay by the unique animating power of the day vampire, consumed the body as it would any Undead flesh. The body first reddened, and wisps of smoke accompanied the stench of burning flesh. Then the body ignited like a piece of meat left on a grill too long and slowly blackened. Finally, when the sun had done its work, nothing was left but gray ash, and this, little by little, was snatched by the breeze and carried off.

Drago had dispatched many a vampire with relish and no remorse, but he felt no joy at Philippe's death. In spite of everything the man had done to conspire against him, Drago had known him for many decades, as a partner and faithful ally.

Soon, though, Drago's thoughts turned to the living—Marya, Adelle and Scott, who owed him more than one explanation. It was for Adelle he was most fearful. He hadn't had time to check on her condition, and his last glimpse of her had shown her prone on the ground. As exhausted as he was, he forced his legs into a run and was back to the van in less than a minute.

The scene hadn't changed. Adelle was still lying on the ground, with Scott kneeling to one side of her and Marya at her other. Drago met Marya's gaze, and the despair and helplessness that swam in the pools of her dark eyes told him enough. He looked to Scott.

The younger vampire rose and met him a few yards from Adelle. "I'm sorry, Drago. There was nothing I could do. Her neck's broken. I couldn't risk moving her, not even to the van. She's been waiting for you. It's all that's kept her alive. I'm glad you made it."

Drago nodded, but made no answer, replacing Scott at Adelle's side.

Scott took Marya's arm. "Come, Marya. Let's leave them alone."

Marya rose silently, and there was suddenly nothing in Drago's world but the woman in front of him. He bent his head down to her, his face only inches from hers. "I'm so sorry, *ma chere.* So sorry."

"Don't be, Leksii. You were right all along—I shouldn't have come. But I have no regrets. There have never been any regrets, ever. I could ask for no better life than loving you." Her once vibrant voice was feeble and faint, and the sound of it tore at him more than the sight of her broken body on the ground.

He leaned even closer and pressed a kiss to her cheek. "These past forty years have only been bearable because of you, *mon chou,* " he whispered. He pulled his head back and frowned. "I've gotten blood on you."

"It's of no matter. But Leksii, they're silver wounds. They won't repair unless you take what you need. I can heal you. Please let me, Leksii. It's the only thing I ask. I took a vow long ago to serve you in any way possible, including to die for you. Let me keep that vow."

"Adelle…"

"Please, do it now. Do it now. Take all you need."

He could let her suffer no more. Leaning forward again, he held his mouth at her ear. "Close your eyes and rest now, my love. You will be at peace, I promise."

He lowered his mouth and did as she had bade him.

TWENTY

When it was over, Drago sat next to her body, lost in a place of blessed insensibility. Her blood had taken his physical pain away, and he rested his mind in a similar nirvana. The unfinished business, however, finally prodded him back to reality. "Scott." The name was spoken softly, but Drago knew the vampire would hear it with no trouble.

"Yeah, Drago."

He could see Scott out of the corner of his eye. Marya was behind him. "I'm going to put her in the van. Get a blanket, will you? If there isn't one in the van, there should be one in my car."

"I'll get it," said Marya.

Drago gently scooped Adelle's body into his arms and lifted her off the ground. He carried her effortlessly to the van and eased her to the floor. Behind him, Marya silently held out a blanket. He took it without a word and covered Adelle.

Turning, he faced Marya again. "Are you all right, *cherie?*"

She nodded. "Your cuts have healed."

Scott came up behind her. "But you look a bloody, god-awful mess, Drago." He tossed Drago a wet cloth. "Here. Clean yourself up before you scare a busload of school children to death."

He washed the blood off his face, getting all of it with Marya's help, and pulled his T-shirt back on. He tossed the cloth back to Scott. *"Merci, mon ami.* Now it's your turn to come clean. Who else do I have to worry about? Who else is in this alliance of Philippe's?"

Scott shook his head. "This was it. Just Chenard, Reno, and myself."

Drago raised his brows. "Not Evrard Verkist?"

"No. Verkist would have never taken orders from one such as Chenard."

"And not De Chaux?"

Scott laughed. "God, no. De Chaux has no higher ambition these days than to watch the sun set."

"And you, Scott? I have to admit, until you recited Voltaire's quote about praying for ridiculous enemies, you had me fooled. I thought you in league with Philippe. But why? Why join this alliance and then save my life, not once, but twice?"

"Someone will be here in a minute who can answer all your questions, Drago."

Two minutes later a gold luxury car pulled up behind Reno's car. A petite, slender woman exited the car, and, with a bride's slow, regal steps approaching the altar, made her way to the group. She wore a short, white sheath dress and a matching fitted white jacket with gold embroidered flowers. Gold jewelry ringed her neck, wrists, and fingers.

"Ah, I am glad to see you alive and well, Aleksei Borisov. And, of course, you as well, Revelin."

With all that had transpired this day, Drago should not have been surprised to see Nikolena, but he was. He couldn't ever remember her coming to the scene of an incident in the States before. *"Madame la directrice!"*

She waved a dainty hand at him. "Oh, forego the formalities, Alek. All but one. Introduce me to the young lady." She nodded toward Marya.

Drago motioned for Marya to come closer. *"Madame,* I am pleased to introduce *mademoiselle* Marya Jaks of Vicksburg. Marya, this is Nikolena."

Marya looked uncertain as to whether she should bow or shake hands. In the end, she did neither. "I'm pleased to meet you, *madame."*

"The pleasure is mine, *mademoiselle* Jaks. I'm afraid I have some business to discuss with Aleksei Borisov and Revelin. Would you mind waiting for us?"

Marya looked at Drago before she answered. By the press

of her brows, he knew she wasn't happy about being excluded, but it couldn't be helped. He nodded to her.

"Of course, *madame,* " said Marya, turning to Nikolena.

"Let us sit in the auto, then, gentlemen. I don't relish standing in the sun in this heat."

They made themselves comfortable in the leather seats of Nikolena's plush car, and she turned on the air conditioning. "So tell me. What is the price of all this joy?"

Drago took a deep breath. There was nothing to do but put the truth on a plate and in turn swallow the consequences. "Two brothers dead, Philippe and David Reno. And Adelle."

Nikolena leaned closer to him and put a hand on his arm. "I'm sorry, Aleksei Borisov. I truly am. I know how close you were to your servant."

"Thank you, Nika."

She dropped her hand. "Yet there is more than grief dominating your thoughts. I sense you are teeming with questions, Alek."

"And I sense your hand guiding all the chess pieces here today, *madame.* Am I wrong?"

She smiled. Not a vampire smile of seduction, but a Nikolena smile of a hundred meanings. "No. The two of you have been my lightning rods for a long time. Alek, you are a magnet for all the crap that flies around the Directorate and Brotherhood. I don't need to do anything but send you out into the fray. That was the case with Verkist. You were the catalyst for that affair with your many harassing phone calls to Curt Deverick and even Scott here. Scott would have gone with you to Phoenix regardless of my orders, I suspect, because Verkist had his apprentice, Callie Monroe, but Scott did have orders. Simple orders, but not so easy, after all—to make sure you came out of *Fata Morgana* alive."

"You assigned me a bodyguard, *madame?* "

Her dark eyes swept him up and down, seeming to reduce his height by at least a foot. "Don't sniff at me with your aristocratic nose in the air, Aleksei Borisov. You needed every bit of his help, didn't you?"

Drago glanced at Scott, who sat alone in the back seat. He

felt no antagonism toward the young enforcer. It was simply hard to admit he had needed help. "But I don't understand this alliance of Scott with Philippe."

"You're my lightning rod, Alek, but so is Revelin. The two of you are opposites. While you are the loose cannon, Scott is my hidden ace. He was a common soldier, not a prince like you were. Scott is seen as used to taking orders, a follower, not a leader, yet ambitious—the ideal candidate for an alliance. Scott has been operating under my orders for years. His job was to join any alliance which appeared to have goals and a modus operandi of violence rather than simple mutual aid."

"Are you saying Scott is your spy, *madame?*"

She bestowed on him another Nika smile, so small, yet full of so many secrets. A glance back at Scott showed a curve to his usual stoic mouth as well.

"'Spy?' Really, Alek. So melodramatic. It is simply that Revelin and I have long had our own alliance. One that takes precedence over any other he may form."

Drago lowered his brows, trying to make order of all these revelations. "Then both of you knew from the outset that Philippe was responsible for the forged order."

"No. Philippe was smart. He trusted no one, not even his partners. I began to have my doubts about him at the same time you did, I suspect—following your return from Phoenix."

Drago turned to Scott. "How did you and Philippe meet? I had never heard of you until this whole affair started."

"Through David Reno. Before he was transferred to the *Coterie,* Reno used to work for the Circle with me. Philippe met him when Reno came to Paris."

"What next, *madame?* Dare I presume my head is no longer on the chopping block?"

Nikolena unleashed just enough of her power to answer Drago's question. The air inside the car became charged, and Drago found it hard to draw a breath.

"You are to make no presumptions, Aleksei Borisov. I think the hue and cry for your termination will die a natural death after this. I will make it known in my own way and in my own words what you did to both Verkist and Philippe. There will be no mention at all of Scott. You, my sweet, will keep your pretty mouth shut. If you ever make any mention to anyone of Scott's role here today, you will answer to me. A small price to pay for the enhancement of your reputation, don't you agree? Are we understood, Alek?"

The royal 'we.' He understood. *"Oui, madame."*

"Good. Revelin, why don't you keep *mademoiselle* Jaks company for awhile? She looks anxious, and I have a private matter to discuss with Aleksei."

"Got it."

Both Nikolena and Drago waited until Scott opened the car door, slid out of the backseat, and was gone with a slam.

"The girl, Alek. She both knows and has seen too much."

He said nothing.

"She has vampire blood, yes?"

"Yes." Drago knew what was coming, but could no more stop the next words than he could stop Philippe's assault.

"She has to die, Aleksei Borisov."

"I won't allow it, *madame.*" There was no hesitation on his part. If she threw a fit, so be it.

But she didn't. There was no lightning bolt drawn from the heavens, only a long, drawn out sigh. "You fought so hard to survive against Verkist and Chenard. You would throw it all away for this mortal?"

Everything became clear for him in that moment. He suddenly knew that he would not have had the strength to prevail against either Evrard Verkist or Philippe if Marya hadn't been there. Nikolena could make all the threats in the world, but he would neither kill her himself nor permit anyone else to harm her.

"I throw nothing away, *madame.* It is what I keep that matters."

"Do you know what you're saying, Alek? Are you so certain of her that you would risk all? You make the supreme sacrifice if you are, and there's no turning back."

"I know what I'm doing, Nika."

He felt Nikolena's penetrating dark eyes burn all the way through him, searching for the truth he saw. After a moment, she nodded. "Very well. I give you until tonight. Sentence will be passed then, Aleksei Borisov. You will pay, and it will be dear."

***

Marya sat in Drago's car, unable to see what was happening two vehicles back. It was just as well. She closed her eyes, hoping to be able to cry. She would welcome the emotional release, but tears wouldn't come. She didn't know what had been worse, watching helplessly as Philippe had cut Drago with the Vampire Hunter, or waiting with Rev and the injured Adelle, praying that Drago would be victorious and return before Adelle lost her fight to hang on. Both events left her numb now, and she knew it still wasn't over.

She couldn't think about what might happen next. She didn't want to think at all. She tried to blank her mind and just relax.

A tap at the window, for all its gentleness, was an appeal she didn't really feel like responding to. But she opened her eyes. It was Revelin. She opened the door.

He flashed her a view of even, white teeth, and the engaging smile was almost enough to lead her past his eyes. She waited.

"Want some company?"

"Will you answer some questions for me?"

His smile widened. "Probably not, but you can ask."

She really wanted to be alone, but the possibility that even one of the small mysteries plaguing her mind might be solved was too powerful a lure to say no. She nodded. "A walk in the shade, then?" she suggested.

"Surely."

He gave her a hand in getting out of the car, and they took refuge from the sun under the awning of green provided by the giant oaks.

She took a deep breath, remembering the fear of the moment displayed by her mind's eye. "After I ran from the car and you grabbed me and threatened to kill me I really thought you were behind the plot."

"You were supposed to."

Her feelings of that moment were hard to forget, even in the light of what happened after. "I hated you then as much as I've ever hated any vampire. But why? Why did you do it?"

"I can't tell you all of it, but basically I did what I did because it was the only way to save Drago."

"You told me you didn't even know Philippe."

Revelin lifted a shoulder. "A lie."

"Why did Philippe try to kill Drago?"

A cock of the shaggy head told Marya that Rev didn't question these things half as much as she did. "Ambition. Jealousy."

"And you yourself don't have those feelings?"

"Jealousy? No. Ambition? Maybe, but not like that."

Marya looked at him. She believed what he said. There was no pretense to Revelin in either his demeanor or appearance. "Did Drago know you were on his side all along?"

"No. Not until I quoted Voltaire. The prayer for making my enemies ridiculous. I wasn't sure Drago would know it was Voltaire, but he did. He told me he understood with the quote about life becoming a disgrace and death a duty. That was Voltaire, too."

She was silent for a moment, digesting everything Revelin had told her. "Is the world of the Undead always like this? Deception and manipulation?"

The white teeth blazed at her again. Flanked by dimples on either side, the look was more an answer than his words. "More like the human world than we care to admit, yeah?"

"You're a very strange man, Revelin."

He scrunched his brows together. "Is that a compliment, Miss Jaks?"

She smiled. "Yeah, I suppose it is." She stepped closer to him, leaned over, and kissed him on the cheek. "Whatever your reasons, thank you for what you did for Drago."

"You're welcome. Come on. We'd better head back. Drago and Nikolena are not patient people."

As they turned back, Marya saw Drago heading for them. As he drew close, she tried to decipher his expression. His face looked strange, as if he were a man who had just aged ten years in the past ten minutes. A ridiculous thought of someone who was well over five hundred years old, but it was true. Gray shadows filled the pockets between his eyes and the bridge of his nose and clung to the planes of his face. By contrast, the rest of his face looked even whiter than usual. Even his lips were bloodless. Marya knew it was the manifestation of the vampire, but it wasn't lust. It was simply as though whatever humanity existed had taken refuge far beneath the surface.

Marya looked at Drago's eyes, but there was no glow to the blue, no brow furrowed in passion. There was only the color, but with no more depth than if the blue had been daubed on with the careless stroke of a paintbrush.

His gaze slipped from Rev to her and back to Revelin. "Time to go. *Mon ami,* one more favor. Take the van and help with Adelle. Nikolena's going to see the body back to France."

"Of course."

There were no more 'thank yous,' hand shakes, or back slaps between Drago and Revelin. Perhaps it was the way of the vampires not to display emotion to each other. Perhaps it was just the lack of amity between the men that had been apparent to Marya from the start. Respect, yes, and a common cause, certainly, but all the *'mon amis'* in the world would never make the two true friends.

Rev turned to her. "Good-bye, Marya."

Well, she was human, and she would show it. She pressed another kiss against Rev's cheek. "Thank you for everything."

His brows as well as the corners of his mouth lifted in bemusement. "You're welcome." Rev glanced once more at Drago, then turned and glided back toward the van.

Drago spoke, his voice as lacking in life as his features. "Come. I'll take you home."

They climbed into the car, and when it became apparent that Drago wasn't going to make so much as small talk, Marya said what she felt she needed to say. "I'm sorry about Adelle. I know how important she was to you."

She hoped he wouldn't think the comment presumptuous. She really knew nothing about being a servant to the Undead, and she didn't know anything of the specific relationship between Adelle and Drago.

But Drago didn't remind her of any of that. All he said was, "She was the light in my window."

It was a very human thing to say, but Marya didn't think now was the time to voice such an observation. She didn't know what was going through that vampire mind of his. Were all his thoughts on Adelle, or was he reflecting on Philippe's betrayal? And Nikolena…what had she instructed him to do? Had she ordered him back to Paris? With that her thoughts drifted to her own feelings, but they were as difficult to make sense of as his were.

He'd be leaving, and soon. Of that, at least, she was very sure. In the face of that certainty, her jumbled feelings shouldn't matter. But they did. If memories were soon to be all she would have, she wanted them to be clear-cut and whole, not blurred by doubts and fears. For the remainder of the ride home, she thought very hard about her past, her future, and the jewel of now, so precious and rare.

***

The arrival at her cottage was as silent as the drive had been. Still, Marya had cherished each moment. If she couldn't have words, she had taken her fill of images, stealing glances at Drago often as he drove, adding the impressions of his profile bearing the healing cut to her store box of memories.

She went to the kitchen now, anxious for a tall glass of iced sweet tea. His first words to her were also of a practical nature.

"Cherie, we must talk, but first I need to take a shower. I cannot abide the stench of vampire blood, not even my own."

She nodded in understanding. As soon as she quenched her thirst with the ready-made tea from the refrigerator, she headed for the master bedroom to take her own shower. But the sound of running water halted her steps and turned her toward the guest bath. A moment later she pulled aside a corner of the shower curtain and stepped inside the sanctuary of the steamy bath.

Drago turned to her, and his eyes widened in surprise,

drops of water glistening on his black lashes like dew on grass. He lifted both arms and swept his long hair back out of his face. The motion tightened the muscles of his stomach, drawing her gaze downward, and somehow the cleansing water cascading over his body like a waterfall over smooth stones made him look young again.

She reached for the bar of soap from its tray and stepped closer to him, sliding the soap over his chest. His raised arms lowered behind her head to follow the length of her hair down to the small of her back. The water from the showerhead pulsed across her body, but it was the pressure from his hands that urged her to lean into him until her breasts brushed against his chest. She moved her hands to his sides, skimming the soap over his back, and her gaze lifted to his face again. She drank in the raw beauty caressed by the thin fingers of water, and when his lips parted, she was jealous of each drop that clung to his skin and trickled over the contours of his face.

He dipped his head closer, and she closed her eyes and waited, the sound of her heart pounding over the pelting of the water. He traced her lips with his as if he were tasting her, searching for the sweetest spot, and the anticipation of being devoured held her fast. But when he kissed her, it was no more than a tug on her lower lip. A second kiss was just as swift and teasing before he pulled away from her. She opened her eyes, and the blue of his, set off by the glittering lashes and brows, was purer than any lake or ocean and no longer empty. She wanted nothing more than to drown in their depths. When he leaned forward again she parted her lips in expectation, but all he did was open his mouth. She expected another kiss, but instead he snaked his tongue out and flicked its tip at the depression under her lower lip.

There wasn't enough water in ten showers to put out the blaze of desire that flared at that small touch. The bar of soap went skittering around the circumference of the tub as she met his next kiss. This time his craving matched hers, and the whole world shrank to a cocoon of wet heat that pulsated all around them. Water ran into her eyes, blinding her, and when her equilibrium deserted her as well, his arms supported her, cupping her buttocks and molding her body to his. She felt him against her, hard and ready, and when his mouth left hers, it was to turn off the water and scoop her into his arms. He stepped out of the tub as if her weight was nothing, and in a few long strides was at his bed. Her back hit the mattress, and his body covered hers immediately. Her entire being felt liquefied, as if she could melt against him, soak into him, and become truly one with him. He was inside her before she realized it, and with his warm, wet body joining hers, the illusion was complete. Only the length of him feeding her hunger, devouring her from the inside out, reminded her that there was solidity to both his body and hers, if not the future.

This time no images of the past came to her mind, no visions at all of the outside world. There was only this one moment, and with the clean warmth and wetness of her body, it was like being born again, fresh and new. Nothing of the past existed or mattered, and the future… She didn't think about the future. Unrecognizable sounds escaped her, asking for something she couldn't express, but Drago understood and gave her what she longed for.

At long last her body relaxed, sated, but the perfection of the moment was marred by her awareness of the tension that still tightened his body. *With every new beginning, a price to be paid.*

"Drago?" she whispered against his cheek.

The sound of his name seemed to pull him back from whatever brink he teetered on. He pulled out of her and rolled to his back, and she watched the beast's need wage war with the man's control. His teeth were clenched, his lips curled back, and his brow furrowed. Finally, she saw his features and his body relax, and his chest rose and fell with measured breaths.

"I'm sorry," she said, grateful at least that this was the last time she'd be responsible for the vampire's agony.

"Don't be, *cherie.* It's not your fault. Besides, your reaction to my touch is every bit as satisfying as blood to me."

Somehow, she doubted that. Still, if he couldn't have her blood, at least he had his fantasy. "It's the fantasy, isn't it?

Exposing a mortal to her ultimate dream?"

"Is that all you think this is, *cherie?*" His voice sounded tired.

"I have no illusions about what it is for you. And you're leaving, so for me it can be nothing else."

"And if I weren't leaving?"

She wriggled under the bedspread, cold without his warmth. "Please, Drago, don't. Let's just leave it as it is."

He turned toward her. "What do you want, Marya?"

She shook her head. "You've given it to me. You've given my life back."

"But what do you want for the future? Come now, the truth. If you could have anything in the world, what would you have?"

She snuggled further down under the cover, as if it could shelter her from his pointless questions. "What I've always wanted. That which I can never have."

"Say it."

She was quiet. *Why does he have to ruin everything this way?*

"Say it, *cherie.*"

Damn you, Drago! "You. I can't have you, but I want you."

"Tell me why."

She lay still for a moment, still angry that her actions in and of themselves hadn't been enough for him to understand her feelings. Gradually, though, the resentment dissipated. Perhaps it was best after all that she spell everything out. She would have her final closure. She would be able to begin her life anew knowing that she had left nothing unsaid, and he would never have any doubts about what he had meant to her. She reached out and grazed her fingertips down his forearm. "Your touch. I can feel your strength, but I also feel everything you've ever felt. Wonder and joy…pain and despair. But your touch also makes me feel cherished, as though you, too, can see everything in my life. I've never had that before. I'm in love with you, Drago, vampire and all. I know love's not a word in the dictionary of the Undead, but…"

"Get dressed."

"What?"

He rolled off the bed. "You heard me. Go get dressed."

She stared at him. She was glad he hadn't dressed up a pretty lie to parade in front of her, but at the same time she had hoped for some kind of acknowledgement of her feelings. She waited, but he said nothing more. When he turned his back on her to get dressed, she silently fled to her own room.

***

An hour later the doorbell rang. She considered ignoring it. She didn't feel like seeing or talking to anyone, but when the bell rang a second time, she went to look through the peephole. *Good.* It wasn't for her. She opened the door and invited Nikolena inside.

"Come in, please. I'll get Drago."

"Oh, but it's you I've come to see, Miss Jaks."

Marya stared at the woman. For all her tiny size, Marya had no trouble feeling the aura of power that elevated Nikolena to far above her physical height. "Me?"

"If we might speak in private…"

"Of course. Come this way." Marya led her guest to the rear patio. Drago was still in the guest room with the door closed.

Nikolena made herself comfortable on a patio chair, looking no less regal than if she had seated herself on a throne. "I'll come straight to the point. I need to know exactly how you feel about Aleksei Borisov. And please don't waste my time or yours with a lie."

Marya's emotions during the past hour had been so much stew boiling in a pot, but it took only a moment now to cool down and serve up the truth. After all, this was about how she felt about Drago, not how he felt about her. "I love him. Is that direct enough?"

The haughty lift of one brow was Nikolena's answer. "And what are your expectations?"

"I have none. He'll leave, and I'll live my life."

"He hasn't talked to you about being his servant?"

"No." The thought had crossed her mind, but apparently

not Drago's. He hadn't mentioned it.

"He cannot make you his servant, even if you both wanted it. You're an aberration. A servant must be able to forge a blood tie. You would not be able to do this with Drago or any vampire. Do you understand, or do I need to explain further?"

"No. I understand."

Nikolena took a deep breath and nodded, not so much in acknowledgement, but as though she had come to some decision. She raised her head. "Aleksei Borisov!" The voice was a command, but not a shout.

Drago evidently heard it. He appeared only seconds later, opening the French doors. However, it was to her he came, not Nikolena. Dressed in black trousers, a flowing white shirt and an embroidered gold vest, he glided first to her side, then moved to stand directly behind her chair. She felt the touch of his left hand on her shoulder.

Nikolena rose. "The two of you leave me no choice. Miss Jaks, you know too much of our ways to be allowed to live freely in the world. Aleksei Borisov, you cannot make this mortal your servant, and you have refused my order to terminate her. Therefore I am forced to impose sanction on you. Are you ready?"

She stiffened, but Drago's hands drew her up out of the chair and turned her to face him. "Do not be afraid, *cherie*. We will face this together, and yes, I do know the meaning of your human word. In giving you your life, you have given me mine." He leaned forward to kiss her softly, but more than either his words or his kiss, his eyes reassured her. Those beautiful blue eyes. She stared at them and saw not boredom, emptiness, or arrogance, but his unspoken word. *L'amour.*

He looked at Nikolena. "We are ready, *madame.*"

She nodded. *"L'enforcier* must die."

***

Marya sat in the art studio of the secluded dacha several miles outside Novgorod. She was more adept at painting people than animals, and she was having a little trouble putting a realistic sheen on the black fur. Even with her concentration on her work, though, she had no trouble sensing that she was no longer alone. The man who was her whole world leaned over her shoulder, and she could feel his breath on her cheek.

"Cherie, I don't know that I like being portrayed as a beast with four legs and a tail."

She smiled. "I think you look very elegant and sleek. Would you rather I give you scaly wings and a tail and have you breathing fire like your namesake, the dragon?"

He turned her head with one finger against her chin and kissed her long and deep.

"No," he whispered, releasing her mouth at last, "but I believe my comment was about putting a rhinestone collar on a big cat, not a creature such as this. Could you not have painted me as a great white tiger?"

She pretended to pout. "But if I had done that, my love, you couldn't very well sit curled up on my lap."

He laughed and scooped her effortlessly into his arms. By the time her paintbrush hit the floor, his speed carried them out of the studio and down the hall to the bedroom.

No more work was done that day on Marya's latest watercolor.

EPILOGUE

As far as the world was concerned, Alek Dragovich was truly dead.

He was killed in the same confrontation that ended the existence of Philippe Chenard and David Reno. That was the official Directorate release. Unofficially, Drago became the Elvis of the Undead. There wasn't a day that went by that some vampire didn't report seeing the black-haired, blue-eyed Anti-God in the company of a beautiful woman somewhere in the world. Notoriety and rumor turned into true legend, and stories freely flowed that Drago had been witnessed doing everything from chewing and spitting out silver bullets to crossing rivers by stopping the flow of the water.

Evrard Verkist relinquished his job as Patriarch and attempted to flee Directorate justice, but after eight months he was located and quietly terminated.

As for Drago's original *alliance*, the Frenchman, Ricard De Chaux, remained the only surviving member. Nikolena tried for two years to convince him to accept the post of Patriarch he had actively sought more than sixty-five years earlier, but Doctor Death would have none of it. Ric's answer was always the same. "What I seek isn't rule over many, but the power over one."

Of Philippe's new alliance, only the Scots-Irish bastard, Revelin Scott, survived. And survive he did. Within two years he was promoted to Directorate status, making him the youngest vampire ever to be among the chosen few. In five years he became the new *enforcier*, and it was rumored that Nikolena had a fondness for Scott that almost, but not quite, matched her affection for the legendary Russian who had preceded him.

Certainly Revelin was privileged to enter Nikolena's sacred domain more often than any of her other enforcers. It was only Revelin Scott, though, who could truly appreciate the new painting that hung in Nikolena's grand office.

Titled "The Secret," it was a full-sheet watercolor depicting a young woman with long, flowing sable hair and expressive dark eyes. Regally perched on her lap was a black cat with haughty blue eyes that wore a narrow rhinestone collar the way a king wears a crown. And if one gazed very, very hard at the painting, the faintest of Mona Lisa smiles could be seen on both woman and beast.

The secret was love.

L'amour. After all, it was what made Eternity bearable.

Don't Miss

Jaye Roycraft's

DOUBLE IMAGE

Dalys Aldgate has been a survivor for 235 years. Life as an Australian convict had sharpened his survival skills, but the bush also bestowed him the ultimate gift of survival—a journey to the Other Side. His soul left behind, Dalys became a mirror for those still human—a polished surface upon which the living can project their fantasies, never seeing the "monster" on the mirror's other side. In present day Mississippi, "Dallas" lives a reclusive life as owner of a haunted inn while trying to forget his even more haunting past.

Ex-cop Tia Martell is now a freelance photographer trying to adjust to life "after The Job" and put the years of violence and death behind her. While on assignment to shoot antebellum mansions in Natchez, Mississippi, murder brings her face-to-face with Dallas Allgate, the coldest, yet most fascinating, man Tia has ever met. Before Tia can unravel the mystery of the man with the hypnotic eyes, a young vampire and his master, Jermyn St. James, seek out Dallas for revenge. St. James only wants Dallas' true death until he sees Tia. Now he wants her, too.

Tia's in danger from St. James, but she's in even more peril from Dallas—the man who knows death even better than she does. In their struggle for life, one of them will have to make the ultimate sacrifice. But will Dallas let Tia make her own choices, or will he bend her will by projecting her fantasies upon his...Double Image.

Available Now from ImaJinn Books

Coming in June, 2002

Jaye Roycraft's

SHADOW IMAGE

Welcome to the idyllic lakefront town of Shadow Bay, where expectation and reality are shores apart. A young woman comes to escape the pressures of the big city, and a very old creature comes to ease himself back into the world of the living…and neither finds what they imagined they would.

Shelby Cort has had enough of working for a big-city police department. Ricard De Chaux, the notorious *le docteur la mort* and ex-Paramount for the Undead in France, has been escaping for years and now reluctantly works his way back into human society. They meet in the small town of Shadow Bay, Michigan—Shelby as Sheriff and Ric as the new county medical examiner.

When dead bodies start to pop up in unlikely places and the killings go unsolved, Shelby comes under attack from town officials, the media, and her own co-workers. She finds an ally in the new ME, both grateful for his support and drawn by his exotic good looks.

But what Shelby doesn't know is that the killer isn't human. What she also doesn't know is that the cool, collected Dr. De Chaux is by night Doctor Death, the new Overlord of the local Undead, whose top priority is to protect his new charges. Doctor Death hides one piece of evidence after another from the Sheriff, as all the while Ric fills Shelby's off-duty time with longing and passion.

When the killer goes after Shelby and all Ric's secrets are on the line, where will his allegiance fall?